The Voluble Topsy

More Handheld Classics

The Voluble Topsy

By A P Herbert

Consisting of

The Trials of Topsy (1928)
Topsy, MP (1929)
Topsy Turvy (1947)

With an introduction by Kate Macdonald

Handheld Classic 34

This edition published in 2023 by Handheld Press
72 Warminster Road, Bath BA2 6RU, United Kingdom.
www.handheldpress.co.uk

ISBN 978-1-912766-46-8

1 2 3 4 5 6 7 8 9 0

Series design by Nadja Guggi and typeset in Adobe Caslon Pro
and Open Sans.

Printed and bound in Great Britain by Short Run Press, Exeter.

MIX
Paper from
responsible sources
FSC® C014540
www.fsc.org

Contents

Topsy, MP

Topsy Turvy

Acknowledgments

From *The Trials of Topsy*: 'I have to thank the Proprietors of *Punch* for their courtesy in permitting Topsy to appear in this dress — A P H.'

From *Topsy, MP*: 'These letters are reprinted here by the courteous permission of the Proprietors of *Punch,* for which I thank them. — A P H.'

Note on the text

While some spelling errors may be spotted in Topsy's letters, they were intended by the author to show the speed of her writing and (probably) her vagueness about her expanding vocabulary.

The text in this edition was scanned non-destructively from first or early editions of the three books, and proofread. Any obvious typographical errors have been corrected.

Some words have been silently deleted or replaced where they would cause offence to modern readers, with the permission of the Executors.

Kate Macdonald is a literary historian and a publisher. She first discovered A P Herbert in the pages of old volumes of *Punch* and has published research on the mechanisms of comic writing.

Introduction

BY KATE MACDONALD

Topsy's letters to her best friend Trix, whom she addresses with gushing endearments such as hen of the North, crystallised cherry, distant woodpigeon, aromatic angel, are a torrent of delightful chatter about the joys and catastrophes of her life. She writes first as a girl about town, then as a *rather* radical Member of Parliament, and finally as a harassed post-war householder. Her letters were published first in *Punch* in 1927, nearly a century ago, but their human warmth and righteous indignation about wrongs to be righted are undated.

Topsy is one of a distinguished line of British female satirical commentators. Her letters preceded both E M Delafield and Nancy Mitford in the interwar years, surely the doyennes of this tradition in British comic writing. Delafield's *Diary of Provincial Lady* first appeared as episodes in *Time & Tide* in 1930. Nancy Mitford's novels deployed Topsy's upper-class idioms and social milieux from 1931. In our own day, Helen Fielding's *Bridget Jones's Diary* from 1995 – also a periodical serial – continued the tradition of recording the private remarks and hapless affairs (not always romantic) of a single woman in possession of a sense of humour who might be in want of a husband.

What makes Topsy so attractive as a character, and gives her artlessly hyperbolic letters their unexpected gravitas, is that she is immersed in the concerns of everyday life. She is passionate about studying the form at greyhound races; she gamely escorts large numbers of unruly children though the London Underground to get them to the train for their country holiday; casting about for ways to earn some money of her own she is employed as a magazine influencer; and she is outraged, often, about the laws of England that prevent ordinary people from having a good time. She serves on a jury, she goes to the theatre, she tries out public speaking and she is an enthusiastic habituée of West End nightclubs and Soho restaurants.

Topsy has no hesitation about trying the new fads and technologies of her day. In 'Flies Half the Atlantic' Topsy accepts sponsorship from a rich feminist to become the first bride and the first lady MP to fly across the Atlantic as a passenger from east to west. In 'Makes Film' Topsy uses croquet to combat her political rival at a health spa, then uses her new cine-camera to film his discomfiture. In 'Reducing' she tries a Turkish bath and in 'Keeping Fit' she catches on to the trend for rolling the abdomen. After the detonation of the atomic bomb, Topsy begins to use 'electron' as an epithet, reflecting a new-found public awareness of the laws of physics. She certainly didn't learn these at school.

Topsy's exuberant letters were published in three waves of volubility in *Punch*, the eminent and very popular political and satirical magazine, at least 50% of whose content was cartoons poking fun at the topics and personalities of the day. The first tranche of letters, appearing from August 1927 to February 1928, were quickly published as *The Trials of Topsy* in 1928, with the replacement of one letter from *Punch* in which Topsy was thoughtlessly rude about Liverpudlians, with a much funnier one. After a six-month break Topsy's letters were back in *Punch* from September 1928 to March 1929, to be published as *Topsy, MP* in 1929. She was then retired to domestic duties. Sixteen years later, in October 1945 Topsy returned to *Punch* for a further 25 episodes until April 1946, to be published in 1947 as *Topsy Turvy*.

Topsy was created by the comic writer, lyricist and novelist Alan Herbert, known to his varied public as 'APH'. He was born in 1890 in Ashtead, Surrey, and after school at Winchester College he took a first-class degree in Jurisprudence at Oxford, during which time his comic verses began to be published in *Punch*. He read for the Bar but never practiced. After marrying Gwen Quilter, the daughter of the Victorian artist and critic Harry Quilter, APH served in the First World War in the Royal Naval Volunteer Reserve. In 1919 he published his first novel, *The Secret Battle*, which attacked the cruel military regulations governing courts martial. In 1924 he was invited to join the staff of *Punch*, which brought him a regular income to support his growing family (three daughters and a son). As well as his verse and regular columns for *Punch* and other magazines, and more novels, APH wrote plays and musicals for London's theatre. After writing satire for over ten years to press for legal reform, he was elected to the Parliamentary seat for the now extinct constituency of Oxford University, sitting as an MP from 1935 to 1950 as an Independent Member. In the Second World War he served as a Petty Officer in the River Emergency Service and later the Royal Navy Auxiliary Patrol in his own boat, the *Water Gypsy*, mine-hunting and fire-watching on the Thames. After the war APH had his biggest theatrical success with *Bless the Bride*, for which he wrote the songs. He was knighted in 1949 in Sir Winston Churchill's Resignation Honours List, the year before APH left Parliament. He died in 1971.

Once installed at *Punch* APH wrote the first of a series of imaginary law reports on Misleading Cases, in which an energetic and public-spirited gentleman called Albert Haddock challenges the English legal system to rule on such questions as what is a Reasonable Man, and whether a cheque written on a cow may be honoured by the bank. These are the works by which APH is best remembered now. David Langford's assessment of the Misleading Cases (Langford 2007) is recommended as one of the very few pieces of critical writing available on Herbert, summarising the range and impact of APH's satire, especially the responses from readers and lawyers outside the UK who failed to spot the jokes. While APH's admirers may know that he was also an MP it might not be known that he wrote the first two Topsy volumes, packed with critical remarks about the state of the law, as well as screeds of Haddockian satirical law reports, before he became a legislator himself. Topsy therefore heralds APH's campaigning achievements as a Member of Parliament by rehearsing in her letters the faults in the law that her creator would later be in a position to do something about. APH's first and most famous legislative triumph was to reform the divorce laws, which took several years of patient negotiation and lobbying in a conservative society dominated by religious considerations of the sanctity of marriage.

Albert Haddock's early legal appearances are closely connected to Topsy's début. In the Misleading Case from 10 August 1927, 'Rex v Haddock. Is a golfer a gentleman?' (Langford nd), the judge giving judgement is Mr Justice Trout. Topsy herself arrived in print a week later, on 17 August, also in *Punch*. The judge quoted the phrase 'Nature's gentleman' in his argument: a phrase used incessantly by Topsy throughout her letter-writing life. Clearly APH liked the sound of Trout as a surname and enjoyed deploying the idioms of the day, but we don't know by which blossom of ingenuity the idea of a scatterbrained yet irrepressibly jaunty English débutante commentating on English daily life sprang into being alongside Haddock's adventures. APH's own autobiography is silent about Topsy, and his biography by Reginald Pound barely mentions her. How could a character so lively and perspicacious, and long-lived, be ignored in the Herbert canon? Haddock himself is a key character in all the Topsy letters, central to her life and happiness. Albert Penrose Haddock is quite obviously APH himself: also a novelist and a playwright, he owns very few suits, roars with laughter when other men would scold, has a passion for campaigning to right legal wrongs, and celebrates the annual Boat Race from his house on the Thames bank with an enthusiastic house party, just as APH was and did himself. Like Haddock, APH also deplored fox-hunting, had an unpredictable income, adored playing pub skittles, swam the Thames from Waterloo Bridge to Westminster Bridge, and noted the new graffiti in the Commons lavatories after the election of a new generation of Labour MPs (Pound 108, 112, 119, 121, 197). Like Topsy he made a sensational maiden speech in Parliament which was complimented by Churchill, endured shattered windows in his house for the duration of the war, and was nearly blown up by a rocket (Pound 137, 167, 191).

Topsy's letters are an anomaly in *Punch*, in that they are almost the sole female voice in a very masculine publication. *Punch* had very few female contributors. Albeit written by a man, Topsy's voice reads as authentically female; she is also young, self-assured, disrespectful and sardonic. She uses swooping hyperbole as an art form, deriving naturally from the slang and convoluted syntax of sophisticated bright young things in her day. Readers may notice that there are over 13,000 italicised words in the three volumes of letters, which produce Topsy's highly distinctive mode of expression. She *italicises* every *important* word that needs *attention*, and the result is *rather* comic genius, lending stress, and directing *attention*, to the less obvious choice of word. The result suggests a delightfully euphonic rendition of the speech patterns of the period. Her voice is unforgettable, and also curiously historic: was this how the chattering classes of her day really spoke? Evidence from the published letters of Nancy Mitford and Evelyn Waugh, for example, might clinch this point.

Topsy is delightful, ridiculous and shamelessly ignorant (especially about her erratic spelling). Perhaps her most outstanding exploit of obtuseness is when she is asked to review a performance of *Othello*. Her criticism of the tired old clichés in the script, the ridiculous plot and poor character delineation, the tediousness of the soliloquies and so on, are not received well by her editor. Yet the reader can see her point. Topsy is an Everywoman for common sense and could never be accused of being pretentious or too learned. She is certainly uneducated, and is utterly at sea about many subjects, but her discourse is so wildly off the point at times that the reader might wonder whether she is making a joke of her own dimness, or was this just Herbert laughing at Topsy's expense?

Is Topsy a snob? She was hardly created to be what she calls proletarian, but she is fervently in favour of doing practical and useful things for the improvement of the lives of the ordinary people, as well as enjoying her titled family's access to what she calls Cadogan and Belgravian parties. Is she shallow? Probably, but she is also very good at heart.

In *Topsy Turvy*, Topsy sounds more frayed than insouciant, because now she is an aggrieved housewife who has endured six years of being bombed and resents that life has not returned to normal now that the bombing has stopped. Her overall tone of controlled exasperation and being resigned to discomfort and shortages is shared by other wartime novelists of domestic life, Angela Thirkell in particular. Yet she remains funny, particularly in her accounts of the builders who do not work, the bizarre episode of the detective novelist looking for copy, and Haddock's appalling behaviour at the Speech Sweep.

After the war, Topsy stopped writing letters, presumably

because Trix, her only known correspondent, had finally moved to London. Captain Haddock contributed racing features in *Punch* and continued his goading of the Law Courts with more Misleading Cases until at least 1963. But Topsy is immortal: her commitment for legislating for the Enjoyment of the People is merely an expression of her enjoyment of life, spilling over into all our lives for the benefit of all.

Works cited

David Langford, 'A P Herbert's Misleading Cases', nd, https://ansible.uk/writing/miscases.html (consulted December 2022).

David Langford, 'The Trials of Albert Haddock', 2007, https://ansible.uk/misc/apherbert.html (consulted December 2022).

Reginald Pound, *A P Herbert. A Biography* (Michael Joseph 1976).

The Trials of Topsy

To William Armstrong
Of the Playhouse, Liverpool

1 A Brush with the Highbrows

Well Trix darling this *blistering* Season is nearly over and I'm
still unblighted in matrimony, isn't it *too* merciful, but you ought
to see poor Mum's face, my dear she's *saturated* with the very
sight of me poor darling, not that I don't try — last night I
went to a perfectly *fallacious* party with the Antons, my dear
all Russians and High Art and beards and everything, wasn't it
too degrading, what I say is why all these sculptors and things
can't be kept in their own holes I *never* know, but there it is,
after my little anti-climax with Toots Mum said perhaps I was
a clever man's woman after all, so I just went to darling Fritz
and I said, Fritz darling will you horizontalise what hair I have
left, and Fritz as usual simply *soared* to the occasion so that I
came out looking like something in the Prussian Guard, and
then I went home and embezzled one of Mum's old dressing-
gowns, cut off the sleeves and sewed up the front, and I went
to Whitworth's and got the *most* disarming pair of sandals for
sixpence, and I apropriated one of those *sensational* red girdles
off the dining-room curtains and let it sort of *waft* about the
hips, and everyone at home said I looked positively *Lithuanian*.

But my dear there's *no* coping with the intelligentsia, when I
got to this party which was in some *desperate* slum in the British
Museum or somewhere, my dear all critics and *bohemians* and
things, well when I tell you that I felt like an Archdeacon's
daughter, because there wasn't a *hair* in the place my dear,
except one or two who had positive tresses, only they wore them
floating round the ankles and everywhere, my dear *too Druid*,
and as for clothes, they all had *bits* of tapestry, and *altarpieces*,
and *Crimean carpets*, and, my dear, anything but *clothes*, so my
poor little dressing-gown struck a note of absolute *tedium*, and
really I felt like an understudy with the inferiority what-name
on the last night of *Chu-Chin-Chow*.

So I just *crawled* into the cloak-room, which was little better
than an outhouse, darling, and I said that KIPLING bit about
the upper lip and counted twenty with the powder and fifty

with the lipstick, and then I felt ready for anything, and when I tell you that before I left I had *two* Jugo-Slovvakians proposing to me at the same time, my dear *too* Bloomsbury for anything, and such *forests* of hair both of them, my dear between them they could have fitted every woman in the room with kiss-curls and a fringe, beards, of course, and I don't think either of them had struck soap since the French Revolution, and really, my dear, to judge by the foreigners one meets in London, well, Europe must be an *insanitary* Continent, however, all this was later, well, it was a studio, of course, and you never saw so many people who looked like *prawns*, of course one cannons into prawns everywhere, but you never see a complete prawnery, if you understand me, well I think nearly everybody there had *gills*, and all the women were *the same shape*, one or two younger ones came in but you could see them growing *more and more* prawny under the influence, my dear *too* scientific and ghastly, as for the pictures, they were nothing but the *most* tuberculous *green* women with triangular legs and blue hair, and always something *infectious* in the background like a stove-pipe or a bowler-hat, really darling I do think Modern art is a bit *septic* don't you?

Well, I asked my hairy loves who all the prawns were and everything and it turned out nearly everybody there was modelling in wax or did secret pottery or something, and it made me feel so utterly *sterile* I nearly cried, so just to get my own back I told Blackbeard just what I thought about the pictures, and, what was so *disheartening*, he told me half of them had been done by Redbeard who of course was listening hard with *both gills*, so I had to tell Redbeard I simply *venerated* his half of the pictures only I didn't know which they were, and of course it turned out that all the most *emerald* women were his, and what with the effort of pretending I preferred to see women with legs like fragments from a *Gorgonzola*, well, really I began to understand how people who live this sort of life all the time grow feelers and gills and things and I began to feel a bit *crustacean* myself.

Well, my dear, by this time both beards were completely *bristling* with passion and I wasn't a bit sure they hadn't both got bombs in their bosoms, and besides there seemed to be an outbreak of *prawn-fever* or something because nearly everybody was sitting on somebody's knee, and I had a sort of *intuition* that Redbeard thought it was lowbrow of me not to sit on his knee because that was evidently the done thing, only he wore velvet trousers and it wouldn't have surprised me if there were *mushrooms* growing on them, so altogether it was a moment of trial for your Topsy, but just then up came a perfectly *magnetic* man called Haddock, a bit brainy to look at perhaps but only the tiniest bit prawny, and not a *trace* of the Lithuanian, well my dear he'd come to my rescue and he told my two prawns they were wanted to sing Folk-Songs or something revolting in the next room, and Mr Slabb or somebody who was the host had sent for them.

So they went off, looking just as if they were going to be *tinned*, and this Mr Haddock sat down and protected me, well I thought probably he'd been attracted by my intellect, because he looked that kind of man, and I thought ten to one he'd painted the other pictures which Redbeard hadn't, so I thought the conversation might be a bit *laborious* perhaps, but I thought anyhow I'll die fighting, so I unloaded a few of Blackbeard's best remarks on Mr Haddock, I said what I liked was the *Pattern* of the picture opposite (which as far as I could see was two green women turning into jelly-fish) and Mr Haddock looked at it for a long time and then he said 'Yes,' and I thought perhaps Mum was right and I'm a clever man's girl after all, well then I said I thought the picture of the tomatoes was a good drawing though it wasn't *like*, because that was what Blackbeard said about one of the portraits. Well, my dear, Mr Haddock simply *ogled* the tomatoes till I thought he'd gone to sleep, but at last he said 'Do you?' in the most *vaccilating* way, and I began to think that perhaps he hadn't painted the pictures after all, but what he did was pottery, and, then I said that what simply *galvanised* me above all things was Significant Form. Well then he looked me in the eyes and he said what the deuce is that, so then I just *tore* off the mask and I said aren't you an intelectual because if not I'm wasting my sweetness on the desert air, so to speak, and he said No and it turned out he'd been terrified of me because of my intelect or rather my dressing-gown, and all he does is write but I don't know what, so after that we simply *thawed* my dear, and I told him about my *unspeakable* loathing for the *entire* party, and he said yes but one of the Russian girls wasn't so bad, so I said yes she was more prawned against than prawning, which means absolutely *zero*, darling, but Mr Haddock seemed to think it was *inspired*, my dear *that's* what I call *magnetic* in a man, so we slunk out into the night and had an absolutely *brainless* supper at Nero's which was such a relief, only my sandals and dressing-gown gave the secretary *such* a kick he made us both honorary members, I do think men are *elastic* don't you, all the same that's the last time I seek a soul-mate among the inteligentsia, so no more now, your *worldly* little Topsy.

2 The Simple Life

Well, night-light of the North, I haven't a *particle* of news, but that shows I'm fashionable, you see down here we're having the *most* heavenly *reaction* against all this histeria and the Press and everything, *you* know all these *pestilent* eclipses and Flights and grey-hounds, and my dear that *fictitious* Wimbledon place, you see nowadays the papers have only to say You *must* flock to Thingummy or Whatname and we all *flock*, my dear it's too gregarious and un-Saxon, and really *nobody's* happy this year unless they're standing in a *quue*, so we've started a perfectly darling movement to *avoid* excitement, when I tell you that we simply *ignored* the Eclipse but next day we all stayed up and saw an ordinary dawn and, my dear, you've no idea what a *sedative* it was, yet Mr Haddock says this happens nearly *every* day and not a word about it in the papers, so *whenever* the papers say that something is *too* marvellous we band together and *shun* it, and when I tell you that not *one* of us have been *near* the Electric Hare, and Toots cut BETTY NUTHALL dead the other day, and *whenever* we meet somebody who's just flown the Atlantic or needlessly swum something we simply *wither* her with a look.

Meanwhile of course my cabbage we have our own little amusements and records and things, but all on the *most* soporific lines my dear, well Toots has a competition to see who can take the longest to drive up Bond Street between twelve and one, and another one to see how long you can drive *round and round* Piccadilly Circus without anybody noticing, and of course that *magnetic* Mr Haddock I told you about, only I do wish his name wasn't Albert, well, whenever some tenacious bore is swimming the Channel or flying from Moscow or winning some *grotesque* championship or record or something and the *whole* of London is massing in a *quue* (how do you spell that?) and swooning with excitement over some *ghastly* tennis-player he gives the *most* Elysian *Chloroform* parties, well we just *congregate* in his garden and gaze at his gold-fish and have no conversation at all, and he has the *most* seductive mussel in a glass tank which only moves once in four days, my dear it's *too* refreshing.

So in a month or two I think you'll find that all this *feverish* Speed business is perfectly *mildewed*, well yesterday Mr Haddock took us a trip in his house-boat on the Grand Junction Canal, which is quite the most *comatical* kind of travel you can imagine, my dear it's too primitive and snaily for words, well, when I tell you that we started somewhere near Ealing and took six hours to reach Hammersmith you must see how divinely *stagnant* one felt, my dear it has the most *amphibious* engine which goes three miles an hour with the wind behind it and *never* starts, and my dear every half-hour the propeller is simply *festooned* with water-lilies and Mr Haddock has to take off his shoes and stockings (my dear he has the *most* musical toes!) and unveil the propeller, well of course me being on board simply *everything* went wrong and the engine got petrol in the carburettor or something so we had to pull the thing along with the most *rugged* sort of *rope*, my dear all tar and everything, and I did the Christian thing and helped Toots pull, and Toots sang the Volga Boat Song, and I felt *too* like the Russian Ballet to breathe darling, though of course my new blue silk was a perfect *sacrifice*.

Well, then a barge caught us up with the most *fascinating* horse and a *celestial* bargee, my dear I fell in love with him at sight, only of course he had a wife and *six* children, and they all lived together in the *weeniest* cabin, about the size of Hermione Tarver's lacquer cabinet, and it was all decorated with castles and roses and *hearts* my dear, and the *most* ornamental *brass* knobs you ever saw, so the barge sort of *towed* us, the *complete* poetry of no motion my dear, because there wasn't a *sound* and every now and then the *divine* horse stopped to eat, and it didn't *matter* at all, my dear the ecstatic *slowness* of it all, except once when the horse walked in its sleep and fell into the canal, because then there was a sort of *refined* excitement, and Toots jumped on to the bank and was *terribly* helpful, but my darling bargee didn't seem to think that experience in the hunting-field cut any ice with a barge-horse, however while they were *enticing* the horse out of the canal with the *most* heavenly language we went on board the barge and my dear you ought to see the way the *bed* lets down out of the wall and how they all manage I *can't* think but I've quite decided I'm going to go primitive and live on a barge and *never* have a bath again, darling, just look at the *time* one wastes!

Well we got to Hanwell where there's a lunatic asylum and seven locks in a quarter of a mile, and when I tell you that it took us a whole hour to go that quarter of a mile, and that was a record, well nearly anybody can fly the Atlantic but as Mr Haddock said seven locks are seven locks and what civilisation wants is a lot more things that can't be done quickly, because of course at every lock the men had to wind up the gates or the slooces or something and it was too utterly restful sitting in the cabin and watching them swear, and Mr Haddock with his hair wet looks *exactly* like a diseased rat, as I told him, darling, and he agreed *unanimously*, well, all this happened under the *wall* of the asylum, and really if anyone had looked over the wall and asked us what we were doing we should have had to say this was a *pleasure*-boat having a *pleasure*-party and then I don't know *what* they wouldn't have said, but really I don't care because really all this *rapidity* is *too* volatile and bilious, and as far as I can see the *sole* point in all this Flight ramp is to let the Americans get to Paris without their wives, and I don't care *what* you say but I won't have any *truck* with it, your rather *torpid* little Topsy.

3 Nature

Trix, dear, I've just had the *most* County weekend at the Antons', my dear it's *too* feudal and humiliating, there isn't a servant who's been with them for less than 27 years and the shrubbery was planted by Catherine Parr, so you can see the sort of *handicap* one has, and between you and me my little complexion does *not* go with woods and spinneys, but there it is I was as good as platinum and went to church on Sunday, though they have such *breakfasts*, well you know my weakness, all those *rows* of dishes, I do *venerate* having about *9* things to choose from, don't you, well, when I tell you that there was kipper and kedgeree and fried fish and bacon and eggs, and bacon and tomato and scrambled eggs, and the *most* Elysian kidneys, and bacon and mushrooms, and bacon and sausages, and porridge and cold bird and *celestial* ham and strawberries and everything, my dear really I could have spent the *entire* morning just *flittering* like a humming-bird from dish to dish, simply toying with them of *course*, darling, but life is serious after all, as Mr Haddock said (my dear, I told you about him I didn't I, the most *narcotic* man!) and I'd hardly got to the kidney and mushrooms when it was time for church. Well I lived through that because Mr Haddock found all the places for me, my dear his *manners* are positively *Bizantine* and when he sings seconds in a hymn simply *everybody* looks round, only I do wish he had two suits but of course it's the *spiritual* side of the man that tickles me, well there was rather an *erroneous* sermon but quite short and afterwards I thought I should have what Mr Haddock calls a nice lay-down before lunch, but in the country as *you* know, you *never* know from one minute to another what *ghastly* event is lurking for you, and sure enough old Anton asked if we'd like to see the New Field which they've just bought or morgidged or something, so of course we all said we were *starving* to see the New Field and of course it was raining, so the old man dug out of a cupboard some *perfectly* mossy old macs, *all* men's my dear, and Dot and I merely *festooned* them round us and hoped we looked like nice-minded Shire girls having clean fun because what we smelt like was a heap of dead leaves.

Well off we all went with all those *unnecessary* dogs, my dear I *do* think that too many dogs can be absolutely *excessive* on a muddy day, don't you, and of course the Shires were a *mass* of mud because they always are when I go to them, well first we had a look at the stables where the horses were when the Antons kept horses only they don't keep horses now so there was nothing in the Stables but an old pram and the gardener's baby, so we all said the stables were *too* attractive, and we went on to the tomatoes because old Anton is rearing *pedigree* tomatoes under glass or something but, I don't know why, I didn't seem to get any *kick* out of the tomatoes though everybody else had all sorts of snappy things to say about tomatoes and the Government and Sir Humphrey Somebody knew all about culture and Denmark and everything, but of course I tore my skirt on some perfectly *redundant* nail and Mr Haddock pinned it up for me with a little gold pin which was rather a flower-like gesture, I thought.

Well, my dear, by this time I was merely *drooping* with exhaustion and *languishing* for food and sort of *stewing* in my macintosh and one of those *irrelevant* dogs had taken a fancy to me, it kept *bounding* up at me out of the *deepest* puddles and Mr Haddock said it showed I had a nice nature which was more than I could say for the dog, so what with my skirt and everything we sort of *drifted* behind the others and talked scandal about May Anton and that refreshed me, well then we *dismembered* the rest of the party and we caught them up at the new Insinerator where they destroy the rubbish and we all stared at the Insinerator and said it was *too* miraculous and my dear the rain *dribbled* down my neck till I could have cried, however the next thrill was the pedigree ewe and old Anton said it might be a little damp underfoot for the ladies but we all did the *Christian* thing and said we didn't care if we had to *swim* to the ewe, well, my dear, what old Anton meant by a little damp underfoot was two fields of long grass up to a girl's knee, my dear I was *inundated*, and at the end was the *most* indecent stile, but when I tell you that the pedigree ewe turned out to be a common or garden *sheep*, my dear the *most* fallacious animal you ever saw, well that finished me, and when they all went off to see the Jersey heffers or something I told Mr. Haddock I should go no farther because ten to one the heffers would only turn out to be ordinary cows, which Mr Haddock said was quite likely, and I said what was more I shouldn't burst into tears if I missed the New Field.

Well Mr Haddock said he was *comparatively* lukewarm about Jersey heffers too, so we sat on the stile which was the only dry place in Sussex, and really I think we might have become *quite* bosoms only of course that *seditious* dog had stayed behind as well and what with its perfectly *mawkish* leapings real conversation was absolutely *prohibitive*, all the same, darling, I found out that we have simply *masses* in common, well he agrees with me that all this Nature is *too* dogmatic and over-rated and he thinks that if Love is not spiritual it's *simply* nothing, which is what I 've always said, haven't you darling, Mr Haddock said he wanted me to be nice to his friend George Rowland (who was there too) because he wanted Mr Rowland to marry and he thought I might kindle the fires of spirituality which from what I can make out are practically *dormant* in Mr Rowland, so I said I'd do what I could but my feet were sopping so we went back to lunch. Well in the evening I had the *most* degrading cold but between sneezes I fascinated Mr Rowland and from what I can make out he fancies himself as a *devil* and has a little money so I'm going out with him on Friday and you shall hear *all* the doings, I only hope he won't be quite so disapointing as the pedigree ewe, your spiritual little TOPSY.

4 Don Juan

Well my little Trix, I promised to tell you about my evening out with Mr Rowland Mr Haddock's friend, and by the way at a certain stage in the proceedings he said are you the kind of girl who tells other girls about the men you go out with and I said *Certainly not*, so if you *should* happen to meet him you must promise not to tell him I told you everything, won't you darling? Well, it was rather a *spineless* evening, I wore my new pink and really I looked *rather* divine and naughty, well, I told you that Mr Rowland thinks himself the last word in 'devils' and from what I can make out he'd had too many late nights and spent too much money that week because the first thing he said was that he'd discovered some *ecstatic* little place in Soho or would I prefer to go to the Majestic. Well it's quite extraordinary darling the *quantity* of young men I go out with nowadays who've just discovered an *ecstatic* little place in Soho where there's no dancing and the wine's two and threepence the quart, well, I wasn't going to squander my new pink on some *insanitary* little Italian ham-shop because really darling all this foreigner business is *too* un-English, isn't it, and my dear a single fly in the soup simply *alienates* me at once, so I said I felt a sort of craving for the Majestic and off we went.

Well Mr Rowland was *Nature's* man-of-the-world with the taxi-driver and the hall-porter and the head-waiter and I expect in the Cloak-Room but my dear there was never a *whisper* of a cocktail and he said he thought perhaps the 'dinner' would be better than à la carte which of course is *madly* more expensive and suddenly it flashed across me that the young man was seriously thinking of taking out your little Topsy on the *cheap*, so of course all the womanhood in me revolted at once, because there's no man living who ever got away with *that* my dear and if a comparative stranger wants to take me out he can take me out or do the other thing, not that it matters a *fraction* to me what I eat and drink, my dear I can't *bear* food, it's just the *principle* of the thing, so I made up my mind that this was going to be the *most* ruinous meal that Mr Rowland had ever paid for. Well, I said that à la carte would be better because I hadn't the *shadow* of an appetite and I couldn't conceivably do justice to a *whole dinner* and really *all* I wanted was a few stewed prunes and a glass of milk, well then of course the waiter began to suggest the *most* complicated and corrupting dishes with *expensive* French names, and I said I might manage *two* sips of a *captivating* soup at three and six and after that perhaps *toy* with a little Sole du Maurier which was seven shillings, after that the waiter began on the *entrées* and I could see my little he-man *peeping* at the prices over my shoulder and simply *deprecating* the waiter with reproachful glances and everything, but the waiter didn't seem to get his meaning, however I said that after the sole I couldn't *look* at anything else but all I wanted was a dry biscuit. Well meanwhile Mr Rowland had ordered nothing but a plate of *radishes* for himself, and from what I could make out he'd lost his appetite too, but I said a grown man must have something *solid* to keep body and soul together and I told the waiter to give him a Whole Young Grouse (which was twelve shillings) and then I said to keep him company I'd nibble at a Whole Young Grouse myself, and after that, I said, I should never eat again, unless perhaps it was a Péche Melba and some *infiniteesimal* savoury, and possibly some coffee and the *tiniest* little liqueur for fun.

Then Mr Rowland turned over the Wine-List in the most *lukewarm* way till he came to the claret page, and then he said wasn't it simply *tragic* that nobody apreciated a good claret nowadays, and I said wasn't it, and he murmured something about number 79 so I took a ladylike peep and I saw that 79 was a four-shilling vintage and really my dear I'd just as soon drink *marking-ink*, so I said I wouldn't take still wine because of my *inconsequent* digestion but if I might have something with bubbles in it like ginger ale or plain soda-water, so he ordered the champagne, and after that my dear he seemed to be plunged in a sort of *lethargy*, and really nobody would have guessed that he was taking out your *irresistible* Topsy for the first time.

Well I toyed with my *celestial* soup and he had his radishes, looking like the last act in a high-brow play, but with the champagne he seemed to cast care aside and after the grouse he *positively* expanded, like a flower my dear, and from what I could make out he must be the *most* injurious and *wild* young man alive, well if I told you the number of *homes* he's shattered and of course mothers simply have to *incarcerate* their daughters the *moment* he crosses the horizon, well he didn't put it so *bluntly* but that was the *impression* my dear, and he said he'd take me to some *abandoned* party where everyone would be utterly *unconventional* and voluptious. Well, it was a gala night at the Majestic, I've *never* been there when it wasn't, so I suppose as *soon* as I arrive they say *Let* it be a gala night and get out the balloons, well anyhow they got out the balloons and the paper-streamers and everything and Mr Rowland threw paper pellets at strange people like a *complete* devil, but as the meal wore on all the *abandon* seemed to be oozing out of him and by the coffee stage it was an *absolute* myth that he was *enthusiastic* well we had one dance but my dear it was too utterly *academic* and refined so I said perhaps we'd better go on to the voluptious party, well they brought the bill and he spent such *ages* adding it up that I thought that he must be the victim of *coma* or something, and then I had *slight* conscience trouble because I remembered I'd promised Mr Haddock to be *nice* to his friend but when he asked me if I could lend him some money to help pay the bill my conscience recovered *too* dramatically. Well after all I'd heard I was quite *aprehensive* about travelling in a taxi with this *assiduous* home-shatterer my dear, so I *cowered* into my corner and talked nineteen to the dozen about vitamins and *fruit* and everything because I was determined to keep the *entire* proceedings on a spiritual plane you see, well he didn't *utter* my dear and I began to have nerve-strain because I thought he must be planning something *passionate* and tiresome, so at last I took a side-long look and when I tell you that the home-shatterer was *fast asleep*, my dear with his *little* mouth open and his *little* chubby hands clenched across his *little* tummy like *Little* Alfred after his *First* Party, my dear it was *too* poignant, and really I began to feel like a wicked woman for keeping him up till a quarter-past ten, so I told the taxi-man to drive to the Cromwell Road where the rake resides in the most *moribund* hotel you ever saw, my dear the sort of place *New Zealanders* go to, and I woke him up and gave him to the porter and I do hope they tucked him up properly, but my dear if Mr Rowland is a twentieth century 'devil' may I never go out with a good young man, no more now, your *pathetic* TOPSY.

5 Good Works

Well, Trix, my partridge, I've just had the most *drastic* adventure, well when I tell you that Mr Haddock used to do good works at some settlement or oasis or something in the East End and every now and then a sort of *nostalgia* for Whitechapel comes over him or else it's a craving for goodness or something, so he goes down to some *morbid* club and plays Halma with the poor, which I think is so *confiding* of them because I'm sure he can't play Halma well one day he asked me if I'd care to go with him, but my dear the very *thought* of Halma merely *decimates* me, and my dear you know I *dote* on the poor but I never can think of a *thing* to say, well then he said would I help send some poor children off to the country, and that sounded more adequate because if you *can't* think of anything to say to children you can always tell them to stop doing what they're doing, and anything that means sending children *somewhere else* must be doing a good action to somebody, because I do think that children are a bit *superfluous*, don't you darling, and besides I wanted to show Mr Haddock that I have a good heart really though I will *not* play Halma if it means a Revolution.

Well my dear it's the most *sensational* movement called the Children's Holiday Fund or something, and they send simply *tribes* of these children to the country for a *fortnight*, and my dear Mr Haddock says some of them have *never* been out of the town though as I said the ones I'm sorry for are the poor little devils who've never been out of the country, because my darling Trix, life in the *country*! Well they were all waiting for us at some *insanitary* school, my dear seventy of them, not one of them more than a *yard* high, my dear like so many *shrimps* and simply encrusted with mothers and aunts and sisters and they were all *festooned* with bundles of clothes and loaves of bread and bottles of milk and kittens and dolls and the most *explosive* bags of gooseberries, and they all had the hugest labels on their tummies with their names and addresses and where they were going, my dear like *Ascot*.

Well Mr Haddock counted them fourteen times and sometimes there were sixty-eight and sometimes there were seventy-four, because they had the most *fraudulent* way of filtering about the yard, and what with the mothers and the sisters, and at the last moment one of the creatures ran home for a bag of *white mice* or a cage of gooseberries or something, but at last we marched off down the *whiffiest* street Mr Haddock in front and me behind and the seventy shrimps sort of *wafting* about between us, my dear I felt like Ulysses leading the three score and ten into the wilderness or something, and all the mothers *prowling* along beside us with *meticulous* glances, I'm sure they thought Mr Haddock was going to *sell* their families into slavery or something though Heaven knows who would have *bought* them, of course they *would* drop their *inconsequent* bundles and all those fallacious gooseberry bags simply *detonated* all over the road my dear if you could have *seen* the procession merely *drivelling* along like the tail of a wet kite and your *fastidious* Topsy carrying a bottle of *milk* and two waifs of the city in *each* hand, and there was one mother kept *goading* me about Little Martha because I was to be *sure* and see that she never had mushrooms which her father died of and she was all her mother had and everything, my dear too *poignant*!

But at last we got to some *squalid* station on the Underground and shook off the mothers which was a mercy, my dear they *swamped* their young with tears and Little Martha was like a *sponge*, no one would have thought she was going to see *real cows* for the first time, and of course on the platform I had *seventy* separate heart-attacks because every single one of the herd was *bent* on electrocution and of course Little Martha dropped her loaf of bread on the line and my dear I do think most of them were *half*-witted or perhaps less, because *nothing* one said to them conveyed the *flimsiest* meaning, they just grinned like little angels and carried on like *fiends*.

Well, my dear, we had *two* changes to get to Paddington, wasn't it *complex*, and every train we got into was like a madhouse, they shouted and sang and swarmed all over the *oldest* old men, gibbering like apes, I was *never* so embarrassed, and, what was so *shattering*, at one station ANOTHER HERD of children got in, can you imagine it, the whole train *crawling* with orphans of the storm, my dear simply *oozing* children at every crack, and Mr Haddock in the next carriage with the other half of our herd, and of course the *other* herd got out before we did and the *whole* of my herd tried to get out with them, and my dear the *difficulty* of sorting them out because my dear simply *all* the children of the poor look *exactly* alike only some had blue labels and some pink, but the *whole* train was held up and some of the passengers were *quite* petulant and my dear I've *never* felt that I wanted to knock 150 children's heads together before.

But of course the *absolute* horror was still to come, well we had to change at Oxford Circus or some prolific place and the herd simply *eddied* up and down those *unreasonable* passages all joyous and singing my dear I could have *cried*, well Mr Haddock had to stop to argue with a perfectly *penultimate* ticket-inspector who insisted on counting the *seventy* tickets twice over my dear simply because two shrimps labelled *Victoria* had got mixed up with our herd, and while we were arguing suddenly the *whole* herd *lost control* and charged past the inspector in the *complete* Gadarene style, well your poor Topsy chased after them, of course it was *quite* prohibitive to catch the front ones without trampling on the ones behind, and when I got round the corner there was *Little Martha* more than half-way up the *Moving Staircase* (!!) and the *entire* herd mounting heavenward behind her, all jambed together and yelling for joy, you never saw anything so *disconcerting*, well of course I knew that something *too* calamitous would happen when they got to the top, and the only way to get to the top myself was to run up the *down* part of the staircase, which my dear isn't half so easy as it sounds and gives a girl the *most* self-conscious sensations if you meet many City men coming down as I did, especially as I fell half-way and got the most *heart-rending* bruises on the shin, so the herd were at the top before me and my dear the front ones seemed to have *no ideas* about getting off the staircase, they merely lay down and caused an obstruction, and what with the others *heaping* up behind there was just a mangled mountain of child-flesh being washed up like shingle, my dear *a complete shambles*! Well I got down to it and *extracted* infant after infant, my dear like *teeth*, of course the whole place was *carpeted* with gooseberries not to mention milk-jugs and white mice and loaves of bread, but none of them seemed to be *fatally* injured, though my dear if ever children deserved *total* eradication those did, well a porter helped me and after a bit Mr Haddock came up and by degrees we *depopulated* the Staircase, and my dear of *course* the very last waif right at the bottom of the pile, was who do you think *Little Martha*, half suffocated my dear and bereft of bundles but *indecently* happy, and the *only* thing she said was Ma says I'm *not* to have no mushrooms lady!

Well they all seemed to think it was the *hugest* joke, quite forgetting the *agony* of mind of your *tender-hearted* Topsy, I do think children are the *most* inconsiderate things in the *whole* Animal Kingdom, don't you, well that's the last time I do good works in the East End thank you, because what Little Martha's mother will say about Mr Haddock and me when she hears the story from Little Martha I *can't* bear to imagine, but when we did get them into the right train at last I did think Well anyhow I've brought some *sunshine* into seventy lives or seventy-two if you count the two that we sent to Hertfordshire instead of to Sussex, and that's more than many a girl can say, and I fancy Mr Haddock was *quite* impressed with a girl's *savoir faire*, so that's that, your little philanthropist TOPSY.

6 Hymen

Trix, dear, I've just been through the *most* agonising of all human proceedings, an English wedding, my dear I shall *simply never* give my girlish heart away because rather than cause a whole day's *suffering* for five hundred wedding-guests well really I'd sooner remain the *world's virgin* for life darling. Well it was poor Ann Atbury that made the trouble and my dear if people *must* be married why *must* they be married in the bowels of the country on a hot day, a complete *slug* of a train and two *diabolical* changes you know my dear all that climbing over bridges for Platform Four and the carriage full of *farmers' wives* and baskets of eggs and everything degrading, well when we got to Stoke-under-the-Wallop or somewhere I was simply *withered* with stuffiness and as for *hilarity*, not that hilarity would have been the right *note* from what I make out, my dear we were twenty minutes too early and I *hovered* about the grave-yard with Aunt Elizabeth feeling *too* funereal and *mothy* for words, and presently the *whole* County crawled into the grave-yard all draped in black and their faces like Liverpool on a wet Sunday morning, my dear they *couldn't* have worn more black if they'd come to see Ann Atbury cremated or electrocuted or turned into a *nun*, it wasn't only the men, they're a one-frock-sex anyway poor dears, but you *would* think that two hundred County beauties could have bought a *dahlia* between them or clubbed together and got something bacchanal in pale grey, but my dear you *never* saw such *masses* of jet, and really my dear the *one* spot of brightness was a darling old Colonel with a lavender waistcoat and a sweet-pea buttonhole, and really *no one* would have said that we'd all come there to celebrate the *gladdest* moment in two people's lives and well-born I may be but I do think top-hats in the country look a bit too feudal and didactic don't you.

Mr Haddock said, my dear of *course* Mr Haddock was *foully* dressed because he said *all* his wedding-garments had been corrupted by moth and he had on his *only* suit as usual, but to show goodwill he wore a butterfly-collar and the *most* ridiculous bow-tie my dear, and he kept his overcoat on so as to make people think he was wearing a tail-coat *underneath*, but of course the whole show was given away by his *hat*, my dear the *most* amorphous, *jelliest*, *dismallest* blancmange you ever saw! Well he said that all this gloom was because of this *putrifying* law about not getting married after three o'clock, because as he said well half-past-two in the afternoon is Life's Barrenest Moment, and how can you expect a Britisher to be merry *immediately* after lunch especially if he hasn't had any, as most of us hadn't because of the *tuberculous* train-service, and I said Well isn't it something to do with religion or something and he said No it's *merely* because of the Nonconformists because they used to have *registrars* when the Nonconformists were married because from what I can make out the Nonconformists had to be treated like so many *wild beasts*, and then a man brought in a Bill, and the Home Secretary and everything, and something about clandestine marriages, well, I didn't understand a word of it but from what Mr Haddock said there's no more religion in it than there is in *lighting-up* time, and the Jews can be married at *midnight* if they like and I do think that what's good enough for the Jews ought to be good enough for a Christian girl in this country, don't you darling.

Well there it is we went into the church, and what I thought was so perfectly *agnostical* in spite of all the black beads and satin and general jettiness simply *none* of the County registered religion, but they all *chatted* and giggled and *peered*, my dear *too* secular, like a Flower-Show or something, well I wouldn't object to a bit of a religious throb in the service provided there was some sort of *worldly hilarity* at the reception, but my dear it was just the other way, the *moment* we gathered in Ann Atbury's mother's mouldy marquee (and I do think a marquee is man's *mouldiest* creation don't you) well a complete *blight* enwrapped the wedding-guests and we all stood on one *leg* and did our best to look County and we all said *didn't* the bride look sweetly pretty though *I* thought she looked like the *Queen of the Fairies* at the Surbiton pantomime, and while Mr Haddock was being matey with the bride no less than *five* of *Nature's* heavy-weights *loaded* me with cucumber sandwiches which always give me a bad night and my dear I do think champagne is life's *dreariest* liquid at half-past three in the afternoon don't you, and as for *wedding* champagne where *do* they find it?

Well at last Mr Haddock came back thank Heaven and rather than look at the guests any longer we went and looked at the presents, my dear the *fish-knives*, there can't be so much fish in all the world, and fourteen photos of Tallulah Bankhead, well Mr Haddock said wasn't it time I was getting married and he knew a nice man he'd like to meet me, and I said *how* Christian but I'm feeling like *Nature's* spinster thank you, and I can get all the fish-knives I want without putting your friends to the trouble of marrying me, well he annoys me when he talks like that, and my dear I was so *tired* I was ready to *yelp* like a pedigree dog, and my dear you know how I *venerate* Ann Atbury, and her young man's *perfectly* congenial, but all I wanted was for the bride and bridegroom to *leave the premises*, which *shows* there must be something *radically* wrong with *weddings* doesn't it?

Well after about two days they did go, well it seemed like that, and there was all that *plebeian* revelry with *rice* and confetti and old *boots* and everything, my dear *nobody* adores clean fun more than I do, but I do think when a girl's best friends are seeing her off into the New Life which stretches before her and everything they *might* think of something more affectionate to do than throw *cereals* down a girl's *back* don't you, but there it is, that's *weddings* and I suppose it's a kind of unconscious *revenge* for all the *sufferings* of the wedding-guests, well there we were, my dear, *suspended* in mid-air so to speak, at Stoke-under-the-Wallop at half-past-five in the afternoon, all the girls half-dead with ices and standing on one leg and all the men half-alive with champagne and no train till 6.15 and two *Satanical* changes at that, my dear *too* pulverising.

Well you know that *morbid* post-wedding sensation when everybody thinks they must do *something* and nobody wants to do *anything* but go to bed or a lunatic asylum, so about sixteen of us went with the best man to Reggie's and worked like *slaves* to be gay, my dear *too* ghastly, everybody tried to be *funny* and nearly everybody was *simply* septic, and we all talked at once and the waiters merely *ignored* the whole party, my dear I was *famished*, and Mr Haddock went on and on about the Marriage Act of eighteen-something and how all this *misery* was simply because you have to be married at the *idiot* hour of half-past two instead of reasonably in the evening, and really I do think there must be something in it and if only there was a *soul* in Parliament with the *guts* of a gold-fish they might perhaps do something about it, but there isn't, so no more now, your devastated TOPSY.

7 Literature

Well Trix dear, what do you think, I've become a *professional* girl, well really, my dear, Mum's got so tiresome about this *boring* marriage business and even Dad's beginning to wear a *martyrish* look, and really I believe if I'm not blighted in matrimony in another fortnight they'll *lock* the front door on me one night, and anyhow as Mr Haddock said in these days economic thingummy is the *sole* criterion or something for a girl of spirit, don't you agree, so I made up my mind to be *Nature's* economic girl and earn some degrading lucre somehow, well, I thought it wouldn't be *too* prohibitive because as Mr Haddock said England may be going to the dogs and democracy and everything but thank Heaven we're all snobs still and if Lady Topsy Trout can't find a niche in the façade of industry who *can* darling?

Well Mr Haddock thought I might perhaps carve a bit of a niche in the *writing* profession because from what I can make out nearly all the writing is done by Society nowadays, it seems you start with advertising a face-cream and by degrees you become a gossip-writer, like Little Lord Fatface (my dear they say his ads for 'Reduce-It-In-The-Home' were *too* exquisite) well my dear I'm in luck because it seems there's the *most* venomous face-cream war going on between 'Queen Cream' and 'Skindew', you see Skindew have just made a *capacious* splash with that Stage Star series and Queen Cream were *just* preparing to retaliate with a Mayfair Flowers series when Mr Haddock happened to mention *me*, and lo and behold your Topsy's the very *first* of the Mayfair Flowers, with a column and a half about How I Keep My Beauty, my dear you can say what you like but it *is* rather a thrill this writing and I can't *tell* you what they're paying me, and *masses* of Queen Cream for life for nothing, of course I'd never *heard* of the stuff before, I *always* use Skindew, but the *most* efficient Queen Cream young woman came to see me with a sniff and my dear a skin like a *sponge*, the *most* deceptive ad for a cream you can imagine and it's just as well they don't photograph *her*, well she read out all the most *litterary* bits she'd written and simply *all* I had to do was to sign it, I must say Beauty and Queen Cream seem to be a whole-time job from what I seem to have written, my dear it's cream before meals and cream after meals and cream between meals and really the actual meals seem to be the only parts of the day I don't spend *creaming*, well it all came out in *The Glass* and next morning the telephone *never* stopped ringing, because my dear simply *everyone* read my article and they adored the photograph all except that *inconsequent* Mr Haddock who said it looked like The Vamp Reformed, so I shan't give *him* one.

But my dear I haven't told you, the *most* fanatical thing happened, *Parker, you* know, my flat-footed maid, well my dear I asked her what she thought of the picture and she said it was sweetly pretty but she was a *wee* bit *difficile* I thought, and the same night she gave notice, my dear I couldn't *imagine* why and you'll never guess, but Mum talked to her and it seems she didn't approve of me writing about Queen Cream when I've used nothing but Skindew since I left the Kindergarten, because she said it was *deceiving the public*, my dear wasn't it *perfectly* sweet, the *ideas* they have! well of course Mum talked her over but I still feel the old thing does a girl's hair more in sorrow than in anger, however, much more important, the next day my dear an *editor* or something rang up from *Undies, the divinest* paper, well I went to see him in the *most* insanitary office, but it seems he was *throbbed* about my article and he was *too* congenial, and they want me to try and do the Mayfair Maiden's page when Hermione Tarver goes to India, well my dear you must say it's *rather* gratifying when you realise I've only just begun, mustn't you darling, they want me to do it as near as possible in the same style as Little Lord Fatface, which is a *tiny* bit lowering perhaps because really my dear *all* he does is to write down the names of *all* the people he met yesterday and fill in from *Who's Who* and my dear if I can't write as well as he does I shall just give up writing, anyhow I've just been practising, what d' you think of this: —

An Ex-Oxonian.
I met Lord Birkenhead in the Park yesterday. He was smoking a cigar. His daughter Pamela was with him. The Secretary of State for India has two daughters, both girls. 'F E' was at Wadham.

Stick-Names.
Mention of 'F E' reminds me that Lord Danver is known to his intimate friends as 'Bubbles'. The nickname was a childish corruption of his first name, which is Charles. These nursery soubriquets often stick to a man through life.

War-Hero.
'Bubbles' owns four thousand acres and is a good shot. He belongs to the Marlborough Club. When I saw him at Hurlingham yesterday he had just had a spill. He was smiling at his mishap. His brother is the Admiral, who fought at Jutland.

Proving The Rule.
There are not many cases of twins marrying brothers. Lord Mouldsworth's daughters are no exception to the rule, for their fiancés *are not related. Both girls are fond of sport. Helena plays golf. They are beautiful.*

A Witty Father.
One day this week Lord Mouldsworth was dining with his family at a famous restaurant. He seemed to be enjoying his oysters. I asked him if he had found any pearls. 'Two', he replied, and smilingly indicated his winsome daughters. He is a yachtsman. The Countess keeps white mice.

Not so bad d' you think darling, as a *matter* of fact Mr Haddock helped me the *flimsiest* bit but he will *not* take it seriously and he does make the *most* naughty suggestions, but I do think that's *just* the kind of simple *sedative* stuff that all those *unfortunate* creatures in Whitechapel are *starving* for on a Sunday morning don't you, well anyhow I'm fairly *launched* on the litterary career and I *do* think it does everybody good if a girl mixes with the life of the people a bit and strikes out her own economic what-not don't you, so if Mr Haddock won't help me I shall go *straight* to that *brainy* Queen Cream woman with the sniff, farewell Trix, your *only* TOPSY.

8 Reducing

Trix darling, have you *ever* been to a Turkish Bath well *don't*, of course if you're *reducing*, but not unless you're *simply* mountainous, and even then, but don't go for voluptious pleasure that's all because my dear it's rather an *erroneous* entertainment, well recently darling I've had the *fraction* of a worry about my little figure, my dear *nothing* spectacular I'm still the *world's* sylph really, but there's just the *teeniest* ripple when I *bend*, and nowadays if a girl can't jump through her garter she's *gross*, well of course I did all those *unnatural* exercises and breathing through the hips and everything, but really my dear what with the hair and the face-cream and the care of the hands it's as much as a girl can do to get to bed as it *is* and if she's going to spend half the night expanding the *lungs* as well, well when *is* a girl to put in a spot of beauty-sleep, so the exercises *dwindled* somewhat.

Well then there's this *affected* fruit business, my dear Hermione eats *nothing* but radishes and she's *quite* invisible but looks like a ghost and my dear I do think breakfast is one of the *few* things worth clinging to in this life, don't you, however I kept on *noticing* this ripple in the bath and that gave me the idea of this Turkish performance because somebody once told me that's the quickest thing ever and they say one of the Duchesses looked almost human after two.

Well I *crawled* in, all by myself, wasn't it heroic, but my dear *quite* petrified and feeling *just* like a human sacrifice approaching the altar, well my dear they take all your clothes away and give you the *most* mortifying garment in *thick* white linen my dear like an abreviated *shroud* or the *Fat Boy's* nightgown, and wide enough for the *widest* Duchesses, so my dear you can *imagine* what your Topsy looked like, well the first place you go into is called the *teppidairium* or something, not very hot but quite hot enough, a sort of purgatory my dear, where you prepare for the bath to come so to speak, well I *crept* in my dear feeling like a dog that's done the wrong thing, and of course the *sole* soul in the place was the *most* redundant woman I know, the widow Wockley, my dear you know I can't *bear* to say an unkind thing but really my dear she *is* quite definitely *unmagnetic*, and my dear she looked like Mrs Caliban in the shroud and her hair like seaweed and she has the *most* unseductive skin, well she was reading *Beauty While You Wait* and from what I can make out she takes a T B once a week, well she was all over me at once, you'd have thought we were *sisters* though really I've scarcely *met* the woman and *never* in shrouds, but my dear the *confidences*, well I gather she wants to get married again or something, though of course my dear she'll *simply* never be forty again, anyhow she plunged into the *most* embarrassing wail about 'Men' and all her *fatiguing* affairs and things, my dear she might have been HELEN OF TROY dictating her diary, Trix darling you *know* I'm not prudish *don't* you but I do think there ought to be some sort of *reticence* in the teppidairium don't you, and all in the *most* baneful we-girls-know-a-thing-or-two-don't-we style, my dear positively *leersome*, and as if she wasn't a *second* older than me, well after a bit something told me I should be *quite* ill *very* soon so I got up in the middle of a sentence and merely *fled* into one of the hot rooms.

Well, you go through a heavy curtain and the *most* awful *blast* of heat *strikes* you in the face, my dear *too* detonating, I just crumpled up and sat down and my dear the seat was *red-hot*, if you could have *seen* me leap up to the roof, well really I thought I should *burst* into *flames*, but rather than go back to the Wockley woman I thought I'd cheerfully be *insinerated*, so I tottered about like a cat on hot bricks, and my dear have you ever been to the *Aquarium* because if you have you know if you look closely into one of those tanks you generally see something perfectly *repugnant* lurking in a corner or sticking to a rock and you can't think *what* it is, it's just a *Thing*, and personally I move on to the next exhibit, well suddenly I realised that this room was full of *Bodies*, and my dear the most *undecorative* bodies, all *pink* and *shiny* with their eyes closed, and not a sound my dear, well if you can imagine a lot of *enormous* dead lobsters with white nighties on and very fat arms and my dear *one* of them was Lettice Loot, you know I do think there's a *lot* of nonsense talked about the beauty of the human form and everything, because really I do think that women are *about* the most hideous things there are don't you darling and that's why we have to be so careful about *clothes*, of course I think these artists are a lot to blame because my dear *look* at the lying pictures of women they do and really if anyone did a picture of a single corner in a Ladies' Turkish Bath well really I think that would be the finish of *matrimony*.

However, well then I took a peep into the *second* hot-room where there were only two dead lobsters, but my dear *too* squalid and the heat was *blistering* so I went back into the first room and my dear *imagine* my horror there was the Wockley body laid out with the others, I recognised it at once, well she opened one eye at me and I was *terrified* she'd *plunge* into her romances again so I escaped back into the teppidairium and read the Directions, well it said you pour teppid water over the *head* and await the *free* outburst of perspiration, and my dear you should have *seen* your poor Topsy sitting all by herself in a fat child's nightie *dripping* teppid water and waiting and waiting for the free outburst and everything, but my dear simply *nothing* took place, and I was petrified because I thought perhaps I was abnormal or cold-blooded or something degrading, well at last the Wockley came out looking *yards* thinner already, my dear she'd practically *disappeared*, but not quite, unfortunately, well she said Have you sweated dear, and that will show you what I mean about a Turkish Bath, because my dear Trix *any* place where a woman like the Wockley can come up to a girl and ask her in cold blood if she's sweated well there *must* be a defect in the *whole* institution. Well I said No I hadn't sweated but I was doing what a girl could, and she said You're in the wrong room, if you don't sweat you'll have *pneumonia*, so I said I'd rather have *peritonitis* than go back into that *insanitary* oven with the bodies in it, and she said Come and try the Russian Steam Bath then, well my dear by this time I'd have tried the Russian

Steam Roller to get out of the place, so she took me into the *most* antagonising cell and let off *masses* of Russian Steam, my dear *too* alarming, but there was a capital free outburst and everything and I *rushed* out just before I was asphyxiated, well after that she began on her *odorous* adventures again and my dear you know I don't blush *gratuitously* but I got hotter and hotter and very soon I said Thank-you Mrs Wockley, your conversation's done the trick, and I walked off, my dear *too* crude, I know, but really!

Well before I could get to my clothes I was caught by an *Amazon* of a woman and laid *flat* on a marble slab, my dear like a *salmon* or a side of ham, and my dear she scrubbed me and scraped me and prodded me and slapped me, my dear *too* humbling, and then she knocked the liver about and stood me up and turned the *hugest* hose on me, my dear I might have been a *conflagration*, well of course you know I'm not *built* for rough stuff and your *ill-treated* Topsy fell *flat* on her face, well then as if that wasn't enough she led me to the *most* barbarous *cold plunge* and said jump in Madam, well my dear only one thing *created* could have made me jump into *cold water* after all I'd been through and at that moment I heard behind me the *leprous* voice of the Wockley woman and rather than share the same *element* with the creature I *dove* into the frozen depths and stayed under water till she'd gone away, well after all this I lost four pounds but my dear I've had *such* an appetite *ever* since that I've put on six, so it's *rather* fallacious in the reducing line and perhaps it will have to be the radishes after all, O *dear*, farewell, your *unfortunate* TOPSY.

9 Going To The Dogs

Well Trix darling at last I've been to these *contagious* greyhounds, and really my dear this *is* the most *unreasonable* country, well the things you *may* do and the *things* you mayn't, in this town one seems to spend one's *whole* life with one foot in the *jail*, well Mr Sweet took me, I don't think I've told you about Mr Sweet darling because, my dear, Mr Sweet is one of my *rather* serious ones, my dear *quite* lamblike and he's been hovering for *years* but my dear *too* shy and *Nature's* breeding, *you* know the Puddefoot Sweets, but only in the Home Office and an *utter* pauper, of course I *rather* wish he wasn't a Civil Servant because as Mr Haddock said it's one thing to marry a Commoner but it's another thing to be tied for life to a Government *Department*, anyhow last night he took me to the dogs or rather I rang him up and said he was to come and I ran him down in the car to save the poor lamb taxis, well we were nearly there when *what* was my horror I remembered I hadn't the *ghost* of a *gasper*, well he doesn't smoke them and Toots had told me that *some* sort of fumigant is *quite* desirable at the dogs, so I stopped at one of those *characteristic* little shops where they sell tobacco and chocolate and newpapers and everything, well my dear the place was *simply* teeming with my favourite fags but *would* you believe it the man said it was *too* felonious to sell us any because it was *five* past eight, though my dear he was *still* selling chocolate and the *most* poisonous sweets, not to mention *stamps* and *newspapers* and *several* guides to greyhound form, and he said he would be selling them till half-past nine but if he sold a gasper or a single match some *superfluous* policeman would be sure to do him a mischief, well my dear Sweet said it was quite right, there's some feeble-minded *law* about it, and all I can say is if there are *still* laws of that kind what *was* the good of women getting the *vote* don't you *agree* darling?

Well my dear more in *anger* than in sorrow we went in to the dogs, and I *insisted* on the five shillings because I knew my poor Sweet couldn't afford the ten and besides Toots said that in the five shillings you get the full *squalor* of the thing, my dear *too* right, however I must say that the first race a girl sees is *too* decorative, well they turn out *all* the lights except the lights on the track, so that *all* you see is just this ribbon of *green baize*, my dear too utterly like a *race-game* or the *hugest* roulette-table, which of course my dear is all it is, and why they don't have electric *dogs* and have done with it I can't imagine.

Because my dear the race takes *thirty seconds* and then there's *twenty* minutes *standing about* and if you didn't bet you'd *merely* perish of *chronic* fatigue, so of course we betted and my poor Sweet was *too* noble, he put *ten* shillings on *every* race, including five shillings for me if we won, only of course we *never* did and my dear I *can't* press money on a man can you so I'm afraid he lost more than I did, my dear we backed *four* seconds and one dog which would have won, my dear the *most* alluring animal, only it was bitten by some other *categorical* creature and came in *last*, and of course every time we knew *perfectly* well which dog would win only it was always odds *on* and my dear *odds on* is *utterly* valueless to your ambitious little Topsy, and if I can't win *masses* I'd much rather lose don't you agree dear?

However after *hours* of this my legs were *crumbling*, so we *crawled* away to Soho, yes I know *too* degrading, but of course we were dressed all plebeian for the dogs, well simply *all* I wanted was a *single* cocktail, but my dear the *foul* man in charge of the place said we *couldn't* have a cocktail unless we had a *ham-sandwich* because it seems there's some *redundant* law which says that, well if you've got to have an unnecessary ham-sandwich you might just as well have a *Christian* supper, so my poor Sweet ordered supper, and my dear if you're going to have a Christian supper you *must* have the *flimsiest* glass of really celestial *wine* so my poor Sweet ordered the wine but my dear *no* sooner had the waiter filled our glasses for the *first* time than he rushed back and merely *snatched* them out of our hands because it was *ten* seconds after eleven or something and there's another nose-poking law about *that*! Well my dear we *slunk* out and went to some *monastic* night-club which Sweet belongs to, my dear *too* Sydenham and they all talk about nothing but *Einstein* and the *new* Prayer-book and *Ibsen* and *Shaw* and all those *miasmal* Czecho-Slo-what-is-its and everything, but my dear the *moment* one sat down it was raided by the *police* because it seems ten years ago there was *another* club there which had a bad book in the library, so we *slunk* out of that and of course there were *four* policemen merely *mustered* round the car because it was facing east instead of west and there's a law about *that*, and anyhow it was in some *criminal* place, well by this time my poor Sweet was blushing all over because he does hate giving his name and address, and my dear it *is* hard because he takes *years* to thaw, and my dear every time we broke the law simply *all* the emotion seemed to *filter* out of him, so I had one of my moments of abandon and I said *Let's* go and have a second's peace on that *romantic* bridge in St James's Park, well we left the car in the Mall and my dear it *is* the most *Venetian* view in the *whole* of London because it was a *unique* night, and my dear the *moon*, and the *water*, and the Foreign Office and everything and not a *soul* about, but of course *rather* Arctic and I suppose I shivered because my angelic Sweet put his *knightly* arm round me, which my dear is the *wildest* action he's *ever* done, so we nestled a little and drank in the night as they say, which my dear will very soon be the only thing we *can* drink, and I was just thinking Well this is the *first* moment we've had that's cost him nothing and isn't against the law, and my dear I *know* he was *quite* liking me, and I do believe he was just going to venture on a *chaste* caress when up came a *reptile* keeper and said Is that your car in the Mall, well my dear it seems there's even a law about leaving my *harmless* little car in the Park for ten seconds at 1 o'clock in the morning so we *slunk* back and there was the *usual* ring of *irrelevant* policemen and my dear *when* you think of the *masses* of murderers they *never* catch, and my dear when you think that all those *obscene* betting-people can do anything they like and the *only* time we were *left alone* was when we were wasting my poor Sweet's money on those *fraudulent* dogs, and of course *the* tragedy is that I hear my poor Sweet is in the *very* Department which makes up all these *nursery* regulations, and my dear talking of Sweet of course the spell was *utterly* broken and I *rather* doubt if the spell will ever be the same again, so no more now, your *revolutionary* TOPSY.

10 Ideals

Trix dear I must write to you or I shall *short-circuit*, my dear I'm *seething*, well it's these *ideals*, I do think people with ideals can be perfectly *undiluted* sometimes don't you, well my dear I've been down here for a week staying with Uncle Arthur and Aunt Margaret, Mum always *exports* me to Whitewalls when she thinks I'm going bad it's a sort of family *refrigerator*, two services on Sunday and everything, of course it's the *most* eligible place, my dear it's *Nature's* manor-house with *divine* low ceilings that *bump* your head and doors that don't *fit* and no lights or lavatories or hot water or anything, my dear too medieval and convincing, but the *entire* place is full of ideals and *stags' heads*, and what I *never* understand about ideals is that anything anybody else feels strongly is *ideals* but anything I feel strongly is *girlish folly* or the Modern Young.

Well for instance a *single* Stag's head alienates me at once, but Uncle Arthur is alienated by cocktails and face-powder, and Aunt Margaret thinks that syncopated music is *too* impure and there's an American judge here who talks *nothing* but ideals and Geneva and some ghastly League or other, and there's the *most* proper young Guardee officer whose *one* idea is to avoid anything *vulgar*, and my dear they spend the *whole* day killing things, well Aunt Margaret doesn't kill anything much except slugs and snails but she kills them in the *most* barbarous manner, my dear if you could *see* her *creeping* round the garden with a bag of salt and *watching* them shrivel, and as for the others, well my dear we have prayers before breakfast and ideals *at* breakfast, well Uncle Arthur reads out all the statistics about *alcohol* and Aunt Margaret reads out *all* the remarks of these *hysterical* centenarians about the Modern Girl, *you* know my dear all this *inconsequent* yap about short hair and short skirts and short lives and everything, and my dear the American reads out anything he can find about this *medicated* League, and the Guardee doesn't read anything but eats *swamps* of porridge in faultless taste, and my dear the *moment* they've digested they get their guns and go out and *slay* something, but of course my dear they all *dote* on dumb animals only it doesn't apply to dumb cock pheasants and voiceless rabbits and perfectly mute fish, and of course it's all done for the good of the country and very often they rout out some *dangerous weasel* and have shots at that for the poor farmer's sake, only I notice they don't waste much time over the homicidal weasel if there's anything *eatable* like a rabbit about. Well my dear *don't* think I'm *sentimental* or anything plebeian, my dear *nobody* adores an *expensive* roast bird more than I do, and I *do* see that anything *too* decorative like a cock-pheasant ought to be exterminated *forthwith*, and of course I can't have my wing of bird if nobody kills it, *all* I do say is that anybody who does bird-slaughter consistently for *fun* had much better be comparatively *reticent* about their *ideals*, and really my dear I don't expect my butcher to give me a *single* lecture about ladylike behaviour.

But my dear that's *just* what happens down here, well so far I've always managed to keep clear of the gun-stuff but this afternoon by request, my dear, I went for a walk with Uncle Arthur and his gun and of course *festoons* of dogs and *all* the time the old boy lectured me about the *snares* of London, and the *healthy* country, and how a girl ought to spend more time with Nature and everything, and he worked up gradually to the cocktail habit and the *mildewed* Modern Girl, of course my dear he's a *complete* lamb and really I don't mind *what* he says, but what was so perfectly *incompatible* my dear, every few minutes he had to stop lecturing to shoot a *rabbit*, my dear I was *quite* ill, and on the word cocktail he let off *both* barrels and *executed* a partridge, well after a bit he said would I like to have a shot and I said No thank you it's *too* saintly of you Uncle but to be *perfectly* frank I'd sooner have the gin-habit than the gun-habit and if he was going to do any more *bird-control* I thought perhaps I'd go back, well I said it *quite* sweetly darling because after all it's *nothing* to do with me what he does, but my dear the poor old thing looked at me as if I was something *unnatural*, the very *idea* that HE could do anything that *I* could disapprove of, however he took it *quite* reasonably and on the way home my dear he never shot a *fly*, well at tea-time as luck would have it the American and the Guardee had the world's kill-conversation, my dear the *fish* they've destroyed and the *bears* they've blown up and the bags and braces and *all* their measurements, and each going *one* better than the other, my dear between them they could have *filled* the *Ark*, well at last the Guardee turned to me and said had I ever shot flying-fish by moonlight because that was *life's* Elysian sport and one night he got twenty, well my dear by this time I was *quite* saturated so I said No I'd *never* seen a flying-fish and if I *did* see a flying-fish my *one* idea would be to let it fly.

Well my dear there was the *most* tropical hush and he looked at me just as Uncle Arthur did, my dear as if I had the *mange*, my dear that's what's so *shattering*, if you let out that you're comparatively *lukewarm* about bird-murder and fishicide they *really* think you must be a bit *unhealthy*, my dear I felt *leprous*, however it all passed off, and the young man was *quite* forgiving because my dear I *rather* fancy he's *rather* attracted, but what with one thing and another I felt rather *cyclonic* and this evening my dear I put on my *naughtiest*, the pink you know, which my dear would be short for the Shires even if it hadn't *shrunk* and I brought down all my *snappiest* records which my dear I've always kept *under the bed* before, well at dinner the men had *two* sips of claret and a *single* sniff of port and there's all that *pedantic* decanter-pushing and *nothing* happens, but my dear *every* time the port came round I filled up my glass, and they all *peered* and at last Aunt Margaret merely *dragged* me from the room, well we always sit in the billiard-room which my dear is *nothing* but stuffed salmon and stags' heads and birds' bodies, a complete *mortuary*, my dear *too* grisly, well we sat down and Aunt Margaret couldn't take her *eyes* off my knees and at last she said Your knees child so I got up and hid the old knees and I put on *Kiss Me Cutie Mother's Coming* which my dear is *History's* loveliest noise, but Aunt Margaret *winced* from the feet up and said Stop it child I want to talk to you seriously, well she began on the Modern Girl and how a quiet young man like the Guardee liked quiet girls with *ideals* and everything, well of course seeing rocks ahead I opened the bag and had a look at the old face, and of course my dear my little nose was too luminous because a girl's nose always is in the Shires, but at that moment *in* came the men and Uncle Arthur said Leave Nature alone Top, well then my dear I *merely* detonated and I sort of *gestured* at the antlers and dead bodies and things and I said Leave *Nature* alone *yourself* uncle, my dear *too* crude, and I said I've got *my* ideals or something and then what was so *utterly* unconvincing I just *melted* into a *pond* of tears and *cantered* out of the room, well of course *ever since* I've been thinking of the *most* napoleonic things I ought to have said, but here I am darling with *no* hot water and this *bucolical* candle is guttering and I *rather* fancy there's a BAT in the room, so shed a tear for your *martyred* TOPSY.

11 The Origin of Nieces

Well Trix darling what *do* you think your *pagan* little Topsy
has become a *doctrinal* controvert, at least I suppose I am, well
anyhow for several days I've been perfectly *emboiled* in episcopal
controversy and my dear my *poor* head's gone *quite* ethereal with
it and I don't know *what* I think or *who* I am and *whether* I exist
and *why* should the Pope and was granny a baboon or a Bartlett
or what, so now as they've all gone bye-bye at last I thought
perhaps if I write to you about it I might get my poor little
morass of a mind a *fraction* clearer, because as Mr Haddock says
the *mere* act of writing makes the intelect function sometimes
when there isn't a cocktail which I think is *so* right, don't you
darling?

Well my dear for *countless* days the *whole* house-party has
been talking *nothing* but *parson*, and by the way I got that from
Mr Haddock, because he says it's the done thing to talk about
parson, like that, and it's an irregular plural or something, like
partridge or *grouse*, well you *never* say *grouses* do you darling, so
I suppose he's right, well of course Aunt Margaret and Uncle
Arthur take parson *quite* earnestly and you know I've *always* said
that I *always* believe in *always* doing the *Christian* thing, and
I must say to me there's *nothing* more arresting than a really
nice he-parson and I've met two or three that I'd just as soon
spend my life on a desert-island with as anybody, well there's
that *atmospheric* Bishop who married Lettice Tarver, my dear
whenever I meet that man I feel *too* saintly for *hours* afterwards,
my dear I *can't* tell you, because of course he *never* talks shop,
but my dear he *just* makes me feel *indecently* good, my dear I
simply want to rub *all* the powder off the old nose and *rush* out
into the street and give my lip-stick to the poor or something,
and my dear it *is* a relief to talk to a man who you *know* would
never notice if the nose *was* luminous or ladders in the hose
or anything, and I think it's *quite* theoretical that if I spent
much time with any of the nice parson I know I should *slowly*

blossom into a nun or martyr darling because you know I *always* respond to personality don't I and I do think that parson as a rule are *too* sensible about nearly everything except religion perhaps, because my dear that's the strange thing, well I don't know if you ever look at a paper but I've had to lately or I should never have been able to *utter* at meals, and it seems that *all* the English parson have *suddenly* gone primitive and started writing to the papers. Well Mr Haddock says that Archdeacon Thing or somebody has been writing the evening papers for *innumerable* years, and now that *dramatical* man the Wireless Dean has taken to writing *all* the papers, and O my dear you ought to look at the *Times* because my dear *platoons* of Bishops are writing *wounded* letters and preaching the *most* personal sermons, and Mr Haddock says it *really* looks as if the whole parsonage had suddenly caught this *contagious* publicity craze and said *Let* us have publicity *too*, my dear he does say the *naughtiest* things, anyhow if so I daresay they're right, because my dear personally I've *never* felt so *esotteric* before, my dear really I've been *too* kindled, and Mr Haddock says I listen to Uncle A arguing with Aunt M with the *most* reverent expression and a *rather* pregnant little pucker on the brow, and my dear it's quite true, I've just looked, there's a definite *line* coming, so that will show you what *masses* of thinking I must have committed, darling.

But my dear what I find so *perfectly* damping is I *simply* can't discover what it's all *about*, because my dear the *extraordinary* thing is that this time it seems it's got *nothing* to do with the Modern Girl, my dear I've read *reams* and not a *hoot* about the Young, and I do wish some *simple* Bishop would write a *simple* letter to the *Times* and *simply* give a sort of *simple* sinopsis, so that people like you and me could *Start Now* like a serial, because of course *everybody* here has been in it from the first and *whenever* I ask Aunt Margaret *doctrinal* questions Uncle Arthur interrupts her and there's the *most* acidulated row, of course Aunt Margaret is *too* severe on the Pope because my dear she had a *Roman* nursemaid who tried to *proselitize* the children while she was bathing them, and was *openly* lukewarm about Protestant fairy-stories, and then my dear there's the Deposited Book and my dear *try* as I will I *can't* make out *why* it's been deposited or *who's* deposited it, and if so *where*, and my dear I do wish people who write to the papers wouldn't *always* assume that everybody else knows everything *too*, anyhow from what I can make out it's all absolutely *germane* to this *inflammatory* monkey-business, well my dear it seems some of them say that Man was *specially* constructed, and the others say that he *merely* evoluted out of an ape-like Stock, and my dear they've had the *most* elaborate *riots* in some cathedral about it, because my dear it's *never* spoiled my beauty-sleep up to now but it seems that if it *should* turn out that the origins of Man were monkeys one *simply* couldn't go *on*, you do see that don't you darling, of course the American here is an *utter* Fundamentalist but I forget which side that is, anyhow some Bishop definitely refuses to go to Tennessee which makes the American *merely* apoplectical.

But my dear the *sensational* thing is that I *do* believe I've *just* got the right idea *myself*, my dear *I* think it's fifty-fifty like everything else, well you see I've *noticed* that they all talk about *Man* this and *Man* that and as usual never a whisper about *Woman*, and well my dear *my* theory is that I shouldn't be a *bit* surprised if Man *did* descend from a monkey but *Women* were *specially created*!

Well my dear don't you think that's *rather* reasonable, because my dear it would be a *melodious* compromise and *utterly* English, my dear it settles *everything*, well I told Mr Haddock and he said he thought it was a *divine* hypothesis but he advised me not to mention it at dinner because they *might* not be carried away by it just at first, my dear *too* right, because my dear my *one* contribution this evening was a *calamitous* flop, well when I tell you that we had *Deans* with the soup and *Bishops* with the fish and *dogmas* with the joint my dear and *monkeys* with the sweet, my dear *too* controversial, my head was like *soda–water*, and at last Mr Haddock said p'raps it would be better if the parson spent less time discussing whether men came from the monkeys and more time preventing them from going to the dogs, well my dear *that* didn't go down *too* well, there was a *rather* cyclonic silence and I thought perhaps it was time for your

Topsy to make a *brief* gesture on doctrine so I said radiantly Well it *all* seems to me to come down to *this*, that I've *always* said that I *always* believe in *always* doing the *Christian* thing — well my dear Aunt Margaret said *too* forgivingly *Don't* talk nonsense dear and Uncle Arthur said That's nothing to do with it child, so perhaps it was *just* as well that I *didn't* explain my *own* theory about the origins of Uncles, however *do* think it over darling and tell me if it makes life any easier to understand and bear, no more now from your *fundamental* little TOPSY.

12 The Superfluous Baronet

Trix darling, star of my night, hope of the Dukeries, *Magnet* of the Midlands, my *heart's* thanks for your *historic* letter and my dear I *quite* agree he sounds *too* adequate for *words* darling, well best of luck my sister soul, as for me I'm 'as you were' still, all the same I've come to the conclusion that I must be the *nation's* lodestar because my dear I've had the *most* unwomaning adventure and really my dear if I can make a Baronet lose *all* control in a place like that well where *are* the limits don't you agree darling?

But of course I haven't told you, well I forget if I've mentioned a rather *septic* Baronet I met at the Antons, some time ago, my dear *too* festering, well he's a financier or a shareholder or something and one *mass* of heartiness, my dear *shouts* at you at breakfast when a girl's not *conscious*, and also he's what I call a *chronic handler*, *you* know my dear simply *can't* keep his hands from pawing and slapping, well my dear by the end of a week-end every *man* in the party is *black* and *blue* with friendly buffets and they say once at a golf-club he *split* an Alderman's *liver* out of sheer *cammaraderie*, and as for women well what with elbow-pinching and head-patting I felt more like a *fox-terrier*, my dear that sort of thing makes me want to *scream* aloud when it's the wrong man doesn't it you darling?

Well my dear I lived through the week-end but I *never* thought our destinies would twine again *etc*, however *yesterday* I went to my *flawless* little dentist and my dear he *simply is* the *Gallahad* of dentistry, because my dear he has the *most* dog-like eyes and really my dear you do feel that it hurts him *far* more than it hurts you which I think is *so* right, and really when Pottler *disintegrates* one of your teeth it's more like a *caress*, only of course I'm *Nature's* coward and I *never* admit that I've not been hurt till ten days afterwards because I do think if a girl does the Spartan mother act they only take advantage of you, so my dear I *always* make the *most* operatical little *yelpings* and *internal* moans my dear *long* before he hurts me just to remind him that

I wasn't *made* for suffering and then as a rule he doesn't hurt me *at all*, however this time as it happened I had a *rather* agonising time, because my dear it was one of those *indecent* teeth *right* at the back and I could tell by the *reserved* way in which he *picked* it to bits that it wasn't exactly a *museum* piece so I merely *closed* the eyes and *whimpered* mouldily now and then my dear *too* pusillanimous I know but *you* are aren't you? Well at last he laid down the pick and shovel, and my dear *do* you know that *collapsing* moment when he lays down the pick and shovel and puts the *hugest* grindstone on the *whirly-whirly* machine well my dear the *moment* he lays down the pick and shovel I always begin the *most* bright conversation, because my dear the *whirly-whirly*, well rather than that my dear I'd talk to *anybody* about *anything*, so I *always* tell him *all* my secrets and really my dear I think it's the *Christian* thing to do, because I do think that young dentists must have the *most* monastic lives, well *emotionally* don't you think, because my dear you can't imagine anyone who spends the *whole* time *poking* about in other people's *mouths* having any sort of *romance* well *can* you darling, my dear *do* dentists marry and if so *who*, I suppose the only sort of *passionate* outlet is when they stop some perfectly *arresting* girl's front teeth, and I'm *quite* sure my poor Pottler is merely *starving* for affection so when I tell him about my *virginal* affairs I do think perhaps he gets the least little second-hand *kick* out of it you see darling, because he merely *toys* with the whirly-whirly and agrees with everything I say, my dear *too* unanimous, and I *rather* fancy he's *rather* attracted. However at *last* he ruthlessly *attached* the grindstone and my dear I simply lay back and *suffered*, because my dear he always says that I have the *most* degrading *wet* mouth and whenever anything complex has to be done he has to fill the mouth with those *inequitable* blobs of *dry* cottonwool and put *two* pumps in it, my dear *whatever* you do don't have a *wet* mouth, Mr Haddock says it *means* something but he couldn't remember what, but from what I can make out it's as bad as wet *hands*, well my dear he *thrust* the whirly-whirly *inch* by *inch* into the very *dome* of a girl's head, and my dear I had the shivers *all* over from the *dry* cotton-wool and my dear my mouth felt so *oblique* that I thought it would never shut normally *again*, and my dear every second I was *quite* satisfied that he was *just* going to hurt me, so after ten minutes of this my dear I *simply* yelled, well just then the Secretary woman came in, my dear *too* Vestal, and said that some Countess had come without warning, so Pottler put something *too* whiffy on my wounds and sent me out to recuperate while he looked at the other sufferer.

Well my dear I *crawled* back to the waiting-room and *merely* drooped over some *disheartening* funny paper, my dear jokes about *dentists* and everything, *too* morbid darling, and of course I was feeling *quite* ethereal, well if you want proof I *simply* hadn't the spirit to powder the old nose, when *in* walked the *redundant* Baronet Sir Charles Chase if you please!! Well darling I didn't exactly *effervesce* with greetings but I wasn't particularly *aprehensive*, because my dear you *would* think that if there's *one* place that *might* be a sanctuary from the Passions and everything it would be a dentist's *waiting-room*, and you would think that if a girl was *ever* safe in this *city* of wolves it would be when she was *merely* moribund with the whirly-whirly and feeling like one huge *antiseptic*, however life *is* the *world's* conundrum as I expect Shakespeare said because my dear that's *just* the kind of thing that *obsolete* man did say, but anyhow Sir Charles Chase *anchored* beside me and began the *most* enthusiastic *paw*, and not only that, well I'll tell you when we meet, my dear *too* affectionate, well I was repugnant but cool darling because my dear *scenes* are quite alien to me, however there was no squashing him, my dear *too* resilient, and I was *just* about to utter a *girlish* scream when fortunately in came the Secretary to fetch me, well my dear I saw she'd seen *quite* enough to make a Secretary talk so of course I told Pottler the whole harrowing tale, and my dear he was *too* contrite because he said he had one or two clients who were *quite* liable to turn *romantic* in the waiting-room, and he ought to have prevented it, well one lives and learns, but my dear I could see my poor Gallahad was merely *incandescent* with chivalry and *suppressed* rage, and my dear he was *utterly* tender with my tooth and everything and never hurt me at *all*, but my dear *what* he did to Sir Charles Chase when he got him in the chair I *can't* imagine but it's *quite* fun trying, and the only thing that worries me somewhat is do you think Sir Charles Chase *always*, or is it that I look that kind of girl, my dear be *cruelly* frank, your *injured* little TOPSY.

13 The Noble Animal

Well Trix dear I do think the *horse* is the *most* unbalanced and fraudulent object don't you, and that reminds me, *masses* of thanks for your *celestial* letter and it's *quite* angelic that you may be coming to London, but *no* darling I do *not* think that Mr Haddock would suit you, well of course it's *too* prohibitive to express in *words* but what I mean is well for *one* thing I *should* hate you to have the *weeest* whiff of unhappiness and really he *is* the most equibiguous man, well for instance, but *don't* think I'm *warning* you off or anything *female* because really my dear I'm *wildly* lukewarm and honestly my dear he spends the *whole* time introducing me to *nice friends* of his whom he'd like me to marry, my dear *too* Christian, and sometimes it *really* looks as if he *really* liked a girl and other times it *merely* looks as if he was merely *evading* her, so that what with one thing and another one *simply* never knows *where* you are, but what I meant about *you* darling, well with *all* his faults he *does* strike a rather *spiritual* note, and my dear *don't* think I'm being the least bit *uncongenial* darling but my dear there *are* people who are obviously *incompatible* aren't there?

Well for instance I was going to tell you, you see after my scene with Uncle Arthur about the stags' heads and the shooting and everything, well whether it was something *I* said or what but this time they asked *Mr Haddock* down here, because really my dear he's the *only* man I know who can look at a cock-pheasant without *wishing* he had a *gun*, and well Uncle Arthur said that since we were both so keen on dumb animals we'd better go *horse-riding* together, which was *rather* unworthy perhaps because as a *matter* of fact I'm not *Nature's* horse-woman, and I doubt if Mr Haddock was exactly *born* in the saddle, however they chartered two *anæmic* creatures from Wratchet-in-the-Hole and this afternoon off we went *hacking* or *hocking* or whatever it is.

Well my dear Mr Haddock had a sort of black creature and I had a blonde, my dear the *complete* image of Catherine Tarver with the same ten-and-sixpenny auburn and the same sloppy eye, but my dear they both looked *Nature's* lambs only as Mr Haddock said for *sheer* hippocrisy there's *nothing* like a horse and he said that lambs or not he has the *most* corrupting influence on them and *nearly* always they do something *perfectly* malignant and unexpected, well my dear of *course* he wore the most *irrelevant* clothes, my dear *grey* flannel trousers and *black* shoes and a pair of Uncle Arthur's gaiters and my dear I do think that horses feel it if you don't dress up for them perhaps, well as long as we were in the grounds they behaved like *nuns*, but my dear the *moment* we were on the road they developed the *most* congenital habits, well my creature had that *adolescent* trick of *tossing* its head back and flattening a girl's nose if you're not very careful and my dear the *whole* time it was wanting to *eat*, and Mr Haddock's horse was *quite* incapable of *trotting* or *walking* it *merely* ambled and my dear *whenever* he said 'Gee-up' or made those plebeian tongue-sounds which my dear *every* horse is supposed to understand it *simply* stood on its *hind-legs* and walked round in circles *waving* its fore-paws and my dear looking *too* self-satisfied, well Mr Haddock retained contact all right and really my dear he looked *rather* County but all the same we decided to cut out encouraging noises with the *result* my dear that we *simply* crawled and the *more* we crawled my dear the more my *sensual* horse was determined to *eat*.

Well Uncle Arthur had warned us not to go through Wratchet-in-the-Hole because it was market-day or something frantic, however Mr Haddock seemed to have a *particular* craving to go through Wratchet-in-the-Hole and call on some friends of his so we went through Wratchet-in-the-H, and my dear the *moment* we were in the main street of W-in-the-H my blonde beast *went mad*, and my dear it *gravitated* to the nearest shop and put its *head* in at the *window*, because my dear there was no *glass* and my dear if it had been a *greengrocer's* one could have *understood* it but what was so perfectly uncanny and *humbling*, my dear it was a *fish-shop* and what *do* you think it *merely* removed the *hugest* tin label with FINE FRESH HADDOCK on it and *lolloped* down the street with this *redundant* object in its teeth, well of course the *entire* population of W followed us, my dear I blushed *all* down my *back* but worse *far* worse was to come, my dear you won't believe me but it went *straight* up to a policeman on point duty outside the Town Hall and *knelt down* on its fore-knees and dropped the FINE FRESH HADDOCK at his feet!!! And *then* my dear it *got* up and *walked on* in the *most* fraternal manner as if *nothing* had happened, well of course the policeman stopped us and he took the names and addresses of *everybody* present, and my dear *when* it came out that Mr Haddock's name was *Haddock* it *all* looked too *utterly* felonious and improper, well when at last we got away Mr Haddock said I know what, *these* horses have been in a *Circus*, and it turned out afterwards that's just what they were, my dear *my* creature had been one of those morbid *mathematical* horses which pick out the letters of the alphabet and everything, and they say whenever it sees *large print* it *loses control*, and Mr Haddock's horse used to do that *superfluous* hind-leg waltzing act when the band keeps time with them, my dear *too* wearing, well they'd told us that the creatures had absolutely *no vice* which was *perfectly* true but my dear I do think that a horse's *parlour tricks* can be just as *anti-social* as its vices don't you?

Well after this we *ambled* along the road some way without a crisis and talked and Mr Haddock as usual said I ought to get married and I said why and he said because I was *Nature's* ray of sunshine and he knew herds of *distracting* bachelors who would *simply* tumble for me, so I said come to that why don't you get married yourself, well my dear he shook his head and looked *too* significant, my dear the *complete* secret-sorrow expression and I was just going to *press* him because I was sure he *wanted* to be pressed when as luck would have it he *sighed* loudly and his horse stood on its hind-legs again, my dear this is *gospel*, so after that we kept off *all* delicate subjects, well when we got to the Greens' place at that moment Mrs Green herself rode out of the gate on the most *expensive*-looking horse and my dear she's the *loveliest* girl, I loathed her at sight, and my dear she looked at me like something under a stone, and suddenly it *flashed* across me that perhaps Mr Haddock had a *hopeless passion* for her, well of course my dear I did the *Christian* thing, I took my horse along the hedge and let it *eat* while they talked, well my dear they *murmured* and all went well but when my *meretricious* horse had eaten *half* the hedge it cocked up its head and saw a large NO TRESPASSERS board stuck in the hedge and my dear without a moment's hesitation it merely *plucked* it out of the hedge and cantered back and *knelt* down and deposited it in front of *Mrs Green* (!), my dear *too* pointed, I was *wrapped* in shame, well of course after that I declined to have any more *truck* with the animal so we left the horses there and came home in the charmer's car, well my dear *all* the way Mr Haddock was perfectly lethargic and broody, so my dear you do see what I mean about your *happiness* darling because if it's a question of a girl's happiness I do *not* think that he's a *fraction* more reliable than that *ruddimentary* horse, and my dear in this life it isn't *enough* to be a *noble* animal and have *no vices*, so you see what I mean your *true* friend TOPSY.

14 The Fresh Mind

Trix darling I've made the *most* voluminous error I've *alienated* the Editor of *Undies* and now I don't believe I'll *ever* be a dramatic critic, well my dear you shall hear what happened and judge for yourself, well I told you he's been giving me *little* commissions to test a girl's mettle didn't I, and the other night he rang up in a *great* state my dear *two* minutes to cocktail-time and said *could* I fly *straight* off to Hammersmith (*Hammersmith*! darling) and go to the first night of a play called Othello, well my dear I'd *just* dressed as it happened but not for Hammersmith which it seems is half-way to *Bath* darling and *quite* insanitary, however that's the sort of horror an economic girl has got to face, well when I tell you that I had *no* dinner and the taxi took me *right* across England, my dear at Hammersmith they talk *pure* Somerset, well of course I was *madly* late and I merely *wriggled* over nine pairs of the largest knees, all in the dark, my dear *too* unpopular, and I had no programme and no dinner and no cigarettes so I merely *swooned* into my seat and prepared to enjoy the new play.

Well after all this *agony* what was my horror, well when I tell you that it was the most *old-fashioned* melodrama and *rather* poor taste I thought, all about a *black* man who marries a white girl, my dear *too* American, and what was so *perfectly* pusillanimous so as to make the thing a *little* less incompatible the man who acted the black man was only *brown*, the merest *beige* darling, pale sheik-colour, but the *whole* time they were talking about how *black* he was, my dear *too* English. Well of course the *plot* was *quite* defective and really my dear if they put it on in the West End not a *soul* would go to it except the police possibly because my dear there were the *rudest* remarks, well this *inane* black man gets *inanely* jealous about his *anæmic* wife the *moment* they're married, and my dear she's a *complete* cow of a woman, my dear *too* clinging, only there's an *obstruse* villain called Yahgo or something who *never* stops lying and my dear for *no* reason at all that I could discover my dear it was *so* unreasonable that every now and then he had to have the *hugest* soliloquies, is that right, to explain what he's going to do next, well he keeps telling the old black man that the white girl has a fancy-friend, well my dear they've only been *married* about ten days but the black man merely *laps* it up, one moment he's *Nature's* honeymooner and the next he's knocking her down, and what I thought was so *perfectly* heterodox he was supposed to be the *world's* successful general but my dear I've always understood the *sole* point of a real he-soldier is that they're the *most* elaborate judges of *character* and *always* know when you're *lying*, and if this black man couldn't see through Yahgo it's *too* unsatisfying to think of him winning a *single* battle against the *Turks*. Well for that matter this Yahgo was the *sole* person in the play who had the *embryo* of a brain and *whatever* he said they *all* swallowed it, but my dear I *do* think that a really professional liar like that must have had *years* of practice and you'd think anyhow Yahgo's *wife* would have known something about it, but *oh* no my dear she went on like the others as if Yahgo was *George* Washington, well so it went on and at last the black man smothers the girl, my dear *too* physical, but of course if *any* of them had had the sense of a Socialist it would *never* have happened, because my dear simply *all* the black man had to do was to say to the subaltern Look here they say you've been taking my wife out, is there anything in it, and he would have said Not likely General, I've a girl of my own, which he had though my dear the young man was *Nature's* fish and only a half-wit would have suspected him of an anti-conjugal *thought*, well then the black man would have said Well Yahgo says you have, and then there would have been explanations and everything, but of course it never *occurs* to the black man to talk to the subaltern, he *merely* goes and bullies his wife, who *merely* crumples up, poor cattle, but if only she'd said Look here less of it what's your evidence, oh yes and I forgot there's the *most* adolescent business with an *embroidered* handkerchief, my dear the wife drops her *favourite* handkerchief which the black man gave her and Yahgo's wife who adores her and looks after her clothes *picks* it up, but my dear *instead* of giving it back to the wife she gives it to Yahgo who puts it in the young man's room, and my dear the young man *must* have known it was the wife's because she *always* wore it, but instead of taking steps he *merely* gives it to his own girl and asks her to *take out* the embroidery, my dear *too* likely, well she gives it back to him in the *public* street while the black man is watching, and when the black man sees *another* girl giving the young man his wife's handkerchief *instead* of saying Hi that's my wife's property how did you get it he *merely* goes off and murders his wife, my dear *too* uncalled-for.

Well my dear when a play is *perfectly* hypothetical from beginning to end I do think a play is a little *redundant* don't you, even if it's very well written, but my dear *this* was written in the most amateur style, my dear never using one word if it was possible to use three, and my dear the *oldest* quotations and the *floppiest* puns, my dear *cashier* and *Cassio, too* infantile, and my dear the *crudest* pantomime couplets at the end of a scene, and immense *floods* of the *longest* words which *sounded* rather marvellous I must admit but my dear meant *simply* nothing, but everyone else seemed to think it was *too* ecstatic so perhaps they'd had dinner, well at the end there was the *most* unnecessary slaughter and the *entire* stage was *sanded* with bodies, because the black man having killed his wife Yahgo killed *his* too because she argued, my dear *too* Harrovian, and really my dear I thought the whole thing was a fraction unhealthy and *saditious*, don't you?

Well at the end there were the *most* reluctant speeches and dahlias and everything, and I stayed for a bit in case the author appeared, because I thought it might be one of those *primitive* women, and then I *rushed* home and wrote down *just* what I thought about it and really I was *rather* proud of it, but my dear this morning the Editor of *Undies* rang up, my dear it's *too* wounding it seems the *whole* thing was written by *Shakespeare* and it's *quite* well-known, well of course my dear I've scarcely *looked* at the man, so I said to the Editor Well you said you wanted a *fresh mind* didn't you, and he said Yes of course but you mustn't have a fresh mind about *Shakespeare*, because it isn't done so there we are, well I rang up Mr Haddock and asked him to buy me a Shakespeare because I want to see if it's true, well he's been in and he gave me *rather* a lecture because he said it's a bad sign if a girl can't apreciate great tragedy because he said Aristotel or some *sedimentary* Greek said that tragedy was better than comedy because tragedy was about fine people and comedy was about mean people, well I said tragedy must have changed since Aristotel then because this play was about one absolute cad and one absolute halt wit and one absolute *cow*, and then suddenly my dear I had emotion-trouble and merely *burst* into tears, my dear what *is* the matter with me I'm *always* liquidating these days, however Mr Haddock comforted me, my dear *too* understanding, and after a bit he sat down and read some Shakespeare to me, which was *rather* flower-like I thought, and really my dear on a comfy sofa in front of a good fire with Mr Haddock and some hot-buttered toast a great deal of Shakespeare sounds *quite* meritricious, so try it Trix, your *cultured* little TOPSY.

15 A Run With The Yaffle

Well Trix darling I've been *quite* heathen but life *is* a scourge my
dear well *isn't* it, and the more I think about *things* and everything
the *less* I seem to see *where* I fit in, well my dear what *is* my
inevitable *niche* in the Universe if you see what I mean, because
my dear I *do* feel that I'm *rather* wasted on Society anyhow
because I'm always *reaching* out for something *bigger* aren't you
darling, my dear *too* intangible *of course* but absolute *aspirations*
and everything, and I do think that if a girl *keeps* on getting sort
of *wistful* yearnings in the middle of some *utterly* Cadogan party
it must mean that she's *rather* starving for bigness or something,
and my dear there's *no* doubt that the life of our lot *is* totally
unspiritual and *alimentary*, my dear life's *one* protracted oyster
for some of us, *isn't* it, on the other hand I'm not *too* positive
that I'm a clever man's woman either because I never seem to hit
many bull's-eyes with triangular artists and the *dyspepsigentsia*,
and the Editor of *Undies* has become *thoroughly* lukewarm about
me, on the other hand our own lot make me feel definitely
brainy, so I do seem rather to *levitate* gracefully between masses
of stools, and I sometimes think that perhaps I ought to seek out
a soul-brother among these cultivated *middle* classes because my
dear I hear they're *too* soothing and *innocuous* without smelling
the *least* bit of the dyspepsigentsia which is what Mr Haddock
calls all these *amorphous* poets and *synthetic* women with no hair
in Bloomsbury, and of course he says that he *quite* understands
I've got a sort of *frustrated* ache for something *utterly* big and he
rather thinks that I may have a genius for *politics* or something,
but he said that meanwhile I must *always* remember that I give a
great deal of *pleasure*, which of course is *too* gratifying but in that
case *why* does he take me to a *Hunt* Ball and *ostracise* me, and
as a *matter* of fact *meanwhile* the *one* thing that's *too* manifest is
that I shall *never* marry into *County* circles well don't you agree
darling?

Because my dear as I've been *trying* to tell you *all* this time, *two* nights ago we went over to the *Hunt* Ball of the Yealm Vale and Fowkeley, my dear pronounced *Yaffle*, Mr Haddock and me and that *rather* antiseptic young Guardee I told you about, Terence Flydde by name, my dear *too* Etonian, my dear *utterly* clean-limbed, washes *all* over and flawlessly upholstered, but of course the *cerebellum* is a *perfect* vacuum, well my dear I've always fancied he was *rather* attracted and of course he's *absolutely* baneless but of course a girl would just as soon marry a *pedigree* St Bernard *dog*, so I didn't exactly propose to *dedicate* the evening to him though I must say those red coats are *rather* decorative, but my dear at the absolute *zenith* of our *very* first dance Mr Haddock suddenly saw that *cloying* Mrs Green woman I mentioned before, my dear she's *ravishing*, and the *most* covetable frock in *firmament* blue, rats bite her nails and lizards eat her young if any, sorry darling but the charmer gives me spleen-trouble, because my dear from *that* moment I merely *melted* off the planet as far as Mr Haddock was concerned, my dear the man's eyes were *too* elsewhere, and when I tell you that was the last dance *we* had, however I had one or two with miscellanous County, red-coats all darling, my dear *too* Bolshie to look at which was fairly comic I thought, but of course the *whole* ensemble *absolutely* ornamental, but my dear all the women *looked* like horses and *talked* like horses and some of them were *dressed* like horses, always excepting the *star-like* Mrs Green, and may *her* nose turn purple, sorry dear but all the same.

Well my dear the *whole* place *stank* of *character* and my dear I'm *quite* sure that Scotland Yard could *not* have discovered the *embryo* of a brain in *that* building with a triple-X-ray, well my partners were *utterly* aerated and sanitary and *up-right*, my dear *too* perpendicular, and *rather* disarming, but of course *moribund* above the eyes, and my dear they *all* said they would send *all* their young to Eton because they might not be educated but dammit it made them *white* men and say what you like a *white* man is a *white* man, my dear as if Rugby and Winchester turned out nothing but *black* men, and of course I lost *quantities* of *caste* because I'd *never* ridden to a *single* hound, my dear *too* heretical and *un*-English, so as I don't know *one* end of a horse from another and *they* didn't know the *beginning* of anything else the conversation tended to be *rather* spasmy and *even* uncontinuous, because my dear after they'd told me *which* people *rode straight* and *which* rode spirally we *simply* ceased to communicate at *all*, and my dear if *my* partners *ride* as straight as they *dance* there must be no brick walls in the county because my dear we merely mowed down the opposition, and everybody making the *most* depressing *tantivy* noises, my dear I felt like the mascot of a *large* Tank *undulating* through the *New* Forest, my dear I've bruises *everywhere*, so *quite* soon I retreated to the faithful Terence who'd been hovering dog-like *all* the time, and we sat out for *simply* centuries on a *rather* suggestive sofa because I wanted Mr Haddock to see us who my dear was permanently revolving with the unnecessary Green thing, my dear she's *electrical*, and I do *not* wish her a *microscopic* harm but I *should* like her to go *quite* suddenly into a nunnery and stay there darling, because honestly my dear she gives me spleen-trouble.

Well my dear it seems *poor* Terence has decided I'm a *high-brow* and my dear *since* we last met he's been reading a *book*, my dear *too* unnatural, my dear one of those *cathartic* female novelists who adulate Sussex and sin and everything, and my dear they're *always* bathing in no-piece costumes, and of course my *poor* Terence was *utterly* baffled because it seems there isn't a *white* man from cover to cover and *no* horses and *scarcely* a hound, well I must say I thought it was rather a lily-white gesture for a subaltern in the Guards to read a *book* for my sake, and you know I *always* say that I *always* believe in *always* doing the *Christian* thing, so I suppose I was rather *unbending* to the troops, especially as Mr Haddock and the Green kept on *swooning* past us when what was my horror I *suddenly* realised that the young man was *tending* towards *serious* amorosity, so I took him into the buffet and we had champagne and the *greenest* ices but that didn't seem to improve the situation because he said *Let's* go into the garden and have a look at *Juppiter*, well my dear in my experience the *planets* are *totally* corrupting and I was *quite* sure that long before we saw a *single* constellation he'd be adumbrating *matrimony*, and my dear I *simply* felt that I *simply* couldn't bear it, well at that moment I had one of my inspired flashes because I remembered that somebody once told me that a young Guardee has to resign or something if he marries an *actress*, so I said I wondered if he knew that I was on the *stage* under a mythical name, well he looked like a goldfish just out of the water and said No he didn't, so I said Yes as a *matter* of fact I'm SYBIL THORNDIKE, because my dear that was the first name that entered my head, and he said Oh that's funny because he'd often seen the name, but he'd never seen me *act*, and my dear it was *rather* poignant because from *that* moment he was *utterly* restrained and *unpassionate* and *nothing* more was heard about the planets, well my dear it was all *rather* unprincipled I *know* but *what* a relief because my dear it *is* so upsetting to have to *refuse* a *white* man because it *only* means that he goes *straight* off to the Congo and *mutilates* some *harmless* lion and you *know* my views about dumb animals, in fact *deep* down darling there must be a lot more *pure* metal in me than many people think because for instance I *had* intended to be *utterly* distant and *corrosive* to Mr Haddock, but as it happened I was *too* Christian and my dear definitely *encouraged* him to talk about the she-wolf, and he *did* enjoy it, and my dear I've *always* said that it *always* pays to *always* do the *Christian* thing because *ever* since he's been too congenial my dear reading *aloud* and everything which is always *rather* a criterion don't you think, so I do seem to give a *little* pleasure, but as for my inevitable *niche* I'm not much wiser, I only know it isn't in the *Yaffle* country, and Mr Haddock *quite* agrees about *that* so that's *one* for Mrs Green, said she tenderly, no more now from your *feminine* little TOPSY.

16 Case For The Defence

No Trix *no* he *never* kissed me or *anything*, well not *really*, my dear I'm *too* deflated about your *wounded* letter because *honestly* my dear there was *merely* nothing between Harry and me and of *course* I'll tell you *all* about it only of course it's *too* esotteric to express in *words*, and of course my dear I *can't* make out whether you're *engaged* to the man or not, because if *not* it all seems *rather* superfluous don't you think darling, and *if* you *are*, well I *never* believe in all this *attitudinous pre*-marriage confession-business, my dear in these days *nobody* wants to marry anybody who's spent the spring-time of their youth in a glass case do they darling, because as Mr Haddock says my dear you *don't* go to a plumber and say *look here* I want you to do the *most* complicated plumbing job only you must *promise* you've *never* done any plumbing *before*, you say the *more* experience the man has had the *better*, and my dear there's *no* doubt that a love affair is the *most* difficult of all human affairs so that it's *rather* infantile to go on as if a man who's *never* had one must be the *most* convincing lover *isn't* it, and as a *matter* of fact as Mr Haddock said *nearly* all soul-mates find each other in the end by *trial* and *error* and the more *trial* the less *error*, you do see what I mean darling, well you *might* say that I was one of Harry Barter's *errors* perhaps, *without* which he'd *never* have realised that *you* were the *only* darling, only *don't* jump to *aromatic* conclusions darling just because it *is* so prohibitive to suggest in *black* ink my dear the absolute *snowiness* of a girl's conscience and everything.

Because my dear in *this* case there's no question of confession or *anything*, and anyhow it was *centuries* ago, well you remember when there was all that *old-fashioned* chat about psycho-paralysis and the *Unconscious*, and it was the done thing to have the *most* insanitary Unconscious, but of course *too* normal on the surface, well my dear I went through the *most* psychalytic phase, and *my* Unconscious was an *utter drain*, I've always said I caught Hermione Tarver's because we were *rather* bosoms at that time, and my dear a really *septic* Unconscious used to run through whole families like a Christmas cold, well she lent me love-Stories by a man called LAWRENCE, my dear *loins* and *glands* and *ganglions* and everything, *too* anatomical, and I had the *most* Cadogan *soul-storms*, my dear *too* chic, well my dear I'd *suddenly* find that I couldn't *bear* the *butler*, or I'd *suddenly* faint at the sight of *porridge*, and then I used to lock myself in my room and read VOLUMES about the *lumbar ganglion* which from what I can make out is some part of the *liver*, and I was always having *debased* yearnings, well my dear I *ached* for *onions*, and I wanted to *ride* on a pillion or go up in a *swing*, and of course the *most* discreditable *dreams*, my dear I *can't* tell you, my dear *umbrellas* and *bowler-hats* and everything *significant*, and my dear I still think it's *rather* stimulating when you think that *Romeo* and *Juliet* and all those *uncontrolled* people in history were *merely* suffering from *gland-trouble* or the *lumbar* thingummy don't you agree darling.

Well of course it *couldn't* go on because my dear I was a *mere* vortex, my dear *too* glandular, and everybody said it was only my unconscious and I'd much better go to somebody and have it taken out, which was what everybody was doing, my dear you *must* remember the *Black* Duchess had *three* Unconsciouses each more festering than the one before, however the *reason* I'm telling you all this is that *about* that time *your* Harry was *rather* a comrade of Hermione T, my dear *utterly* boy-and-girl-and-no-nonsense of *course*, but *he* caught it *too*, and well it *so* happened that he went to the same psych-merchant as me, my dear the *most* monastic-looking little man with a mind like a *canal*, called *Slivers*, well he asked the *dingiest* questions, and my dear he'd *suddenly* look right into my *soul* and say 'PRAM!' and my dear if I said 'BABY!' that meant that my Unconscious was *utterly* Continental and *suggestive* darling, and my dear I always did because it made him *simply* purr and you know I *always* believe in *always* doing the *Christian* thing and giving pleasure *wherever* feasible, well my dear after about *eight* visits he discovered that I had the *most* revolting *suppressed exhibitions*, which *means* my dear that *when* I wanted to *fling* the chocolate shape in the *butler's* face I *sat* still and did *merely* nothing, my dear *too* right, because my dear that's the *detonating* thing it was utterly *true*, oh and of course I forgot, I had to tell him all my dreams, because my dear the *whitest* dream means something *too* foul, but my dear either it was always the *same* dream or I *couldn't* remember it or I was utterly *dreamless*, so I used to leap out of bed in the *middle* of the night and write reams in my dream-book before I forgot and then the cold snap came so I had to *make* them up, because my dear nobody got their money's worth unless they had the *smelliest* dreams, well my dear my *favourite* dream was about *three* black women in *green* satin who used to *ride* about on bicycles singing *Land* of Hope and Glory, and my dear the *whole* time I was *trying* to think of the *next line* and *never* could, my dear *agony*, well it seems *that* sort of dream is *too* revealing and my little wizard took the *gravest* view, because my dear it *so* happened that *Harry's* pet dream was utterly the same breed the man said, well *he* used to dream about *being* at a railway-station when the *roof* fell in and he had another about an *old* peeress who kept on bursting into *flames* at meal-times, my dear *too* alarming, and it seems *that* means that Harry's Unconsh was in the same state as mine only *complimentary* you see, sort of twin souls *reaching* out, my dear like two bats in cages, and my man said that if we got together and were *utterly* frank probably *all* our exhibitions would *cancel* out and be *quite* liquidated, so we did but my dear you *do* understand that the whole thing was perfectly *medical* and on the soul-plane don't you darling?

Because my dear we used to meet *once* a week and exchange exhibitions and everything, and my dear whenever we had an *unsavoury* yearning we merely *yielded* to it, my dear we used to *slink* away to *Soho* and Palais de *Danses* and everything plebeian, and my dear we started a perfect *cult* for celery and dough-nuts because we found they had the *most* aspirin properties if you eat them slowly out of a *paper-bag*, and then of course I was *quite* rude to the butler and he left, and after that I became *too* normal again, but meanwhile my dear *don't* think we'd been a blest pair of sirens or anything because as a *matter* of fact the *whole* episode was *rather* wearing because my dear we had the *most* antagonous rows *always* because it was only our Unconsciouses that were a *fraction* harmonious you see, because *in the flesh* we were generally *hating* each other, but of course the *two* planes are *so* mixed up my dear that one can't always keep them apart, and my dear I don't know *what* he's told you *exactly* but of course it's *quite* possible that he *thinks* he remembers some things happening on the *earthly* plane which were really going on in the *Unconscious*, if you see what I mean, well it's *perfectly* true we went down to Brighton one day because my dear that was one of our suppressed *exhibitions*, my dear we *both* had a *low* craving to look at those penny-in-the-slots on the pier about what Tommy saw at Paris, and my dear *one* pennyworth cured the *two* of us, my dear *too* healing, but of course *as* I said my dear this kissing idea is *utterly mythical* because anything of that kind must have been definitely in the Unconscious department which of course nobody's to blame for, and by the way darling it's only fair to mention that his was *quite* cured too, in fact I should have said that he was *totally* normal now, so I do wish you *every* happiness and you do understand *don't* you darling, *celestial* luck from your rather *hurt* little TOPSY.

17 Good Women And True

Trix darling my *heart's* apologies. I've not written to you for an *epoch*, and no wonder, my dear when I tell you, well for *five* days I've been *incarcerated* in the courts and my dear I *rather* think I've *rather* inserted my fascinating little *foot* and it's *quite* possible my *next* letter will come from Holloway *Jail* or somewhere, well my dear some time ago I ran into *poor* old Rosemary Dune and my dear she was an utter *blancmange* of emotion because after *thirty-five* years of *patient* endeavour she'd at *last* got blighted in matrimony or rather she's *just* about to but of course on the *same* day she had a summons to serve on a *foul* jury, my dear *so* like men *no* tact or *humane* feeling anywhere, well of course I did the Christian thing and said *Let* me do it for you, because my dear *nobody* ought to function on a *British* jury who's thinking the *whole* time *What* undies shall I buy and *where*, which my dear from what I can make out is the *sole* thing these brides on the brink *do* think of don't you agree darling?

Well my dear of course the poor bat merely *liquefied* with gratitude, so I put on my oldest and left the nose *quite* luminous and I *answered* winningly to the name of Rosemary *Dune*, well the old man *ogled* me somewhat but he didn't *say* anything and after *centuries* of *sitting* about *in* I walked to the jury-box and *there* I sat for *five* days, my dear the agony, the *hardest* wood, like sitting in the *Strand*, well there was only one other doe, and she sat next to me, my dear with the *possible* exception of the widow Wockley the *most* emetical creation since the *jelly-fish*, my dear a *crustacean*, I christened her the *Whelk*, my dear I can't tell you, *coated* with *jet* and *black* velvet *tickle-me's*, my dear definitely *unmagnetic*, and of course the moment our *hips* touched there was a sort of *mutual* spasm of *utter* repugnance, my dear I'm *positive* she writes *righteous* postcards to the BBC, *that* kind of ullage, well I'm sorry to say that it was a congested *Divorce* case and *rather* unsuitable, my dear *too* French, but my dear I must say I do think that lawyers can be *rather* atmospheric, because my dear the judge was *divine* and not the least bit *gagga*, and of course the *husband's* barrister my dear I surrendered at *sight*, with the *most* morocco *skin*, for a man, and the *most* insinuating *dove-like* voice, and of course those *wigs* are *indecently* becoming, well *whatever* he said you felt was *too* equitable, and they all have darling little snow-white *bibs* and my dear they *all* look as if they washed *thrice* daily, before and after meals, which is more than I can say for the wife, well *rather* hairy at the hocks darling you know the type, well she said he beat her and as I said to the Whelk Who *wouldn't*, but my dear she *quivered* at me, *too* antagonous.

Well my dear on the *second* day I *rather* lost control and powdered the old nose in the middle of one of the judge's *longest* interruptions, because my dear what with the *intense* tribulation of *sitting* on mahogany I *had* to do something or scream like a woman, well my dear the *judge* gave me the *most* ecclesiastical *look* so I smiled *radiantly* at him till the *Whelk* inflicted on me the *cruellest* prod with her totally unupholstered *elbow*, my dear returned *cum* dividend, so the *next* day I thought better be hung for a *sheep* etcetera so I put on everything pearls and all and the *new* cami-*underloons*, my dear *have* you seen them, well *after* that I may have been wrong but it *seemed* to me that the case was attracting more and more interest because my dear absolute *troops* of *seraphic* young barristers merely *thronged* into the court, my dear *standing* for hours and I should have said *staring*, of course Mr *Haddock* says, who *by* the way my dear was once *called* to the bar but it seems failed to turn up, *too* characteristic darling, well he says that the handsome lads must have merely come to study law-points, but I don't know darling I *rather* fancied they were *rather* attracted, anyhow my dear the *more* expensive and virginal I looked the more embarrassed were the *KC's* because my dear whenever they had to be at *all* French they *kept* apologising with their *lovely* eyes, my dear like *dogs*, and they tried so hard to express everything *too* nicely for me, only the judge kept *chipping* in and said he would *not* have a *spade* called an *implement* of a *certain nature*, however most of it was about his beating her and whether it was *cruelty* to read in *bed*, and so it went on, well my dear the *husband's* KC made an *infatuating* speech and I was utterly convinced that *he* was *too* right, only the wife's KC *rather* persuaded me too, and of course after the *judge* I was a *mere* muddle of conflicting hypothetics anyhow at last we *retired*, my dear the *dingiest* sort of *third-class* waiting-room with nothing in it but a *jug* of tooth-water, my dear *too* masculine, however I thought one can at least have a *smoke* and attend to the old face, but my dear you should have *seen* the Whelk's expression especially as some of the men heaved *sighs* of thanksgiving and produced their pipes, well my dear the foreman was the *merest* blotting-pad and the Whelk took charge of the *entire* proceedings, of course she was *utterly* for the *injured* wife and my dear by the end of my *first* gasper they'd *all* decided to divorce the *husband*, and my dear I've often wondered *how* it is that you can always get *twelve* people to agree about a law-case when I've never met *three* bipeds who could agree about *anything*, and the *reason* is I suppose that *every* jury has it's particular *Whelk*, only fortunately it *doesn't* have its particular *Topsy*, because my dear none of them seemed to be exactly *absorbed* in my opinions so when the foreman said We're *all* agreed then, I said no we weren't because I said if the man was floppy enough to want to adhere to *that* woman, then let him *adhere*, sensation darling!

Well my dear the Whelk *detonated* and she said Perhaps you're not a married woman so I said No perhaps you never had a father, my dear *too* crude, well then she said she had a luncheon appointment and I said I wasn't interested in her meals, and she said I couldn't possibly understand a case like this so I said if she meant I had a *nice* mind she was *too* right but weren't they allowed on juries, and I said anyhow I understand the wife *quite* lucidly because I know the type, well then we got down to it, talon and tooth darling, some of the men became *too* courageous and began to argue with the Whelk, and my dear we were there for *five* inflammatory hours, *no* lunch, *fainting* for tea and I *rather* think the Whelk was one of these *orange-juice* breakfasters, so *what* she was feeling, however I was *quite* remorseless and my dear *one* by *one* those *gelatinous* men came round to my side, because my dear some of the younger jurors I *rather* fancy were *rather* attracted and the others were yearning for Surbiton Home and Beauty, and my dear *last* of all the Whelk yielded *also*, my dear *rather* poignant because she was *so* shattered with nerves and famine she could only *hiss* at me but at *four* o'clock I said O gosh tea-time and my dear *at* that she suddenly became *too* unanimous, well we trooped out into the court and during the verdict and everything the Whelk hissed at me *Chits* like you ought not to *be* empanelled at all, so I said *Too* right, I wasn't, I'm doing it for a *friend*, well then she asked questions and I was *girlishly* candid and my dear she *rose* in her place like *Joan* of Arc or one of those flapping *infallible* females and told the *whole* story to the judge, *can* you believe it, sensation again, and my dear it seems the *whole* trial may have to be *re*-done because the Whelk said I'd *corrupted* the jury by *brazenly* exploiting my personality, and Mr Haddock tells me it's a *miss*-demeanour at *Common* Law punishable with imprisonment for *simply* ever, so pray for me darling though of course the really *black* feature is that *when* I think of the *Whelk* I long to do it *again*, so farewell Trix your *felonious* little TOPSY.

18 Charity

Well Trix darling *pity* the poor aristocracy I'm *quite* debilitised
from singing *carols* for the poor, my dear as Mr Haddock said
about the aristoc we may have no Faith and not much *Hope* but
if we have not *Charity* it's not for want of *Committees*, because
my dear all these *hysterical* pre-Christmas weeks there's always
the *most* malignant *epidemic* of goodness and really my dear one
scarcely dares to *eat* if it isn't *in aid* of something, and my dear
this year it's been *more* fierce than ever because of course it's
one *protracted* battle between the *Black* Duchess and Caramel
Lion to see *who* can have the *most* Committees in her handbag
and if the *Black* D raises a *halfpenny* more than Caramel for a
single matinée there's *grinding* of teeth in Berkeley Square, and
my dear we all hope that *this* year may be their Armageddon
perhaps because we're all *quite* terminated with being *charity*
mannequins and *charity* tea-girls and *charity* coster-women
and I think if one of them were to burst at a Bazaar there'd be
comparative calm in the best circles darling.

Well of course *last* year the *Black* D had the *most* hydraulic
scoop with her Grosvenor *Carol* Singers and since then *poor*
Caramel has never smirked again because my dear the *Black* D
pouched *fortunes* for the Boilermakers' Orphans or something
and of course *divine* publicity, so this year Caramel retaliated
with a rival outfit called the Berkeley Belles, well I was roped
into it through Mr Haddock and he was roped in at the last
minute by that Mrs Green who was Caramel's *conductress* and
is on the stage it seems, my dear she sings like a canary, *curse
her*, because I've never known *one* note from *another* only I have
a *rather* attractive eupeptic *chirp*, but that's the *bizarre* thing
about today *isn't* it darling, because it seems *what* people like is
to see people doing something they *can't* do, well my dear they
adore to have boxers *acting* and actresses *journalising* and typists
swimming and Society girls doing *simply* everything, however
well we *all* massed at Caramel's *palacious* house and had two

or three *Paradisical* cocktails, because my dear as Mr Haddock says Charity covers a multitude of *gins*, and as a *matter* of fact Caramel made *rather* a point of it because it seems the Black D's carolling is *too* ascetical, with the result my dear that Caramel has *enticed* away *three* of the Duchess's *pet* sopranos and *almost* all her Basses so my dear they say the *bitterest* remarks are heard in The Dukery.

Well my dear nearly *everyone* was there, *Pearl* and Imogen, Toots and Hermione Tarver, Tiger Trant and Iseult and Mewmew, my dear *30* sopranos and altos, *eight* basses and one rather bronchial *tenor*, all in *coal*-black, my dear I wore the *most* provocative black mantilla with the hugest *comb* and they say I looked *too* Andalusian, of course we spent *years* adjusting our *masks* because my dear they *adhere* to the eyelashes and *tickle* the ears, my dear *agony*, and we all wore the *most* disarming little *silver* bells, to suggest *winter* and everything, well *after* that we had a sort of *stirrup-cup* of some quite drinkable champagne because *as* a rule my dear I think it's a rather *inflated* beverage, and then we *practised*, but luckily we only had time for about *five* minutes' practice because my dear whenever I *expanded* in a *soulful* chirp the Green creature fixed me with a *toxic* eye and said *Flat* Sopranoes, and we *all* had to begin *all* over again, and my dear we were utterly and *mutually* repugnant which was *slightly* pathetic perhaps because *poor* Mr Haddock has an *infantile* desire to *bring* us together, my dear *too* Mahommedan, however at half-past-six we *went* out into the night, my dear in the *most* elephantine *Saloon* cars to the Dowager Bottleby's *expensive* residence, and my dear *all* the females arrived in one herd and swarmed into the Greek Hall and *burst* into song, my dear King *Wenceslas*, which was rather deplorable because when the males arrived they merely huddled on the doorstep with the Press and the photographers and *madly* detonated with Noel *Noel*, well my dear I'd sort of *hovered* behind because Mr Haddock had all my music you see, and I kept on vociferating *Wenceslas* in his ear, but my dear there's no stopping a British bass once he's away, so *what* it sounded like I *can't* imagine, however the Dowager stood up the *spiral* staircase and showered *fivers* on us, my dear she gave us *fifty* pounds and the *dream* of a cocktail so that noblesse *does* oblige don't you agree darling?

Well then we journeyed on to the Mowbrays who gave us twenty-five and said we needn't bother to sing because they had sandwiches and *hot* soup ready, and Fanny said it was *too* heroic our *pluck* and everything, and then the Friths and Carlton House Terrace, and honestly my dear after about *three* Wenceslases and four Martinis I *did* begin to feel *rather* a Christian, because my dear *outside* the Maltravers where we had the *most* heavenly caviare we were photographed in *full* song *under* a lamp-post, in masks of *course* because we were *all* supposed to be *too* anonymous, only *as* it happened some fiend gave all our names to the papers, Mrs Green I expect, and my dear what was *rather* humorous I thought, at *that* moment I *happened* to be next to *Mr Haddock* because we were *sharing* a copy of Heavenly Bird and he was *rather* smiling into a girl's eyes and everything because I'd *just* said *Don't* you think that Caramel's voice is a *little* attitudinous, and my dear I chirped my loudest for the Green to notice us which of course she did and my *darling* what a scowl, so if you see a photo in the papers you'll be able to read between her lines — laugh darling.

Catty, my dear doubtless, but who cares, as a *matter* of fact she's *rather* a dove, but I *do* feel a fraction that if *Mr* Green was cremated tomorrow I shouldn't see *quite* so much of my equibiguous *Haddock*, however well after that we did the *hotels*, my dear the *Superb*, and *George's* and the *Fratz*, *rather* a martyrdom darling because we'd had *no* dinner and we massed among the tables between armies of *eaters* and my dear it's *too* embarrassing to sing Come all ye faithful to a lonely Colonel *three* inches away and golloping *oysters*, of course we *totally* obstructed the waiters and one or two of the *fleshlier* diners were *almost* petulant about it, however Caramel made me take round the *hat* and my dear they *machine-gunned* money at me because my dear I *rather* think some of them were *rather* attracted, only what was so painful, *would* you believe it, *five* men recognised me, under my mask, my dear *too* undesirable because whatever the Black D does *my* motto is Do good by Stealth isn't it yours darling.

Well my dear the worse we sang the more money they seemed to give us, so I thought I might just as well let my little treble be *heard* and let the Green woman *scowl*, because my dear I may not be *musical* but I do like making the *most* emphatic *noise*, however on we went to the *Murillo*, and my dear I ought to have told you Caramel had *suggested* to the Black D that they should *divide* up the West-End into *respective* areas so as not to *clash* you see, my dear like the New York bootleggers and everything, and *Caramel* says the Murillo was one of *our* preserves *definitely*, because my dear you remember the *two* entrances and my dear she had a *spectacular* plan well we all *formed* up in the street all military and everything, and my dear *marched* in at the back entrance singing Hark the herald angels darling, and all our delicious little bells *jingling* at the ankles, my dear *honestly* it was *rather* a throb, well we marched on sweeping all before us footmen waiters and guests and everybody *through* the grill-room and *into* the dining-room, singing like fifty of the *most* exuberant blackbirds, my dear C B COCHRAN has never done anything *like* it, and *would* you believe it at the far end of the room there was the Black D and the *whole* Grosvenor lot *yelling* like lunatics God rest you merry gentlemen, well my dear Caramel wouldn't *stop* and her Grace wasn't going to move so we marched *clean* through them and out at the far side, my dear the *most* elaborate insult and they say *duels* are threatened and my dear the hotel-people were *too* alienated, however we cleared two hundred for some perfectly darling charity only I never discovered the name of it, farewell, your rather *laryngical* TOPSY.

19 A Real Christmas

Well Trix darling I do think *Christmas*, of course this one was infinitely more afflicting than *ever* before because my dear I *haven't* mentioned it because well but now it's *too* public, my dear the *fact* is *Mum's* gone primitive and taken *horse-glands*, or rather the other way round, because my dear for some years she's been *utterly* anæmic and *decayed* violet and the one thing that seemed to bring colour into her life was the *spasmodic* hope of *planting* out your unwanted little Topsy, and it was *rather* poignant because you know my poor Dad is a *heavenly* fox-trotter and can *almost* Charleston if he has a vast open space only of course he can't *bear* to go out without Mum, and she wouldn't, and so at *last* he promised her she should have *horse-glands* for Christmas which was *rather* touching and monogamous don't you think darling?

Because my dear *horse*-glands are the latest ever for the withered ancestor class and there's a *most* magical Lithuanian called *Whoff* who does it, and of course *monkey* ones went quite out after that *rather* squalid affair at the Bilberries, well then there were *sheep*, and of course quite a lot of people still swear by sheep, in fact they say very soon you won't be able to get *sweetbreads* or *livers* or any odd sheeperies to *eat* because they'll *all* be wanted for re-stringing the peerage, however well now *Whoff* comes along and my dear he's *quite* young and they say *plays* the piano like a syncopated angel, well of course *he* says that monkey-glands and sheep-glands are utterly unfounded because my dear he says both the creatures are *quite* peppy no *doubt* but look at their *characters*, *too* undesirable, while of course the *horse* is not only peppy but is *Nature's* gentleman as well, my dear *noble* and everything, well of course everybody knew that my dear it's the *mossiest* cliché, only *until* Whoff happened *nobody* had thought of pretending it was *scientific* which of course as Mr Haddock says is the whole *secret* of science, anyhow Whoff has got away with it and my dear you can imagine there's the

73

most rodent anxiety in any family which has gone monkey or has a *single* sheep-case, well for instance *darling* old Thirlworth has started *climbing* things, my dear *too* gruesome, they say one night he *swarmed* up a pillar at the Old Yeoman, my dear the *only* habitable dawn-place in London, and simply *swung* himself from rafter to *rafter*, my dear *too* prehensile, and the *next* week the Dowager Dish showed the *most* suggestive *sheep-symptoms*, well whenever she saw a *quue* she *merely* went and *huddled* against it and they say the *most* significant passion for *gates*, so that *ever* since *all* sorts of the *very* best have had to be *observed* quite continuously, and it's *rather* a suspense poor dears because you see the *real* transmorphosis *may* not happen for four or five years but simply anything may set it off *suddenly*, well for instance they *never* let Thirlworth go near a *tree* which is a *little* cramping isn't it in this country darling, and there are the *wildest* bets about *poor* Ronnie Carraway who'll be Lord Chancellor one day because they think the *moment* he sits on the woolsack he'll turn into a ewe or something, *rather* macaber isn't it darling?

However *meanwhile* the *intriguing* Whoff has utterly put the *horse-gland* across, because for one *thing* it's the *first* convincing excuse for *horse-racing* and everything because of course all this ulterior yap about keeping up the blood-stock and all that has been wearing a *little* thin lately hasn't it, my dear, well for all practical purposes they might just as well keep up the blood-stock of the *yak* because my dear what *is* a horse for, however *now*, you see, the best-bred horses earn *simply* fortunes for the *merest* little gland, because of course the better the breed the *nobler* the animal, and my dear they say it's the *most* painless little operation, like having a tooth out with a local thingummy, and some horses are all the better for it, of course if you can afford a gland or two from a Derby winner you live for *simply* ever only it *costs* quite thousands, well poor Dad couldn't run to that but he bought up the *very last* glands of a *rather* temperamental *race-mare* called *Flat Iron* which was third in the Oaks once by a fluke and was *always* going to win *everything* afterwards only *something* nearly *always* happened so it became a selling-plater or something and I believe sold *masses* of plates, anyhow it looks *too* athletic and winning because Whoff gives you a photograph with *every* gland and Mum carries hers about in her bag, *rather* mawkish but still.

Well, I must say the *effect* was *quite* plausible because my dear *this* Christmas Mum's been a *different* woman, well for *years* past we've almost *ignored* the festival because I do think *Christmas*, and so did Mum, well generally I give *Mum* a new record and she gives *me* a new record, and we both give *Dad* a new record we want and that's about all we do in the home, only Dad likes to go to *all* the Hotel galas and throw paper streamers at strange virgins, and he had Mum *glanded* quite early in the month so as to be in fettle for the galas I suppose, well when I tell you, my dear she's *simply* blossomed in *all* directions, and my dear *too* noble, well for one thing she's taken to *utterly* adoring me, which is *rather* a menace, because my dear life's onward march is difficult enough without having one's mother *perpetually* clinging, however that's not the worst, of course she's developed the *most* fatiguing *energy*, my dear she *quite* never stops *bounding* about, my dear *too* mobile and buoyant and everything, and my dear *what* was my horror, well *three* weeks ago she *suddenly* said *Topsy* darling we'll have a *real* Christmas this year, and my dear I *merely* dissolved, because my dear a *real* Christmas, well *you* know, to begin with the *presents*, well she made a *list* of everybody in Who's Who and *lists* of relations, and *lists* of children and *lists* of servants, and *lists* of the poor, and we've been doing one *elongated stagger* from *shop* to shop *ticking* off these *calamitous* lists and *benefacting* the whole of London, my dear the *agony*, if you could have *seen* us in some of these *delirious* bazaars choosing *clockwork* elephants and *electric* cows and the *Child's* Packet of *Practical* Jokes, my dear *too* lowering, and my dear *loaded* with parcels and even *holly*, can you *see* the picture, because of course the *grimmest* feature is that she's gone all soupy about *children*, and my dear you know *my* policy about children and Mum's *always* coincided but *this* year, *conceive* it darling, we gave a *Children's* Party *Christmas* Tree conjurer and all, and my dear your *suffering* Topsy distributed the presents *disguised* as a fairy with a WAND O *gosh*!!

Well my dear the *tragedy* is that, well I told you about *Flat Iron* and it seems that *whenever* Flat Iron was *certain* to win a *dog* ran through its legs or some other horse *trod* on her or something uncalled for, so she *never* did, and my dear I do think that all this must have gone to Flat Iron's *glands* perhaps, because my dear *poor* Mum's *noblest* efforts always seem to go *septic* somewhere, well for instance, *nearly* everybody got the *wrong* present, my dear she *sent* the kitchen-maid an *ivory* bridge-marker and a copy of *Black Beauty* to Hattie Demerara, who my dear is *madly* woundable and won't even have black *coffee* in the house, well then at this party of course most of the little ones were *quite* viperous and wouldn't play anything Mum suggested, the *meringues* ran out, the *Christmas* Tree caught fire, and my dear the *last* straw they sent the *wrong* conjurer, a sort of *Men's* Entertainer with the *broadest* back-chat, my dear *too* smoking-room, and after about six mothers had taken their offspring out, Dad had to ask him to *cease* functioning, and of course the remaining little angels were *too* mutinous, however nothing seemed to discourage Mum and the *next* thing my dear what was my horror, there she was on *all fours* with *seven* devils on her back *wallowing* round the drawing-room and perfectly *neighing*, well my dear I don't suppose she's been on her hands and knees since she was *one*, and of course it's *utterly* explainable at a *children's party*, but my dear *what* if she goes horsy at the *Diplomats'* tonight, because my dear it's the *most* expensive *gala*, and I'm *too* solicitous, so pray for me Trix your *tormented* little TOPSY.

20 The Ephemeral Triangle

Trix darling I *must* tell you about New Year's Eve my dear I *can't* tell you I shall *never* forget it, well I *think* I told you about Mum in my last letter because *since* she took *glands* my dear she's been *quite* unavoidable, well she's joined *all* the night-clubs and *goes* to all of them *every night*, my dear *don't* think I grudge her a *molecule* of pleasure because I do think it's *too* nutritious to see one's ancestors having *clean* fun instead of *decaying* over a *smoky* fire and picking the poor wee modern girl to pieces, and really I do think the seductive Whoff (my dear I've *met* him!) who *invented* horse-glands ought to be utterly *knighted*, because my dear nothing gives me a deeper *throb* than to see *old* people totally enjoying themselves because after all my dear it's a gruesome thought but *sooner* or later we shall *all* be wearing the moss and mildew, and besides now-a-days Mum is *too* harmonious in the home and the *sole* trouble is that a girl can *hardly* ever get out of it *without* her, which *is* a bit penal as you must admit darling.

Because my dear in the *old* days if nowhere *else* one *could* count on a little peace and quiet at an abandoned night-club, but *now* of course no sooner has one made preliminary soul-touch with some acceptable he than *in* walks one's *mother*, my dear *too* hampering *either* with Dad, who of course is glandless but a goer only he can't keep it up like Mum without horse-glands or with poor Dad's understudy the *most* verminous *Black*-bottoming *poodle-dog* called *Chickweed*, and of course now-a-days at the *creamiest* dance-dens a couple under thirty is *almost* invisible and *rather* demodified, and I do think the ancestors ought to have absolute *haunts* of their own, because my dear they merely *dominate* the band and one *never* gets a *balloon* or anything.

Only of course the *sour* fact is that it's the *ancestors* who have the *silk-shares* and keep the pleasure-places *solvent*, however one or two of the Indigent *Young* have started a new place called the Colts and Fillies *intended* solely for revellers under *forty* only of course they can't put it in the *rules* because the man who cashed up for them is a hundred and three and dances nightly (goat-glands they say darling), of course they've circulated a *whisper*, and now and again a few William the Fourthians do drop in but it's *generally* feasible for a *raw* juvenile like yours devotedly to get Charlestoning room on the actual dancing-floor, and my dear there's the *most* Elysian band of one piano and one drum and they play *quite* inaudibly which as Mr Haddock said is just how *Jazz* music *ought* to be played.

Well my dear *as* I was saying on New Year's Eve Mr Haddock gave a *perfectly* doomed party at the C and F, *me* and *he* and the *dispensable* Green woman who as Mr Haddock said was to bring Green or a man, my dear I've *never* seen Green but they *say* he adjusts *averages*, day after day, well I forget if I mentioned that my *poor* Mr Haddock has the *most* touching *baby* idea of making me and the Green creature *utterly* adulate each other, my dear *all* girls together and everything, *too* understanding, and *this* party was to be the *crowning* climax, which of course it *was*, however I was *late* of *course*, and when we got there there was the Green thing *waiting*, the least bit *sultry* I thought however we kissed *too* passionately, and Mr Haddock was *utterly* buoyant, my dear quite *cork*-like and bubbulous *all* over, and of course to see his two girl-colleagues *definitely* embracing *is* rather illusionary for an untrained male, and my dear I *don't* blame him, but of course *what* happened was that the Green thing's partner *failed* to eventuate, and there we were *we* three, so at last we ate, and of course Mr Haddock said something *airy* about the *Eternal* Triangle, and if you could have *seen* the secret looks between the Green thing and *me* my dear as if we'd *both* said *Eternal*? O *Gosh*, O let us part at *once*, however we had the *most* enticing *frogs'* legs and some *ineffable* Burgundy so things relaxed somewhat and we talked about *Mozart* and all those *albuminous* composers because my dear as I think I told you the *Green* object *sings* and Mr Haddock says she's absolutely *sui* generis, whatever that means, well so it went on and my *deluded* Mr Haddock was *too* radiant about his *triangular* little party, but of course after about twenty minutes of *unleavened* Good Music I was the least bit saturated with Good Music and everything, because my dear I've *always* said that Good Music is *too* defensible on a gramophone when you can *turn* it off at *once*, and my dear I do *not* believe that Mr Haddock is quite so fanatical about *Good* Music as you *might* suppose from the way he talks about *Good* Music to the magnetic *Green* female, so my dear I *blush* to say it but I began talking *family*, and *hinc* illæ *ructions* as Euclid remarked knowingly.

Because my dear you know I *never* talk family without the most *hydraulic* provocation, but in *this* case well my dear the Green's *voice* and everything may be *too* ecstatic but I *suspect* that her *birth* and everything is *perfectly* opaque because my dear she *dwells* in Chelsea which is only *one* better than *Hammersmith* if that, and my dear as Napoleon said a girl *must* mobilise her natural defences, so I kept asking her if she *knew* people I *knew* she didn't know and of course she *never* did, which my dear is the *most* leopardy but *insidious* gambit, well you see she was all *musical* and I was *quite* Berkeley and *whenever* she played a composer I threw off a *Duchess* and if she *breathed* a sonata I interrupted with a *week-end*, so that my dear by *about* the coffee-stage *things* were beginning to be the least bit *tropical*, however my *myopic* Haddock was *too* unaware because of course the *more* we loathed each other the *more* the Green thing and me merely *nestled* together and my dear *I* would say DARLING you *must* know the Bilberries and *she* would say But ANGEL Topsy you've *surely* heard some flatulent man who played the *oboe*, and Mr Haddock *wallowed* in our divine *sympatheticness* and everything, and so it went on, however it's a long triangle which has no ending and there comes a moment when the *best* Mahommedan begins to realise that he *can't* dance with *two* fairies at the same time *doesn't* he, and of course the *moment* Mr Haddock suggested exercising with *either* of us we *both* said we'd be *boiled* in *hot* vinegar rather than *desert* the other and we smiled *carbolically*, and I think the *pathetic* male at *last* began to *smell* something, *rather* astigmatous, aren't they darling?

Well of course *meanwhile* there was the *most* tailor-made *festivity* proceeding, my dear the *whole* of the Tribe of Cadogan throwing *paper* about and *blowing* squeakers and wearing *blue* balloons, my dear *flat* soda-water from first to last, and *our* little cat-party merely festering in the middle, my dear goodwill to all *men* more or less but no quarter for *women*, because my dear there was *no* doubt that I'd *rather* drawn blood, so I talked *too* foxily about Hermione Tarver and *Cowes* and everything, *repugnant* darling but war *is* war, only of course just when I was absolutely *oozing* family, what *do* you think, *in* walked Mum with the *uncataloguable* Chickweed and merely *gravitated* to *our* table, well of course as you know my dear Mum's a *cherub* but my dear *no* amount of family-chat will make Mum *look* family *escorted* by Chickweed and inspired with *horse-glands*, my dear *too* humbling, the *divine* old thing was *lyrical* with excitement, she chose the *most* virginal cracker-caps and popped *everybody's* balloon, if you could have *seen* the Green's *compassionate* glances, my dear she whispered *so* many times your mother's a *darling* darling that I nearly had control-trouble, however at midnight my dear they had *Big* Ben on the wireless and we all clasped hands, my dear all comrades and solemn *too* Ramsay Macdonald, my dear the *Green* and I *clutched* each other like the *dearest* bosoms, only of course at the *very* climax of the Midnight Hush my *lost* Mum *neighed* hysterically and pulled a cracker with the Chickweed, *quite* wrecking the whole atmosphere, my dear *everybody* glared and *immediately* afterwards the Green went home, calamitous my dear but I *rather* think that's *rather* the end of poor Mr Haddock's eternal triangle, farewell darling your *horrid* little TOPSY.

21 Engaged

Trix darling I've come to the conclusion that I'm a *born* misogamist, well my dear what with the New Year I've been thinking *too* deeply about marriage and everything and I do think that perhaps *some* girls' destinies are *definitely* celibatic don't you, and if so it's *quite* sterile to shut the old eyes to it, well my dear here I am twenty-one already and not a *tinkle* from the village bells, though really my dear I *am* one of the rages of the city and when I think of the *platoons* of poor fish who merely *flounder* in my wake, not to speak of what I call the *rather* eligible danglers, but my dear the *utter* fallacy is that *whenever* I begin the *gentlest* heart-beat about a man he *merely* evaporates but the ones that go soupy about me are nearly always *absolutely* dispensable, my dear I find it *too* prohibitive to take the masculine gender seriously when it begins to *flabbify* don't you, on the other hand of course my *only* Patrick went off to India without so much as a parting wireless, and ever since the Park episode my *poor* Sweet has *dwindled* back into a walking Plato, my *unique* Nick *shuns* me, and my *unimpeachable* Wog does nothing but tell me about his *latest* proposal to the *noxious* Margery, my dear that *deluded* youth has been dangling from the *cradle*, and I do think Margery Pooks is perfectly *unclassified* don't you?

And of course Mr Haddock is a *chronic* enigma, well there you are my dear, either the male merely *gravitates* at me or he merely *gallops* away, but always the wrong ones, my dear it's *too* inequitable, because my dear the *rows* of men who've *departed* to India and everywhere *just* as I was beginning to think they were *rather* tolerable, really darling in my humble way I'm *quite* populating the Empire, because my dear I do seem to have a gift for *dissipating* the flower of our youth to the four corners and everything while I *rally* about me a *complete* herd of the most *toxic* scions of the upper classes, and my dear I do think some of our aristocracy are *perfectly* unvaccinated, so it's all a little *morbid* you must admit and what with one thing and another and everything I might just as well decide on misogamy and have done with it, because my dear from what I see of marriage it's the *most* hypothetical of all human proceedings, well look at the *Featherlegs* who do nothing but *impeach* each other in public, and *look* at the Merridews who do nothing but *venerate* each other in public and really I don't know *which* is the most emetical, you know my dear I *can't* bear these *varicose* emotions, and besides I *rather* fancy that perhaps my real destiny is just to be the *world's* ray of sunshine, not anybody *particular's* darling but utterly communal, well what I mean is that I *rather* see myself *drifting* radiantly from *life* to *life*, my dear a sort of *universal* electric butterfly, well I should *flit* in at the Featherlegs and make the moribund Featherleg see that *after* all there is something in life worth living for, my dear *too* spiritual and everything of *course* but when I flut away the *poor* lamb would be *utterly* reconciled to existence and Hattie F and then I should merely *waft* in and out of the *Merridew* ménage and *shake* up that *sedimentary* man till he saw that *after* all there *is* something worth looking at besides his *totally* oval and methylated *wife*, my dear it would do the pair of them a *mountain* of good and my dear think what you like but *doing good* would be the *dominant* note of my *whole* policy and I do think there's something *rather* valid about the idea don't you darling?

Because my dear there's *no* doubt that married life *is* definitely a *dungeon*, and unless it gets *continual* rays of sunshine from the *outer* world well the whole thing becomes *too* unhygienic and fungy, and I do think that perhaps it's the *duty* of a really *unusual* ray of sunshine to keep herself available for *general* sweetness instead of wasting herself on a desert husband if you see what I mean, so I shall just *float* about the world *brightening* the lives of *despairing* widowers and suicidal City men, my dear *quite* fairy-like, and of course what's so remunerative one would keep the old figure for perfectly *ever*, and I *rather* see myself as the *most* heavenly old maid don't you darling, my dear the *nation's* godmother, always doing tapestry *cushion-covers* over the fire at house-parties, and my dear saying *sagacious* things about *Life* and everything, and of course my dear the *Young* would worship me because I should be *too* advanced and understanding about the *Young* and my dear always help the Young to marry each other *whatever* their *foul* parents said, and my dear the *most* blossomy nieces would cluster at my knee and say *Wasn't* there ever a *Man* in your life Aunt Topsy, and I shall say Well darlings I did meet a man once only the letter wasn't delivered and we *drifted* apart and everything, and p'raps I shall tell them how my *poor* Sweet took me to the greyhounds once, only of course by that time it will all sound too fragrant and Victorian, and I shall drop *two* tears on to my tapestry p'raps.

But my dear the *real* reason of all this philosophication is that I'm expecting Mr Haddock ANY minute, my dear he *rang* up this morning and said he had a *rather* serious proposal to make and my dear I'm in a *virginal* dither from floor to ceiling, because my dear well Mr Haddock has *never* yet turned oozy like most of them, he's *always* been a sort of *salubrious* background, and my dear if he does turn oozy I'm not *sure* that I can bear it, on the *other* hand darling it *isn't* like him and if he *should* suggest anything in a *disarming* way I've a *gnawing* fear my dear that I may have a moment of *girlish* abandon and utterly forget about misogamy and everything, because my dear with *all* his faults, O snakes here he is, pray for me darling.

Later.—Well my dear I'll tell you what happened, he didn't ooze a *fraction*, my dear too restrained, but he made the *longest* speech about my arresting *qualities*, well he said that I might be the *tiniest* bit superficial on the *top*, but he knew perfectly well that *deep* down I was *utterly* fundamental, my dear heart of gold and everything, because he said that he didn't care *what* these *fermented* centenarians said, *my* type of Modern Girl was the *penultimate* flower of *evolution*, which is what I've *always* thought haven't you darling, well he said that what he was going to propose might p'raps seem strange to a girl of my position and everything, and my dear I was just working up for *acute* emotion-trouble, my dear I felt like a *blancmange*, when he said the *fact* was he'd just been adopted for a *Parliamentary* Candidate and he wanted me to be a sort of extra-special super-Private *Secretary*, my dear *too* flattering, of course he'll have some plebeian creature to do the typing and everything *menial* but he wants somebody *rather* Cadogan to help in the *policy* department and *fascinate* the electors because it seems it's the *most* industrial neighbourhood, Burbleton or somewhere, my dear *too* democratic, but he says they're *all* snobs and adore Beauty, and he says he *rather* thinks I have a *flair* for politics, and he's *quite* sure that when it comes to it I shall have some perfectly *strategic* ideas, and it seems there may be a bye-election *quite* soon so we're to go down for week-ends and *nurse* the constituency, my dear it's *rather* a throb *isn't* it, well of course after the first shock I said I'd do *anything* because my litterary career does seem to be *procrastinating* somewhat and I do think a girl ought to do *something* for her principles and the country and everything, of course it isn't *quite* what I expected but it never *is* with men *is* it darling and anyhow it's *quite* compatible with *utter* misogamy so farewell my sister soul, your *single* but nevertheless secretarial little TOPSY.

22 The Untrained Nurse

Well Trix my distant angel I *must* tell you we're just back from our *first* week-end *nursing* Mr Haddock's constituency and my dear I've made my *virgin* speech, my dear *too* kindling, well I'll tell you, we *all* went down to Burbleton on Saturday, Mr Haddock and his *two* Private Secretaries, me and Taffeta Mole who my dear is the *menial* Secretary for typing and everything, my dear *too* forty and efficient, *utterly* harmonious but *definitely* celibatic, in fact *rather* a prawn darling, but of course the *most* convincing chaperon which I gather is *quite* vital in Burbleton, my dear *poor* Taffeta has been a P S to nine Members of P, and there's *simply* nothing she doesn't know *except* the love of a clean-limbed Britisher, my dear it's *rather* poignant, but if you *will* wear pince-nez and *brown* boots and the badge of the *Guild* of *Godly Girls* it does make it *difficult* for destiny doesn't it darling?

Of course *just* at first I thought Taffeta was a *shade* reluctant to take your political Topsy *too* seriously, my dear it's the *old* story the *trained* nurse and the VAD, but ever since my speech we've been *absolute* bosoms because my dear the *Cause* is totally *Life* to Taffeta and it's her *heart's* pride my dear that she's *never* lost an Election yet, so of course at the *first* sign of adequateness in your little Top she *merely* melted, well my dear on Saturday there was the *largest* meeting to introduce Mr Haddock to the *toxic* electors of Burbleton, *South* I think it is but it may be *West*, and we dined at the hotel with the agent and the Chairman and the Vice-Chairman, all *rather* spherical darling but *moderately* innocuous, and then Taffeta and I and the agent went to the meeting in one taxi and Mr Haddock was following with the Chairman, but my dear to shingle a long story somewhat Mr Haddock *didn't turn up*, and my dear the place was *teeming* with the *most* manual labourers, my dear *too* impatient and unrefined, but at last the Chairman arrived and said that *poor* Mr Haddock had got *locked* in a bathroom or somewhere and we must keep the meeting going till they'd *excavated* him, well my dear we filed on to the platform and the old tub talked for *countless* hours, my dear *too* sedative, all *principles* and the *Gold* Standard and everything phenacetin, and after him an *unthinkable* Alderman got up and went *on* and *on* about the *new* fire-engine, and then a perfectly phlebotomous man got up and was *funny*, my dear *too* laborious, and my dear the proletariat *merely* objected to him, and after that they *lost* control and *vociferated* for the Candidate, well the Chairman kept saying that Mr Haddock had been detained at a Committee-meeting but was *just* coming but my dear the situation was *quite* parlous and my dear the *most* democratic remarks so at *last* he said perhaps Lady *Topsy*, Mr Haddock's Secretary would give us *her* views of the political situation, well my dear I was one *Gargantuan* dither because you know I've never *whispered* in public, however the blood of the Trouts and everything so I *smiled* winningly and took a peep at the old nose, well my dear they *roared* at that and then I felt ready for anything, so I took off my cloak because my dear I'd taken *particular* trouble to look *rather* fairy-like and expensive because Mr Haddock says that all this *creeping* about in *old* clothes is *utterly* mythical and doesn't go down the least bit with the poor, because he says they *venerate* lords and pretty frocks and everything, and anyhow he says that anyone who *doesn't* like to see a *disarming* girl in a *seductive* evening-dress is a biological case and no good to the Party.

Anyhow my dear I'd put on my *new* blue, and my dear it *is* the *world's* dream and I *rather* think I was looking *rather* lovable, well my dear it's cut straight across the front, I don't like a 'V' do you darling, and the *tiniest* shoulder-straps made of the *most* invisible little roses, and my dear a *celestial* fit *everywhere*, however well the *moment* I stood up they *merely* yelled, and my dear the *most* odd whistles at the back which the agent says is what they do when they want to be *too* complimentary, though I thought they sounded *rather* equibiguous, well my dear I didn't blather about the bush like the Chairman but I said straight out *Poor* Mr Haddock is locked up in the bathroom or somewhere, well my dear they *roared* again, and after that they totally fell for me, so I said but *meanwhile* I *merely* want to say the *weest* word about Mr Haddock and everything, because I said he's the *most* boracic and *melodious* candidate, and I said perfectly everyone *dotes* on Mr Haddock so perfectly *everyone* ought to *vote* for him, well then some *scorpion* at the back shouted *What's* his policy lady, so I said Well of course he's a *Tory Anarchist*, because my dear I heard him say that once at a night-club, well for instance I said he thinks that the Constitution is *too* divine, but he thinks that *lots* of Tories are utterly molluscular and ought to be *quite* painlessly dispensed with at once, and *as* for the Labour Party he thinks they mean well think badly and talk worse, because he says they've got *one* idea and that was mildewed about seven thousand years ago, and he says the Liberals have got *two* ideas only they cancel out and the Tories have got *no* ideas which is *too* desirable, because as *soon* as politicians get *big* ideas they rush to the head, well I said all this *promiscuous* gup about *nationalisation* and everything, one side saying it must *never* be done and the other saying you must do *nothing else*, well as I said it's *just* like cooking eggs sometimes you boil 'em and something it's best to *poach* 'em it depends on the *eggs*, but I said *nobody* outside politics would *think* of saying It's *utterly* fallacious to *boil* an egg, they'd have a look at the eggs *first*, but that's what all these *incurable* politicians call a matter of *principle* so I said if *you* want a man of principle *don't* vote for Mr Haddock because those sort of principles give him the *most* awful *mental* indigestion, and I said the *reason* he's a Tory is that they have *fewer* principles and get more done, and the *reason* he's an Anarchist is that they never do what *he* wants!

Well my dear by *this* time they *nearly* all worshipped me, of course some of the things I said caused *microscopic* riots in one or two corners but my dear whenever some *inflated* man at the back interrupted me about *six* darling blacksmiths who adored me merely *knocked* him on the head and he was *carted* away, well then I said And of *course* Mr Haddock is *utterly* vinophilous and at the *first* sign of *vinophobia* he merely detonates, because he says all this *pragmatical* yap about *tea* being a necessity and *beer* being a vice because he says when *tea* came in the *doctors* and everybody said exactly what they're saying now about *beer*, my dear *sapping* the stamina and all that, and as a *matter* of fact tea's far more corroding to the national life because *whenever* two women sit down to tea they talk *sickening* scandal and the *most* felonious *gossip* but when two men have a beer they get more and more *Christian*, and I said Well Mr Haddock *always* says that he *always* believes in *always* doing the *Christian* thing, so you can take it from me that *his* motto is *Better* beer and *larger* glasses, and as a *matter* of fact his *first* action will be to *abolish* the Licensing Laws, and stop all these *flatulent* interferences with private life and everything, because he says it's the *most* staggering nonsense that an Englishman's thought fit to choose his own Government but he *isn't* thought fit to choose his own food and drink, well don't you agree darling?

Well my dear they merely *ululated* and by this time I felt *too* rhetorical and satisfactory, my dear I'd *no* idea that public speaking could give you such a *throb*, well I had *masses* more to say but just then Mr Haddock arrived, and my dear he had the *loveliest* reception, *all* because of me some of them said, and my dear he was *too* moved when he heard about it and the Taffeta cried on my new frock which was a bit uncalled-for perhaps, of course I *rather* gather that the Chairman didn't exactly *rave* about some of the things I said, but Mr Haddock said he agreed with every word of it, my dear it's *all* reported in the Burbleton Post, my dear *Promising* Recruit to *Public* Life, the *only* worry is that some of the other speakers got muddled and *would* keep talking about *Lady Haddock*, my dear *too* embarrassing, however the great thing is that I'm a *public* woman and the *Joy* of Burbleton and really my dear I *do* begin to think that I'm *rather* a darling, and so farewell your little fairy TOPSY.

23 Politics

Well Trix darling I haven't a *second* to write to you my dear I'm
quite frenzical but I *simply* must, well I suppose you've seen in
the papers only of course you don't read the papers but anyhow
here we are in the absolute *throes* of a *bye*-election because Sir
Roger *Stuff* my dear resigned his seat after his *Christmas* dinner,
my dear *too* thoughtless, and *here* we are as I said before, Mr
Haddock and Taffeta Mole and your *political* Top, and my dear
it's *too* lowering but in *spite* of Taffeta *such* is politics that already
from what I can make out there's the *most* definite little *breath*
of scandal in the noxious air of Burbleton, however well when I
tell you that the moment we got here *poor* Mr Haddock merely
disintegrated with flu so of course Taffeta and I have been *madly*
drafting the Election Address, we didn't *quite* harmonise so
we each did one well I finished first, and my dear you know
you *never* can tell about litterature until you see it in *print* so
of course I sent mine straight off to the printer's which it seems
has *rather* alienated the Committee and people because the
Chairman was *too* forbearing but he said my address was the
least bit erroneous in punctuation and a few things, however *I*
thought it was *rather* winning but they wouldn't even show it to
Mr Haddock because of his temperature, well I'll send you one
but no more now darling because we're a *whirl* of deputations
and *wounded* constituents and *importunate* Societies for the
abolition of *everything* and now I must fly because Mr Haddock
wants to dictate a letter to the Society for *Increasing* the Death
Penalty or something, farewell your *distracted* little TOPSY.

(Enclosure)

Mr ALBERT HADDOCK'S ELECTION ADDRESS
To the Electors and Everybody

Too RIGHT.

Darlings I do hope you'll all vote for me because I may not be *orthodox* and everything but you'll find that *nearly* always I'm *too* right.

POLICY.

Well of course I *always* say that I *always* believe in always doing the *Christian* thing and that's the main thing in this life *isn't* it, apart from that I think the British Constitution is *too* adequate, well no one's thought of a better one *have* they, and of course we *must* have a *Navy* and *Army* and the *Police* and the *Fire-Brigade* because you've only got to *think* what would happen if we didn't, but of course don't think I don't *adulate* the poor because I *simply* do only the people I pity are the *Middle Classes* who of course *pay* for everything and *get* nothing and *why* they do it I *simply* can't imagine and my advice to them is to pay *no* Income-Tax until they've one foot in the jail.

PEACE.

Of course I *adore* Peace and Disarmament and everything, but what I always say is well, what about *pirates*?

WAR.

I think War is *utterly* anomalous but so are burglars.

FOREIGN AFFAIRS.

I'm *too* saturated with foreign affairs, my dears I *don't* want to hear a *single* word about the *hairy* Lithuanians or the *scrofulous* Croats or the Poles or the Yaks or *any* of these *redundant* Europeans, because of course they're *not* white men, they *don't* care *two* hoots for us, I don't care *half* a hoot for them, they're *miles* away, they *don't* shave, and *why* we should waste *ten* minutes *oozing* about in their *malarial* affairs I *merely* can't imagine so what I've *always* said is *Let* them *wallow*, because *why* we should be the *scullery-maid* of Europe when *meanwhile* we've got the *most* disarming *clean-limbed* Empire *utterly* far-flung and *starving* for a matey glance, and if you ask me *my* Foreign Policy is eliminate the Foreign Office, because my dears merely *all* they do is to make *jobs* for themselves and *trouble* for us.

SECOND CHAMBER REFORM.

Well of course we *haven't* got a Second Chamber and it *doesn't* want reforming, because my dears I think the *House* of Lords is *too* sagacious, they're the sole people who *know* their job and have *no* publicity so of course they've *nothing* to do, which is *too* English and utterly right.

BAZAARS AND EVERYTHING.

Well I'd better tell you at once that *if* I'm elected it'll be *too* fruitless to write *carbolic* letters to me about the way I *vote* because of course I shall be *utterly* plastic and vote *just* how I feel in the mood for *always* and of course *don't* expect me to *snow* money on all your *sickly* Bazaars and superfluous bicycling-clubs and everything, because I will *not* open Shopping Weeks, I will *not* spend week-ends *smarming* about in your *ulcerated* town, because and my dears we'd better be *too* frank from the soup-stage, and the *fact* is I've always said that *constituencies* are the *most* unsalubrious places in the *whole* United Kingdom and I'm *not* asking you to elect me to Burbleton but *Westminster* and my dears supposing you do I shall park there *permanently*.

VINOPHOBIA.

But my *angel* electors I *can't* tell you how I *abhor* vinophobes and all these *vociferous* busies and scorbutic nose-pokers, and my dears that's the *main* plank in my *whole* platform because nowadays whenever there's a clear case of *feverish* vinophobia or unnecessary nose-poking in the Spinster of Parliaments there's *merely* nobody whose *first* idea is to *merely* jump on it, because *all* these *gelatinous* Parties are equally bad, they *all* go pale at the sight of a postcard, and even the Liberals, well all that will be *my* particular heartburn because I think all these laws about selling meat-pies and everything, and after all *did* we or *did* we not win the Great War for Liberty, well look at London and look at *conquered* Berlin *and* then look again, I *ask* you my dears.

DEDISTRIBUTION AND ALL THAT.

And *all* that of course leads up *too* fluidly to all *this* doesn't it because of course the *sole* trouble with Parliament is that it *simply* never has time to discuss anything that anybody really cares about, because of course they spend *weeks* on *Trade* and *Disarmament* and *Unemployment* and all those *extensive* things which of course are *too* cardinal only of course *everybody* knows that *nobody* in the world can do *anything* about them, so of course *what* happens is that we have too much legislation all about *nothing* because *meanwhile* darlings they never have time for all the *wee* small things that really might be done and even *they* could understand, poor blotting-pads, so of course what I've *always* said is that there ought to be *two* Parliaments, one *large* one where they could talk *politics* and have *amendments* and all that *attitudinous* yap about *Nationalisation* and *Free Trade* and everything, and another small one where they could get small things *done*, well my dears things like *Stonehenge* and *Hospitals* and *Theatre* Rents and *buying matches* and a boat-service on the *Thames* and when you can get *married* and when you can eat and *drink* and all these *Bridges* and *Dora* and the *dogs* and my dears *all* the things that everybody in the world is talking about except Parliament, and of course if we *can't* have two Parliaments *all* I can say is that *this* Parliament ought to *start* work at ten in the morning and go on till it does something *sensible* because I've always said that *nobody* who starts work at *three* in the afternoon is likely to do *too* much in this world well *are* they?

THE SURTAX.

Well of course you've all heard of these *Christian* highwaymen who *only* robbed the *rich* and were *too* idealish only I never heard it called *Social Service* before and I *never* heard that the poor got offensively *fat* on their proceedings. However.

MR BALDWIN.

All the same I *do* rather think that it's *almost* about time that my *divine* Mr Baldwin *cleaned* his pipe or did *something* about *something*, because of course I *do* see that all this immobility is *rather* intriguing but of course as *I* said in one of my *arresting* plays I *do* think it's *rather* a case of

> Man, like a pebble on a glacier,
> Moves imperceptibly but always down.

Your only ALBERT HADDOCK.

24 Scandal at Burbleton

Well Trix darling I've been *too* peccable but my dear *what* a throb, well of course I don't know *where* to begin because my dear the *truth* is that *ever* since the Election began I've been the least bit of a stumbling-block to Mr Haddock it seems because my dear you've *no* idea what *sedimentary* minds the electors have, my dear *quite* creamy people go *perfectly* Foot and Mouth the *moment* they touch politics and my dear you'll hardly believe it but it seems absolute *things* have been *definitely* said about Mr Haddock and me, my dear *simply* because *when* he was convalescenting he used *too* occasionally to *dictate* a letter or two to the Amalgamated Aunts or the Society for Keeping People *Too* Virginal or something from his sick-bed to *me*, well of course he dictated *reams* more to Taffeta on every sort of subject from the *same* situation but nobody seems to *fret* much about what Taffeta does, my dear *too* inequitable, however there you are and of course the *point* is that the other candidate the *most* elastic man called Antony Buffle has absolutely pocketed *not* only the Mothers' Vote but the *Pure* Vote as well and my dear *those* two together have the last word in *this* country, *believe* me, especially my dear if absolute *things* are *quite* definitely *said* darling as they have been because my dear these *politicians*, my dear they all go round shouting NO PERSONALITIES at *this* Election when of course there's *nothing* they enjoy like a *sulphuric* little scandal, well my dear when I tell you that it seems the Chairman gave Mr Haddock the *nudest* hint that it would be *just* as well if his *principal* private secretary retired to London or looked a little less magnetic, so my dear I *offered* to wear cotton stockings or a *veil* or anything but of course Mr Haddock was *too* adamant because he said if *I* didn't mind *he* merely thrived on it and he says that for every Pure Vote I alienate I shall probably inspire ten of the Apathetic Vote to go to the poll for the *first* time which is *too* plausible because there's no doubt I'm the *hugest* draw with the great heart of the people and as for the proletariat it *adulates* me darling.

Well my dear I've been too precautious and utterly *prim* in the grill-room where my dear we all eat together in *one* vortex of *suggestive* glances, however all went well till *yesterday* when my dear the *most* prawny deputation came to see Mr Haddock from this Society for Keeping People *Too* Virginal, my dear *six* of them all with *antennæ* and my dear they looked at me like so many *scorpions* and of course they were *too* unsatisfied with Mr Haddock's attitude on vinophobia and everything because they're all misovinists and of course Mr Haddock is *frankly* vinophilous, so they said they were *too* reluctant but they were afraid they'd have to give the Virginal Vote to Mr *Buffle*, well of course my dear Mr Buffle is staying at the *same* hotel and as a *matter* of fact I happened to hear from a *mutual* chambermaid that *Mr* Buffle isn't *quite* such a vinophobe in private life as he is during an *election*, and is also *quite* a philogynist, so my dear in one of my moments of girlish abandon it suddenly occurred to me, Well if I can compromise *poor* Mr Haddock well why shouldn't I compromise the spurious Mr *Buffle* and strike a *blow* for Mr Haddock and my dear I *happened* to hear that this *anæmic* deputation was visiting the Buffle at 6 so my dear at about half-past 5 I put on an *extensive* black hat and the *most* mystical veil which I had for the Christmas carol-party and I *tripped* up to Mr Buffle's rooms on the next floor darling hoping for the worst.

Well my dear *too* fortuitous the man was in and mixing a cocktail, quite an endurable fellow darling with the *most* Celtic eyes what I call rather a *smoking-room* man, well not married of course because I should think he's too fond of the ladies, anyhow my dear I *rather* thought that he was *rather* attracted because my dear he adumbrated a gin and mixed *almost* at once, well we toyed with our refreshments and I let on that I was the *most* gushing constituent who was *too* anxious for him to do something in Parliament for the dear *birds*, my dear municipal haunts for *nightingales* and titteries in the Parks and everything, because my dear I *simply* couldn't think of a *thing* to say, so of course he was a bit mystified but utterly *clasped* my hand and said he'd do merely *everything* for the birds if I said so, well my dear just as I was becoming *quite* wordless and I *rather* feared that he was *rather* tending to be *rather* affectionate, *in* rushed a Secretary, a *male* ewe darling, and said the *Deputation* were looming, and my dear the Buffle went all agitato and said he was *too* occupied but couldn't we meet again while my dear the Secretary *madly* concealed the gin and things, however I wasn't to be eliminated *quite* so easily so I said I had *masses* more to tell him about the poor birds and couldn't I wait till *after* the Deputation, and my dear *while* he was saying he was too devastated but etcetera etcetera I merely tantivied through the *nearest* door which happened to be Mr Buffle's bed-room and at the same moment through the *other* door *in* came the Deputation from the Society for Keeping the Empire *Absolutely Virginal!*

Well my dear I listened *unscrupulously* and my dear *when* I heard him *address* the deputation merely *all* remorse *oozed* rapidly out of me because my dear he was *too* pure and misovinous for *words*, my dear I can't *tell* you, and of course they utterly *lapped* it up and my dear *when* I heard the *Chief* Spinster say that the *whole* Virginal Vote would go simply *solid* to Mr Buffle I *merely* lost control and I yelled *Tony, Tony* there's a *mouse* in your *pyjamas*, with *which* words darling I *tottered* into the sitting-room and *fainted* in Mr Buffle's *reluctant* arms before the *whole* deputation, shouting at the same time darling *Where* is the GIN, well of course human life comes before everything *doesn't* it and the Secretary instantly unveiled the restorative to the *intense* collapse of the *Deputation* not to mention Mr Buffle because my dear only a *moment* before he'd been telling them that the *Modern* Girl and the cocktail habit were *Imperial* menaces, however my dear I kept on coming to and *requiring* succour and *fainting* piteously again till my dear a *little* pointedly the Deputation *evaporated*.

Well then my dear I recovered *too* suddenly and of course the situation was *rather* vulnerable because of course the man was *quite* florid with rage and at the same time *rather* tending to be *rather* passionate only fortunately the *Secretary*, well he said I'd lost him a thousand votes and I said many people thought I was worth more than that so he said *Too* right and wouldn't I *discard* the veil because *after* the Election we ought to have supper or something and meanwhile we ought to be friends and everything, and my dear *things* were beginning to be *faintly* difficult because of course you'll understand I had *slight* conscience-trouble, however *fate* intercepted because my dear the *divine* telephone rang and the Secretary said it was the *President* of the *Virginal* outfit so of course he *had* to go and my dear *while* he was in the middle of the *most* protracted explanations I merely *glided* into the passage and *gravitated* to my room, my dear *too* jeapardous the whole thing of *course* and if Mr Haddock was to hear I don't know *what*, however I do feel that I've struck the flimsiest blow for moderate vinophily and honesty in politics and everything, and the one canker is that I *rather* feel that if I'd met Mr Buffle in *lay*-circumstances so to speak, I *rather* think that he might have been *rather* congenial however such *is* this *scourge* of a life *isn't* it darling your *defamated* little TOPSY.

25 End of Act One

Well Trix my *heart's* balm so at last it's happened and of course you *would* have appendix-trouble and miss it, my dear it's *too* damping I *did* so yearn for you, and of course you've heard nothing but my wire well I'll try and tell you everything only of course I'm a *mere* vortex and I never could write my *lucidest* in bed, however I'd better get on with it before Haddock wakes up, my dear I've decided I *can't* call him Albert or *even* Penrose so I'm *hovering* rather between Haddock and *Fin* however there hasn't been much time for details yet, my dear I *simply* can't realise it only happened *yesterday*, however I'd better begin at the beginning, my dear I've *just* upset my coffee over my *delirious* new nightie *too* sobering, so that's what comes of writing to *you* darling.

Where was I well I *think* I told you about the Election tending towards a certain *acidulosity* towards the end what with the Pure Vote and the Mother's Vote being rather *massed* against Haddock on account of his rather discussable little Secretary because my dear quite *things* I believe were positively *said*, only it seems after my visit to *Mr Buffle* in the black *veil* the *same* sort of things began to be *rather* muttered about *him*, the only difference was that *he* was *too* resentful about it but Haddock cared not one molecular *hoot* neither did I because of the great heart of the people being utterly attached to me, my dear I've made *rows* of *sensational* speeches and *wherever* I went I had a perfect bodyguard of *adhesive* weavers and congenial loom girls and my dear the handsomest fellows with *cotton-hooks* who whenever some stoat of a man so much as interrupted me they merely *carved* him into *small* sections, my dear I do think the proletariat are *rather* winning if only you can manage to creep into their hearts don't you find that darling?

Well on *Sunday* morning my dear feeling the least bit blotting-paper after all this *throbbery* and *jading* labour Haddock took me over to *New Brighton* in a *bijou* ferry-steamer for ventilation and refreshment, my dear you go *right* down the Mersey rather scenic the whole thing darling because it was an *electrical* day though of course *too* Polar, my dear the *azurest* sky with those *divine* little kiss-clouds, and my dear you know how I respond to Nature when I'm in the mood, well I wore my fur coat and a rather inflammatory little hat in high-brow green with a *silver* fish in honour of Haddock and the *chastest* little feathers which my dear sort of *trespass* on to the cheek and madden the male, well Haddock says so, and of course the cold was *too* brutal so at New Brighton we merely *cantered* along the sands to get warm, *hand* in *hand* darling because I nearly always fall down when I canter in high heels, *rather* a fragrant picture don't you think because my dear we were *utterly* alone with the sun and the sand and the Mersey and everything, *too* lyrical, and I remember having that *esotteric* feeling *you* know my dear when *something* tells you that *something* is *simply* going to happen *quite* soon, my dear *too* right because just then I did fall down, and that's how things *matured* because I was convinced I'd shattered my ankle and of course a bitter East Wind does give a girl rather a *radiance*, anyhow Haddock said I looked *too* adorable, like a *frozen rose* or something, so we sat on the sand and he went suddenly soupy for the *first* time, my dear he said the *most* lovely things about me, and it seems he's really rather *ached* for me from the *very* first at that prawn-party only he's always thought I was too *Cadogan* for him, so of course I said I was an *utter* reptile and bound to ruin his life and he said he was *too* spurious in every possible way so I said in that case we were *too* suitable and of course I'd marry him, only I said What about Mrs Green and he said well she was more like the Christian religion to him while of course I'm a pagan but unperishing *passion* which was rather flower-like and satisfactory I thought, so my dear we nestled restfully beside the septic Mersey and merely *gazed* at the factories and cranes and everything, and we picked up *pink* shells, and my dear you know I'm not sentimental but I don't think I shall ever see a *dredger* or a *distant* crane without thinking of Haddock's first *virginal* salutes at my darling New Brighton.

Well then my dear I had one of my *inspired* flashes because of course we'd settled nothing about *when*, only *suddenly* I said *why* shouldn't we be married at *Burbleton* on *polling-day* because *what* vinegar it would be to the Pure Vote and all those *drainy* Societies, and of course *ecstatic* publicity because *no* candidate has ever been blighted in matrimony on polling-day *before*, and they say a married man gets away with the Mothers' Vote *too* always, well my dear it was just the sort of *demented* idea that utterly magnetises Haddock, my dear like me he's his own self-starter which my dear is *one* reason why we're *rather* gloves, so he registered an affirmative *quite* instantly, bless him, of course we had to get the *most* special and expensive licence and what with the Election the trousseau was somewhat a scramble, especially in Burbleton where my dear I got *everything*, simply *every* shop in the borough provided something, *including* my dear the *most* Burbleton undies which I *rather* doubt if I shall wear *very* continuously *outside* the constituency, my dear *too* uninspired, however the Undy Vote was ours to a man likewise the Milliner Vote, well my dear the *note* of the dress and everything was *blue* because of our election colours, my dear *ivory* charmeuse with the *most* maidenly turquoise girdle and forget-me-nots on the train, ditto the chaplet, my dear *too* alluring, with the hugest bouquet of *painted* lilies, the bridesmaids in butterfly-blue velvet and enchanting blue *muffs* with *secret* pockets for *all* the Prayer-Books whether deposited or what-not which was Haddock's present to them, my dear there were *twenty*, one from every Ward, so of course the *whole* constitt came, Dad gave me away, my dear *too* alacritous, and a man called Rowland was best-man who I had a rather fallacious evening with once you remember, he smiled wistfully and I *rather* thought he was *rather* kicking himself because my dear they say I did look *really* disarming, well I don't know about other brides but I utterly adored the *whole* proceedings, my dear the church was *thronged*, all my loom-girls in the *most* characteristic shawls and afterwards my devotional bodyguard tied absolute *ropes* to the car and simply *processed* us round the voting-places, me beaming darling like *absolute* Royalty, with the *result* my dear that more people voted than *ever* before and of course the *entire* Mother and Pure Votes merely pendulised over to Haddock because crowns may fall and everything but the g h p does like a *wedding*.

Well of course you saw my dear we had a *flawless* majority, but my dear now for the *cankers*, well first of all Mr Buffle *recognised* me at the counting, my dear my *blushes*, only he was *too* Gallahad and says he'll *never* divulge, and *secondly* and *ghastily* it seems one of Haddock's agents or something who quite venerates me has been doing *corrupt* practices, my dear *beer* and everything, all for *my* sake of course but there's going to be an *expostulation* or something and they say my *poor* Haddock is sure to be *unseated*, *can* you conceive it, only in that case they say that your little Topsy is sure to be elected *instead* to keep the seat warm because they *do* idolatrise me and it's the done thing nowadays, however all that's *too* unponderable at the moment because *what* matters is that *here* I am my dear feeling *quite* ethereal and bubbulous with bliss, my dear like the *most* frothy meringue it's *too* narcotic, when are *you* going to be blighted darling, I'm *too* deflated to hear about Harry, however there's lots of good fish and the *moment* you're antiseptic again you must come and stay with us because I do want you to like my Haddock only not too much, because I do think he's *rather* adequate in his erroneous little way and he does adore me, well no more now, we're off today, of course it's an utter secret *where* in fact we don't know ourselves *quite*, anyhow *too* far away, so farewell my fallen lily. I do wish your trials were over too, take care of the old tummy and one day soon p'raps you'll get the *most* matronical letter from your sober little TOPSY—*MP*!

Topsy, MP

1 Becomes A Member

Trix, my cruel angel, I will *not* be upbraided in that *corrosive* way, my dear how *could* I write to you, if you *will* go *wafting* about the world in *yachts*, my dear I've started the *longest* letter *oceans* of times, but then I always thought O well where *is* China, and by the time she gets this she *won't* be there and anyhow the news will be *too* obsolete, so in the end the pen *quite* fell from the little fingers, besides darling you know you never *uttered* yourself except that *rather* aloof picture-postcard from the ROCKEFELLER yacht, but *don't* think darling there's the *palest* cloud between us, because we're the old old bosoms still and you shall hear the *whole* proceedings *daily* darling.

But my dear it's *too* dreary to hear you're still a Vestal, I did think you'd magnetise in one of those tropical climes, however life *undulates* before you still darling so don't hurry the stroke, because my dear I'm *satisfied* that matrimony is a thing a girl ought to commit *once* only and then well, as for me I'm the *born* matron already, well no tiny tots yet for which thanks be, but my dear utterly *poised* and *mature* and my dear *too* wifely, my dear we're *crazily* harmonious still and we've only had the *most* trivial tantrums except one which was rather cyclonic, I'll tell you one day, but as far as I can see the *sole* flaw in conjugality is that at *any* moment a girl may be guilty of *twins* because my dear I'm *quite* sure that your generous Topsy is the type that *twins* if anything, so you can understand they *are* rather a *background* to a girl's thoughts, and that will explain if I seem a *fraction* more esoteric and autumnal in tone from time to time these days darling,

Well of course we had *Earth's* rosiest honeymoon since ADAM and EVE, my dear *Jamaica*, *too* voluptious and historical, you have *nothing* but *yams* and *rum-punch* and *bread-fruit*, and my dear the *humming*-birds are *quite* electrical, well we stayed at a *divinely* lotos-eating little place called Montego Bay, my dear if *ever* you descend to matrimony you *must* go there and *merely* mention my name because I *rather* think they were *rather* attracted, well we had *Elysian* rooms with the widest balcony *quite* over the sea which my dear is the *most* theatrical blue with *intoxicating* coral reefs, my dear *live* coral sort of openwork rock in *pink* and *too* ornamental, and the *most* tropical little *aquarium* fish all topaz and purple with orange stripes and everything, and of course the water is *too* diaphanous, well when I tell you that I dropped a looking-glass from our balcony into six foot of sea and attended to the little nose in it *quite* adequately as it lay at the bottom, and my dear the bathing was *dream-like*, you lie on this miraculous *white* sand with *secret* bottles of coker-nut oil and merely *cook* the little frame by sections, my dear like something on a spit till you go *pure* antelope *all* over, only of course the *hilarious* thing is that the *local* white virgins utterly *shun* the sun and merely *lurk* under umbrellas and everything for fear they'll go dusky and be taken for *Nature's* Jamaicans, my dear *too* delicate the whole situation, however you recline *comatically* and watch the fifty-fifty girls, my dear the *most* enticing cinnamon colour and *what* figures, doing the *highest* dives upside-down and everything, and after that you sort of *wilt* into the water which is like *blue* velvet a cat's been lying on, my dear it's *so* buoyant you're sort of swimming in the *air*, and of course I had a *languishing* costume in *Cambridge* and ivory with a *marked* absence of *back* darling, and I gave Haddock an *emerald* garment in wool, because my dear I *do* resent this *mourning* uniform men wear in the water, and I do *not* see why one's nearest and dearest should always look like a *wet* hansom-cab horse on the beach, do you darling, however *this* one I must admit was the *faintest* shade too *garish* for a male, because it was the last in the shop and quite *remarks* I believe were definitely passed on the sunlit strand about it, however Haddock didn't seem to care a *cabbage*, which only shows you darling what *Love* can do to a lord and master, don't you agree?

So what with everything I don't want to hear a *single* word about your *populous* Lidos and *teeming* lingerie parades, because think what you will of me but my dear this tender plant does *not* blossom in *herds* and *hives* and places where they *swarm*, no darling I am *not* the human bee, but small and congenial which was what we had there, because there were a few quite endurable *voiceless* Britons, who *murmured* Good-morning and *whispered* Good-night but didn't utter between, also some *rather* creamy Americans who paid for the rum-punch *quite* always, my dear *too* amenable, however *that* leads me to the *solitary* canker, because one of the Americans was *rather* magical, my dear a *definite* witch, called Mrs May, and we became *quite* bosoms, only as luck would have it the nymph reminded Haddock of that *Green* attractor I've told you about, and my dear she was *rather* litterary and constantly read *books*, my dear *quite* nothing in it of course only there *was* a second or two when your *radiant* Top felt she had to *definitely* make an effort to *command* attention, and *that* my dear is *not* marked on the map of my life, but *don't* think darling that I'm going to be one of those *bilious* wives, because I've quite decided that if *ever* there's the shadow of Delilah-trouble I'm going to be *too* Christian about it, because my dear you know I *always* say that it *always* pays to *always* do the *Christian* thing.

However no more of that now, because my dear of course I've forgotten to tell you the *real* throb, my dear in *case* you haven't seen I am *litterally* a Member of Parliament, well it was just as we expected, my *poor* Haddock was *unseated* owing to some weasel of a man who gave *beer* to the populace, however your Topsy was elected *too* unanimously instead, my dear a walking *weed* did stand against me, but he quite lost his deposit and everything and was *practically* stoned to death, well it all took *months* to fructify and now I can't take my little seat till next Session, of course my poor Haddock is *faintly* wounded I'm afraid, because meanwhile he'd made *history's* virgin speech and was once ejected from the House for calling the man HICKS a cow in a china-shop, so he was *rather* popular, however he's writing a tragedy or something now and we've taken a house in *my* constituency, only outside Burbleton because my dear *Burbleton*, *too* morbid, of course one faint flaw is that the *finances* are the least bit tremulous and on the debit side, so Haddock's doing some ads as well, well no more now darling, O snakes I nearly forgot, my dear talking of finance there's a *misty* chance of my *flying* the large Atlantic, but not a *whisper* darling, because not even Haddock is to know, more later, your *constant* angel TOPSY.

2 Goes Shooting

My *soul's* thanks Trix for your *fragrant* letter, but my dear I do wish you wouldn't *exaggerate* so, I can't think *what* I said to put such *moonery* into your head, because of course my dear there was *never* a 'row' or 'incident' or anything, I *told* you we had *history's* halcyon honeymoon, my dear *too* serene, in fact *some* girls *might* smell the breath of cattery in your suggestions, but I know you don't mean that, however *since* you ask me darling I *will* tell you one thing that happened because it was *rather* laughworthy and I think might be a help and sign-post to *you* darling if ever you snare something as far as the altar.

Only my dear you must register a *virgin's* vow to *never* let my Haddock guess I tell you a *thing* about him, because I *rather* think he'd *rather* resent it, however well my dear the *moment* I saw that he was *quite* noticing this Mrs May the American, and I must say darling she had high sight-value, though a bit on the *bijou* scale, besides of course reminding Haddock of his Green fairy, the pure passion of the past, my dear they *both* have eyes like the *largest* lavender pearls, my dear my pathetic little orbs are the merest *beads* beside them, however, thanks be, I am *not* the height of a small-size marionette, *no* darling I'm *not* jealous, I *am—not—a—jealous—woman*, it *merely* isn't in my *nature*, of course a wife has her *amour propre*, but *what* happened was that, well *Mr* May who was an Englishman and *rather* a savoury fellow, only he's one of the gun-brigade my dear *never* happy unless he's *supplying* the fish-course or murdering a bird, and of course Glory, that's the wife, yes darling *believe* me *Glory* was the charmer's name, well she was quite a one with a gun as well, my dear she knew about *butts* and she'd *landed* fish the size of herself, *sardines* I suppose said the young wife tenderly, well my dear on our *last* day in Jamaica she turned her lavender lamps on Haddock and said *would* we like to go and shoot *alligators* with them, because *if* one shot any they made the *most* Parisian shoes.

Well of course my dear *my* reactions were *too* negative, because you *know* my attitude to gunnery, my dear don't think I'm flabby about alligators or anything only I definitely had *no* feeling against the alligators of Jamaica because it seems they lead *aloof* lives in the mangrove swamps and *quite* never invade the home, besides I *rather* wanted to have a farewell sun-debauch on the sands, well of course Haddock and I are absolute gloves on this subject as a rule, but what was my stagger and dismay when I saw him utterly nibbling at the alligator notion, well my dear I did the *Christian* thing forthwith and said that *Haddock* must go alligating and *I* would stay and suffer on the beach by myself, well then of course Haddock said that a barrel of *rubies* wouldn't induce him, etcetera, so then I did the double-Christian and said well we'd *both* go on the shoe-hunt, and Gosh it was so.

Well darling the alligator may be seductive *footwear* but he lives in the *most* alluvial and un-salubrious places, my dear have you *ever* been in a mangrove swamp, my dear Nature at its *most* revolting, well we *all* got into an almost invisible little *flat* boat, my dear a mere *plank*, well *two* would have been a crowd but we had a jet-black Britisher as well to row, May had a gun of course and so had Haddock, but my dear *too* reluctant because it seems he hasn't fingered a firearm since the Battle of *Arras*, and had *quite* forgotten how most of it *functioned*, however he didn't dare to say so and of course Glory insisted on his having her gun, and my dear I did do *rather* an astute chuckle within because I thought he was becoming *rather* lukewarm about the entire proceeding, me likewise darling, well there was a frantic wind and in *two* whiffs we were blown round a corner into the *bowels* of this *insanitary* swamp, my dear I *always* thought a mangrove was a sort of *plant* they put in the chutney, but *these* were absolute *trees*, my dear if you can imagine the *smelliest* forest merely growing in a *deep* drain, and of course the *most* emetical *red* and black *crabs* quite clambering about the branches, my dear too *ventrifugal,* so there we were my dear in that *festering* corner, entirely surrounded by the *slimy* mangroves, sitting in a *hot* draught, *inhaling* malaria, *black* with mosquitoes and *looking* for alligators, O Gosh!

And if that isn't life's most *lowering* situation I don't know what, *because* my dear it seems the *sole* thing you *ever* see of an alligator is *one* eye popping out of the water, and what with the water that day being *too* ruffled by the wind and *fish* popping in *all* directions one saw *platoons* of alligators only they *never* were, and my dear one couldn't *respirate* or blow the little nose for fear of upsetting this *precarious* boat, in *which* case of course there being no ground visible one would *merely* cling to these indecent mangroves and have the legs chewed off by submarine reptiles and the *upper* parts by mosquitoes and crabs, O yes and by the way darling they said that the *pet* habit of the alligator is to pop up *too* near the boat and merely *flick* it over with *one* flick of the scaly tail, my dear I *never* knew a place where there were *so* many agonies at the *same* time, because of course at *any* moment one might be *shot* to death by my *dejected* Haddock, my dear he *sat* there looking *too* unmilitary with the gun on his knees, my dear like a man left alone with a *baby*, and my dear I did pray that no alligator would do the popping act *his* side of the boat because I was *quite* convinced that long before he found the right trigger and everything I should have lost *both* the little uninsured legs.

Too right my dear, because *meanwhile* the May family were merely *living* for the *chase*, my dear *too* voracious, the male May kept whispering *There there* and *hoisting* his weapon, my dear my *nerves*, but it was always only a *tarpon* or something and the Glory creature kept hissing at Haddock *Shoot* man *shoot* and my poor Haddock would peer *too* ferociously in the wrong direction and do *quite* nothing, well at *last* Mr May *suddenly* made a film face and blew off his rifle, my dear *too* alarming, the boat rocked *madly* and some of the drain came in, well my dear nobody else had seen the *smell* of a reptile but he was *too* sure he'd hit one, an old hen alligator it seemed darling, and we could have the skin, only it wouldn't come to the surface for *two* days, so I said *Too* thoughtless we're leaving tomorrow, and of course *Glory* after this was *more* bloodsome than before and *more* and *more* unsatisfied with Haddock, my dear she saw alligators *everywhere*, but *nothing* she said could induce my Haddock to part with his bullet, and what with the *wind* and the *whiff* and the *mosquitoes* and the *crabs* I thought that at *any* moment I should have to *scream* like a spinster, my dear *too* right because just then one of these *obscene* crabs fell *plop* into the boat out of a tree, and my dear I am *not* accustomed to a shower of crabs so I *merely* yelled, the boat *heaved* and my dear *at* that Haddock's gun went off at *last*, well the black man disembarked the crab and my *poor* Haddock looked the *least* bit evasive but he swore he'd seen *two* reptiles and *definitely* hit *one*, well we all said it was *too* bad it wouldn't come up for *two* days, however *Glory* my dear looked *too* incredulous and *disillusioned* and I doubt if they'll *ever* be *quite* bosoms now, however after that we merely *crawled* out of the swamp *against* the hurricane, my dear *torture*, and my *poor* Haddock couldn't remember *how* to *unload* and everything, well we *both* agreed that it had been the world's *most* noxious expedition and it was a lesson to both of us, but of course the *real* message for you darling is *as* I say that it *always* pays to *always* do etc, so take it to heart your *Christian* little TOPSY.

3 Flies Half The Atlantic

Trix my darling have you *ever* flown the Atlantic, well don't, of course it was all *so* secret I couldn't wire you, and my dear there was no time for *letters*, and of course I *never* know how *much* you read the papers, if any, anyhow you haven't seen the whole story, at least, hopes be, so here's the whole *degrading* narrative.

Well my dear I *think* I told you once about a *congenitally* redundant Baronet called Sir Charles Chase who showed affection in the dentist's waiting-room, my dear one of the *few* definite *surprises* in this worldly little life, well our paths have never intersected since then, my dear *too* deliberate on my side, but this dog-fish has a son called *Claude* whom I'd cannoned into once or twice at routs and swarries, quite a congenial cub about supper-time darling only he *will* yap on about these *repugnant* aeroplanes and *dedicates* his life to *zooming* and *stalling* and all that ullage and he was always *yearning* to take me up because my dear from the very first it was *rather* manifest that he was *rather* attracted, only of course Haddock is *too* alienated by the air, to say nothing of Claude, and I've always been *rather* unanimous so I spurned the youth's petition on monogamous grounds.

However *meanwhile* my dear he got a grip somehow on this moon-affected female you've read about perhaps Miss Lotweed, who has a weakness for all this *neurotic* air-stuff and also for the Rights of Woman and everything, and it seems her *life's* ambition is to finance the *first* London girl to *fly* the Atlantic from *east* to west, because it seems that's the *one* thing wanted to put the *entire* feminine gender on its feet, well of course Claude told her that I was the *world's* little woman for the exploit because I was the *utter* prize-winner in the modern doe class, and besides I should be the *first* bride and the *first* woman MP to do the idiot's trick and shatter *masses* of records with a *single* gesture.

Well my dear I met her by chance and the Lotweed *totally* agreed with him at *sight*, my dear *too* impressed, but of course I was *perfectly* aloof about it, because I knew my poor Haddock would *merely* detonate, only my dear *then* it came out that the moon-woman wanted to pay positive *sums* of money to the First Girl etc, my dear she *started* at a thousand, and of course I told you that the Haddock finances have just a *paltry* touch of instability and vagueness, so my dear I began to *dimly* ponder the thing, but of course *too* reluctant, and my dear the woman *sweats* money, and I pointed out I should have to *deceive* my poor Haddock with the wedding-bells still trembling in the belfry, so the price leapt up at once, and so then I said I was *rather* lukewarm about going to America *at all*, and well to shingle the story somewhat the price leapt *quite* frequently, and at last I got one figure for hitting America, and another for half-way, and another for leaving the planet at all, my dear *too* satisfactory, and that was that.

Well then of course I had to tell my *poor* Haddock my *first* evasion, about a long week-end in my *importunate* constituency or something, my dear it was *rather* poignant, but I sent him the *most* penitent letter from the thingummy-drome, but of course *quite* making the point that it was all for *his* sake and now he'd be able to give up doing advertisements and write *synthetical* novels or any garbage he liked, my dear Gertrude says he merely *howled* like a dog and *flung* the gold-fish-bowl out of the window when he got the letter, *rather* moving darling, wasn't it, however all's well etc.

Well, my dear, *picture* your little Top at this *draughty* drome at *five* in the morning, *blue* with cold and *lemon* with aprehension, and my dear a criminal eyesore in *chestnut* leather, my dear I looked like a new suit-case *bulging* with a body, however, thanks be, there were no witnesses except the Lotweed who my dear was *too* cylindrical and clinging and nearly drowned me in the generous bosom, however I came up the third time so we climbed into the Spirit of Woman and abruptly left the planet, and of course never go *near* the air, it's as *cold* as a carcase, and the *noise*, my dear like *forty* motor-lorries in a telephone-box, and the *vibration*, my dear it's like sitting on a mechanical *drill*, and of course the *barbarous* thing was that owing to the rush and hushery of it all I'd *merely* never been up *before*, of course

I'd had a *sly* suspicion that I wasn't exactly *Nature's* bird-girl, my dear *too* right, because we'd scarcely soared for *ten* minutes darling when I was as sick as an *Aunt*, my dear *too* humbling, because it wasn't a case of Now we *are* sick and done with it, but utter high frequency and *protracted* agony, my dear I was sick *all over* the Western Counties and three parts of Ireland, but of course the *moment* we saw the unnecessary Atlantic I was so petrified I forgot about the old tummy, well darling I thought of you and my poor Haddock of course, and had *rather* conscience trouble, and I merely *lay* on the floor with the spanners and the sandwiches and *prayed* and *prayed* for thousands of miles, but of course *quite* fortitudinous on the surface, because whenever Claude wrote me a note, my dear that's the *fallacious* thing about the air, you merely can't *utter* because of what they call the *hum* of the engines, well he would write down HOW D' YOU FEEL, LITTLE WOMAN and I would write back TOO BUOYANT OLD SNIPE or something sparkling like that, but my dear feeling like a *rubber sponge* inside and the little bosom heaving with *girlish* tears, my dear I've realised one thing what absolute *girls* girls are, don't you agree darling.

Well my dear after about *three* thousand miles I got used to the horror and was *merely* bored, my *dear* the boredom, because the *whole* Atlantic is nothing but *wet* clouds and you can't see a thing, and of course the *moment* I wasn't frightened I was sick again, and so it went on, however *about* midnight I saw that Claude was *practically* asleep poor sheep, so I thought I'd do the serviceable hero-girl and keep him conscious with *hilarious* stories, my dear I wrote down in capitals all the *most* drawing-room ones I know, not naughty of *course* darling but definitely Continental, however he didn't seem to get much of a *kick* out of them, so at last I told him about Papa Chase at the dentist's, my dear *rather* crude I know but *consider* the circs, well *at* that he laughed and laughed and laughed till I thought he'd fall into the sea, my dear *too* right because just then whether it was his laughing or what, the Spirit of Woman merely kicked up its heels and *dived* through a cloud, and we fell *flop* on the foul Atlantic, my dear *too* alarming.

Well darling I powdered the little nose and everything, however I must stop now so ask me no details, *suffice* it to say that *years* passed and *there* we were, but my dear the *bizarre* thing is that in *spite* of the utter *squalor* of it all I was *too* convinced that all would be well still, but on the other hand the masculine male had gone all sepulchral and *no hope* whatever, well of course we rather *nestled* together because of the brutal cold and sort of *discussed* our pasts and everything, and *suddenly* my dear, my dear you *won't* believe me, but the man went *suddenly* soupy and said I adore you little woman, my dear don't *ever* tell anyone I told you this, so I said, O *gosh* like father like son, because my dear you *would* think that at four AM on a dark night with one small plank between a girl and the Atlantic she *might* be safe from the major passions, but my dear he wanted to utterly *lash* the bodies together and *drown* together in a fond embrace, my dear my *blushes*, but I said *Too* romantic but *how* embarrassing if we *don't* drown and me a bride and everything, well just then the dawn began to happen, thanks be, and there was the *most* opportune Cunarder about *two* waves away, my dear *too* well-arranged, well it only shows my dear that a girl can *simply* never be too careful, my dear not a whisper of this because my darling Haddock has been a *unique* saint about it all but if he knew the *whole* story, anyhow I've got the halfway prize and *hydraulic* publicity but no more bird-work for your *terrestrial* little TOPSY.

4 At The Prunery

Well Trix darling no doubt you'll *chuckle* somewhat at the address, but *here* I am my dear *definitely* interned at Doctor Bootle's *Prunery* and have been for a week, well you see after the *afflicting* strain of *almost* flying the Atlantic my *girlish* nerves were *utterly* twanging, my dear you'd only to *contradict* me and they played a *tune*, and of course I must be *quite* pepulent by the time the *Session* sits, and the Press were being *rather* importunate about the *flight* and everything, my dear as Haddock said a public woman these days has no more privacy than a *goldfish*, so what with everything he thought I'd better go into a *retreat* or cloister somewhere and *quietly* decarbonise the neurotic system, and at the same time *incubate* my Parliamentary programme.

So here I am my dear sort of *sitting* on my policy and eating *nothing* but prunes, my dear you *must* have heard of this place it's *the* Cadogan health-hell at the moment, my dear they charge you *fortunes* and *as* I say give you *nothing* but prunes, because of course *orange-juice* is *quite* vieux jeu by now, and my dear *don't* think we're stinted, we have the *most* protracted dinners, my dear *prune* soup, and *fillet* of prune, and *prune* cutlets, and after that *Roast* prune, and then as a rule we have prune à la *créme*, and as often as not some sort of a *prune* savoury, no coffee of *course* but they have the *most* exhilarating prune *liqueur*, oh and I forgot, there's generally some nice *prunes purées* with the joint, also on Wednesday we *each* get a banana to ourselves, and on Sunday night which is *rather* an orgy we have beetroot salad *instead* of the savoury.

Well darling as you *know* I'm not a *congenital* herbivore, but I must say the *effect* is *rather* ethereal, and personally I'm doing the thing *too* fanatically, well so far I've *refused* both *beetroot* and *banana* and am utterly *loyal* to the prune, in fact in a day or two your misunderstood little friend will be 100 per cent *prune*, because my dear it's *too* discouraging to think that all these *æons* have fluttered by in vain before Dr Bootle discovered it, but it seems the little *prune* is *Nature's* nourishment, my dear *nothing* else was ever *meant* to be eaten, well it's got *more* vitamins than the orange, my dear somebody's *counted* them, and more *hypo-cardrates* or something than the *banana*, and *no* alkali or *starch* or uric acid or *anything*, my dear *did* you know that if the *British Army* had been fed on *nothing* but prunes the *War* would have been over in *1916*, well that's what they say, and my dear it's *rather* a scandal when you come to think of it, of course Dr Bootle says that *all* other food ought to be utterly vetoed by law, because he says that in the end the *Prune* Peoples must come out on top, so of course he's got a *big* kick out of an *authentic* legislator like your Topsy coming here, you know my dear they can say what they like about the *decay* of representative what-nots and everything but there's *no* doubt that being an MP *does* give a girl a sort of phantom importance, only I do *rather* find that people expect one to *bleat* about politics from dawn till dream-time, and of course all these infatuated *womanly* women who want me to be the absolute *battle-axe* of the *Woman's* Cause, my dear they *molest* and *mob* me *already*, and even in *this* concealed turning, because there are two *analogous* friends of the *Lotweed* object here and *whenever* they can they merely *herd* me into a corner and *snuffle* at me about some *rancid* aspect of the *Woman's* Problems, my dear I'm *too* laconic with them and it's *even* come to my *hiding* in the bathroom, because as I've *always* said there's never been more than *one* Woman's Problem and that is *Man*, and in *my* opinion the pathetic shrimp has already gone down for the second time and there's no hurry about the *third*, anyhow I'm *too* clear that I am *not* going to be a sort of whining-trumpet for the jaundiced doe, because *love* is the note of *my* life, and as a *matter* of fact I *rather* detest *all* women, don't you agree darling?

Well my dear as you may imagine the *other* inmates are a *shade* apocryphal and miscellaneous, of course there are some of the *more* cylindrical *Cadogan* matrons busy revising the measurements, and a lot of *anæmic* citizens acquiring *flesh*, because my dear that's the *radiant* thing about the prune, it doesn't matter if you're too *fat* or too *thin*, the gifted little prune will do the necessary, my dear it's *ambidexterous*, and of course anything like *lassitude* or *blood-pressure* or *flatulence* or *tennis-elbow* is *utterly* prunable, which reminds me *who* did I find here but Councillor Mule, well I forget if you know about him but he's the absolute *Voice* of the Crêpe Vote in Burbleton, my dear *too* sunless, the *world's* vinophobe, and he's suffering from cubic capacity insomnia *and* nerves, which is not *much* of an 'ad' for the Chocolate-Suckers, well of course I'm having to step *rather* delicately because of course we're *quite* cat and dog, my dear *this* is the fungus who suppressed the Burbleton *band* on Sundays, and we're going to have the *rudest* battles about that and a few other outrages, my dear I'm so *tired* of all these *railing* sin-seekers and sucking Savonarolas, however *at* the moment my policy is to *rather* win him with *sweetness* and disarming glances, but my dear *too* impervious at the time of writing, however nous verrons.

Well *meanwhile* darling as for myself I must confess I'm a mere *bubble* of well-being, thanks to the plucky prune, my dear sort of *rarefied*, well I feel that at *any* moment the little head might *float* off the little body and merely *waft* about the firmament, if you know what I mean, and of course the girl's complexion is *too* diaphanous and satisfactory, my dear I *rather* think I'm looking *rather* lovable, and it's just as well perhaps there's no male inmate under the buriable age, however fortunately I feel more *valetudinous* than anything, because having at last a little time on the hands I've been *cherishing* the frame in every direction, my dear I read *all* the advertisements in *all* the hen-papers and send for *simply* everything, because my dear it's *quite* alarming when you realise how we all *neglect* the body, my dear I've bought *brassières* and *cuticle* removers, and *things* for the *lips* and the *dandruff* and the *nails* and as for the *skin*, my dear *toning* creams and *tightening* creams, and *skin foods* and *muscle* oil, and then of course there are the *mouth*-balms and the *eye*-preservers, and *things* to put in the bath, and *garden-rollers* for the little tummy, and of course the exercises *quite* always, so altogether I *do* see now that if a girl can keep the body clean and sweet it's *about* all she's time for on *this* planet darling, and I *rather* fear that when I'm a busy public woman again I shall become a *mere* mass of *degenerate tissues*, and *flaccid muscles*, and *fatty accumulation*, not to speak of *impure pores* and *embarrassing odours*, with probably a touch of halitosis and lethargy, my dear these advertisements, *too* upsetting, however I'm *determined* to have a good pure *prune*-foundation for the winter months, so I'm going to suffer for another week here, if only to irritate Councillor Mule, though I must say I'm *quite* beginning to pine for my Haddock and as a *matter* of fact the *tiniest* beaker of juniper-juice and Italian would be *rather* like the ripple of a cooling stream in the *fatiguing* deserts of Sahara, and of course *what* Haddock is going to say about the *bill* my dear, because as far as I can see it *works* out at *about* a guinea a *prune*, however no more now darling, your *austere* little prunatic TOPSY.

5 Makes A Film

Well Trix my hidden wildflower *here* I am at the health-hell still, but my dear *since* I wrote to you things have been *rather* tending towards a certain mobility and *stress*, well I *think* I told you about Councillor *Mule* being here, my dear the *King* of the vinophobes in *my* constituency, President of the Anti-Smile Society and *death* to anything that *might* bring a spark of joy into the *dogmatic* gloom of Burbleton life on the Sabbath-day, well my dear he's taking the prune-treatment to diminish his *specific* gravity, my dear *too* right, because my dear *quite* annually he does the *foulest* yap in public about the young girls' *bathing* uniforms and everything, *little* realising, poor drain, that he's the *most* indecent spectacle in the industrial *North*.

Well of course *blood* my dear is *definitely* going to fly between us before *I* cease to be Member for Burbleton (West), however I thought I'd better give him a chance so I *began* by disarming the stoat with sweetness, my dear *too* abortive, my dear I've *never* exerted the wistful charms before without *some* sort of a reaction, and it was *rather* humbling and salubrious I suppose, however that being a flop I swiftly mobilised the reserves, and of course I *ought* to explain that the effect of *two* weeks of *nothing* but prunes is *too* different from *one*, well after the *first* week as I told you a girl feels *rarefied* but by about half through the *second* one's *merely* anæmic and we sort of *hover* about like semiflated *airships*, well what I mean is that one's *mainly* sluglike but at the *faintest* puff you go *quite* up in the air, *rather* intricate darling I'm afraid but I can't stop to explain, well *tempers* and everything, you do see *don't* you?

Well my dear the *sole* blood-sport played at the Prunery is the *dyspeptic* game of *croquet*, and while I was still hoping to sirenise the Mule thing we put in a good many totters round the course together, *rather* a martyrdom darling because I had to keep the *tightest* rein on the little self, because my dear croquet as *you* know utterly *draws* out the *vilest* passions of the human system, especially played with the antique rules and of course like many of the virtuous ones the Councillor *cheats* at games, my dear *too* crude, and he used to *too* brutally *bash* me into the *snailiest* bushes, however I used to *frolic* after my ball with a *Christian* smile, but my dear on *Sunday* the agony was *too* much, well there he was my dear sort of *floating* round the lawn like a *captive* jelly, my dear like an *extinct* monster in *aspic*, my dear like a — however, and of course what with ten days of prunes I was feeling *rather* giddy about the knees and a little *inflammable* in the head, *you* know my dear when you feel that the *next* minute you *must* short-circuit, my dear *too* right, because at *last* I'd managed to *quite* hit the municipal ball, and my dear *as* I stood there with the little foot poised ready to do that *uncivilised croquet* proceeding a fuse did burst in the little brain darling and I saw *bright* scarlet, well I said, *Well* Councillor we're having *rather* a hilarious Sunday afternoon aren't we, and I *do* hope you're *adoring* the game, but *what* about all those *hereditary* blotting-pads who have to fester in Burbleton all day, and *can't* play tennis because of *you* Councillor, and can't go to the pictures because of *you* Councillor, and can't listen to a band because of *you* Councillor, while *here* you are Councillor gadding it at croquet with a *married* girl, well, if you ask *me* Councillor you're a periphrastic *Pharisee* or something of that sort, and *then* my dear, *rather* hysterical I know, I *raised* the mallet with *both* hands and merely *mutilated* my own pathetic *foot* with it, my dear I'm *lame* for life, however the blood of the Trouts and everything, so I bit the little lip and took aim again, and *this* time my dear I utterly *lashed* the Mule ball *through* the shrubbery and down the *longest* bank into the *ornamental* water where my dear it *floated*, and next to *puncturing* the man himself with a *pointed* spear *quite* nothing could have been such *anodyne*, my dear there *is* that to be said for croquet isn't there?

Well my darling you *may* blame me but *if* you do it *simply* means that you *don't* understand *psycology*, because my dear the effect of Councillors on a *pruny* stomach, well anyhow for the rest of the game I *merely* behaved like a *rogue* elephant my dear *never* trying to penetrate a hoop myself but always *wickedly* torpedoing the Mule out of position, well he was *mute* and suffering and of course he won the game in the end, *too* like a man, and afterwards I *rather* apologised, however the next day I had one of my *inspired* flashes, because my dear Haddock's *just* given me one of those *bijou* cinema-machines and *in* the bath darling the little brain said suddenly why not do a *film* of the Mule horror, because my dear the truth as somebody said *is* indefatigable, and the *more* people realise that the *more* people are like Councillor Mule the more people *look* like Councillor Mule the *less* I mean the *more* people will utterly *strain* the nerves not to *be* like Councillor Mule if you see what I mean darling.

Well my dear I began the *very* next day when the *Mule* thing was taking the afternoon prune with a few of the more *globular* inmates on the verandah, of course they were all *too* hungering to be in it, so the Mule *couldn't* take umbrage, and besides I was being rather bright and boracic again, anyhow after a few mass-effects like that I began doing *solo*-studies of the Councillor, but always utterly by *request* my dear and *too* complimentary, my dear I got him reading *White Lives* which is the absolute *organ* of the Antimacassar Vote and writing an anti-article to *The Burbleton Post* and chewing a lonely prune my dear in *cyclist's* knickerbockers and a gentleman's boater, my dear I took him *walking*, from above, and *cheating* at croquet, and of course *quite* numberless close-ups, my dear a close-up of the Councillor is just like looking into an Aquarium and *suddenly* seeing something which is not quite *nice*, my dear he *is* the human octopus, my dear his *eyes* are the sort of thing that makes divers *ignore* the specie and *rush* to the surface, however of course I kept telling him that he had *Nature's* film-face and how *throbbed* his friends would be to see the new VALENTINO, but after a bit my dear he became *rather* terse and reluctant about sitting, so I said I was *too* contrite and would *never* molest him again, if I might perhaps sneak an *occasional* picture when he wasn't looking.

Well then began the absolute *cream* of the campaign, because my dear *wherever* the yam went I followed afar off and movied him from astern, and of course whenever he turned round suddenly and saw me I produced one of my *winning* little smiles and said he was to *quite* ignore me, and of course it *ought* to be rather a compliment if a *magnetic* girl keeps on taking your photograph, so no umbrage was *definitely* taken, however he began to shun me somewhat and took to roaming secret in the woods and spinneys and my dear peeping *too* nervously over the shoulder every ten yards, and my dear I was nearly *always* there, and of course some of the photography in this film is *quite* German because my dear he's lost *tons* of flesh here and his *ghastly* clothes are perfectly *festooned* about the body like an *empty* balloon, and my dear if you can imagine the *zymotic* object disappearing down the leafy vistas with *guilty* backward looks, as if the Flying Squad were after him, *reel* after *reel* darling, my dear I don't know *what* the *Pure* Vote of Burbleton will think!

Well at last he began to wear rather a *hunted* look and on Thursday he *madly* packed and shambled away to Burbleton, so *last* night I *released* the little film to the assembled inmates and my dear it *bit* them, they *merely* howled, of course I've put in the *most* professional captions and things, my dear *Councillor* Mule Seeks Truth In The Forest and Councillor Mule *Fretting* about the Sins of Burbleton, my dear *too* crude, however I *rather* think that when the Mule and I meet at our own little Waterloo the Mule Animal Picture is going to be *rather* a weapon, however no more now darling, your little crusader TOPSY.

6 Goes Hunting

Well Trix my crystallised cherry I'm completing the cure down here at the Dilvers' my dear I'm having *rather* an orgy of air and exercise, disgusting for the brain darling, I can scarcely *think*, however I do feel less like a dried prune, anyhow we've had the *longest* paper-chase over absolute *hill* and bog and my dear whether it was the prunes or what to my *frank* surprise I discovered that *running* was *rather* congenial, because I have rather an antelope action and breathe *plausibly* through the nose, and my dear there's an *angelical* man here called *Colonel* Candy, my dear too boyish and beamy for a Colonel and he commands the *Guards* Cavalry or something, well he was a hound too and we *practically* caught the hares together only not quite because at the crisis I bounded gracefully into the *profoundest* brook, anyhow he said I was *Nature's* gazelle in the running department and I *rather* thought he was *rather* attracted so the next day I challenged him to a *handicap* Marathon round the private lake, which my dear is *quite* miles so of course he gave me the *most* benevolent handicap, I was half out of *sight* because of the shrubberies, but you know there's *no* doubt that girls were *not* designed for mobility in skirts, so my dear after about *half* a mile what with *agony* in the chest and the little breath *oozing* in *pitiful* sobs I paused at a convenient bush, discarded the lower garment, and darted on in my Parisian bloomers, *chaste* darling but of a *tangerine* hue, however *such* was the relief and I got my second wind, but my dear *what* was my horror when *thus* arrayed I crashed round a corner and met *one* Duchess and a Lady-in-Waiting taking a walk, my dear my *blushes*, and of course *what* they thought because by this time the Colonel had nearly caught me and my dear being *Nature's* knight he'd picked up the skirt and it seems was cantering behind me with the garment on his *arm*, however I waved *cheerily* to the ladies and panted on, my dear *too* insouciant but far from convincing.

However darling as if *that* wasn't enough *yesterday* I took the

Colonel to an absolute *fox-meet* in the car, because it seems he's a *casual* hunter but had brought no spurs or anything, so he said we might follow on *foot* perhaps, well darling you know my views but I thought it was rather my duty to litterally *see* what happens, and of course the *magnetic* smile of the man, however Catherine Dilver said I wasn't to go unless I swore to be *too* restrained and not *head* the foxes or shoot them or anything, because she didn't want to lose caste with the Master and everybody, so I utterly swore because when you're a guest one must *rather* behave, whatever one's principles well don't you agree darling?

Well my dear it was the *rudest* day and raining *too* cruelly however I must say the meet was *quite* pictorial, only of course it was *rather* difficult to see the horses for the cars, and my dear the Colonel says there are *some* Hunts now where they don't allow horses at the meet at *all*, however the red-coats and everything and those *divine* dogs, which my dear I *patted* tenderly to placate the Master, but my dear *too* unresponsive I thought, the Master I mean, and of course I do *not* think that the British girl looks best in a *bowler*, not to mention a *veil*, my dear Margaret Dilver looked *quite* another person and *as* I told her I preferred the original, of course *quite* piquant and so forth but my dear as I said *why* must the fox-field be the sole place where the men dress gaudy and the girls go *plain*?

And my dear the whole thing was *rather* alarming because nearly *every* horse had a *red* ribbon on the tail to show that it kicked and scratched and was generally malignant, though of course if a horse had *blue* ribbons *all over* I wouldn't trust it *very* fanatically, and my dear as all horses do nothing but go round and round in the *most* suggestive circles one gets quite giddy with edging away from the scarlet sterns, however at last the dogs departed and we *spludged* after them along an *obscenely* muddy lane and I lost the Colonel almost at once in the crowd, and they all disappeared, so my dear forlorn and lonely I merely *waded* along till I saw a *distant* red coat beside a wood or spinney, which of course taking it to be the Master or something I *plunged* across the filthy fields through *streets* of barbed wire and two definite *morasses*, and when I tell you that it turned out to be a woman in a *red* mackintosh, my dear *too* galling, well after that I sort of *swam* back to the road where far away on the other side I saw *one* man with a *reluctant* horse constantly trying to jump the *same* fence, so then I crawled back to the car and merely flopped on the cushions to wait for the Colonel, my dear *quite* moribund, and now comes the drama, because my dear the whole time one could hear the dogs *vaguely* barking afar off because it seems if was one of these *circular* hunts, anyhow as I lay gasping with the door open what *do* you think the *largest* fox jumped into the car, my dear *quite* out of breath and *smelling* horribly but with the *most* appealing eyes, well my dear the little brain worked swiftly and I thought Catherine or no Catherine I *can't* have all those *dogs* in the car, so my dear I *closed* the door and I said to the faithful Parker *rather* casually Drive on.

Well darling we drove on slowly about *two* miles up the longest hill, me patting the fox and everything which apart from the smell gave *no* trouble at all, and of course it was rather a dilema because after what Catherine said I didn't think it fair to utterly terminate the hunt, so my dear the fox having rather a *moulting* tendency I plucked a fluffy bit from the back now and then and merely threw it out of the window, with the *result* my dear that *when* we Stopped at the top of the hill I looked back and saw the whole *herd* of dogs quite pouring up the road and *one* man in red absolute *miles* behind and *rather* wildly playing the cornet.

Well then my dear foreseeing trouble and stress I told Parker to have *no* mercy on the accelerator and we departed at about sixty into the *heart* and bowels of the *next* county but *one*, where my dear at a *convenient* copse I opened the door and gently tried to *disembark* the fox, my dear *too* fruitless because the *wistful* creature declined to budge, so I thought perhaps in its *home-county* it would be more amenable, and of course I had to retrieve the Colonel, so my dear we slunk back by circumsical routes but my dear *what* was my horror when suddenly round a corner we ran into the *entire* hunt drawing a spinney or something, however no dogs in sight, so I threw a rug over Reynard and drove past warily, well I picked up the Colonel who my dear had had *quite* enough of hunting on foot, and we'd just started again when out of the spinney came the principal dog, and my dear it gave the *loudest* sniff and bounded after us with alarming noises *followed* rapidly by *all* its colleagues, because it seems a bit of the fox-fluff had stuck to the *back* of the car, so I said Faster Parker, well my dear what *was* I to do because at *that* point *could* I eject the creature, well of course the Colonel was *too* mystified so I said quietly I can't explain but as a *matter* of fact there's a *fox* in the car and at that moment he put his foot on the fox and it nipped him *rather* familiarly in the calf, but my dear he *is* a *complete* lamb because he laughed and laughed only he said the whole proceeding was *utter* blasphemy and I ought to stop the car and explain to the Master, so I said that would be *too* fatal because of Catherine Dilver and everything, because probably I shouldn't tune in with the Master and anyhow it was MY car and for that matter it was MY fox, but if we could shake off the dogs then nobody would *ever* know, so my dear we drove like tigers along the *tiniest* lanes and at last escaped, only so hot was the hunt that we couldn't stop to evacuate the fox till a *secret* shrubbery on the Dilvers' own drive, and *now* my dear I hear that seven of the *prize* pullets disappeared last *night*, my dear *too* wearing, because I *did* mean to behave so *utterly* well, Oh dear, farewell your *misfortunate* TOPSY.

7 Passes Poxton

Trix my poppy I find the *jading* thing about being a *public* woman is that one feels responsible for *quite* everything, and of course *all* a girl's constituents write *sulphuric* letters to her *too* daily, my dear I've come to the conclusion that *my* constituency is THE cradle of the nation's half-wits, my dear there seems to be a *definite* race of *moonmen* who dwell at Burbleton and write *imperative* postcards, *women* principally of *course*, my dear you've no idea what absolute *cabbage-water* the minds are made of, and the *baffling* feature is that *at* the Election they seemed *too* normal, however the moment people begin to write letters they do rather tend to give themselves away *doesn't* one darling?

Well my dear *at* the moment I'm *moved* to the core about the cancerisation of England, my dear have you read that *luminous* book England and the Octopus or something, you *must* buy it I haven't myself because Hermione Tarver is going to lend me her library copy, however I've read bits and it's *quite* inflammatory, it's by WILLIAMS ELLIS that *rather* Celtic architect we met in a bathing-dress somewhere, well anyhow he's *too* right because my dear *last* Saturday I and my Haddock motored all the septic way from Dover to Worthing, of course you'll say But *why* motor from Dover to *Worthing* and my dear you *may* say it, because my dear *Worthing*, and my dear *Brighton*, and *Hastings*, and *Bexhill*, and *Seaford*, and *Newhaven*, and *Rottingdean*, and *Shoreham*, my dear *uncataloguable*, however the facts are as stated so *don't* ask for the grisly details, well my dear an *old* friend of Haddock's called *Rowland* drove us, I *think* I've mentioned him before, well he'd have been *quite* an endurable fellow darling if only the *internal* combustion engine had *never* been invented, but since it has been he's a human *epidemic*, my dear he's the *kind* of distemper who actually *likes motoring*, my dear he *lives* for his next car, my dear call me crude if you *like* but his breath *does* smell of *petrol*, my dear he *is* definitely a *carburetter*, and of course my dear you know *my* attitude to motoring, it's merely an *epileptic* way of getting from one place to another, but as for pleasure, my dear you can't *read*, you can't *think*, you can't *smoke*, you *must* talk if there's anyone there, you *must* look at the scenery *however* nocuous, and my dear at *every* corner you *merely* oscillate from prayer to thanksgiving, and of course my dear in an *open* car where the *whole* time you have *one* eye screwed up and the other full of winged creatures, my dear after *five* miles I want to resign my seat and this was a *hundred*, however off we went, and my dear it was the *pearliest* morning with Nature *quite* at the top of her form, which is more than I can say for the efforts of *Man*, well when I tell you that in the whole *hundred* miles you hardly go *one* without seeing something that merely *blisters* the eyes with cheapness and hideosity, my dear you know that *optimistic* yap about Kent being the *Garden* of England and everything, well along the South Coast it's much more like the *Backyard* of England, or the *Garage* of England, or the *Servants' Bathroom* of England because my dear you know the Romney Marshes which of course are *too* atmospheric and flat but at present the *only* atmosphere is supplied by *motor*-spirit, and the *entire* coast is a *chain* of motor-parks for bathers and *motor*-shops and *motor*-advertisements, and loathly *tea-shops* for the motorist, and gruesome *warnings* to the motorist, and my dear *when* I realised that I was being a motorist myself I merely *blushed* for shame all down the little back, do you ever do that darling?

However compared with Fair Sussex by the Sea the Backyard of England is almost *amenitous*, my dear I'll pass over *Brighton* and *even Hastings*, because of course I suppose all these *teeming* Britons with families *must* have their annual wash and brush-up by the sea, and my dear *that's* the sardonic thought *isn't* it that it's the pure old sea is responsible for all these putrefying places, however one's got used to the larger blots, and *parts* of some of them are less agonising than others, but my dear it reminds me of poor brother Phil who, my dear it's *rather* a crude allegory but he used to have the hugest *boils* after the War from *iron* rations or something poor lamb, scattered *all* about the body, my dear he was *too* patient with them and we used to have *names* for them all, my dear one would be Brighton and another *Bexhill* and one absolute *carbuncle* was Hastings, well that was bad enough but it was *rather* much when he began coming out in *small* spots everywhere *in between* the major boroughs, well we had him inoculated and *swamped* him in orange-juice which *quite* cured him only of course then he had *jaundice* and was *too* bilious for *years*, sorry darling this is rather a *realistic* letter perhaps, but you *do* see my point, it's the *creeping* spottery is the *ghastly* symptom, my dear at *Shoreham* there's the *most* awful *nest* of bungaloid ulcers, and of course *when* you come to *Poxton* you *merely* yearn for the *invasion* of England by history's most destructive *Huns*, though of course I'm *too* sorry for all the poor dupes who've been *lured* into living there by some *wart* of a financier who *doubtless* lives elsewhere.

Well my dear *meanwhile* the Rowland was being *rather* a burden because the *whole* time he talked of nothing but the *internal* organs of his unalluring car and wondering *what* was rattling and *why*, when of course the *entire* machine was one *tautologous* rattle because he will keep seeing if he can get sixty out of her on a bad road, and my dear what with *wasps* in the little eye and *inhaling* the exhaust of those *maternal* motor-coaches I was *quite* saturated *too* soon, and of course I kept on *yelping* with anguish at the sights I saw, but my dear this *mechanical* fellow saw *simply* nothing but his *felonious* speedometer, my dear *too* unmoved, my dear as long as it's a *road* it can run between *dustheaps* for all he'd care, and *when* we got to *Poxton*, my dear, *as* I say, *Poxton*, my dear the little hand trembles as I write the word, my dear it is the *world's* sight-restorer because you may have had *no* views before but *when* you see *Poxton* you have the *most* æsthetic *abdominal* pain, like someone getting religion, especially if you knew those *rather* seductive cliffs a few years ago *before* they broke out with these *gangrenous growths*, my dear it *is* definitely the *bungalonic plague*, well not even *bungalows* often, it's a mere multitude of *bijou* shacks and garagettes *dropped* on the innocent downs out of a *sack*, and my dear I hardly saw *one* of these pustulous little dwellings that didn't advertise *something*, one wants to fly up and down in an aeroplane and *spray* the place with a good strong weedkiller, one *aches* for an *earthquake*, however I hear the *tragic* inhabitants are beginning to take some *steps* at last, only of course probably the *best* thing would be to utterly *preserve* Poxton just as it is, my dear a sort of *grisly* Peace Memorial, and have absolute *free* expeditions from all over England to *show* people what's going to happen everywhere if *somebody* doesn't function *quite* soon, because at the moment as Haddock said the disease is *galloping* destruction, but of course all *Rowland* said was we'd better *stop* here for *petrol* O gosh!

Well my dear *when* you think of the *things* you're not allowed to do which do *no* harm to anybody, and Auntie Jix tearing her suffering hair over twenty Britons in a night-club, while my dear a *herd* of mouldy little builders can take *chunks* of the Sussex Downs and turn them into a festering eye-sore for *quite* ever, and nobody can stop them, well of course they *can* really, only what *is* the good of these balloon-bellied councillors, have they *never* heard of an *architect*, of course they're too busy peering at a girl's *skirts* and *censoring* the bathing-dress, my dear as Haddock said they can't see the wood for the *knees*, and if only they'd realise that a bad girl dies but a bad building lasts for *centuries*, and of course all this *bat-eyed* bleating about the *declining* Birth-rate, my dear the Birth-rate ought to be *stopped*, well anyhow the moment the House sits I shall go to the PRIME and say *Darling* STANLEY *put* the old pipe down and have a Mussolini morning about this, farewell now darling your *shocked* little TOPSY.

8 Is All For Al

Trix my angel *all* my thanks for your *cherubic* letter but I can't answer *any* of your questions now because I'm *too* worked up about my darling AL, and of course the *fiendish* thing is that I suppose you've *no* idea who my darling AL *is*, my dear I do wish you'd take a *sporadic* glance at the morning papers, because my dear I *quite* admit that most of the Press is *rather* sea-weed, on the other hand there are one or two things happening on this over-rated planet which are almost worthy of a clean girl's attention, well anyhow AL SMITH darling wants to be absolute *President* of the United States, and so does a perfect *paper-weight* of a man called HERBERT HOOVER, my dear you can say what you like about the decline of England but I do *not* think that in this decrepit country a man would dare to put up for the President of the *Fire Brigade* if he had a name like HOOVER, with HERB in the prow, my dear *too* facetious, don't you agree, darling?

Only my dear *don't* think I don't utterly *adore* Americans because I merely *do*, and of course Haddock knows some perfectly *blossomy* ones, but that's the staggering thing about them, my dear you *meet* them in London and they seem *quite* lambs and then they go home to America and gun at each other, well anyhow this AL SMITH's a Democrat, my dear it's *rather* sweet he used to be a *paper-boy*, and HERB HOOVER's a *Republican*, or else it's the other way round, because my dear I *never* can remember and *nobody* knows the difference, my dear it's like saying that one man's a *herring* and the other's a *bloater*, only there's *rather* more in it *this* time, because my dear HERB's a Protestant and a *Prohibitionist*, which Haddock says is a contradiction in terms or something, because he says the *whole* idea of Protestantism was against unnecessary *bossing* and *erroneous* doctrines, however AL's a Catholic and a *moderate* Wet, and my dear *that* will show you the utterly *degrading* effect of having these *feeble-minded* laws, because my dear you probably don't know that the population of the States is a *mere* hundred million, and my dear *when* you think of *all* those people *electing* a President, which with the *exception* perhaps of a *Boxing* champion is *about* the most important thing a man can *be*, and instead of the candidates being called ALBERT the *Just* or HERBERT the *Peacemaker* or anything they're labelled Moderate *Wet* and Bone *Dry*, my dear like peas or something in a grocer's shop, well as Haddock said it's utterly *debasing* the currency of *politics* or something, because my dear it seems they're both the *world's* flawless fellows and have done *quite* miracles but the *sole* thing that seems to matter is this *nursery* question of *diet*.

Because my dear it isn't as if AL wanted to *flood* the Continent with *gin*, my dear *all* he says is that he wouldn't be a bit surprised if there were *one* or two Americans who might be *safely* trusted to have a little *white* wine and *lager* beer with their food, if it was *sold* by the State in *sanitary* bottles *one* bottle at a time, in which case of course there'd be far less whisky imported than there is now, anyhow my dear this is *definitely* the *Lager Beer* Election because *nobody* cares what the *pathetic* men think about Peace or War or anything, the one thing is *Is* Lager Beer safe for the *democracy*, and my dear *don't* accuse me of *superfluous* interference with the affairs of a friendly nation, because my dear this is matter of *common humanity*, my dear like *slavery* or the mutilation of *bishops*, it's a crime against *nature*, my dear a man in Michigan has just got imprisonment for life for *merely* possessing a *pint* of gin, and of course the *moment* the Eighteenth Amendment oozed into existence the *whole* civilised world ought to have utterly *broken* off relations, my dear like Russia, sort of outlawing the Government but *too* sympathetic with the martyred populace, instead of all this *poltroonery* about *moral experiments*, my dear what *is* there *moral* in *not* having what you can't *get*, my dear what's *moral* is when you utterly *wallow* in temptation and emerge *too* spotless, and *that* my dear as Haddock said is what *moulds* the character, because of course it's *quite* theoretical that *wine* like women was *merely* created to sort of *test* the human engine, and if you take away *all* the temptations you *simply* don't know *where* you are, and of course where *is* it to *stop*, because my dear *speaking* of women, well there's *no* doubt that *Love* leads to *more* unpleasantness than anything else my dear it's responsible for *all* the divorces and *nearly* all the murders, *three-quarters* of the stealing and *all* the over-population, and *that* of course means unemployment and *slums* and misery and Bolshevism, so that you *might* say that Love was the absolute *root* of all evil and of course it *nearly* always begins with *kissing*, so my dear I shouldn't be a *bit* surprised if the Twenty-first Amendment was against *kissing*, and then of course there'll be a Kissing Election, and one of the candidates will be a *Petting* Democrat and the other will be a *Platonic* Republican, *unless* of course my darling AL gets in this time because I do think *he* might be able to strike a *note* of sanity perhaps, my dear *don't* be *aloof* about this because it's *too* cardinal for *us* because the foul breath of the joyphobes is *already* wafting over the ocean towards us, you can smell it EVERYWHERE, my dear *do* you know that there are *261* societies in England and Wales *all* beavering away for Prohibition and kindred horrors *just* like America, of course I know you think I've got a bee in the little bonnet about this, but as Haddock said I'd rather have a bee in the bonnet than absolute *fungus* on the brain well don't you agree darling?

However my dear I'm *rather* aprehensive for AL because of the POPE, you see there's *quite* nothing people *won't* say in politics, and it seems they're *all* saying that AL is going to *put* the POPE in charge of the American Navy, my dear *too* unsuitable, but it *simply* isn't *true*, because I'm perfectly convinced that AL would *never* do it, anyhow there's this *irrelevant* religious chat, and they have absolute *pamphlets* to say that my *poor* AL stands for the Vatican and the vine, my dear POPE one pocket and *port* in the other, isn't it *too* cruel, you know my dear I *do* adore religion but I do think that religious people are *too* un-Christian sometimes, and my dear I do believe if you had absolute *statistics* of all the *unnecessary* unpleasantness there's *ever* been you'd find that these sort of woolly-headed well-meaners had been responsible for *more* unnecessary unpleasantness than anything else, except Love perhaps, because my dear they can't even have *private* conferences without calling each other the *most* venomous names, my dear *Erastians* and *Apollinarians* and *Monophysists* or something, *too* alarming, *and* my dear *not* content with making the *mouldiest* muddle of their own affairs they *must* keep *crashing* into politics and everything with gratuitous suggestions, and as for these *Jeremiacal* preachers, you *can't* keep them out of the papers these days, my dear the *moment* they see somebody dormatose during a sermon they think civilisation's cracking and nobody's pure, and the nation's pagan and literature's foul, and Bolshevism's looming and the Modern Girl's a degenerate wasp, however if you ask *my* opinion *nearly* everybody's much more Christian than they used to be, except some of the wowsers perhaps, and *nearly* everything's much better than it used to be, except sermons perhaps, and anyhow what HAS the POPE got to do with my *poor* AL being President of America, my dear I'm going out now to send him a *tender* telegram because I *know* he's done for, so farewell now darling your noble-hearted TOPSY.

9 Takes Her Seat

Trix my darling wasn't it *too* tragic about AL, however I was right of *course* so let that be a warning to you, well you *mere* elector *here* I am at last *litterally* writing to you in the *House* of Commons, and my dear it's *rather* intimidous the *whole* place smells of Gothic and soap, I don't know if you've ever been in the building but one seems to be utterly *inhaling* disinfectant, however here I am in the *Does'* Dungeon where the hen-members have truck with their secretaries, I've just sent Taffeta Mole home to her Vestal pillow, my dear she's *fabulous*, of course she *venerates* the place, she *stalks* about it as if she was the Prime, she knows *quite* everything and has already draughted *seven* Questions for me to ask, only of course as she *will* try and translate the *Taffeta* thought into the *Topsy* prose, dear cow, I don't know *what* the Speaker will say, especially as I believe he *abhors* adjectives, which is going to be *rather* a handicap isn't it darling?

Well my dear *what* d'you think, NANCY ASTOR is sitting at the *next* table dictating the *loudest* letter about farinaceous food, however I must say in spite of her *gruesome* views about the vine and everything she's *rather* a winner, I *quite* expected a slightly *sulphuric* reaction because of my vinophilous policy but she didn't seem to resent it a fraction and has been *too* matey, my dear I'm sitting next to her in the Chamber and she makes the *most* hilarious *rude* remarks about some of the *yams* and *loofahs* of the Party, my dear those are my names for *two* species of the redundant male, well for instance a *yam* would be a *spherical* heavy-weight like Councillor Mule and a *loofah* is one of those *stringy* wearinesses with a face like a long sponge, in fact a *loofah*, and my dear the *rather* macaber thing is that we came to the conclusion that seventy per cent of our *own* Party were *either* loofahs or *yams*.

However, my dear, I was *introduced* by two *utter* old doves, *both* knights darling *and* Privy Councillors Sir LESLIE SCOTT and Sir WILIAM BULL, my dear *Nature's* godfathers, *too* courtly and staunch, because Haddock said I'd better *enter* the House by the Cadogan door if I *am* evacuated from a back-window in the end, well my dear I *do* believe I looked *rather* radiant, anyhow I did what Paris could do for me, because my dear I'd *quite* determined I would *not* dress up as the *first* feminine undertaker like most of the hen-members, my dear NANCY was rather *astringent* with me about the little outfit because of course she's *too* correct and wears a sort of *black* biretta, becoming but on the *medieval* side, and as I said to her sweetly it's all very well at *your* age, but why not do the thing thoroughly and *festoon* the frame with *jet*, because my dear I said *either* a girl is a ray of sunshine or she is *not*, and if she is it's *too* unwomanly to come into a perfectly *miasmal* place like this disguised as a *dead tree*, because my dear with *seven hundred* male things all in the same *fuliginous* uniform well *what* an opportunity for a *small* splash of virginal *colour*, and I do *not* see why the *Mother* of Parliaments should dress like a *widow*, and if *that's* the mentality, O gosh Haddock says that's an erroneous word, well no wonder the debates are more like dirges, don't you agree darling?

Anyhow my dear it's the *most* mellifluous garment in *the* printed velvet which is utterly the worn thing these days only of course printed on the *wrong* side darling because that gives the *nebulous* effect, my dear *extremely* lush and *caramel*-beige, because say what you like my dear you can *not* beat *beige*, and it has the *most* wistful little *flower* design in cinnamon and burgundy and *firmament*-blue, *rather* less of the little knee showing than latterly darling because of the surroundings and a *boyish* fit to show the girl means business, but I had an Amami morning and the hair was *dazzling*, my dear Haddock said I looked like a cameo cornfield from the Gallery, well anyhow *thus* arrayed I *twinkled* up the floor between my two darling old sheep-dogs, all bows and benevolence, my dear it felt *rather* like a wedding without any women, and my dear the SPEAKER was too pastoral and the Prime utterly *beamed* at me, and they *all* made the *most* odd noises in the throat, my dear *yer-yer-yer-*YER it sounded like, but I've *since* discovered it means Hear hear and this noise is *one* of the things that women can't do, however the *intention* it seems was absolutely congenial, and afterwards I met WINSTON and Sir ROBERT HORNE, both *rather* attracted I think darling and both *quite* charmers themselves in my opinion, well they were all *too* chivalrous, my dear I *even* caught the eye of Auntie JIX and I rather thought the eye became *human* only I've *since* heard she had three *stainless* constituents from *Twickenham* in the Gallery, so I must have erred, and of course I've *totally* surrendered to one of the younger ones I met in the Lobby a friend of Haddock's called *Captain* EDEN, my dear the *nation's* loveliest legislator, my dear six foot of *slender* elegance, *too* Etonian and the *most* Berkeley moustache, my dear I *ached* to sit on his *knee* only it seems he's a Parliamentary Private Sec or something and parks just behind the Prime and the Foreign Footler so *that's* an idle dream, and of course I could see at once that the little charms were *rather* fruitless because he's utterly *embalmed* in his job and is one of those rather *alibiquitous* men, my dear *too* elsewhere when you talk to him and you *know* he's thinking of the Polish Corridor or some *septic* crisis among the Bulgs, so the only hope I can see is that WINSTON or the Prime may make me *their* PPS, because if we're legislating hand-in-hand as it were one *might* make more of an impression perhaps, only of course if I have the *smallest* discord with the Whips or anything I shall go *straight* off and sit on those cross-benches and be cross.

And of course I *quite* adore WINSTON who gave me an *imperial* twinkle and said something witful about the House having had just enough Haddock to sharpen its appetite for *Trout*, well I met some of the Labour men who were quite *disarming*, my dear like *tame* bears, and I dined with Haddock in the *Harcourt* Room, which is *rather* stimulating because my dear there's a sort of *tape-measure* in the wall to show who's yapping in the *Chamber* and it's *too* tickling to know that some *absolute* loofah is speaking and merely go on un-Christianly *absorbing* oysters, my dear when Auntie JIX's name went up I ordered the *hugest* rump-steak at *once* as a *gesture*, well then the *Division* bell tinkles and of course one pretends to your guests that it's a *pulverising* bore having to go and vote but of course in the secret bosom feeling *too* legislative and important, though I don't know how long that lasts, of course the food's *rather* poisonous but altogether it's like the *largest* country-house party, *you* know my dear where you don't know the names of *half* the people and *never* need speak to your host, well I feel quite the little House of Commons girl *already*, and watch the papers darling because it's quite feasible I may make my virgin speech on the Address or something, in *which* case I *rather* fear I shall have to be *rather* rude about the *Royal* oration so pray for me darling your little Stateswoman TOPSY.

10 Hauls Down The Gold Standard

Trix darling I don't know if you saw but I'm afraid my virgin speech was a *classic* fiasco, my dear *too* chastening, however here and there the proceedings had fun-value so I'll nought conceal because my dear the Press were *too* Christian and I don't suppose you *take in* Hansard exactly, by the way darling I *do* hope you're utterly *preserving* my letters because it's *occured* to me they might be *rather* cream to the autobiogmongers some day, and I don't know if you've noticed but I've been *rather* pedantic about spelling and everything lately for that reason, well I *nearly* always get *aprehensive* right and *even* esotteric don't I darling?

Well of course it's a fraction *intricate* this macaber tale if you *don't* understand the geography, anyhow it was *quite* arranged that I was to *catch* the SPEAKER'S *fictitious* eye after the Honourable loofah for Ullage Boroughs and I must mention of course that the House was *crammed*, my dear *too* insanitary, of course if you *will* have a House of *seven* hundred and a Chamber that holds *four*, *how* like men darling, and as I will *not* have truck with that *degrading* scramble for seats before *breakfast*, my dear *imagine* me standing in a queue with the man HICKS at six o'clock in the morning, and of course some *maggotty* constituent came to see me about *Sunday* osculation or something, so what with everything I lost the little seat, however I thought in *case* I said anything about *vinophobia* it might be just as well not to be next to NANCY in case she pinched the little legs or anything, and I was *quite* determined to be rather *carbolic* to the Government about the Gold Standard and everything, so I took a seat on the *cross*-benches *quite* under the Gallery, my dear *whispering* secretly in the palping little bosom, *Mister* Speaker Sir the *Gold* Standard is the banner of the nation's wretchedness and the gilded ensign of our *defeated* industries.

Because my dear that's how Haddock *told* me to begin, of course usually I don't concoct a *syllable* beforehand but merely bubble on *fortuitously*, only one's virgin in the House is *such* an event that we thought I'd better *mesmerise*, and I'd mesmerised the *entire* speech, my dear *calamitous*, however well you see the *Gold Standard* was the absolute *note* of the speech, of course I don't *really* understand the Gold Standard, but as I said who *does*, anyhow all this *deflation* is *utterly* spurious, my dear it's *rather* difficult to explain to you because I suppose it's *just* possible you haven't *studied* deflation much, well I *think* deflation is a sort of financial *banting* and *inflation* so the inflaters say means feeding the nation *up*, but of course the other people, that's the *deflaters*, say it means national flatulence, so it's all rather *intestinal* and complex, and my dear you've *no* idea of the *things* a public woman has to keep in the little cranium, however darling *don't* read that bit again because I don't *quite* know what I am but the *point* is *too* simple, you see all this *deflation* they say and the Gold Standard and everything means we have the *most* convincing *credit*, and as I said what is the good of braying about your *credit* if you have *millions* of unemployed, and what *is* the good of the Gold Standard if you *never* see a sovereign, and *what* is the good of having *cheap* food if people have *no* money to purchase same, my dear as *I* said *if* you have the *most* convincing credit what does a girl *do*, one *rushes* out and gets all sorts of *utter* necessaries you *can't* afford *now*, which my dear is *just* what the *Government* ought to do, because my dear *look* at all the *remunerative* things they won't do because they're *short* of money, my dear *roads* and *canals* and Channel *Tunnels* and growing artificial *forests*, and harnessing the *tides* and *all* sorts of *water*-stunts, because my dear there's no doubt that *coal* is *too* obsolete, and gosh you'd think there was enough *water* in this country to run the *universe* by electricity, and of course *as* for the money they've only got to have the *world's* seductive loan *specially* for unemployment, my dear call it the Peace Loan, get a good publicity man and the trick is *done*.

Well my dear that was the sort of *Message* of my speech, only of course my poor Haddock *would* mutilate it into these *dyspeptic* sentences about *banners* and things, well when the loofah for Ullage Boroughs had ceased uttering, which my dear was the *sort* of relief you get when an *engine* stops blowing off steam at St Pancras, well I bounded *nimbly* to the little feet and smiled my winningest at the Speaker, but my dear *what* was my humiliation when he called upon a Conservative yam from Yorkshire instead, well my dear I *wilted* like a frozen daffodil into my seat and a rather kindly balloon came up and told me I *couldn't* speak from there because I was *behind* the Bar or under the Bar or something puerile, my dear you've *no* idea, the place is like a *girls'* academy only *nobody* knows the rules, because *another* Samaritan came up and said I was *utterly* orthodox only the Speaker *couldn't* have noticed the slender frame, my dear *too* flattering, anyhow I wasn't going to be muted by *that* schoolgirl stuff, so after a bit I *glided* up the little Staircase at the back into a sort of overflow gallery at the side, and my dear I'd *hardly* had time to attend to the haggard features when the yam subsided and I *leapt* to the perpendicular again, well my dear some beetle said Order order because it seems *nobody's* spoken from the Gallery except a man called HEALY *centuries* ago, however *nearly* everyone else made Yer-yer noises and the Speaker called on me and I moistened the little lips and said *Mr* Speaker Sir the *Gold* Standard.

Well my dear I *stop* there because that's just where I *did* stop, my dear I couldn't *utter*, I merely *looked* down at a sort of *sea* of jelly-fish *glaring* up at me, and they say I was *rather* a Ruth-like and poignant little figure sort of *quivering* alone above the alien gasteropods, of course they were *foully* polite, my dear if they'd *only* been *rude* I'd have been a different woman, but I *could* not remember a *single* word about the Gold Standard, I don't know *what* I said in the end, my dear *too* brief, some sort of *Christian* babble about the Prime I believe however darling let us draw a veil.

Well my dear I *faded* out of the place and had a juniper-juice for the stamina, and I went back when the Prime got up, who my dear *quite* brought tears to the little eyes, my dear *too* magnetic, however now for the fun-stuff, well just before the Prime stopped a perfectly *tropical* loofah who sits for Scotland or somewhere and had the *most* offensive snivelly cold *got* up, my dear, and said Mr Speaker *is* it in order for the Honourable

Member for Burbleton to *powder* her nose during the Prime's remarks, my dear *sensation*, I blushed *all* over, well the Speaker said something pedantic about *non sine pulvere* being no doubt applicable to feminine conquests but he thought the *sense* of the House was that Honourable Members should in the Chamber confine the arts of adornment and decoration to their *prose* or something, well they all yer-yerred and cachinnated, and my dear I was *so* staggered I could think of *nothing* to say, because my dear *after* all *what* century *are* they living in, however well the Prime stopped and *while* the Speaker was doing the clear-the-lobbies ritual the noxious loofah aforesaid gave the *most* hippopotamy *snort*, so my dear I had one of my inspired flashes, I *got* up and I said On an absolute *point* of order Mr Speaker, but of course *just* then it seems the first Division bell rang, and the two yams beside me utterly *pulled* me down and said I could only put a point of order *sitting* with a *hat* on, because my dear there's some *nursery* rule about that, however I said Can't you see the girl's *hatless*, and then somebody gave me Sir WILLIAM BULL'S *topper* and I utterly yelled Is it in order for the Honourable and Bronchial Member to attend to *his* nose in a *hydraulic* manner, only of course I doubt if anyone heard because I was *drowned* in the hat, my dear *right* down to the little shoulders, my dear they *roared*, because of course they're *Nature's* infants and I must say *rather* congenial, well Haddock says that after the hat-exploit they'll *quite* forget about my virgin fiasco, and I *quite* think that some of them are *quite* attracted so all's well etc, farewell now your *rather* pathetic TOPSY.

11 Has Words With The Whips

Trix darling as I *rather* expected I'm having *rather* trouble with the Whips already because my dear the *perverted thing* is that the *one* thing they don't like a legislatrix to do is to *legislate*, my dear a *private* Member's Bill utterly *sends* up the little temperatures because *all* they want you to do is to *always* be on tap and occasionally *filter* through the Lobbies like a *performing* microbe, well my dear I've *quite* determined that I'm *not* going to be a mere automatic divider, especially as they *will* talk about nothing but *politics* in Parliament, my dear all this *phlegmatic* chat about the *rates* and everything, you know there's *no* doubt that politics are getting *more* and more *materialistic* and gross, because the *sole* thing they *ever* discuss is *bread* and *butter* and *wages* and *trade*, and of course it's all *too* cardinal, but my dear *after* all man does *not* live by bread alone, except in politics, because my dear they've *no* time for anything which is not *utterly* £ s d, however personally I'm going to strike an absolute *note* of idealism, and I've draughted *rows* of *immaculate* Bills already, my dear I've a Bill to Preserve the *Beauties* of England, and a *Bill* to Start a National *Theatre*, and a *Rent Restriction* Bill for Theatres, and a Bill about Architects, and a Bill to have a Boat-service on the Thames, and a Bill to Reform the Divorce Laws and another for the *Betting* Laws, and of *course* the Licensing Laws, and a Channel Tunnel Bill, and a Bill to Harness the *Tides*, and a Bill about *Forests*, and of course my Peace Loan (Unemployment) Bill, and a Bill to *Nationalise* the Bar, and another for the Hospitals, and a Bill about Sunday and a Bill to *Reduce* the Age of Magistrates and Councillors, and a Bill to Improve the Pub, and a Bill to Reform the Second Chamber by the Creation of *Young* Peers, my dear people like Haddock, and a Bill to Assist Music and one or two more.

Well my dear *some* of these have already been *quite* printed and read a First Time, which is *rather* a throb, only of course the Prime has pinched *all* the private Members' time so *quite* nothing can be done worth doing, but my dear these *pussilanimous* Whips utterly *swooned* when they saw my little Bills because they'll be *too* popular and *embarass* the Gov, my dear you've no idea what absolute *lizard-livers* they've got, and my dear the *toil* I've had to get people to *back* them, because they all say they're *too* right but will *alienate* the local yams, my dear as *if* that mattered, however the Whips said they were all *too* heinous and if I wasn't careful I should *lose* the Whip so I said who *wants* your dismal Whip and that's how it stands, O snakes a Division, no more now darling but I'll send you my Sunday Bill and I think you'll agree that the *preamble* anyhow is *rather* plausible farewell your *refractory* TOPSY.

(Enclosure)

A BILL TO IMPROVE THE CONDITION
OF THE PEOPLE ON SUNDAY AND FOR THE INCREASE OF
JOY ON WEEK-DAYS

WHEREAS notwithstanding the passage of time there is a *noxious* species of municipal yam which lives in the year 400 AD and feeds on antique regulations and *barbarical* taboos, and whereas together with another *medieval* kind of weasel called the Licensing Justices the yams aforesaid have made the Lord's Day a day of wretchedness and undiluted *gloom* in the larger towns of these teeming islands, especially the North, well *have* you been to Burbleton on Sunday, and whereas the said yams and dog-fish having comfortable homes have no itch to go to the *pictures* on Sunday or listen to a *band* in the parks and don't see why anybody else should, and anyhow they can play *golf* if they like, and whereas being too antique and shaggy to have a best girl it doesn't occur to them that other people *may* have, but whereas the poor having *small* homes cluttered up with mothers-in-law and dirty plates after lunch do proceed into the streets for recreation but there is no recreation, well in a place like Burbleton there are *no* cinemas open, and *no* concerts, and Councillor Mule has stopped the band in the Park, there is not one *note* of music all day except hymns though of course it's *too* lawful to read these *corrupting* Sunday papers, but whereas nobody can go to church *all* day, and whereas by reason of the mothers-in-law and best girls aforesaid the poor dupes must go *somewhere*, but there is nowhere to go except the museum and the pubs, and whereas it is unlawful to hold hands in the museum, and therefore they walk *drearily* about the Streets and there is a great deal of promiscuous clicking in the High Street, and of course if it rains they probably go into the pub, in *which* case the aforesaid yams are responsible, and whereas for these reasons the said yams and Councillors have shown themselves unfit to govern the recreations of the people on Sunday or any other day, and anyhow they were only elected to manage the drains, and whereas there is nothing in the Holy Scriptures to say that Sunday should be one long funeral, and whereas the aforesaid Licensing stoats have certain powers concerning the issue of licences for music dancing and other guileless amusements which powers for similar causes as aforesaid they have abused *most* foxily,

Be it therefore enacted by the King's *most* Excellent Majesty, by and utterly *with* the advice and consent and everything of the Lords Spiritual and Temporal, and of *course* the old Commons, in this *present* Parliament assembled and massed, and by the authority of the same as follows:

Definitions

1. In the construction of this Act the following words and expressions have the following meanings, unless excluded by the context, and anyhow it's *too* obvious what they mean, that is to say:

   The expression '*yam*' means a spherical growth like Councillor Mule of the Burbleton Town Council who has somehow *clambered* on to the Council by *weaselish* work in the *provision* world and knows about the trams and things, for *which* reason he *sees* himself as a censor of plays and books and bathing-dresses and *general* Mussolini of Burbleton morals.

The expression '*loofah*' means much the same thing only the face is *oblong* and *as* a rule has the *most* lachrymose moustache composed of *rotting* straw which goes *dank* like seaweed when there is *rain* in the *air*.

The expression '*stoat*' is *too* similar but has an added significance of Purityrannical *venom* and *un-Christian* prejudice because of course it's *nearly* always a Licensing Justice who is *Vice*-President of the Milk League and deprecates fun.

2. Notwithstanding any flatulent bye-law it shall be *quite* lawful everywhere for the pictures to be open on Sunday evening, also to play games (if any) in municipal parks and things the same as a week-day.

3. No municipal yam or loofah shall have anything to do with the recreations and pleasures of the people, which shall be governed where necessary by a Joy Committee of the Council, elected absolutely *ad* hoc and consisting of *two* men and a virgin, *one of these to be under thirty and the others under forty*.

4. The Joy Committee shall organise a *good* band and make it play on Sunday afternoons.

5. Every town shall have Sunday concerts in the winter months.

6. Every town shall have a public swimming-bath which shall be open on Sunday afternoons.

7. Mixed Bathing shall be *quite* lawful and any contagious comments by yams or loofahs shall be punishable with *utter* imprisonment.

8. It shall be lawful to play bagatelle and billiards the same as golf on Sunday and sections 10–14 of the Gaming Act 1845 are hereby totally cancelled likewise any similar blather.

9. The Joy Committees shall take over the powers and duties of the Licensing stoats in relation to the recreations of the people.

10. All Prohibitionists and such-like fanaticals shall be excluded from the Licensing Bench the same as the brewers, well isn't that *too* reasonable?

11. Councillor Mule shall be washed *weekly*.

12. This Act may be cited as the Sunday (Diminution of Gloom) and Recreations of the People (England and Wales) Act 1928.

12 Knows Too Much

Trix you small snake, I will *not* be stung with *mordant* reproaches, how *could* I write to you, my dear I'm *supine* on a bed of sickness and having the *most* complicated sufferings, but of course, if you ask me *what*, well the *doctors* call it the *rudest* name, but my dear the *nude* fact is that the doctors know *nothing* and I was *utterly* saved by a *Medical* Dictionary, because my dear one night at the American Embassy I suddenly asked loudly what a *sweetbread* was, because *at* that moment we were having one of those *inflating* farinaceous foods the Americans eat and I thought a sweetbread was the same sort of thing, my dear like sweet *corn* or sweet *potato*, *too* fallacious, because there was a *steamy* silence, and afterwards Haddock said that every public woman ought to know about the *facts* of the stomach and everything, which of course were *quite* Greek to your innocent little friend, so the other day I saw this *divine* book and bought it.

Well my dear I don't know if you've ever looked at a Medical Dic, my dear too *disintegrating*, though of course just at first it's rather a *hilarious* work to sort of *merely* loiter with, well you keep on coming across things like OESOPHAGUS the technical name for the gullet *which* see, and then you look up GULLET and you see Gullet or OESOPHAGUS is *merely* the *food* canal, and my dear KING'S EVIL is an old name for Scrofula which seems rather uncalled-for don't you think, well of course I looked up SWEETBREAD for fun and it said *See* PANCREAS, and my dear it's *rather* a shock to find that the *whole* of one's thoughtless life one's had sweetbreads and pancreases and things and known *nothing* about it, my dear I don't want to *agitate* you but as a *matter* of fact you've got a sweetbread *too*, however *don't* speed off to the doctor or anything because it isn't exactly a disease, though of course as far as I can see the *whole* of life may hang on a girl's pancreas, my dear it's a *digestive* gland which secretes the *pancreatic* juice into the *small* intestine, and my dear when I tell you that it may be the seat of *cancer* and the formation of tumours which are called pancreatic *cysts* you'll understand that the sweetbread isn't *exactly* the sort of subject for table-twitter at the American Embassy, nor *yet* darling for reading in *bed*, which was where I stumbled on the murky truth, especially my dear as *besides* all this it's the *assiduous* pancreas that pours into the blood, *your* blood darling, a fluid that regulates the consumption of *sugar* by the muscles, and my dear *if* it fails to do that it says you have *one* form of diabetes, only one darling but one would be enough, I thought, and my dear if I *have* got a vice it's *sugar*, because I always have a *sweet* Martini and *never* a dry, so of course I turned to DIABETES with dithering fingers, and my dear *imagine* my horror when I found that the symptoms were *thirst* and a *voracious* appetite, and *either* loss of flesh *or* obesity, complicated my dear by *mental* depression, my dear *too* convincing, because of course I eat and drink like an emu, I've *flung* away flesh since I was in the House, my dear I'm *puny*, and as for depression there are times as *you* know when I feel that there's *nothing* for it but the gas-oven, only of course I've always been *terrified* of gas.

Well my dear by this time I was *quite* spongy with *intestinal* pains but I said nothing to Haddock about the diabetes, although that night the little eyes did *not* close till about half-past cockcrow, well the next day I *simply* cut sugar and starch and flour and thick soups and oysters and liver right out of my life, but notwithstanding the *next* morning after rather a dawn-party at Bow-wow's I had the *most* suggestive *symptoms* in the *back* of the head, my dear a sort of cross between an *ache* and an inflammation, well I looked up HEADACHE and my dear there are *twenty-five* reasons for having a headache, from overwork and alcohol to blood-clots on the brain, *poisonous* circulations and *tumours* in the skull, my dear *too* gruesome, and of course the *blood* may be contagious through abscesses or scarlet fever or else *chronic* Bright's Disease, and my dear it *might* be the beginning of *apoplexy* or cerebral thrombosis or *brain*-fever or *water* on the brain, which I didn't think I'd got, but anyhow the *divine* thing was that *nothing* was said about diabetes, at which I perked up buoyantly and put the whole thing down to overwork and worry, so my dear I expelled Taffeta Mole, neglected the *entire* correspondence of Burbleton, telephoned to Lewisham that I could *not* lay the foundation of the new roller-skating rink and *super*-cinemadrome, asked the Whips for a pair and pranced out to the Zoo to have a *girlish* holiday with Georgie Rowland, who has popped up again my dear only more of a Topsiphilist than *ever* before!

Well of course the *first* person we met coming out of the Monkey House was *poor* Jack Lantern who mumbled brightly at us that he'd had *all* his teeth out, which he said was *too* marvellous and *quite* everybody ought to have *all* their teeth out because he'd had no more headaches or inferior nights and bounced out of bed as fresh as a *bulb* in May-time, because he said it's the known thing now that teeth are so many *toxic* growths which merely *pollute* the blood-stream and bring on permanent *septicanemia* or something, my dear *too* lowering, because of course from *that* moment the buoyancy sank to *absolute* zero, I had lassitude and debility and the *acutest* pains in the back, however my dear I crawled on bravely as far as the Reptiles, and *there* we met little Ivory Doon who had just discarded *her* teeth and was in a *rapture* about it, so my dear seeing it was the done thing I *abandoned* George in chagrin and the Snake House, *flew* to my dentist and implored him to dismantle the *poisonous* mouth, however he said the little tusks were quite too taintless and utterly declined, so my dear feeling more and more rickety and mucous and everything I *slunk* home and retired to bed with *abdominable* spasms and the Medical Dictionary, because I was *too* determined to find out myself *exactly* what was the matter with me, although by this time the little head was a *mere* ferment, *agony* darling.

Well my dear in about ten minutes I found I was suffering from a *long*-neglected *kidney* complaint, *rather* aggravated by *cirrhosis* of the liver, as a *result* of which it said death *generally* supervenes, and of course with the *pancreas* not functioning as well you'll get *some* idea of the *condition* your poor little blossom's arrangements were *in*, my dear *don't* go on with this letter if you'd *rather* not, only I *rather* think you ought to, well anyhow I phoned *feebly* for the doctor and lay there shivering and alone because Haddock was making a speech at the Mansion House to *all* the solicitors, well of course the doctor was out and meanwhile darling I found the *most* sinister little swelling in the neck which was *probably* goitre or else *tuberculous* enlargement of the *lymphatic* glands, so my dear I sent for Annie and dictated the *most* wistful little will, I left you *two* frocks, darling and all my *celestial* new *undies*, however the doctor came at last and said he thought I should live with *complete* rest and *no* parties for a *whole* week, only he heartlessly deprived me of my dear little Dic, which only shows you darling the *jealousy* in that profession, because as *I* said if I hadn't *known* what a State I was in I should probably have dropped dead in *harness* at the House of Commons, however Haddock said he was *too* right, and since then he's been sending *anonymous* Medical Dictionaries to all the people he *can't* endure, with the *result* my dear that there's been an absolute *crop* of nervous breakdowns among the yams and loofahs and prawns of this island, my dear Councillor Mule himself wrote me a *poignant* farewell because he said he was just off to the doctor having found he had *incurable* myxœdema and nephritis or something, and I see that four or five notorious nose-pokers are in the invalid list with complaints unspecified so there *may* be something in it, only as I told Haddock I still think his reasoning's mouldy because what *I* think is that one ought to utterly *face* these things because my dear health *is* everything, well *isn't* it, and my dear *without* knowledge how *can* you hope to keep a *complex* arrangement like the feminine body in order, anyhow I've told Hatchards to send you a Medical Dic for your birthday darling, so *be* good and keep well, your rather *anæmic* little TOPSY.

13 Wins Bread

Trix my poppet I'm *rather* prostrate once more, I've been doing the *most* exhausting *practical* study of the absolute *life* of the people, well you know it's the done thing nowadays to have *served* in front of the *mast* or resided in *tenements* or laboured in the *mines* and things so that one can tell the Labour Party they know *quite* nothing about it, and of course I've always wanted to have a *rather* deeper understanding of the democratic strata especially the toiling girls of our land, however I thought it would be *too* drastic and repugnant to serve before the mast or behind a counter or anything, and one day I had the *most* plaintive epistle from a girl at Grunton who was a sixpenny partner in the Palais de Danse, because she said her wages were *too* harsh and she had *quite* nothing over after paying for her room and everything, so my dear I thought I'd *explore* the Sixpenny Partner stratum because if there's one thing I *can* do as *you* know darling it is footwork at the ball, and anyhow I'm *too* saturated with the House and all these *clammy* incantations about quinquenniums and the rates.

Well my dear I went down to Grunton but of course *too* incognito in black silk with a lot of sixpenny lace about and saw this girl who was called Elspeth something and was *pure* fluff, my dear *too* peroxide, however *quite* matey, and she told me there was a new Sixpenny wanted and there was an absolute *audition* or something the very next day, well there were *six* other candidates, all blonde as barley-sugar, and we all *pranced* round the *spacious* floor with one of the *he*-partners, but my dear almost the *moment* the manager saw your alluring little chum he merely *stampeded* across and engaged me on the spot, of course I had *rather* conscience-trouble about the other poor females, however in a good cause and everything, anyhow Elspeth got me the *drabbest* little room in the same house as hers, my dear a mere *call-box* with the *frigidest* lino, two pound ten darling bed and board including *one* bath on Fridays, so I left all my luggage at the Metropole except one *sparse* little tin-trunk I borrowed from Annie, and settled down to a life of *utter* poverty and wage-earning, and if you could have seen me *weeping* myself to sleep with nothing but *one* wee hot-water-bottle between me and suicide, because of course *no* fire in the bedroom, my dear *too* harrowing.

And of course my dear I found that Elspeth was *too* right about the economics, because my dear it *is* complete servitude to be a Sixpenny, well we all sat in a *pen* darling, *twelve* of us, like performing dogs, of course they were all rather *curious* about your elegant Top, not that the others weren't elegant, my dear *too* ladylike, and the *most* expensive *names*, my dear *Iseult* and *Auriol* and *Lillith* and so forth, but *quite* darlings and thoroughly genial, to begin with anyhow, all except two called *Amethyst* and *Elaine* who were the two *princesses* of the pen, and rather *sniffed* about me, however I arranged with Elspeth that I was a clergyman's orphan with utterly *no* means of consistence, anyhow the *sole* salary you get is *ten* small shillings a week, my dear *too* inadequate, only of course every time a customer pays sixpence to dance with you you earn *threepence*, so that you see it *all* depends on *how* much you magnetise the male, my dear absolute payment by *results* which is *rather* brutal, because my dear some afternoons the place is *too* unpopulated, and of course it isn't everybody who can afford *many* sixpences for *one* dance and an attenuated encore, my dear *never* more than about *two* minutes together, so it's *quite* a costly luxury, anyhow most of the girls reckon to make about three pounds or under, which after the rent and everything *doesn't* leave much for silk stockings and frocks and the *pictures*, *does* it, *which* latter my dear is the *sole* thing they think about, my dear it's *too* staggering, like you darling they never *peep* at the papers and my dear there were three girls *definitely* who'd no idea who Mr BALDWIN was, which is *rather* fragrant and refreshing in a way don't you think?

And of course it's the *most* menial and *lacerating* labour, my dear 3 to 6 in the afternoon and 8 to 12 at night, not to mention giving *lessons* in the mornings which some of them do, and if you danced *every* dance it would mean 70 dances a day and four hundred and twenty a week, my dear *imagine* the horror, and all with the *strangest* men, *some* of whom seem to think because they've bought you for two minutes they've a right to you for *life*, my dear I had two or three perfectly *septic* partners who made the *most* alarming proposals, my dear it's *too* extraordinary the number of little *frog*-men there are who seem to have *nothing* to do but *prowl* round a Palais in the *afternoon*, and they dance *too* well only in a *leprous* style, my dear they have hands like *newts* and they *clutch* your fingers in the *most* messy *professional* grip as if they were holding a snake by the tail, and my dear at *any* moment one of them may utterly purchase you for sixpence, and then of course there are the *primordial* monsters with *hypertrophy* of the abdomen as my Medical Dic would call it who merely *trample* on you like intoxicated *Tanks*, so my dear the whole thing would be *too* murderous if it wasn't for what the girls call *regular* clients, because my dear it's the done thing to have *favourite* youths who buy *blocks* of tickets and utterly book you for the evening, because *then* my dear you can *insist* on sitting out now and then and have *Vanilla* Sundaes, my dear *too* poisonous, only you get the same fat fee for sitting out as dancing, which is *rather* hard on the client perhaps, especially as the management is *too* severe, my dear one's not allowed to so much as *smile* at an old customer across the floor, *too* monastic, and personally I found most of my clients were *quite* reluctant to sit out at all.

However my dear it was this *exquisite* system that led to the *trouble*, because my dear I was a *blazing* success and was scarcely *ever* left forlorn in the pen, which was *rather* warming in a way, because my dear it *is* nice to know that one's appeal is *really* universal and *democratic* and everything, like SHAKESPEARE I mean, and my dear as one dragged the *bleeding* little toes to bed it gave one *rather* a glow to think one was definitely a *working-*girl, but then *why* is it that *whenever* I try to do good the *worst* seems to occur, because the *dire* thing was that *half* the girls' *particular* clients switched over to *me*, and especially *Amethyst's* and *Elaine's*, my dear *too* fatal, because *what* was I to do, you can't *refuse* to dance if you're a sixpenny dancer, well you can understand there was a certain *petulance* in the pen, and my dear I *can't* tell you what I heard Amethyst say to Elaine when Amethyst's elderly *pet client* who comes down from town booked your *well-intentioned* Topsy for Saturday afternoon *and* evening, and he was *rather* a dove darling because he only wanted to dance about once in ten, the slow waltz being his strong suit, and he bought mountains of chocolates and *gazed* yearningly only then he started to tell me about his wife and 8 children who spent *all* his money and *never* understood him, so it was all on the *difficult* side, and what with Amethyst looking *vitriol* at me, however believe me or not I stuck it for 8 days, though *so* tired darling that in the mornings I had to *creep* into the Metropole and have a Christian bath, however at last my Elspeth who was *too* loyal said if I stayed much longer I should get a hat-pin in the midriff from Amethyst or Elaine, and my dear I was ticked off *too* barbarously by the manager for being five minutes late one night, so my dear I waited till Friday when they have a sort of *Staff* meeting for complaints and everything, only nobody dares to complain, and *at* that I rose up and said that *all* the girls were *too* exploited and they ought to have an absolute *basic* salary because *how* could a girl be lady-like *and* pure for that money, not to mention *free* tea in the afternoon and something to eat at night, sensation my dear and the next day I was *quietly* sacked with a week's wages ten bob darling so that will show you, rather a *degrading* climax perhaps, however all the girls quite *wept* on my neck what with wonder and gratitude and even Amethyst relented meagrely, and my dear I *do* know now how it feels to be a *mere* wage-girl and of course if *ever* there's a Debate about Palais de Danses or the wages of girls I shall make the *most* electrical speech, no more darling your *martyred* little TOPSY.

14 Behaves Badly

Trix darling I've *behaved* like an *utter* scorpion and I'm having *rather* conscience-trouble, however not *too* collapsing, because my dear I'm *beginning* to think that in the *lonely* crusade I'm waging almost *any* kind of injurious witchery is justified provided it comes off, my dear it's *no* use *playing the game* with rattle-snakes, well *is* it darling?

Well I've told you didn't I about the *austere* little Bills I've draughted and especially my disarming Bill about the Crêpe Sunday and the Recreations of the People, well my dear the Whips are *sizzling* with rage and of course the moment the Antimacassar Vote in Burbleton heard about it they rushed as *one* antimacassar to the writing-table and spat *anonymous* postcards at me, my dear *too* uncontrolled, my dear the *queer* thing is that everything the other side say is *too* right but everything *I* say is *base* 'propaganda', however the absolute *azimuth* of impertinence was reached when I got a challenge from Councillar Mule to *debate* with him at the Annual Dinner of the Burbleton Branch of the Total Abstinent Sons of the Salamander, which my dear is the *gross* body of the Crêpe Votes and is against *quite* everything from *silk* stockings to sun-bathing.

Well my dear Haddock and my agent and everybody wanted me to take a *spurny* line about it, but the blood of the Trouts rather reacted to the tocsin, and besides I *always* believe in meeting the Amalekites face to face because quite often you find that the most repugnant of the species have some *compassionate* feature when witnessed in the flesh, my dear *too* right, because, well anyhow I accepted, and my dear I can't *begin* to describe the company, my dear you know I'm a *comparative* fundamentalist in dogmatological matters, don't you, but my dear it *is* hard sometimes to believe that Creation was an *ordered* plan, well there were about two hundred of the tribe of Salamander, and my dear if you'd *seen* them, well if you can imagine a *hundred* whelks having dinner with a *hundred* underdone *prawns*, of course it was all a bit *poignant* really because my dear I know you've *never* understood psycology but the whole thing was *too* pellucid to me, my dear as Haddock put it people with fat ankles do *not* approve of short *skirts*, and that's *most* of this municipal fussery in a nut-shell, of course there were one or two *divine* old angels with GLADSTONE expressions whom I *quite* adored and a lot like Councillor Mule who do this sort of thing for the *mere* love of nose-poking and power, but the *yellow* residue my dear were *merely* sour with hereditary frustration poor things, my dear the very *veins* are vinegar, my dear *born* jilted, and my dear it's no good saying that appearances aren't everything, because I *always* say that beauty will out if there is any and if you see *nothing* but eye-blisters in a place there must be something *radically* spurious about the whole institution.

However what with everything I took rather a *Christian* attitude to the rank and file, but of course I've *always* had a *rodent* suspicion about the *malignant* complaints like Councillor Mule, and as a *matter* of fact my agent has been making rather *inquiries* lately, *whereby* darling hangs this crepuscular tale, well for *one* thing darling it seems he has the *most* Continental *library*, however I sat next to the yam and my dear he ate *too* hoggily, as total abstinents very often do I'm told, my dear the food was *poison* and we drank *hot* water, but I must say *quite* genial, well he evidently thought he was going to *flog* me in the debate with his loyal Salamanders to hold his hand, but my dear *while* he was worrying a *rump*-steak and utterly *beaming* between bites, my dear it's *rather* crude but you know the old story and of course you must censure Haddock and the agent as well as your peccable Top, well anyhow he was handed a note on his *own* paper on *which* was written in *block*-letters as I *happened* to know DO NOT COME HOME THE POLICE ARE HERE.

Well my dear the effect was *immediate*, the sparkle faded in the spongy eye and from *that* moment the edibles lost their *pristine* charm, my dear the yam peered *guiltily* in all directions toyed *apathetically* with the steak and would *not* be tempted with a *vanilla* ice, well I was *too* solicitous and kept *hoping* there were no bad news from home and everything, but he got paler and paler, my dear I thought he would *faint*, and at last he sent out for a *brandy*, well my dear the thought of me driving the *king* vinophobe to alcoholic indulgence which is what they call a drink was *rather* hilarious, but I had conscience-trouble because I thought he really might have done a murder or something, however in *sepulchral* tones he called on me to speak and I said Well my poor miseries, *don't* think I blame you because I know *just* what's the matter with you, you're a *pathetic* collection of dogs-in-the-manger, you're *incapable* of joy, you *don't* like beer, you've got *fat* ankles, you don't *stir* from your antimacassars on Sunday and you don't see why anyone else etcetera, only of course the real *sin* is that you call all this jaundice and jealousy *virtue*, and you have the *utter* impudence to say that you know what's good for the *poor*, well I said let me tell you my bilious women that I don't call un-Christian *gossiping* virtue, and I don't call systematic *nose-poking* virtue, and I don't call dyspeptic *inertia* virtue, and what's more, I said, you don't care two *toots* about the poor, you only care about yourselves and your own *mingy* ideas, and besides *half* of you have got *horrible* vices, you poison your systems with tannic acid and tittle-tattle, you *peep* behind curtains, you're *too* petulous with servants, you're *mean* about money, you've no bowels of *love* or mercy or anything, and you may die sober but you'll die in a *septic* condition of envy hatred and *all* uncharitableness, however I said as I said before I'm *sorry* for you, and *believe* me darling I *was* sorry for them, but I said there's *still* a hope for you if you'll *only* come out of your *righteous* holes and *mix* with your *contaminated* fellow-creatures a little because I said you'll find they're *much* more congenial than you *think* and in most ways *much* more moral than you are, and anyhow I said I'm going on with my *flawless* little Bill so there, and then I sat down.

Well my dear none of them actually *threw* things at me but the air seemed cloudy with *invisible* missiles and the applause was *perfunctional*, my dear *too* tepid, but of course *when* the Mule thing *climbed* on to its feet there was an *absolute* hurricane of *anæmic* aprobation, however the Mule was like a *whispering* jelly my dear all the accustomed vinegar and wizardry were *utterly* missing, and my dear whether he thought he might perhaps get me to *bail* him out or what, but anyhow he spent about *five* minutes *burbleing* compliments at me, to the *intense* discomforture my dear of the *daughters* of the Salamander, especially my dear as *about* this time, my dear believe me or not but I am *not* to blame for this, anyhow *all* the male Salamanders began to receive *stealthy* telegrams or notes or letters according to circs, my dear my *agent* is a *fiend* of efficiency, and they all said I HAVE DISCOVERED ALL or NEVER DARKEN MY DOORS AGAIN or COME AT ONCE YOUR WIFE KNOWS or YOU WILL NOT BE WANTED AT THE OFFICE TOMORROW, etcetra, and of course some of them darling absolutely *signed* and everything, I've no *idea* how it was done, anyhow one by one darling the *male* Salamanders rose up and merely *wilted* out of the room, and my dear I don't know if you've *ever* spoken but of course the effect of even *one* person rather drifting out of earshot is *fairly* lowering so *what* it must be when you see a *hundred*, especially as I suppose the Mule thing imagined that they'd *all* heard about the police in the home and everything, anyhow just as he was lumbering towards the *point* of his speech about the sixty-seventh man went out, the Mule gave a *garotted* groan subsided into his seat and then passed out into the night, and *so* much darling for the *consciences* of Salamanders.

Well darling I *rose* up and said a few *gentle* words to the residuary females who by this time were totally kickless, well I said My *pitiful* back-biters the truth has *evidently* prevailed but I *won't* rub it in, you'd better *creep* home now and *try* to be a little more *Christian* in the future, of course the *Press* were there and they described the debate as an absolute *massacre*, so in spite of the little conscience it's *rather* satisfactory and *after* this I hope to make it up with the Mule and come to a *melodious* compromise about Burbleton life, no more now your Machivellian TOPSY.

15 Plays Golf With Nancy

Trix darling, I'm *stricken*, I've played *18* holes of golf with NANCY ASTOR, and of course if you *don't* know NANCY you've *no* idea what that means, my dear she's a *walking* dynamo, my dear *volcanic*, and I must say she's the *most* convincing advertisement for vinophobia and *no* smoking as far as *energy's* concerned, but of course as *I* said to her about the *12th* hole the question is *is* so much energy *desirable* on this planet, because my dear I've *come* to the conclusion that a certain amount of spasmodic *inertia* produces the *deepest* philosophy and meditation and everything, because it's *too* obvious that if you're always *bounding* over fences you've *no* time to *absorb* the scenery, and therefore it's *quite* hypothetical that beer and tobacco may be the absolute *foundation* of British wisdom, well don't you agree darling?

Only my dear *don't* think I'm being the *least* bit corrosive about NANCY because I *do* think she's a *miraculous* person and *rather* maligned, because what *I* like about her is that *like* me she doesn't care *two* toots *what* she says to anybody, in fact in her case I should put it at *one* toot, or even less, and my dear everyone thinks she's *too* fanatical, and of course she *is* fanatical in a *cerebral* sort of way but not *personally*, well I mean she doesn't utterly *spurn* a person because you don't agree with her, like some of these completists, though of course she'll make the *most* explosive remarks about you, but my dear *quite* genial because I think she's *always* thinking she's going to *convert* you, which of course I *now* see ought to be *just* my policy to Councillor *Mule* and Co, and *by* the way darling I *rather* fancy I've made the wee-est *impression* in that quarter, well anyhow my dear *this* morning NANCY rang me up and said *would* I go down to *Warpsand* with her and *bring* my clubs because she was *too* saturated with this *mephitic* town and she was taking BERNARD SHAW to see his *first* game of golf and she *must* have a chaperon because he's the *most* dangerous centenarian she knows, well my dear it sounded *rather* a party though a fraction *intelectual* perhaps for your rustic little friend, so I dug out the old clubs which my dear were utterly *draped* in rust, and we all drove down in the *vastest* car, *me* my dear a *melting* little sandwich between NANCY and the great man, my dear *too* bizarre.

Well my dear *what* a journey, because of course they *quite* never stopped talking and I *simply* didn't utter, my dear I felt like a *very* small horse with troopers *firing* over my *body*, though in a way it was more like *two* people letting off *rockets* at the *same* time, because *first* of all BERNARD would explain that he was *unique* among mortals and long before he'd finished NANCY would point out that *she* was *celestial*, my dear they were *too* witful only I can't remember what they *said*, and I must say that NANCY *quite* held her end up, as she generally *does*, well anyhow they tore each other into *small* pieces all the way to Warpsand, at *which* place they suddenly discovered your *immaterial* Top lying like a *crushed* strawberry *between* them, so I then *faded* into the picture with a definite *remark* about something, and they *both* began talking about something *quite* else, my dear *too* flattening.

However it all had rather throb and fun-value, and at last we stood on the first tee, *me* my dear with my *three* pitiful *red* clubs and *one* slightly superannuated ball, because of course I've *never* had truck with *classical* golf I haven't played for an *epoch* and then only at Mullion, where my dear you stop at the *seventh* to pick mushrooms and at the *12th* for tea, I should think my handicap is about 57 and *as* a rule I *carry* my ball for the last few holes, so my dear *when* I tell you that Warpsand is a *haunt* of tigers with *red* coats and utter *armouries* of irons, not to mention *sponges* and *wind-gauges* and *wooden* clubs in *tropical* profusion, and of course *too* populous, my dear *platoons* of plus 5's *clustered* on the tee, well some of them tried a little twittery on NANCY and in about two sentences she laid them *quite* horizontal, my dear one of them said Why don't Americans practise their *principles* in England LADY ASTOR, so she said Why don't Englishmen take their *morals* to *Paris*, which my dear I thought was *rather* rapid and pertinent, however after that she gave the caddies a *brief* homily about their *private* lives and arranged for *all* their children to join the *Band* of Hope, and then *off* she went like an *electric* racehorse, with SHAW *striding* beside her like a *Norwegian* god, my dear *too* perpendicular, and making the *most* carbolic remarks about golf, and of course your *frail* little friend trotting *feverishly* behind them from one gorse-bush to another, can you *see* the picture?

Well my dear I did the first six holes *running*, my dear mere *hockey*, because *wherever* there were brooks or bunkers or bushes or roads or *out* of bounds or *heaps* of stones or anything *quite* there I went, and of course whenever I *did* trickle back to the fairway I'd see NANCY and BERNARD absolute leagues ahead discussing Christian *Science* on the green and the *hugest* men waiting *patiently* behind me, so I *picked* up the fragments of my only ball and cantered on to the next, I think the *10th* was the first hole I definitely *finished*, and of course the girlish stamina surrendered *quite* soon because my dear the course goes up and down over the highest mountains, the little wind grew *sparse* and the little legs became two *lean* and protracted *aches*, but of course NANCY and SHAW never *turned* a hair, and I must say that G B is the *most* plausible ad for vegetables and everything, only as *I* say darling well *is* it worth it, well my dear they marched *all* over the mountains flinging *wit* at each other, never *pausing* for breath or *me* or anything, and on the *twelfth* tee SHAW said it was no good NANCY trying to be a *Joan* of Arc because she'd *never* hear any voices but her *own*, so NANCY said she didn't *intend* to be a *Saint* because somebody like SHAW would go and make money out of her, so SHAW said he could never write a play about NANCY because his *appeal* was to the *intelect*, and just then I took my baffoon and drove my *only* ball over the *cliff*, my dear *too* disheartening.

Well then NANCY lent me a new ball and began on me about vinophily and everything, because *at* the moment she's *too* whoopy about HOOVER, and *whenever* I missed the ball *too* totally she said *That's* what happens to the *cocktail-girl*, so we *galloped* along my dear *she* shouting congenial abuse about alcohol and the *brewers*, and me panting insults about horse-races and *betting,* with which as a *matter* of fact she rather agreed, only of course SHAW said we were *both* erroneous because if only it was compulsory to read *his* plays nobody would want any other pleasures at *all,* and my dear the *whole* time we were *utterly* chasing a rather *Gothical* foursome of circular old men, my dear *too* skilled but *praying* over their putts and everything, and my dear NANCY was *yearning* to *trample* over them but of course your little Top was *rather* a handicap, however when we came to the down-hill holes I got my fourth or fifth wind and played with one club only to save time, so we *sailed* through and left the round ones *petrified* because NANCY gave them a cheery little lecture about their *physique* and the brewers and everything and SHAW said his life had been in vain if grown-up men were still *squandering* their minds on a game like *golf,* however NANCY said that if SHAW played games he'd have a sense of *proportion* and his plays would be shorter, and SHAW said that if she read his plays she'd have a sense of power and her drives would be *longer,* and so we *charged* along the long sixteenth because we had to get to the House, but my dear for the last two holes I gave up *all* pretence and merely kicked or carted the ball, and my dear I arrived in a *complete* lather but the others of course were *too* tireless and *fresh* as fairies, so I shunned the House and had a *mustard*-bath, and my dear *here* I am *quite* moribund in bed, however I must say it was *rather* a party, only before I go roaming the hills and dales with *those* two super-creatures again I shall have a *long* dose of vegetables and *quite* no gaspers, farewell now darling your *dormatose* little TOPSY.

16 Solves Everything

Trix darling I haven't a *moment* to write to you, my dear life's a *cataract* just now, well my *new* house-parlour's given notice because of the *stairs* and of course they've put me on one of these *yawny* Committees about the *chaotical* Rates, and now I've got to *fly* away and lay the *foundation*-stone of a Palais de Danse, my dear *too* miscellaneous so no more now, how *are* you poppet, and *would* you like to read my *deserving* little Bill about Betting and everything, my dear the *Whips* are *incandescent* about it, anyhow *here* it is, farewell your little *reformer* TOPSY.

(Enclosure)

A BILL FOR THE ABSOLUTE REFORM
OF THE GAMING LAWS AND ALL THAT,
TO SWELL THE EXCHEQUER AND MAKE PROVISION FOR
THE UNEMPLOYED

Preamble

WHEREAS the Briton is *born* betting, and *can* you wonder in a climate like this where *quite* nothing is certain, and anyhow it was the gambling spirit that utterly *made* our ubiquitous Empire, and if you ask me when it comes to it the British race will be found *buoyantly* betting on the *respective* numbers of the sheep and the goats, because *quite* nobody can stop them and *what* is more I notice that none of these *drastic* Savonarolas has the *nerve* to suggest it, on the contrary the Sunday papers which have the *most* Puritanical *leaders* have the *widest* pages at the end about *winners* and prices and odds and everything but of course the *rude* truth as I always tell NANCY is that *over*-betting is *just* as fallacious as over-drinking, in fact *worse*, because beer *is* definitely a food but backing a winner is a *mere* vice and of course backing a loser a *sin*, besides depriving the children of their crusts and everything, well anyhow it can't be stopped, but whereas we spend £200,000,000 per annum on betting, not counting all these *corrupting* competitions in the papers which my dear are *mere* lotteries in fancy-dress, and of course the Insurance papers are just as bad, my dear it's all the *same* thing, *Money* for Nothing, but what I say is *can* you blame the poor because of course for *herds* of people all this betting is the *sole* romance and radiance they *have?*

AND WHEREAS the *grim* thing is that of all the *millions* they spend only about *eightpence* goes to the State, and of course it's *too* saponaceous to talk about its being a *septic* matter for the State to touch, because whereas *when* you think that Westminster Bridge was *merely* built out of the *contagious* proceeds of *State* Lotteries, and *there* it is day after day utterly *contaminating* the eyes of our *cow-hearted* legislators, so if they're at all genuine the first thing to do is to *demolish* same, only it seems to be a fairly substantial and clean-living bridge, and likewise also the British *Museum* was begun with a State Lottery and what about *that*, anyhow whereas it is expedient that the national betting itch should have an outlet *somewhere* and at the same time benefit the Exchequer, and whereas there are many and *greivous* evils arising out of betting, well I mean street-bookies and child-messengers and all that, but they can't be stopped because of the *bat-eyed* law, whereas of course it is much easier to *control* a thing if it is lawful than if it is *not*, well look at Prohibition, and anyhow what *I* say is that betting ought to be like motoring which is *too* lawful only you can *only* do it if you have a licence and pay taxation and *quite* behave yourself.

AND WHEREAS besides at the present time the Gaming Laws are a *suppurative* muddle of hypocrisy and injustice, well isn't it *too* childish when you think that *credit*-betting's lawful and *cash*-betting's a crime, because after all cash-betting means that you lose the money you've *got* but the other way you can lose a fortune you *haven't* got, but there it is the *rich* man's bookie does everything over the King's most excellent telephones and my dear *what* about the Stock Exchange, but the poor man's bookie is chased about the back-alleys by the King's most excellent policemen, and if you call that *justice*, but whereas of course the *thing* to do is to stamp out street-betting by having *licensed* betting-places for the poor the same as the rich and give absolute *years* of hard labour for street-betting afterwards.

AND WHEREAS the principles of this Act are therefore to
    Control betting by regulation
    Keep it clean by the *most* malignant penalties
    Discourage it by cruel taxation (like drink)
and get a *mere* £20,000,000 out of it for the suffering Exchequer,

BE it enacted by the King's most Excellent Majesty, the Lords and Commons and everything, by and with, accordingly, and inasmuch, as follows: —

1. It shall be lawful to bet and gamble, except where specially forbidden, well I mean roulette and all that, and street-betting, and at football matches and things.

2. (1) No person shall make or take a bet without a *Licence*, which licence shall be endorsed or cancelled if he robs the children's bread, or steals or welshes, or fails to pay up or anything.

   (2) These licences shall be renewed *annually* and any person found guilty of betting to the public danger shall not get *another* licence for at least *two* years.

3. The penalty for street-betting or betting without a licence shall be *two* years' hard *without* the option.

4. There shall be licensed and registered betting-offices for the poor the same as the rich, but limited in number and the whole thing *rather* inconvenient.

5. It shall be unlawful for *any* newspaper to give *money* to its readers on *any* pretext except *litterary* competitions and *perhaps* cross-words, provided that

   (1) There shall be a *State* Lottery *four times* yearly, the *proceeds* to be devoted to Unemployment works, and

(2) *Local* lotteries and sweepstakes shall be allowed by *special* licence for the Derby and everything. The tax to be 10% on all entrance money and 123% on all prize-money, like they do in Tasmania.

6. (1) The Betting-Tax shall be *much* higher because of course it's *too* inequitable to charge 2 per cent on a bet and 16 per cent on a Theatre Ticket, and 200 per cent on whisky, well anyhow it shall be 5 per cent on the course and 10 per cent *off*.

(2) The cost of a betting-licence shall be five shillings, and for a book-maker on the course £50 and off the course £100.

(3) Race-courses and other people permitting people to bet on their premises shall have a special licence and tax and be responsible for the said people.

7. (1) No newspapers published on the Lord's Day shall publish the odds on any horse-race or offer any aids or incitement to bet and gamble, but their reports of race-meetings shall be a *mere* record of what has happened, like divorce cases.

(2) Any Sunday newspaper contradicting this section shall be *deemed* guilty of an act calculated to *corrupt* the morals of the people and shall be utterly proceeded against as for a *misdemeanour* under the *Obscene* Publications Act 1857.

8. It shall *not* be lawful to gamble on the Stock Exchange.

9. All previous *erroneous* legislation on this subject is hereby utterly washed-out repealed and abrogated

Provided that nothing in this Act shall prevent a chap from having a friendly bet in the home about the date of WILLIAM THE CONQUEROR or something, or *even* on a round of golf, *provided* that no such bet shall exceed the sum of £1, which I think is *reasonable* don't you.

10. And that's about all I think, only of course this Act may
    be cited as The Gaming Laws Unemployment and Sunday
    Newspapers Reform Act 1928.

17 Converts A Whip

Trix my little snowdrop *all* the compliments of the season and *how* have you survived the digestive season, I *do* hope you got the Sunlight Lamp because I could think of *nothing* else to comfort you in the *bestial* months that are before us, my dear Haddock and I have a *ten* minutes sun-debauch every evening before bed, only of course *Science* changes *so* often these days and the *latest* my dear is that sunlight and fresh air are *definitely* baneful and there's some new doctor who shuts *all* his sufferers up in a *dark* room with a bad smell, and they say it's *too* salubrious, however unfortunately I'd *bought* your present before I heard this, and of course after all the trouble we've had about the *revoltage* and everything I *really* can't start pulling the house to pieces again to instal the Stale Air System, and if you think the Lamp's *too* old-fashioned you'd better *hide* it away darling till Sunlight comes in again.

Well my dear we've had the *most* tribal and alimentary Christmas, my dear I do think that Christmas is the *one* season that ought to *always* be spent in the *home* but if possible somebody *else's* because here we are at the Antons' and my dear it's *too* reposeful *not* having to *calculate* foodstuffs for *six* days ahead, and of course I *rather* adore all the orthodox Yulery as long as somebody else has the *jading* labour of getting it ready, my dear you know I *always* respond to mistletoe and holly when it's *there*, but as for *climbing* up ladders with *bosomfuls* of greenery, my dear *too* Scandinavian, and of course a Christmas-tree *intoxicates* me *provided* I haven't had to *stand* on tip-toe and tie those *combustible* glass bobbles on to it, not to mention candles which will *not* be perpendicular, however well the Antons have their *principal* orgy at *lunch* because of their *herds* of young so of course by about tea-time there was rather a *lethargic* reaction in the house, especially as Haddock would keep playing *folk-songs* on the organ which is *quite* Paradise to Haddock but mere anguish to the *entire* vicinity, in fact at four-thirty a *most* expensive guest who is lacerated by the *best* music merely ordered his car and drove *petulantly* back to London, so what with everything the *old* problem arose *Shall* we raid the Barnacles and if so *how*, because you know there's an *age-long* feud between Beaver and White Ladies and they're always playing the *most* mature *practical* jokes on each other my dear *one* year we *all* went over to White Ladies and dressed up as the *domestic* staff and utterly *waited* at lunch and everything, and my dear they had the *hugest* house-party and *nobody* spotted us till the *liqueur*-stage when as *luck* would have it I gave *Admiral* Flabb a *crème d*e menthe instead of cognac or something, my dear *too* unsuitable, however it only shows how little people notice the *menial* beings who hand them food, well *doesn't* it?

Well my dear *this* time we were all *quite* planless and not a *mind* would function, but of course I was *too* determined on witchery of some sort because Ronnie Barnacle is one of the Whips and has been a *complete* blanket about my little Bills, anyhow at *last* I had a brain-blossom, and I said *Let's* be a kind of *prawn-faced* deputation from Ronnie's constituency, because of course he's *too* pussilanimous and knocks at the knees at the *smell* of an elector, well my dear it *was* so and we all dressed up like *congenital* glooms, my dear *beards* and spectacles and *clusters* of jet and *veils* and everything, and we *flashed* over to White Ladies seven of us in the *middle* of dinner-time.

Well my dear it was arranged that *I* was to be the spokes-girl, *Mrs* Thimblefoot of *West* Wockleham, and my dear *when* Ronnie heard that Mrs Thimblefoot of *West* Wockleham was waiting he quite *torpedoed* out of the dining-room with the *pinkest* cracker-cap on and my dear *pursued* by two *inflammable* fairies trying to hold mistletoe over his head, my dear *too* corybantic the whole thing, so we all looked *rather* forgiving and said we'd come over from *West* Wockleham to wish our Member a *Happy* Christmas, only unfortunately we'd *missed* our connections and things were *days* late and had had *nothing* to eat, so of course the least he could do was to ask his *starving* constituents into the feast, to the *intense* disgust of his *assembled* revellers, because my dear we looked like *seven* black stalactites, my dear *too* baroque, my dear *even* in Wockleham there can *not* be seven people like the people we were like, however Ronnie seemed to think we were *too* normal and representative, which as I told him afterwards is the *kind* of mistake the Whips *do* make, well of course the place was the usual Christmas shambles and mess, my dear *almonds* and *raisins* and cracker-caps and *bits* of turkey and *mince-pies* and mottoes and *broken* glasses and balloons and everything, so of course we were *too* shocked and cast a *cloud* of sorrow by refusing champagne, and then *Foxy* Fortescue, who my dear was made up like ABRAHAM LINCOLN said suddenly *Peace* Pagans have you no SHAME and so *then* my dear I *rose* to the little feet and made the *most* spiritual speech about the absolute *significance* of Christmas, because I said *Brothers* and Sisters *this* is no way to celebrate a *sacred* season, *what* brothers is all this grapery and crackerdom, these salted almonds and *crystallised* greengages, *what* are these fleshly berries suspended o'er the threshold and for *what* this heathen foliage on the walls, O tear down the paper streamers brethren and O my sisters utterly *pop* the blue balloons, because after all this is a *rather* serious day and I do not think that the Mayor of Wockleham would like to think of their Member commemorating same in festoons of coloured paper and the *most* Mephistophely *mask* and blowing a *penny* trumpet, not to mention a *bunch* of raisins over the *left* ear, unless of course he went to *church* this morning, because my dear Ronnie I *know* quite *never* goes to church except to marry a wife or christen a baby, or *unless* he's caught in Wockleham on a Sunday because he's *too* dependent on the Pew Vote, well my dear meanwhile the *whole* of our party sat scowling over their eatables like Savonarola at breakfast-time, and of course the Barnacle party were *too* mute and remorseful and you ought to have seen them *one* by one *stealthily* discarding the cracker-caps, well I said *when* we came to wish the Members happiness we meant happiness of the *soul* and the after-life and everything and not the *carnal* merriment of port-wine and mistletoe, because I said we'd *rather* expected to find him singing *hymns* with the servants or working out a scheme to amend the *morals* of Europe, but *as* it was we felt we were *rather* redundant and had better leave them to their godless revelry, and with *these* words darling we *rose* up and marched out into the night leaving a *clammy* silence at the festive board.

Well my dear we *listened* outside the dining-room window and after about *five* minutes the sounds of hilarity began again, but *rather* tremulous because my dear I heard afterwards that poor Ronnie was perfectly *dank* with aprehension because of the gossip-writers in the Wockleham papers, so then we began singing carols, at least we sang King Wenceslas because that was the *only* one we all knew, and after we'd sung about that *over-rated* monarch about seventeen times poor Ronnie came out and flung *pocketfuls* of money into the darkness, but we said *Keep* your contagious lucre Squire, *all* we want is to save your *soul*, and then Foxy in the most rustical dialect began to absolutely *pray* for Ronnie's soul, which of course is *about* the most *carbolic* thing that one man can do to another in public, so my dear Ronnie fled *blushing* into the house and we sang Wenceslas a lot more and after about the tenth time somebody poured water on us from upstairs but missed, so we *all* prayed loudly for Ronnie again, and hoped that some kind angel would utterly *wean* our good young Squire from his *corrupt* companions and *flighty* London-folk and everything, so at last the *whole* house-party rushed out with the *most* homicidal umbrellas and things, so I gave a girlish shriek and we tore off our make-up *just* in time to escape a massacre, because my dear Ronnie's guests were *practically* incandescent with rage, well then we all went in and found Ronnie *quite* hysterical in the billiard-room, my dear *gulping* hot cocoa and muttering *bits* out of the Catechism which I *rather* fear is all the Scripture he remembers, well he was *too* relieved, and after that of course we had a *magical* party, *rather* a decadent tale perhaps darling however many a true word's spoken in jest they say and I *rather* think that Ronnie will be *too* devout *next* Christmas, in the morning anyhow, no more now your little missionary TOPSY.

18 Is Unlucky

Well Trix my aromatic angel the photographs are *divine* but why oh *why* have you removed the *fringe* because my dear in your style definitely brows are *not* the worn thing now, however they're *rather* winsome, I *adore* the upside-down ones, but my dear you *must* be done by this new man *Moult* who does everyone in *Shakesperian* characters, my dear I've been done as Ophelia and NANCY ASTOR is *Nature's* Portia and they all want HICKS to be Malvolio or somebody only I never heard of the man, did you?

However darling one smiles through one's miseries but as a *matter of fact* I've been having *rather* a rancid time, by the way *do* you remember when we were tots at Beaumanoir that *morose* episode of the *head*-gardener whom we all abhorred, and one night we played *witches* and pretended that one of my dolls was *him* and stuck absolute *pins* into it and wished horrible wishes and finally *burnt* it in the nursery fire, and of course *two* days later the *un*Christian fellow got treble pneumonia and *perished* miserably, my dear I shall *never* forget it I didn't smile for *days*, and of course *ever* since I've utterly *shunned* magic, however about a fortnight ago darling, I forget if I told you, I went with Haddock to a 'surprise' party at Mew-mew's, and my dear *to* my horror I found it was one of those synthetic *thirteen* parties *you* know my dear where you do everything *unlucky* you can think of, well of course my *first* instinct was to fly, because my dear I'm *too* superstitious, well I can *just* walk under a ladder if urgent, but I do *not* go about looking for ladders if you see what I mean, and Haddock rather agrees, however of course Mew-mew said the whole thirteen idea would be shattered if there were only eleven, and my dear *then* it turned out that that Mrs Green was one of the party, *after* which Haddock was *much* less reluctant, so what with everything I said I'd go through with the agony because I always believe in *grasping* the nettles of this nettlesome life, don't you darling?

Well my dear the whole thing was *too* provocative, they gave each of us '13' brooches and *necklaces* of opals and little cocked hats in the *most* unlucky green, we walked into dinner under a *green* ladder with Florio's band playing *all* the inauspicious tunes there are and my dear a *mechanical* magpie fluttering on the left, well when we sat down we found *all* the knives crossed and the *hugest* salt-cellar in front of everybody to upset, and my dear the curtains weren't drawn so the *whole* time you could see the new moon through *glass* which of course is *too* unpropitious, well my dear the first thing was that we *all* had to utterly *upset* the salt-cellars and *not* throw any over the shoulder but *help* your neighbour to salt instead which you know is a *deadly* thing to do, my dear I was *emerald* with aprehension and of course the *really* unlucky thing for me was the *intense* proximity of Mrs Green, who my dear was *next* to Haddock, while I had *Mr* Green and a perfectly *deciduous* youth who the whole time *ecstasised* about the Russian Ballet, my dear he could *think* of nothing but a single ankle-waggle which Calomelovksa or somebody used to do in *Apéritifs*, which left me *too* lukewarm especially as every two minutes one had to do some *injurious* act, my dear the butler brought us each a cameo looking-glass which we had to utterly *smash* with a hammer and throw into a basket, well my dear that was *merely* more than I could face, because my dear *seven* years is *rather* much, isn't it, so I *missed* my mirror and slipped it into the basket *unshattered*, only of course Mew-mew was *too* nosy about shirking and everything so she *inspected* the fragments and found mine and it all came out and I had to, my dear *too* humbling, and of course what was such *vinegar* was that *there* I was my dear chattering with terror and moony with boredom about the Russian Ballet but all the time Haddock was quite *swimming* in the liquid eyes of the Green siren, and my dear having *such* fun that he didn't care *what* he did, my dear mutilating looking-glasses right and left and *dissipating* the salt and utterly bubbling with ill-omened quotations from Macbeth or something and of course the *solitary* balm was that instead of drinking to people's *good* health and everything it was the done thing to utterly *curse* them, though of course *quite* jocular, so my dear you should have heard me *showering* ill wishes at the Green attractor and *meaning* every word.

Well my dear and so the *ghoulish* meal dragged on, my dear we sang *Three* Blind Mice and lit *three* cigarettes with one match, and said optimistic things without *ever* touching wood, and they brought in a *live* peacock, my dear I don't know how the others felt really, but as for me all the *feasible* misfortunes merely thronged in the little brain, and of course you know that *if* you're thirteen it's the first person who gets up perishes or something, well my dear I was *quite* determined that whatever happened it wouldn't be *me*, because my dear there *are* limits, and I think perhaps Mew-mew had the same idea, anyhow *when* she caught the eye of the females we both *began* to get up and then subsided swiftly and looked for lipsticks under the table, with the *result* my dear that the *Green* thing was *quite* the first riser, my dear *too* malignant, but I thought no more of it and after a few tiresome unlucky games I tore Haddock away and *speeded* home, *expecting* my dear to find the *house* in flames and the bailiffs *massing* round the ruins, however all was reasonably tranquil, except that all the *dankest* people in London had rung up meanwhile and asked us to dinner, and as a matter-of-fact for a brief space afterwards the gods seemed to really be rather on the Haddock side in one or two ways, and my dear *Mew-mew* says she's backed *nothing* but winners since and *all* her shares have gone to twenty-seven *eighths* or something.

But my dear *what* was my horror, well when I tell you that a few days later Haddock came in with a *church-yard* countenance and said that Mrs Green had gone into a Home and was *at* that moment *discarding* her appendix, my dear *imagine* the condition of the guilty bosom, because of course I saw absolute *visions* of your innocent little Top decorating the dock and suspended from *giblets*, because I was *quite* satisfied she'd have peritonitis or blacken my life by dying under the dope, and of course the *savage* thing was that we couldn't *approach* the creature for two days, my dear I went about *wilting* from policemen and took to reading poetry in bed, which Mew-mew says is always a bad sign, and of course I *couldn't* tell Haddock about my *acute* conscience-trouble while of course *he* thought it was *too* Christian of me to be so concerned about the witch, my *dear* how I suffered, well the *second* she was visible I bought *all* the grapes in the Metropolis and van-loads of flowers and rushed to the bedside, and my dear *there* she was looking frail and enchanting in a *cloud* of hair, but of course heartlessly *well*, my dear no *tubes* or complications or anything and not a sign of slipping starward, however I didn't trust her an inch, because I know the type, my dear I was too sure she'd have relapses and quietly *drift* away, so of course *ever* since I've been like a guardian bee about the sacred bed, my dear busy with *books* and *scent* and *sweetmeats*, my dear I rang up twice nightly and I sat with her for *weeks*, *too* jading, because my dear you know what an *advantage* an operation gives a girl particularly if you can look like a tropical *lily* on the pillow, my dear that sort of *succulent* allure like *printed* velvet, *too* lush, and of course those *lavender* eyes, my dear I do *not* blame Haddock a *fraction*, only of course *he* didn't see much of the magnet poor dupe because there were always platoons of men in the queue, however she and I became *too* fraternal and kissed like *bosoms*, only of course *when* she talked about *how* to manage Haddock and everything it was *rather* torment because I had to sit there and merely *beam* at the little afflicted angel while of course utterly *aching* to tear her from the bed and *beat* her, however my dear all's well etc. because she's going home today I think, but my dear that's the *last* time I play the wanton with superstition and everything or wish the *flimsiest* harm to my foulest enemy. *Later*, O *gosh*, darling I've just rung up and what *do* you think, the witch has gone and got *complications* and the temperature's bounding, my dear that's *just* like her, I *know* she'll die on me, my dear I must fly and get a *hundredweight* of grapes, *what* a life farewell now and pity your palping little homicide, TOPSY.

19 Converts the Councillor

Trix my little ring-dove it's *too* sensational I've *practically* converted *Councillor* Mule to *moderate* sanity well my dear I *know* I told you about my rather *skunkish* conduct at the Salamander dinner, well my dear he was *so* beflattened that the little *feminine* heart was *totally* melted, and besides it's *quite* my policy to conciliate rather than *inflame* the foe, that is of course if they're not too *utterly* impalpable, because my dear that *is* after all the absolute cream and *redolence* of practical politics, well don't you agree darling, anyhow *soon* after that in a fit of *girlish* remorse I *invited* the repugnant person to *dine* at the House and mutually examine the *comparative* absence of cordiality between us, and my dear I apologised *winningly* for my *rather* cod-like behaviour at Burbleton but adding of course that *quite* nothing but his *abnormal* toadery could have provoked a gentlegirl to *such* proceedings, anyhow he came and of course my dear you can say what you like about *despising* politics but there *is* just *something* about the House of Commons which utterly disarms the ravening lion, my dear I've seen *constituents* come there quite *oozing* at the ears with poison and splutter, my dear *too* Vesuvial, and they *go* away like performing pigeons, but my dear whether it's the architecture or the girlish charm, anyhow the *Mule* came and he *wolfed* his whitebait and adored the *entrée*, my dear the food was *uneatable* as usual but he knew no better, and of course I introduced him to everybody who came in, my dear *Councillor* Mule the Burbleton Dynamo, which gave *definite* pleasure though rather bewildered because I made most of them Lords or Cabinet Ministers, so that *about* the savoury the iceberg melted and it came out that he was *faintly* wounded with his own fanaticals because it seemed there'd been sulphuric whisperings and utter innuendoes in the camp, my dear I gather it was *even* suggested that he'd *rather* surrendered to *my* pagan fascinations, anyhow I was *too* compassionate but tactful darling, well I *merely* said Well it *only* shows you, and *what* a warning to have *no* truck with the fanatical fowl, and so we parted in a sort of *septical* neutrality.

However my dear strike while the victim's *tottering* is my motto, so my dear to Haddock's *intense* reluctance I invited the Mule to stay the New Year week-end with us, my dear the *suffering*, but of course I wanted to show him how *too* innocuous are the worldly pleasures which *so* upset the tribe of Salamander, so we took him to one of the more *ascetical* nightclubs where the sole sign of revelry is the hoarse laughter of the police, and of course he expected to see *drugs* and *dice* and *debauchery* and *drinks*, and *vampires* and bat-women and *carnal* dancing, but of course what he *did* see was a few *stilted* suburbans doing *clockwork* waltzes in *slow* time and a few *austere* theatricals drinking *coffee* and orange-juice because it was after hours, and my dear the whole thing like a choir-treat which is *not* going *too* well, well my dear I introduced him to Bryan Bare and his lady who my dear are in *Ibsen* just now and they were eating a *dangerous* kipper after the labours of the day and we discussed the *Repertory* Movement and the influence of *Checkov* or somebody and *what* is genius and *has* Music a *meaning* and everything, my dear, you never *heard* such *ventrifugal* talk and as for the Mule, well my dear Brian and Pearl explained that they *never* could eat before doing a high-brow play because it turned the food sour and they had *agonies* of heartburn in the fourth or fifth Act, and just then Miles Anderson came in who my dear is on one of the papers and had missed his dinner through having to write the *longest* leader about the *Church* crisis, and also Twiggy Marlow and Marion Flake who'd been rehearsing a film without food since daybreak, so they all had kippers which of course was all *rather* tuneful and opportune darling, because as I observed to the Mule there *are* people who practically *have* to eat at midnight, and anyhow why *not*, because *what* has it got to do with anyone else, well the Mule *quite* concurred and Pearl was *too* benignant to him because I *think* she thought he was a *wealthy* cotton spinner going to put *money* into the Drama, and meanwhile the atmosphere of kipper was *so* pervading that even the Mule succumbed and kippered, and my dear *such* is the effect when Pearl turns on her *plausible* little lamps that by about half-way through the *second* kipper his *whole* life-policy about actresses had changed, and he'd *quite* decided to have Repertory Movements *all over* Burbleton and Pearl had promised him an absolute *box* for *Ibsen*, and that my dear was absolutely *that*.

Well my dear on Sunday *flushed* with triumph I proceeded with the selfless mission and took him to a *Sunday* Concert of *Good Music*, my dear *too* lowering, especially as Haddock declined to come because he said there *were* limits, anyhow we two went and my dear I could have screamed with lassitude, my dear the *most* amorphous little *German* songs and *protuberant* contralto women sort of *heaving* about *fairies*, and *anæmic* Andantes and things on the piano, my dear I *swear* to you there wasn't the *taint* of a tune from beginning to end, however as I said to the Mule there *are* people who openly *enjoy* that sort of noise, and *if* so why *not*, because it does *nobody* a mischief but of course in Burbleton *all* music is *too* illegal on Sunday, anyhow my dear tireless in well-doing *that* evening I took him to the *nearest* cinema, and my dear *all* this time by the way the melting monster was *rather* beginning to *rather* like me because of course he's accustomed to the *sourest* females, well there was the *most* uplifting film about a business man who *utterly* made good and didn't go off with the stenographer after all because at the *critical* moment he *suddenly* remembered his mother's knee and how he was taught the *Catechism* and everything, my dear *pure* suet but of course the Councillor was *too* impressed, and my dear we were *quite* surrounded by the *tender* proletariat, so I said *how* much better for the great heart of the people to be able to *hold* hands in here and see a film with an *antiseptic* message instead of having to cuddle in passages or crawl about the streets clicking or merely *dwindle* into the pub like they do at Burbleton, well he said there was something in that only of course they oughtn't to want to hold hands on Sunday, so I said not before lunch perhaps but if they'd been to church in the morning a little *Platonic* clinging at the pictures in the evening wasn't a menace and he said *Too* right but *had* they?

However my dear the change in him was quite *chemical*, because every *hour* he was away from the vinegar-women of Burbleton (West) he *increased* in charity and *loving-kindness*, and my dear the last night we *quite* persuaded him to make a *personal* visit to the *Black* Swan which my dear is the *most* darling old pub round the corner with a *floral* garden where they have the *most* medieval *skittle* alley at the back and Haddock's the absolute *President* of the Skittles Club and thinks he's *too* important, well of course they have *Associations* and matches and things and *that* night there was a match between the Black Swan and the *Full* Moon, and my dear it's like the *most* County cricket, you can hear a *germ* breathe, and my dear I don't really understand it but I do try, anyhow they play 8 a side or perhaps it's 9 and they have 9 sort of *nine*-pins, unless it's 8, and it's all *too* athletic and scientific, because they throw the heaviest kind of flat round thing which my dear is called a *cheese*, and my dear the *real* throb is when they knock *all* the 8 9-pins down with *utterly* one blow of course it's all rather like *golf* really only I can't explain, anyhow they're the *most* cordial and disarming fellows and *too* sober because of course you can't throw a cheese straight otherwise, however of course there was *beer* and my dear in the interval we had *pickled* onions and *bread* and gherkins, consumed in the fingers, my dear *too* democratic, well the Black Swan won and my dear last year it seems they won a *silver* cup, anyhow there were cheers and speeches, *too* Eton and Harrow, and my dear the Mule sat *gaping* because of course his *one* idea was that *nothing* happens in a pub but *alcohol*, and my dear knowing nothing of his *repugnant* past they were *too* sweet to him, because my dear they're *Nature's* gentlemen, and the Captain asked him to make a speech, and what with the New Year and goodwill flowing to such an extent he *actually* gulped a *glass* of beer, after which my dear we took him home to bed, and this morning darling he said he'd had his *life's* holiday, so I said Well *darling* Councillor *do* try to think more about the pleasures of the people and a *little* less about the ideas of the *Aunts*, and he said he definitely would because he said his eyes had been *quite* opened and henceforth he'd be a *complete* moderate like me, and *then* darling the obese old thing utterly *kissed* my hand, *rather* moving my dear because I do believe that the life of Burbleton is going to be changed for the brighter, *all* owing darling to your *laborious* little TOPSY.

20 Starts A Salon

Trix my little sunrise you were *rather* a toad not to come down for my *inaugural* salon, however of course if the foxes are becoming *such* a menace that you can't spare a *single* day from *nobly* destroying the same of course I *quite* understand, only what I *do* say is *why* not do the thing *scientifically* darling, because what *is* the use of *modern* artillery and *poison gas* and everything if you have to spend absolute *months* of the year *defending* the poor farmers and have *quite* no intercourse with your own true friend?

However *your* loss my dear, because really it was the *century's* party, though not *quite* according to *plan* perhaps, well my dear I've *always* meant to have an *absolute* salon but of course *too* original and not all this *undiluted* peerage-cum-politics stuff, because my dear you know what *most* of these Cadogan crushes are like, my dear nothing but *sedative* Under-Secretaries and the *teeming* daughters of the *danker* Duchesses, my dear you'd *think* that *politics* was the *one* thing that anybody *did*, whereas of course only about *one* Briton in every thousand ever *thinks* of the things, and of course they all *hover* about in *Garters* and Decorations and whisper *municipal* jokes about the *Local* Government Bill, anyhow I was *too* determined that my salon should be *quite* heteraneous and *representative*, so my dear I had sort of *two* parties in one, well first I asked all the *right* people my dear *Ministers* and *Whips* and *all* the congenial KCB's and *quite* unmarriageable Belgrave beauties, and *then* I asked a herd of *unCadogan* but first-prize people, my dear editors and barristers and doctors and *novelists* and ARNOLD BENNETT and everything, and also about ten of the *most* vociferous Labour Members, my dear MAXTON and KIRKWOOD are *Nature's* lambs when you know them, and then a perfect *shoal* of rather *Bohemian* people acquainted with Haddock, my dear actors and actresses and the *shaggiest* painters, of course *utterly* respectable up to a point but definitely *tainted* with the arts

and in fact most of them *rather* living by their *wits*, as they say
rodently in the police-courts, however well anyhow Mum let me
have the feudal home for the night and for the sake of harmony
we *bisected* same and we labelled that *desert* of a drawing-room
Olympus which was Haddock's idea and Mum's sort of Studio-
music-room beyond it we called *Arcadia*, and of course *Olympus*
was intended for the Blue Blood and Garter Brigade, where my
dear I had *gold* chairs from the Stores and the *most* ranunculous
orchestra who played *ethereal* chamber music by a man called
Spotti or *Batti* or something, and of course *no* food but the
most invisible sandwiches and a *rather* anæmic claret-cup, so
that in between these ghastly sonatas and things the Orders
and Decorations could stand about like animated waxworks
and discuss the Housing of the People Act and your *bromidical*
hunting-stuff in the usual salonical way, but of course anybody
who was *too* alienated could creep off into Arcadia, where my
dear the commisariat was sausages, vulgar my dear but *quite* hot,
with *mash* and everything, not to mention a *degraded* barrel of
Lager Beer, of course sausage-parties are the done thing now, but
I've been giving them for *simply* years, and of course cushions on
the floor for the seats of the weary, and my dear the *quaintest*
girl called ELSA LANCHESTER who sings those *bizarre* songs
of the Albert Epoch and does low life and everything, *rather* a
melodious arrangement don't you think darling?

Well anyhow at first it worked *too* flawlessly my dear the
PRIME came as a *unique* favour because of course he utterly
shuns parties, but I'd told him it was *quite* likely it would turn out
to be a pipe party in the end, also WINSTON and H G WELLS
and quite *herds* of highlights, my dear I can't tell you the crush
was cruel and the tiaras *blinding*, but of course nearly all the
Haddock contingent took *one* look at the Duchesses and things
and *slunk* on into the other room, likewise the Labour lads, who
my dear I'd told particularly not to dress unless they wanted, and
only my *rugged* KIRKWOOD stayed behind and had the *maddest*
argument with ELLEN WILKINSON who my dear is rather a
bosom of mine these days because she's the *most* miniature and

sagacious little witch with the *most* ornamental hair, my dear *too* auburn, well my dear our minds are gloves about nearly *quite* everything and we'd *just* agreed that Spotti's music was *too* meagre and *tinklinabulous* when suddenly I *looked* round and found that the room was *half*-empty, imagine my horror, because my dear the PRIME had vanished and WINSTON and everybody and of course I thought O gosh the Spotti sonatas have *revolted* the Cabinet, but my dear at *that* moment in rushes Haddock in an *emotional* state and says *All* is lost because the *sausages* are running out, sensation darling!

Because of course I *knew* I'd ordered enough sausages to feed the *entire* tribes of Bohemia and Bloomsbury, however I *cataracted* out into the other room, and there *what* do you think, my dear *more* than half of the haughty Cadoganry had *slunk* away and joined up with Bohemia and there they were my dear, *golloping* sausages with ill-concealed ecstasy, my dear as if they'd *quite* never had food before, *Garters* darling *tiaras* and all, my dear *too* unsuitable, there likewise also was my dearly-beloved PRIME merely squatting on a cushion against the wall, puffing at the old pipe and looking *far* far happier than I ever saw him before, because my dear *quite* nobody was paying the *tiniest* attention to him which must be *pure* balm to a PRIME don't you think, in fact I saw one of the hairier Nohomians go up and ask him for a *cigarette* of all things thus *rather* demonstrating my dear that he'd *no* idea who the gentleman *was*, and my dear you should have *seen* the PRIME's seraphical smile when he realised that at *last* nobody wanted to get *anything* out of him except a cigarette which he *couldn't* supply, well my dear there too also were WINSTON and H G WELLS and the LORD CHANCELLOR in the silkiest breeches because he'd *just* come from the Woolsack or somewhere, all clutching *sausages* darling and *too* engrossed in the LANCHESTER girl who was singing the *most* plebeian song about charwomen or something which Haddock wrote for her, only of course meanwhile the *sausage* situation was *too* precarious so I fled to the kitchen and organised a kipper or two, and my dear *when* I got back the party was in *full* flower because they'd started dancing and of course the *one* canker was that the *withered* orchestra in the *other* room were still *grimly* playing the *vegetarian* compositions of Spotti and Batti to about seven depressed Dowagers and Charles Street chaperons who were repelled by sausages and would keep sending *sulphuric* messages to their wandering girls who of course were utterly *embedded* in Bohemia, however having extracted and evacuated same I comforted the musicians with *mundane* refreshment and the party settled down to a *flawless* rhythm, I had a dance with WINSTON, my dear *too* vigorous, and then we had the *world's* chic cabaret, my dear ARNOLD BENNETT sang the *sweetest* song about a youth and a maid sucking cyder through a straw or something, and MAXTON did his piratical turn, and Haddock sang a *deplorable* ditty my dear I can't *tell* you and NANCY imitated a hunting *peer*, and crowds of others only I can't remember, and of course *simply* everybody got on with *quite* everybody, my dear you saw the *strangest* couples, *Tories* and Socialists, theatricals and KCB's, and my dear *there* sat the PRIME all beams and baccy, sort of presiding happily over a *united* nation, because really my dear it *only* shows you what *comparative* flip-flap politics *is*, because you *merely* need a little sausage and bonhomie and the heart of the Empire utterly beats as *one*, anyhow they all said it was a *historical* party and *my* salon darling's going to always be *quite* miscellaneous, farewell now your rather *exhausted* TOPSY.

21 Trouble In The Home

O Trix my fortunate spinster I've had an *epileptic* day and I *must* unload the lacerated soul, of course the *truth* is that the *throes* of being a public woman are quite enough for one mortal my dear *without* having to cope with a *private* life to boot, and my dear I'm *beginning* to think there *may* be something in all that *avunculous* chat about *woman's* place being in the home and not in the House, and *what's* to happen when the twins arrive if any, I shall have to utterly *park* them somewhere or retire to the Chiltern Hundreds or something.

Well my dear it *began* at 9.0 this morning when I had to *sack* the cook, my dear *agony*, or rather it began about *1.0* this morning when Haddock started to *read* in bed, because my dear you know I'm utterly for self-determination and everything but I *have* begun recently to rather *mould* my Haddock, only my dear he's *rather* unplastic I find and he has the *most* unorthodox habits, of course I know that writers are never *too* normal but I do think the mate of a public woman ought to shave when he gets up instead of just before *lunch*, don't you darling, only of course I do *rather* sympathize because I'm *never* conscious till an hour after breakfast myself, and my dear the *torment* of ordering meals in an *utter* stupor, however then there are his clothes, of course since we were blighted I've *insisted* on his having *two* suits but my dear in *three* days he can make the *newest* suit look like a bagful of *bulbs*, because my dear he puts *all* he possesses in the pockets and *all* the letters he's ever received, my dear his note-case is one *protuberant* mass of *everything* except notes, so about *once* a week I have a *bird's-nesting* day and ruthlessly evacuate the *loose* tobacco *and* pipe-cleaners and *patent* medicines and *pieces* of string, my dear *too* miscellaneous, and then my dear he's *indecently* untidy about the house, my dear he leaves everything *quite* everywhere, my dear there are always *pipes* in the bathroom and pyjama-fragments in the dining-room, and little *deposits* of tobacco all over the house, I have to sort of follow him about like one of those *mechanical* reapers *picking* up the sheaves, and of course the staff gets more and more subversive, and my dear the cook has been *too* democratic about *late* meals and because Haddock will burgle the larder and *mutilate* the cold bird at midnight, so my dear *yesterday* I utterly determined to hand the harpy her passport and give Haddock rather a *lecture*, because my dear for the first few months the best brides *procrastinate* somewhat, but there comes a moment when one has to merely assert the little self as you'll find darling.

However easier said than done, because my dear I was *all* prepared with a rather *moving* little homily when Haddock bounded into bed and said *Did* I mind if he finished his *book* which was that *Octopus* book I told you about, well my dear I was *rather* wounded because my dear he's never read in bed *before*, of course we *both* read at meals if we're alone which is rather a *sagacious* habit don't you think my dear we sit and masticate *too* mutely over blood-yarns and the like, and I'm *quite* sure that if *all* connubial couples, however when it comes to reading in *bed*, because my dear after the bath and the breathing exercises that's *just* the time the little brain is *utterly* prolific, my dear I *burgeon* with ideas and luminous hypothesises, my dear *what* a word, because sometimes I've made notes of the absolute *theories* I've had on the snowy pillow and in the morning they're *too* inspired still, so you see one rather *counts* on Haddock to be *rather* receptive just then, well my dear as usual my *worminous* good-nature betrayed me and I said *Too* welcome, and of course meanwhile such was the shock and chagrin I'd *quite* forgotten about the *lecture* darling, however never go back on your word when dealing with a child or husband, so I lay quiet and suffered, my dear *rather* pathetic because I had a *sudden* attack of *morbid* wisteria if you know what I mean, well I *quite* felt that this perhaps was the absolute *beginning* of the end, my dear I must have been dormatose because I sort of looked down the vistas of the years and saw Haddock reading the *whole* of the *Encyclopedia Britannica* for *quite* ever and *me* my dear lying *neglected* under the first five volumes, however I *bore* the vision for a long time bravely, my dear with scarcely a *sigh* or a weary turn-over, which is what I sometimes do when in the martyr-mood darling, because anyhow Haddock was too impervious, my dear perfectly *embedded* in architecture, and at last my dear I suddenly found myself *whimpering* mouldily into the dewy pillow, well then of course he was *too* concerned and utterly *flung* the Octopus away, only as luck would have it I rather *blurted* out a few puss-remarks about that Mrs Green, who my dear was at the Antons' the other day and of course a *whole* week-end gave me *rather* spleen-trouble because my dear she *is* magical, only thanks be Haddock doesn't like her new hair-policy, my dear *drawn* back and the ears naked, the woman's *moony*, with *that* face, however the *igmonious* thing was that I'd *quite* intended to be *too* Christian only I wasn't, so we had rather a *tropical* little talk, my dear utterly harmonious in the end of *course* only what with the vipers of remorse and remembering *all* the things I *ought* to have said I *merely* didn't close the eyes till those garrulous birds began their *redundant* anthem to the dawn and everything, while of course *Haddock* slept the entire night like a *new* kitten only noisily, my dear *too* insouciant, that's men all over darling.

Well my dear blithe virgin that you are, *imagine* after a night of suffering having to *totter* kitchenward and sack your *first* cook, my dear feeling *exactly* similar to an *under-done* egg, my dear *no* solidity and *liquid* at the top, of course there's *no* doubt that I'm *far* too Christian for this world darling, because my dear she's *behaved* like a beetle, her *cooking's* primeval, she *banquets* the tradesmen, she has *pains* in the back and sides and will *not* do the doorstep properly, my dear *forgive* these utterly *plebeian* details but that's the holy estate of *matrimony*, anyhow I was *quite* macadamous and I drifted in like a *relentless* jelly-fish with the cruel words *tip-toe* on the little tongue, only of course she *would* choose *this* morning to be *too* boracic, my dear *no* pains in the back and *yearning* to do my *favourite* casserole and looking forward to *Easter*, and my dear *mock* and corrode as you will but I was *totally* disarmed, and of course she was our absolutely *first* cook and welcomed the bride home and everything, anyhow I was feeling *such* putty that I postponed the *whole* thing till lunchtime, well then my dear *Taffeta* Mole must ring up and say she's not the right temperature and can't function today, so my dear Haddock having gone out rather *tersely* to a publisher I had to face the *whole* correspondence of Burbleton under my own steam, and my dear I was *just* mastering the *most* suggestive letter from the Vigilance Committee about *three* girl stowaways who went to South America or Bristol or somewhere when *up* comes Hetty to say the *scullery-drain's* stopped up and Annie's come over *queer*, my dear how I *abhor* women.

Well I telephoned *tenaciously* and was put on to everyone in London except a plumber, and of course meanwhile that *demented* fellow came from Fluke's about the dining-room chairs, my dear he's *nailed* on my *unpriceable* tapestry *upside-down*, however I hunted the girl to bed with aspirins and menaces and *rang* up specialists and of course *when* a man arrived to *tune* the piano I merely *babbled* at him, my dear I felt like a *congested* pin-cushion and one more stab made utterly no difference, well it turned out that Annie had *scarlet*-fever and of course *at* that moment it's announced that *all* the water's to be turned off and they've got to *excavate* the street, so my dear we had *cold* mutton for lunch which is Haddock's *pet* horror, the cook came up and was *too* ungenial because she said there was damp in the house, and my dear *having* lost Annie so far from *sacking* the adder I had to utterly *raise* her wages, and of course the *whole* time that bestial fellow was *torturing* the piano, well then Haddock comes back and says brightly that he's *just* run into Mrs Green on the Tube, however darling *don't* think I'm *weakening* or anything, *only* I think perhaps sometimes when a virgin rather aches for the altar she doesn't quite visualise the *wintry* future, and I think there may be something *quite* consoling about being an old maid, however tomorrow doubtless I shall be your own sunny bubble again, so farewell now your rather *tragical* TOPSY.

22 Asks Questions

Well Trix my little gilliflower it's *rather* a throb, you remember last November I told you about the *hat-trouble* I had in the House owing to some *babyish* rule about raising a point of order *sitting* down with a *hat* on and I hadn't a hat, well my dear now the Speaker has *scotched* the said rule so I haven't *quite* lived in vain, however I *do* believe I'm going to *lose* the Whip, my dear I'm *too* unloved, because well the House is quite *gangrenously* boring at present, my dear they *drone* along with these *suety* Government Bills which *nobody* understands except the *Civil* Servants who are the absolute *kings* of the castle these days, my dear Haddock says we're not a limited monarchy or democracy or anything any longer but an unlimited *burocracy*, though I don't suppose *that* will keep you awake darling anyhow the *private* Members can do *quite* nothing except *waddle* through the Lobbies *whenever* the bell rings like perfectly drilled ducks, except of course that we're not allowed to *quack*, and my dear it's all very well for the Gov to say they must have *all* the time for their *adipose* Bills, but what they don't seem to realise is that if they can't keep the *Members* interested in the mouldy Parliament how *can* they expect the man-in-the-Tube to be, and the *nude* truth is that *nothing* people talk about in the home is ever *mentioned* in the House, well my dear you remember what *mustard* I was to begin with but of course now I merely *trickle* into the place about as brightly as a stagnant pond, and almost my *one* amusement is to *suddenly* crash into the Smoking-Room and see *all* the male legislators dry up with their mouths open in the middle of a *masculine* story, my dear *too* unwelcome.

However darling even that's rather a *palling* pleasure and I thought that *somehow* I must get my money's worth out of the club so I've taken to *tormenting* the man HICKS with *Parliamentary* questions, of course I know you think I'm moony about HICKS, and people keep *goading* me to *leave* him alone, but my dear he's like a *baby* the *moment* you leave him alone he does something *too* ghastly, my dear I hadn't *uttered* about him for *weeks* when suddenly he erupted with three perfectly *flatulent* speeches about Dora being *dead*, and of course the very same day I saw a man was fined because the number-plates on his car were too *large*, and also a *stainless* publican was prosecuted *merely* darling because somebody played the piano in the *bar* and the criminals present joined in the *chorus* and the man hadn't a *music*-licence and of course there were *three* detectives sniffing *busily* at the window, can you *see* the picture, so *English* darling, because my dear it seems if one man sings at the piano it's *too* lawful but if *three* men sing it's felonious, well darling I put down a question about this mean and *smelly* affair and HICKS as usual said it was the *law* of the land and he couldn't interfere, so my dear I started *pelting* the person with *Supplementaries*, and I said Well if *that's* the law had he taken *any* steps to have it altered during the last four *years*, and he took six words to say *No* as the *loquacious* custom is, so I said *Is* it not a fact that the *sole offence* in this case was that people were *enjoying themselves* and did he *still* think Dora was *dead* and he said Certainly, so I said Well *does* the Right Honourable HICKS know the song about John Brown's body lies a-mouldering in the grave but his *soul* goes utterly *marching* on, because my dear *that* is the crystal point and of course the *whole* House broke into a *bronchial* cheer and Auntie refused to answer, though I thought the discomforture was *too* too noticeable.

Well my dear *thus* heartened I made the holiest kind of *vow* to ask him at *least* one question a day, though of course it's all *so* difficult, because you have to submit *every* question to the *Clerk* at the Table who is perfectly encrusted with the *most* kindergarten *rules*, well you *mayn't* ask a question which is *hypothetical* or a statement of *fact*, or contains arguments or inferences or imputations or *epithets* or controversial or ironical expressions, which doesn't leave *much* well *does* it darling, for instance if I put down a question like this

> To ask the Home Secretary if he is not a *well-meaning* but *inflated* solicitor

this *pedantical* Clerk would merely scratch out *well-meaning* and *inflated* which of course *are* utterly the *operative words*, my dear how *can* you discuss HICKS *without* using a *sporadic* epithet or two, my dear the man's *too* negative as it is, my dear he's one protracted NO, *too* marvellous at stamping the heavy foot, but *where* is the helping hand, well my dear what *has* he done except *trample* on the pathetic Bishops and *tread* on the Trade Unions and *prance* about on the publishers, *turn* out the Russians by the raid on Arcos and *keep* out the Americans by the raids on the West End, my dear his *one* idea is raids and regulations, my dear as Haddock says he has the *raid-mind*, he is definitely the *Raid*-King, but as for *creating* anything, well my dear you *won't* remember but in 1924 he announced with a *loud* bang that he was going to utterly *clean up* the nightlife of London because of Wembley and the *chaste* Colonials and everything, and my dear *here* he is in 1929 still *loudly* announcing that he is *definitely* going to utterly *clean up* the night-life of London, and the *sole* fruit and blossom of four years' *hysterical* cleaning is that the police are in a *septic* mess, my dear it's *rather* hilarious when you come to think of it, *half* Scotland Yard quite *swearing* before the Police Commission that the police are *too* impeccable and the other half *nose-deep* in the *most* insanitary police scandals, and my dear *do* you remember how *poor* TERENCE O'CONNOR was *stamped upon* by Hicks for merely suggesting that a Metropolitan cop was *capable* of bribery, however, but meanwhile as for Home Affairs, of course you *might* say the Virgins' Vote came out of the Home Office though that was the PRIME really, and I can't think of anything else but the Shop Hours Act which had to be *rammed* down their throats and anyhow was the permanent *incarnation* of Dora, except that you *can* buy chocolates at a theatre now, but my dear it took *ten* years' yapping in the Press to get *that*, my dear that *Department*, it's like an elephant giving birth to a *mouse*, too reluctant, anyhow my *next* question was *How* long has the H S been in charge of Home Affairs and *is* he satisfied with the *festering* condition of our *diseased* Betting Laws, only this *bigot* of a Clerk scratched out *both* festering and diseased which of course was the *entire* gist and *flavour* of the Question, well I appealed to the Speaker and he rejected the *whole* Question because he said it was asking for an expression of *opinion*, my dear *that's* the kind of *Roedean* regulation a public woman has to face, however I altered it to *Has* HICKS done anything during the last four years and does he *propose* to do anything during the next four *months* to reform and codify the BLs, well my dear he *bleated* in the negative as usual, so I said *Doesn't* he think this *malarious* and *national* mess is *more* important than the *night-life* of London, but my dear *too* mute, so the next day I did the same about the *Divorce* Laws and the Licensing Laws and I said *Will* the Right Hon Sec for *Home* Affairs take his mind off *Soho* and get down to the *Home*, because my dear *think* what a real he-fellow could have done in *four* years with *that* majority, so and then the other day I asked *Has* he considered the question of suppressing *Stag-hunting* and he said as usual there was *no* public demand, so then my dear I rather *lost* the little head and I *leaped* up and said *Will* the Right Honourable *Humbug* say if there is any public demand for prosecuting people who play the piano in *pubs*, well *then* darling there was the *most* vociferous scene and I had to *withdraw* Humbug, and now the Whips are at me and I'm getting the *most* malevolent letters, however I'm *too* undeterred because my dear the man's a *menace*, and Haddock's going to utterly *stand* for Twickenham as an Independent and *split* the Tory vote so as to *save* the nation from another Jixennium, *too* right, farewell now your rather unpopular TOPSY.

23 Loses The Whip

Well Trix my rustic little lamb if you *only* knew how I sometimes envy you, *ignoring* the world's news, not caring a *twopenny* hoot about the *Gold* Standard or anything, and *merely* living for the death of the next fox, my dear I *do* see how elemental and satisfying it must be, whereas *here* am I darling *hip*-deep in *acrimony* and correspondence and brain-strain, my dear I *think* I told you how I had *words* with the Whips because I *would* put *sulphuric* Questions to the Right Honourable HICKS, well my dear they said I was *quite* undermining the Cabinet because the *whole* of the Cabinet utterly agreed with me but they thought it was *too* perilous to even discuss my pet questions *however* cardinal, so they wanted them all to be left in a state of purulent placidity till after the Election, my dear *too* pussilanimous, and *especially* it seems because of the *new* virgin voters, though my dear *why* they should think that *all* the flappers are *Nonconformists* and wouldn't like to see some sanitary *Betting* Laws for instance I *merely* can't imagine, however and of course they said that anyhow it was the *done* thing to treat JIX as a joke so I said that's *just* the danger because the man HICKS and his herd were *serious* menaces to the *character* of the race and the *happiness* of the people, my dear *too* eloquent, my dear I do think my *style* is a bit more *dynamic* and fluid than it used to be, don't you, though of course what do you care, well anyhow darling they said if I put down *one* more *irreverent* Question I should definitely *lose* the Whip, but they said if I was honeyed and obedient I might be a Parliamentary Sec or something in the *next* Parliament, and I *rather* gathered I should *probably* rise to Cabinet rank in the first few *weeks*, well darling poor shrinking doe though I am I did *not* propose to be bribed or brow-battered because my dear they knew *too* clearly what the little platform was when I was *elected*, not to mention my Haddock, so the next day I put down the *most* mutinous questions to *half* the Cabinet, I forget what about but *nearly* everything, and sure enough I got the *most* pompifical letter to say that in future I should *not* receive the *Party* Whip, my dear *too* paltry, so I wrote back tersely who *wants* your tiresome Whip, and my dear as a *matter* of fact it *is* rather a *boon* to be Whipless, because normally you have to get absolute *leave* to leave the House, and if they say you *can't* go out to dinner or anything my dear you *merely* can't, *too* galling, but *now* of course I *prance* out airily *whenever* inclined, cocking a *phantom* snook at the Whips as I pass darling, my dear *too* satisfactory.

However my dear what I *faintly* forgot was my obese and woolly-witted *constituency*, because of course the faithful commons of Burbleton are *always* titilated to see their little Member in the papers, *whatever* she does, but my dear my *Executive* Committee, being all *quite* circular and medieval were *too* unamused, because they said it meant they were practically *de*-franchised and anyhow it was giving Burbleton (West) a *bad* name, my dear *too* sensitive, and anyhow it's *rather* a tender moment because everyone's busy *adopting* candidates for this *promiscuous* General Election, and my dear it seems there's a *toxic* clique on the Executive which is *beavering* away to have a *pursy* businessman called *Poop* instead of me, my dear *too* rotund but merely *dripping* with dividends and bonds and things, so they've been quite *nosing* about in what they call my *record*, my dear totting up my *divisions* and speeches and everything, and likewise of course, and my dear *this* is the *real* rankle, how much *money* I've spent in the blood-sucking Borough, because *between* you and I darling we haven't spent *too* much, not *having* too much, and my dear it was an absolute *plank* in the little platform at the *Bye*-Election that they were *not* to regard me as a kind of *milch*-elephant like most of the Tories, because I said if you *must* have *clubs* and *bazaars* and *new* wings to the library and everything I'm *too* throbbed about it but you'll have to pay for them *yourselves*, because I said *my* motto and maxiom is *service* not *shekels*, so don't elect *me* if *what* you want is an animated *cash-box*, which of course is *exactly* what they *do* want, and *that* my dear is going to be the *penultimate* bane of the *Conservative*

Party, my dear they *expect* their Member to be a sort of *Fairy Godmother*, with birthdays *weekly*, however to continue the sombre story I was summoned to Burbleton to give an account of myself at a sort of *secret* Inquisition, where my dear it was hinted *too* nudely that I should have to *spend* better and behave more *balmily*, because my dear *another* complication is that now I'm in such *swampy* odour with the Whips and Government the *Central* Office are *threatening* delicately that *funds* perhaps will *not* be forthcoming at the *next* Election like they did at the last, my dear *too* despotical, because *that* of course has *radically* shaken some of my orbicular Committee, so that what with everything unless I become both *rich* and respectable it *rather* looks as if the *next* Member will be Sir *Horace* Poop, who sells bowler-hats and hose darling and *already* I gather has *busily* manured the entire constituency with *life*-subscriptions and *new* wings and has quite *sworn* to build chapels and wash-houses *all* over Burbleton, well of course it's all *too* salubrious for Burbleton, but my dear what *is* the good of my poor little PRIME making those *sweet* speeches about yearning for *Youth* in the Party if any mature but *mindless* merchant is allowed to *buy* a constituency with *two* chapels and a public *lavatory*?

However my dear I *faced* up to them after dinner like a hen-bison at bay darling in the *arresting* black-and-gold I told you about, and Haddock says looking *rather* like the Queen of Sheba at the *first* Solomon party, anyhow whether it was the frock, my dear there's the *phantom* touch of a *hoop* in the skirt which gives a *dominant* effect but at the same time rather a *nun-like* note, if you know what I mean, and I carried a fan for imperious *gestures*, well I told them tersely my *compassionate* opinion about them and the Poop creature, and I said If you *want* a dead hatter *have* Horace by all means, and if you want a live Member behold your *immutable* Topsy, but *don't* expect any free sewers or public brine-baths from *me*, well don't you think I was *right* darling?

Anyhow my dear a little on the *cowed* side they agreed to a sort of *armistice*, and I think all would have been well, only *meanwhile* my dear I've made the *most* luminous but *alienating* speech in the House, my dear we had a debate about Afghanistan and that *fatiguing* ULLAH family, well you *wouldn't* understand darling but it was all about *black* men wearing bowler-hats and *trousers*, well my dear I *rose* up and said there ought to be an *absolute* law of the League of Nations to stamp out the trouser traffic, and I said all these *missionaries* and people ought to be *too* discouraged who go about the fair places of the earth spreading *plus* fours and *braces* and celluloid collars, because my dear it *only* means that the *blameless* black man gets *tuberculosis* and a *swelled* head, but my dear *when* I tell you that Burbleton *mainly* exists by exporting bowler-hats and trousers and other *degrading* garments to the innocent blacks you'll understand that I've *rather* inserted the pretty little foot again, and you'll also gather the *kind* of bunkers which beset the course of an *independent* girl not constructed to pattern, my dear the *only* thing these days is to be *mass*-produced, farewell now your *excommunicated* little TOPSY.

24 Trouble In The House

Trix my sweet bosom this is going to be rather a *difficult* letter, yes I *know* it's a long while since the last one anyhow, but *don't* be carbolic with me, because my dear the *fact* is, O gosh I can't tell you even *now*, well as a *matter* of fact, I've been *deceiving* you for some time, because my dear I don't know why but I *merely* couldn't tell you, and even now the very *ink* is blushing, well darling the *truth* is I *am* going to have *twins*, well when I say twins the doctor doesn't *know* for certain, but I've told him it *is* twins *definitely* because I've always said it would be didn't I darling, anyhow don't be alarmed because it isn't for *years* yet, but my dear it is rather radiant and embarassing *isn't* it, of course I know it's happened to *herds* of other people but somehow it didn't seem quite like *me*, and my dear the whole thing seems to me rather old-world and *gauche*, don't you think, because what *is* the good of all this *science* and stuff, my dear *have* you read about EINSTEIN's *new* theory, well of course *nobody* understands it, but it seems he's reducing the *whole* of Nature to about *one* formula my dear x equals y or something because he's proved that *nearly* everything is *quite* the same, well my dear *electricity's* the same as *gravity* and Space is *merely* another name for *Time*, though my dear we did *not* need a German to tell us *that* because haven't we *always* talked about *knocking* a man into the middle of next *week* and everything, and of course you *know* darling *don't* you that you're nothing but a *bundle* of atoms like a table or an ash-tray, so I *suppose* an ash-tray is a bundle of *nerves* like *us*, however my dear *what* I was going to say was that in spite of all this brainery and simplification of the Universe and everything it seems *just* as complex to become a mother as *ever* it was, my dear it's *just* like these *motors* well they can invent a car which does 250 in the heart of the *Sahara* but has to be *towed* on a Christian road, but my dear as for anything *useful* like a *self*-starter which will *start* itself or a wind-screen wiper which will *wipe* the wind-screen for *more* than a minute, my dear not a *hope*.

However my dear one day I suppose we shall be able to step *lightly* into the *fourth* dimension and have babies by algebra with *no* trouble to anyone, but meanwhile darling I've *quite* vowed that I'm *not* going to *crumple* up and disappear *months* too early like the best-bred mothers, because my dear these *poor* proletarians have to continue functioning till the last moment *don't* they, so why not *me*, well my dear I was determined to *cling* to the House as long as feasible, however what's *rather* confused things is that meanwhile darling as perhaps you've seen I've been *confined* in the Clock Tower, *no* darling *no* don't leap to conclusions, I mean *shut* up, *incarcerated*, it's a parliamentary expression, yes I know it all sounds a muddle but that's *just* what it is, but my dear forbear a brief space and all shall be plain, where was I, well my dear I suppose this twin-business may have made me the least bit *hysterical* and balloon-witted lately, anyhow I told you about my trouble with the Whips and the Party popes at Burbleton, and of course seeing the *legions* of the male massing *more* and more against me did *not* tend to placify the combatious little soul, well my dear one day there was a debate about Unemployment and my dear just before I'd shown my *attractive* little Bill to the Clerk at the Table about *making* the LCC have a boat-service on the Thames, which of course is one of Haddock's pet notions and would make *quantities* of work in a small way, anyhow *that* darling is the *kind* of thing that *somebody* ought to do only of course all these *distended* old men have such *rows* of good reasons for *not* doing anything, well the Clerk said my Bill was *frivolously* expressed *and* out of order, so my dear I was *so* saturated with the Government and the medieval male generally that in the *middle* of the debate I *pranced* across the floor and made the *most* spontaneous and lyrical speech from the *Labour* benches, well my dear on *that* subject we *quite* harmonise so *why* not say so, anyhow sensation darling and an *absolute* ovation from the Opposition, well after that I *again* took my wistful Bill to the Clerk and he *again* spurned it, my dear *too* polite of course but I'm *sorry* to say that what with my speech and the twins and everything I *suddenly* saw scarlet and *smote* the man in the face with the said Bill *ferociously*, my dear *too* unrestrained, and it wasn't even *typed* which perhaps made it worse.

Well darling the SPEAKER saw the barbarous act, so of course I was *named* and *suspended* and *expelled* and everything, and what was *rather* poignant my pet Winston had to *move* the motion which he *quite* detested, however *there* I was my dear the *first* girl Member to be suspended, which you might say would be about enough for one woman, only of course you *don't* understand the effect of *twins* darling, and besides it's *too* clear that the *one* way to get things done is to *give* trouble, because my dear the *next* day everyone was saying that I was *too* right about the Thames Boats and the Unemployment Loan and things and I now hear the LCC are at last *stirring* in their sleep, anyhow that afternoon I don't *quite* know why darling but I proceeded *casually* to the House after Questions, *tripped* past the policeman and *took* my seat, my dear *too* unsubordinate, because *that* of course was absolute *contempt* and flouting of the *august* authority and everything, so my dear *quite* rightly I was *committed* for contempt, *arrested* by the Serjeant-at-Arms and *deposited* in the Clock Tower, my dear up 496 stairs *right* under Big Ben in the *most* Arctic and carpetless little room where it seems *nobody's* been put since a man called LABBY, but only for the afternoon my dear to break the little spirit I gather, because of course in these days they'd get *no* servant to carry the meals up 496 stairs, and my dear *one* night of those *revolting* bells just above the bed would send *anyone* moony, so in the evening I was confined in a *civilised* room at the bottom of the Tower till I *purged* my contempt with apologies at the Bar and so forth.

Well darling by this time I was beginning to *somewhat* regret the girlish impetuosity, and I wasn't quite sure that it was all *too* good for the twins, which by the way my dear *nobody* knew about, because so far as usual I've managed to be *too* unusual, so I confess I had a *slight* sob when Haddock came to see me, however my dear torments *and* scorpions could not induce me to *humbly* apologise before 700 male legislators, so on the second day I sent a *polite* note to the Speaker to say I should *never* grovel and I was *too* sorry but if I wasn't released *forthwith* I should linger there tenaciously and have *twins* in the Clock Tower, which would make the Mother of Parliaments look ridiculous for *quite* ever.

Well my dear the result was *utter* panic in the high places, I believe they had a *special* Cabinet Meeting, my doctor was sent for, and my dear I was released *forthwith* with *no* purgings or apologies or anything, though of course I'm still *totally* suspended, *rather* a triumph for the lone female don't you think darling, because it *does* show that we have still an argument or two with which to pulverise the brutal male, though on the other hand the *twins* perhaps show up rather a *weakness* in the female *politically* because now I suppose I shall have to abandon the seat whether they want me or not and *dedicate* the promising life to motherhood, no more now. darling your little blossom's *rather* faded and HADDOCK's going to read to me something suitable out of KEATS, HADDOCK by the way darling is *quite* too aprehensive about becoming a father but is bearing up bravely, farewell fond one your at last *interesting* TOPSY.

25 Does Needlework

Well Trix my distant delight I'm *rather* afraid that this will be *about* the last letter you'll have for a *long* time, not that you'll care, my dear from some of the *obstruse* things you say I believe you *skip* my profoundest passages, anyhow darling the twins are *definitely* in the offing though *rather* reluctant, my dear it's *too* protracted and wearing, there's been some *gauche* error about the *date* and we've had a nurse in the house for a *whole* fortnight, my dear the *expense* not to mention the conversation, my dear the *torture*, because of course she's a pearl of a person, *quite* placid and fussless, and I know will be a *complete* angel once one's in bed, only my dear you know what they are in the small-talk department and the *dear* thing *bubbles* on about nothing but *births* and deaths and *major* operations, with *all* the details and complications, my dear *too* technical, and of course she has the *most* Belgravian connection, my dear she's ushered *half* the peerage on to the planet, so that *what* I don't know about the insides of the aristocracy and their *habits* in the home, my dear the first week we went through the *whole* list daily, till I felt *too* intimate with people I've *never* set eyes on, my dear I could tell you things about the *Black* Duchess's internal arrangements which she doesn't know *herself*, *rather* macaber darling well don't you agree?

Well that was the *first* week, and *then* my dear we began on *hospital* shop, my dear I know the names and hobbies of *all* the doctors and half the nurses, likewise my dear the *frailest* phantom of a scandal or two, and of course I've *quite* fallen for a magnetic doctor called Bobble or something who's Nurse's Apollo, does *radiobology* and sounds *irresistible*, and meanwhile my dear I've learned *masses* of Latin and all these *gruesome* initials they have in hospitals, my dear BID is a *Brought In Dead*, and BBA means *Born* Before Arrival, yes it *sounds* difficult my dear but it *merely* means that some *careless* infant arrives before the nurse does, though *that* as Haddock said might be better than a case of Born *weeks* after arrival, and of course the *peak* and climax was today when my dear the *divine* thing picked up some paper and saw Haddock's initials, and my dear she murmured *Oh* yes, Funny, that's Ante Partum Hemorrhage, my dear I *don't* know much Latin but Haddock says at the present crisis that *particular* remark was *too* unsuitable, so my dear *what* with all this and *periodical* panics about the twins you'll understand that the *taut* little nerves are faintly on the *frayed* side, and of course we've *quite* got operations and things on the *brain*, my dear the other day Haddock was *dreamily* carving a chicken when suddenly he said, Will you have the *femur* darling or a bit off the *tibia major*, my dear *too* alarming.

Well my dear *try* to imagine the *jading* nature of everything, however we smile *darkly* through our tears darling, only I *can't* believe that this sort of thing is much of an *encouragement* to the twins, oh of course and that's *another* worry, my dear *nobody* but me believes that it *is* twins, not even the doctor, well he's *too* nebulous and my dear *most* people seem to think I'm being *amusing* about it, my dear *too* likely, and anyhow I *never* can understand why twins should be *funny*, my dear I think it's the *most* economical and *disarming* arrangement, however *knowing* I'm right I've been perfectly firm and we're *madly* organising *two* of *everything*, because *that* is the practical point after all, but my dear they *actually* wanted to *wait* and *see*, because it seems that's the done thing in dubious cases, however, the idea of the *tragical* other one with *quite* nothing to wear was *too* much for *this* tender heart, so here I sit *needle-working*, my dear the *most* laughable little socks and things about the size of *egg-covers*, at least Nurse and Mum do most of it because knittery was never my strongest suit and I drop *so* many stitches and things that my *pathetic* garments look more like *nets*, of course one thing we've got against the twins is that they've *rather* brought Mum back into our lives, my dear you know I'm *too* filial, but of course she and poor Haddock are like the grater and the cheese, and my dear having just been made *Vice*-President of a Maternity Centre she thinks she's *practically* a doctor and is *quite* burgeoning with advice and theories, and my dear everything she says reminds Nurse of some *grisly* anecdote about a local *anaesthetic* or the Black Duchess's *liver* or something, and of course they both rather *resent* each other so they have the *most* protracted *obstetrical* battles over my suffering little body, my dear I could *yell* sometimes and the *sole* silencer I have is to make Haddock read to me out of KEATS and DICKENS and WINSTON and people and sometimes one of those *flawless* little *short* leaders in *The Times*, because my dear I want the twins to be *too* litterary, and of course *whenever* there's anything about the Tribe of HICKS I have it read *over* and *over* again because they must be *born* rebels in that department, only Mum is rather a Hicksophil because of the POPE, so she *will* interrupt with one of her *clinical* remarks and then Haddock looks *beetles* at her, and my dear the *atmosphere* is *too* unmotherly.

Well darling I don't know if all this gives you any kind of a *picture* of your little blossom's tribulations, but if so have a *quiet* little cry for me won't you, of course as I've *told* Haddock if the twins survive *this* they'll be *quite* supermen, well there's *no* more news I think, I see the House is still *feebly* functioning without me, my dear the bizarre thing is that I find myself *rather* itching to be back in it, my dear it's like a *drug*, however of course I'm still *totally* suspended, though I expect after the twins I shall be I readmitted and everything, because that's just the kind of *sweet* but rather *sloppy* thing they do do, however meanwhile I get one of my bosoms there to put down my *daily* Question to the man HICKS, my dear I've just done a *dazzling* one about gas-ovens, my dear it's to ask him *whether* his attention has been called to the number of people who *commit* suicide by putting their heads in *gas-ovens*, whether it is not the case that *more* people perish from gas-ovens than from alcohol, and if he will take steps for the *prohibition* of *gas-ovens* or anyhow have *licences* for them and *rows* of *astringent* regulations, Oh and of course I've forgotten to tell you about my *divine* Society, my dear I did tell you once that there are *261* Societies all *beavering* away for Prohibition and such-like *alien* atrocities, and somebody's sent me a sort of *catalogue* of them which has *marked* fun-value, my dear they have the *most* baroque and *buffoonable* names, my dear there's the United Kingdom Alliance for the Total Suppression of the Liquor Traffic by the *Will* of the People, well *there's* a sweet little nickname for you, and the Society for the *Study* of *Inebriety*, which runs a paper called the *British* Journal of Inebriety, my dear can you *see* the old darlings somewhere in Portland Place all *morbidly* studying *inebriety*, I suppose they *meet* on Boat-Race Night, however then there's the United Order of the *Total* Abstinent Sons of the Phœnix, and the *Juvenile* Rechabites, and the *Wigan* Parent Total Abstinence Society, and the *World* Prohibition Federation, and the National British Women's Total Abstinence Union, which has a paper called *White Ribbon and Wings*, oh and *herds* more only I'm too tired now darling, well of course in this world *anybody* may be right, but my dear the question *does* arise, can anybody who can *solemnly* give themselves names like *that* be right about *anything*, and of course it's *too* easy to laugh but with all you *flappers* getting the vote *quite* anything may happen, anyhow the *point* is that I'm founding the *most* magical Society called *Topsy's Own*, only of course it has a *superb* long name as well, since that's the done thing, my dear it's Topsy's Own Society for the *Propagation* of the Sense of *Humour* and Proportion and for the *Increase* of *Innocent* Pleasure and Joy among the People, and my dear *you* shall be a Vice-President, O dear I'm shattered and weary and I *suppose* you think I'm a *wee* bit hysterical, well maybe I am, but if *you'd* heard what Nurse has *just* told Mum about *what* happened to Connie Fitlow so would *you* be darling, no more now, pray for me, your rather *terrified* little TOPSY.

26 Becomes A Mother

Well Trix my poor spinster *here* I am a British matron at last, thanks be, looking *pale* and ethereal on the snowy pillow, and *here* they are my dear two *revolting* little bundles of *thick* white flannel, *two* darling yes because of *course* I was right, my dear if *only* the world would take me seriously *instead* of treating me as an *irrelevant* bubble, however it's boy and girl, as *like* as two electrons, and the *whole* tribe thriving and buoyant, *even* my poor Haddock who my dear is *much* more dilapidated than any of the party, though of course he merely *fled* out into a taxi during the actual proceedings, told the man to drive *round* and round London, and my dear what with the *protracted* fussery and vacilation of it all he fell *fast* asleep in the cab and *woke* up, like BYRON or somebody, to find himself a father and *five* pounds seventeen and eightpence on the clock!

Well my dear whatever I say, and of course you know I *can't* blow froth about these *embarassing* events, but as a matter of fact I suppose it is *rather* a throb and land-mark in the little life, but my dear *don't* think that I'm going to be one of those *wallowing* mothers who make one blush *right* down the back to hear them *speak* of their young, because *quite* definitely the twins are *perfectly* revolting, my dear the *most* amorphous and *unfinished* little objects, my dear mere *studies* as the artists say, and my dear Haddock stands over them and sort of *mutters* dumbly, my dear *too* mystified, as if he was thinking O *gosh* did *I* do that, which I expect he is, though of course he tells me daily that they're *quite* exquisite and then *flies* out of the room, well my dear when you come down for the christening if I *once* tell you they're exquisite or anything in their present condition you shall have *three* new *frocks*, my dear they're *grotesque*, however I must say they have *rather* heart-rending little *toy* hands, my dear *too* pathetic, like a *fairy* frog's, and of course *delicious* little tuffets of hair, *coal-black* darling which was *rather* a shock to your tawny little friend, however Nurse tells me it will all be changed, but my dear it's *too* extraordinary to see how the *character* comes out already, because my dear the boy is an absolute *replica* of Haddock, of course the *eyes* are mine but you can see the germs of the Haddock nose *too* manifest though I *rather* hope that it won't spread to the girl, and my dear I know you'll think I've gone *soupy* suddenly, but honestly the *first* words the boy said, well not *words* precisely, but the nurse took it away from me and my dear it *clenched* the little frog-fists, *frowned* ferociously and made the *most* mutinous noise, my dear I *swear* it said JIX, *too* uncanny but *rather* encouraging because there's no doubt that it's going to be the absolute *hope* and HAMPDEN of the twentieth century, well the *girl* on the other hand is *quite* think going to be *musical*, my dear she's *too* intelligent and has those *long* tapering *piano*-fingers, well of course not *now* exactly but you can *see* them coming, and my dear she's *too* sensitive to *sound* and rhythm and everything because the *moment* Haddock puts on the gramophone the *sagacious* little eyes open and she's taking the *whole* thing in, and my dear her *pet* record seems to be a *Symphony* or something by a Belgian or somebody, which Haddock says is a *little* significant, so my plans are rather to finish her off with *two* years' concentrated music in *Paris*, though of course Haddock wants her to go to Oxford and take *Law*.

However we needn't decide that *yet*, and *now* darling about the *names, about* which we've had some rather *umbrageous* arguments, however I've told Haddock that as you were to be the principal godmother you ought to have a sort of *casting* vote, *assuming* of course darling that you cast on *my* side, well Haddock began with the *most* un-Parliamentary suggestions, my dear he wanted to call them TRIX and JIX, to sort of *allegorise* my public career, but rather hard on the boy I thought, so I suggested Sherry and Soda, to symbolise *his*, rather sweet don't you think, and he retorted with Sausage and *Mash*, and *Sankey* and Moody, and Derry and Tom and Adam and Eve, my dear the naming of twins would be an *inspired* paper-game for one of those *facetious* house-parties, however Haddock suddenly went all fastidious and now he'll have nothing but *hot-house* names, like *Tristram*

and Iseult and *Geraint* and Enid and Coral and Amber and *June*
and January, my dear *too* aspic and fragile for me, because what
I want is something *quite* normal and *unCadogan*, well William
and Mary or *George* and Joan, however I'm *rather* wedded to
JACK and JILL, because I think Sir *John* Haddock sounds *too*
tenacious and reliable don't you, well my dear *if* you agree you
might send Haddock the *most* emphatic telegram, but if you
don't don't bother, do you see darling?

Well my dear the Nurse is massing against me again, and your
little song-bird is feeling *rather* droopy, besides I expect you've
had *quite* enough of my young, so no more now, by the way I've
quite decided that Jack will go to Winchester, a scholarship of
course, and *then* I think Oxford, a little trip round the world and
the *Bar* for fun, though of course it's *too* obvious that he's going
to *write*, my dear if you could *see* the imagination in that *bulbous*
little head, though my dear *how* we're going to afford another
writer in the home, however you'll see at the christening, my
dear if you *miss* it I merely *root* you out of my life, it's *too* moving
to think you're going to linger in London a bit, because I shan't
have to think every minute *Have* I written to that *voracious*
hen, by the way you might bring any old letters of mine with
you because Haddock says they ought to be used as a *scourge*
and pamphlet at this *dreary* Election and given to *quite* every
elector, so that all these *cowering* candidates will have to at
last face up to the Topsy Policy and *swear* to pass my flawless
little Bills, my dear *did* I tell you that *since* the twins I've had
the *sweetest* telegrams from the PRIME and the SPEAKER and
absolute *entreaties* from Burbleton to stand again because the
great heart of the people is *too* kindled and it seems that merely
becoming a mother has put me right with the yams and loofahs,
and besides they say the only Member who's just had twins is
certain to hold the seat, however I don't think I shall because it's
too discouraging, my dear what *can* one do, one's like a flea on
an elephant, my dear Parliament's a *pachyderm* and always will
be as long as *everyone* in it is *over* forty when the *soul* fossilises
and you begin being *careful* about the body, *and* everything else,

my dear this Democracy would be *too* satisfactory if the *young* did the governing and the *old* did the work, instead of vice versa, however at least I've left my mark upon *Burbleton*, because I hear my *dear* Councillor Mule has been doing *quite* marvels, my dear they have *music* in the Parks and *Sunday* Concerts and the pictures open and they're making a *mixed* Swimming Bath and *improving* the pubs and *cleaning* up the Licensing Justices and everything, so I mean to be buried in *Brighter* Burbleton, my. dear the *whole* town my *smiling* monument, and meanwhile I shall cherish and cultivate my *exquisite* babes, O gosh darling I owe you *three* frocks, farewell now your *musunderstood* little *matron* TOPSY.

Topsy Turvy

To
JACK and JILL

1 Peace!

Trix, my restored exile, do you see a *ray* of hope, I mean all this *cosmic* acidity and gloom, it's *too* fraying, however *one* gleam is that you're back from Medicine Hat at *last*, or was it *Moose Jaw*, I forget, and I *do* grovel about my *utter* reticence while you were distant, only I merely could *not* write letters to the *remotest* places like Canada, I mean across *oceans*, and of course everything went round by *Cape* Horn or *Lapland* and took a *century*, so one thought Well, if *ever* this does touch Medicine Hat the chances are that *all* one's windows will have been detonated *again*, and the little old ashes may be at Golder's Green, *too* misleading, so it seemed the kindly thing not to utter at all, if you see what I mean, *not* to mention that *when* I imagined you and your *over-rated* young at work upon a *peach-fed* ham while *poor* Haddock and me were *prowling* hungrily from dust-bin to dust-bin, the little stomach missed *five* beats and the pen fell from the malnutritioned fingers, *besides* darling, you *must* comprend, life in the big city during the late conflict was a shade distractious and unadapted to *protracted* correspondence, my dear you *can't* imagine what the *doodle-bugs* were like, *quite* the most *unfriendly* gesture of the whole series, my dear Haddock and me were mere *magnets* for the pests, it seems they had a *wireless* attachment and simply *hounded* some people about, the ones on the Black List I mean, which Haddock was it seems, and of course the instant one sat down to write you the *longest* letter those *emetical* sirens performed and one had to keep away from the *glass*, when we had any, and lie *flat* on the floor, but of course not *too* flat because of the blast effect on the old abdomen, the *most* complicated drill, darling, with the little rump *uplifted*, well if you scorned the action it was *too* likely you found yourself standing in the street with *utterly* no clothes on, my dear I've been prostrate in *all* the *wettest* gutters from the

Savoy to *West London, rather* a strain on the wardrobe because of course *no* coupons allowed for gutter-work, but my dear Hermione Tarver, you remember her *surely*, she must be eighty now, was *too* meticulous about her *one* frock and was blasted *quite* naked in Church Street Kensington, *too* embarrassing, so it only shows, then of course we had *four* incendiaries on the roof, a *normal* bomb at the bottom of the garden, and the *most* malignant *rocket* three hundred yards away, however belay there, as Haddock says, I must desist and withdraw, because my dear, Haddock's already started this *morbid* anniversary habit, my dear the last fine Sunday we had which was *months* ago he came down to breakfast and said *Five* years ago I tied my ship up to a buoy marking a *mine*, to which of course the *one* response was How careless darling, which didn't ring any bells, and the next Sunday it was the *entire* Surrey Docks in flames, or the House of Commons *eliminated* or something, and my dear what with the anniversaries of the *last* war and the war before that, there's practically *no* day now which doesn't begin with some *gruesome* reminiscence, but my dear does he *ever* remember the twins' *birthday* not to mention his countless god-children's, not *ever*, not *utterly* ever, however *all* I was trying to say was, *Don't* be *too* wounded about my war-reticence, you do understand *don't* you poppet, then of course there was *security*, but I won't go into that now, only there was *literally nothing* you could say which mightn't give *nearly everything away*, even the *weather* was a septic theme, *except* in the Straits of Dover, and that I expect you saw in the papers.

It was *too* galling not to see you as you *flashed* through the city, but of course *if* it means you took *one* look at London and said to Henry, Gosh, no, *remove* me rapidly, I couldn't abuse you less, my dear isn't it the *zenith* of agony, or do I mean the *nadir*, anyhow I don't suppose for a moment you could have secured a *couch* anywhere, you have to give *years* of notice and then it's a guinea a minute, with 10 per cent for service and *no* service, and my dear of course *we're* utterly couchless because the *builders* are in, my dear they've *just* got round to the last bomb but one, not counting that *unethical* rocket which I must say they did

alacritously, or some of it, but of course now I've painted the
two top rooms for the twins they're *opening up* the roof and the
entire sky will enter from now till Yule-time, *what* a life and
it's the *most* seductive *cerulean* blue with *indications* of toe-nail
pink, and then of course the *food*, my dear, I can't recall when
I ate *last*, I mean *ate*, though of course doing *all* the cooking I
never *want* to eat extensively, unless it's a *boiled* egg and we get
them once a month *some* months, my dear *do* you remember the
days when one tried to get the evening meal *too* late at some
insanitary little hotel in a *cathedral* town and they said Sorry
we've *only* got *breakfast dishes* and one turned up the little old
nose at them, Gosh *only* breakfast dishes! *only* bacon and eggs
and *kidneys*, and *do* you remember the County breakfasts when
one *stalked* up and down the sideboard, *peering* haughtily at
dish by dish, *spurning* kidneys on toast, *shuddering* away from
fried fish and utterly *debating* whether one would *stoop* to a little
sausage and bacon or stave off famine with *buttered* eggs and
mushrooms, *Oh* dear of course Haddock says he doesn't think we
shall *quite* ever see civilization again, well, not in *our* time, and
by civilization Haddock means *hams*, I think he's *so* right for
once, I mean a real *total* ham on the sideboard *always*, so that
whenever the pangs of famine occurred one could *mutilate* the
ham a piece and win through till the next meal, which *reminds*
me darling of Haddock's *pet* song, I Do Like a Nibble in the
Night, do you know it, because in the old days when he was *too*
inspired he used to write novels and things *all night*, only when
the *afflatus* failed there was always the *hugest* ham in the larder
or at least a cold but enchanting leg of bird, and after a nibble
and a noggin or two he'd perpetrate *four more chapters*, as it is the
poor dear slinks muttering to bed and writes *practically nothing*,
so perhaps there *is* something to be said for having *special* rations
for *literary* households, however of course one can always *crawl*
out to a restaurant, *if* you can get sitting-space, I don't say *food*,
because my dear the *most* imperceptible gin costs half- or *three-
quarters*-a-crown, and *if* they add the tiniest adjunct in the
shape of flavouring, my dear the mere *dregs* of the grape-yard
after the women have stamped out everything else with their

contagious feet, well that sinks *four* shillings for a *single* sniff, and as for eatery one consumes *practically* nothing but *cats* and *dogs*, my dear *fried kitten* is *too* succulent *actually*, but one has one's *principles* well mustn't one, darling, and then of course *no* help in the home, when I tell you that *since* Alamein I've had *one* daily for two precarious hours, no more, and now of course what with her *redundant* husbands and sons all *swarming* back from the wars my *angelic* Mrs Bee is *so* fussed with feeding the soldiery that she has less and less time for your pathetic T, who is a blue mass of *varicosity* from *excessive* standing at the shop or sink, as of course are *all* the nation's matrons, but darling *don't* think for a *moment* that I'm *wilting* about having you, because *do* come *whenever* you like, of course it *won't* be the same as Medicine *Hat*, or was it Moose Jaw, but we'll manage somehow, and we *must* have the cosiest chat, O Gosh I've not told you a *thing* about the *twins* yet, and if one *can't* get a table anywhere one can nearly always find a *free* seat on the *Victoria* Embankment or Sloane Square Station, and Haddock says I *do* make the most *filling* sandwiches out of *completely* nothing, so do come soon darling, farewell for a fraction, your *devoted* TOPSY.

2 Consolations

Well Trix, my *top* female, I've *just* a moment while the vegetables are doing, *no* I haven't, there's that *magnetic* dustman with the whole sack of *manure* he promised me from that *prolific* municipal horse sorry.

Here we are again, well I think you're *so* wise not to *think* of coming to stay in London *too* soon, because honestly *some* days one does *not* detect a *single* ray of hope, and as a *matter* of fact there's *no* doubt that *nearly* everything is worse than it was in the *war*, though as Haddock said during the late conflict, and my dear he has a *foul* habit of being *too* right, he *never* expected it to be anything else, of course the *bottom* blunder was to liberate that *tiresome* Continent, my dear you know I never did exactly *dote* on the foreigner, except the French perhaps because of *omelettes*, but really the *way* they're *all* behaving, my dear those divine but *inflated* Russians, and to think that we've to feed and foster the *obscene* Germans, who as Haddock said are the *sole* architects of the cosmic mess, well when I tell you that I still can't plant a *single* cutting or extract a *weed* without lacerating the little fingers with *broken* glass, we've collected *tons* but sometimes I think it's taken *root* or something and *grows*, well you'll *begin* to comprend perhaps how an *emaciated* matron feels when she reads *group*-letters asking her to *petition* the Gov to *reduce* her *too* imperceptible ration and send more to that *unnecessary* Continent, my dear of course you know my motto, I *always* say that it *always* pays to *always* do the Christian thing, but when it comes to *fats*, my dear *did* you know that we're sending absolute *tons* of fats abroad, when my dear if you gave me the *most* authentic and virginal *Dover Sole* tomorrow I could no more fry it than I could split an electron, *utterly* fatless, but my dear *what* do the French do except *consign* it to the *Black* Market, which is the *sole* thing it seems that my *adored* French are capable of *united action* in, and as for the *fraternal* Russians they *merely* remove everything they can see *fraternally* to Russia, my dear Haddock says we're the *Suckers* of the *World*, and of course if our wide-hearted *Americans* are going to weary in well-giving, and *could* you blame them, my dear that far from unmagnetic Mrs May we met in Jamaica *centuries* ago has been sending us fortifying little parcels *throughout* the conflict, well but *if* they do I suppose we shall *all* crawl about queueing for sea-weed and *dandelions*, which they say my dear are quite *startlingly* nutritious and everything, only even then I expect we shall send *most* of our sea-weed crop to that fallacious Continent, by the way darling you *know* my principles about bird-murder and everything but I'm absolutely open-minded when the bird's in the *oven*, so one day if Henry comes tottering home with any *superfluous* feathered things from the moors or spinneys you *won't* forget the wolf at a certain door in West London, will you?

However darling *don't* think for a moment that I'm weakening, or anything, because there *are* one or two quite *positive* consolements, well, for one thing the twins are safe thanks be and blooming, and then nowadays one need *simply* never listen to the News *at all*, because you know for *certain* that there *can't* be any *good* news and the one wagerable thing *is* that you'll hear some lugubrious trumpet of the people miffling away about everything being *too* impossible and we must tighten the old belt *again*, well my dear if you could *see* the little belt it's *nothing* but holes and *nearly* goes *twice* round the midriff, my dear yesterday I *weighed* the meagre body on Haddock's *parcel*-scales and it seems I could be posted for *about* fourpence-halfpenny, besides if you *do* listen it's practically bound to be that dogmatic *announcerrr* who talks about Russ-i-a, puts four r's into *destroyerrrr*, and one into Malaya-r, only of course *when* in a hurry he *forgets* about his r's *like* you and me, which only shows how *fundamentally* bogus, however then I *must* say there *is* a *touch* of anodyne in going to bed *undressed*, *not* expecting to hear *rude* explosions or be blown into the *basement*, and *not* leaving the bath-water in the bath for *incendiaries* which looks *too* degrading and *insanitary* in the

cold wet *dawn*, and of course *no* black-out which *is* my dear
the absolute *ecliptic* of bliss, which perhaps will *show* you *how*
low we've sunk in these *barbarous* years, because I mean *literally*,
no Haddock says I mean *actually* if anything, I *never* look at a
lighted window without a *positive* thrill, and my dear to this *day*
if I come home latish and switch on the *smallest* light I still think
O *Gosh* the *police* I *never* did the fatiguing *black-out*, and of course
not having to creep about *stealing* electric torches, *colliding* with
lamp-posts, falling over *sand-bags*, or butting into the bosoms of
revolting strangers, my dear it's *Paradise*, the only bleak point in
this Borough is that they've given us the *most* bilious *blue* street-
lighting, which makes the *whole* population look like film-stars
made up, my dear the lipstick goes *quite* black, too macaber, of
course I dare say *all* this sounds *absolute* bats to you, because
I suppose the black-out was comparatively *formal* in Medicine
Hat, or *even* Moose Jaw, but *six* years darling do seem to go on
for *quite* a time and *this* frail matron has *never* left the risky city,
so you'll comprend perhaps our simple pleasures, personally of
course I *sometimes* sigh for the bad old days, I mean the peak-
weeks of the *doodle-bugs* or the 1940 *winter*, when swarms of
the citizens were rightly *too* elsewhere, one could *move* about
the city and even from time to time secure a *meal*, my dear in
the doodle-days I've seen the *Savoy* Grill *half* empty at 1.30, and
Haddock says *one* day he went into a club and they positively
thrust fried sole and *salmon* at him, *now* of course the *entire*
town is *one* mass of *redundant* personnel with *nothing* to do it
seems but *swarm* about the pavements, *monopolize* the taxis,
congest the Underground, and *minister* to the alimentary *canal*,
my dear *where* they've all *emerged* from and *what* they're all *for*
I definitely can *not* envisage, of course it's *too* futile to *think* of
lunching much after 11.30 anywhere, and by that time the main
dish is *generally* off, and as for *movement* well the *bizarre* thing is
that the *more* Americans go away the *fewer* taxis and *one* theory
is that they're taking them *home* with them, and *as* for the
Underground they used to talk about the *Rush-hour* but which
it is now it's *too* impossible to say, and my dear all the *largest*

soldiers accoutred with *everything* poor pets, which reminds me darling when you *do* come up I can't *utterly* guarantee that you won't have a *rather* shattering *voyage*, if I were you darling before you start I should *train* for the train, I mean *stand* for an hour or two in some small asphyxiating *cupboard* to get the corridor-technique and *fortify* the unaccustomed legs, and *don't* on any account let Henry take *Firsts* because they're all occupied by the *most* carbolic and unmelting types with Thirds, there'll only be *needless* antagonism, and Henry will have *frustration* as well as the cramp, *too* lowering.

However angel in *spite* of all the *turmoil* of Peace you'll find us *quite* bonhomous and even *jocular*, that's one thing, when you *know* you've *nothing* to look forward to it's so much less of a *worry* isn't it, I mean than when you're always *hoping* for the next thing like in the war, because now one sort of *trickles* about in a *genial* coma, *utterly* thankful for *small* things like *stewed* cat or switching on a light, and my dear I must say the people on the whole are *quite* wonder-worthy considering all things, *not* forgetting the *worn* legs and varicose veins, I mean *how* the bus-conductors stand it I *cannot* guess, and you can ask almost anyone the way without getting a rude response, which is more than I can say about the General Election, I must tell you about *that* degrading episode, but no more now, because my *vegetables*, farewell, and come when you can, your suffering TOPSY.

3 The Suffrage Episode

October 24, 1945

Trix, Hen of the North, *uncountable* thanks for the poor wee feathered thing, which was *absolutely* eatable and cheered these jaded *œsophaguses* noticeably, yes darling I *know* you sent a *brace*, but only *one* got through a *little* mangled, however that's a pretty high proportion for these days, *after* all it's *fifty* per cent isn't it, and I found two moving little *shots* in my piece which made me think of Henry *slinking* through the spinneys in that *filth* of a coat, the bloodthirsty old bag, however top salutes to both and Haddock says he's not against bird-murder *any* more.

But I promised to tell you about that *rancid* Election, my dear you know I've seen a good deal of the suffrage-stuff in my time, and of course one does *not* expect an Election to be as *boracic* as a charity bazaar, but honestly *this* time the old fatherland did touch bottoms for behaviour, I don't mean the *result*, but my dear *one* minute the whole nation were beavering away together, *quite* bosoms except for a few carps among the politicos, and the next there was *mass*-rudery and vinegar *everywhere*, my dear a *railway*-porter at Burbleton told Joyce Pennant who's *half*-crippled she could *carry* her *own bag*, my dear the *sweetest* porter with *velvet* manners as a rule and now *all* smiles and service again, which thanks be goes for most of the populace, but *for* a period it was *too* like *shaking* a bottle or stirring up the mud-bed of Haddock's *newt-pond*, the *most* unexpected *smells emerged* from the mere dregs of the Island character, my dear the most *brutal* tale was about John Penny, *you* know the blind *Member*, well he was answering some imbecile questions quite bonhomously as he *always* is, my dear he *is* Galahad, and he said to one man I *think* I see what you mean, *whereupon* some young Briton at the back sings out, You can't see *anything* You're *blind*, my dear *can* you imagine such a mind, and of course as Haddock says if *that's* the fruits of seventy years of free State *education* it may well be that our *arrangements* need *drastic* attention, I mean, he says, look at *Newfoundland* where education is *too* far astern according to *us*, because it seems it's all run by the Churches, *three* in number, *not* counting the Salvation Army, so that the *minutest* village has three or four little schools with not enough teachers or money or *anything*, and it's all *too* overlapping and undeorientated and everything, on the *other* hand there are *no* policemen and *no* crime, there's *one* murder about every ten years and the *whole* population have manners like *Archangels* or spaniel puppies, so it *may* be the old State doesn't know *quite* all it thinks it does, do you see what I mean darling?

However where was I, well to go back to this *leprous* Election, well my dear as a *matter* of fact, I wasn't *fanatical* about Haddock standing *at all* this time, after all we've each had *five years* in that Place, and after all this war-nonsense it's *high* time he settled down and wrote a trilogy or something if only to nourish the suffering *twins*, after all my dear I married a young *barrister*, but what happens he takes up this precarious *writing*, then without warning he became a *politico* the lowest form of vegetable life, *not* content he goes for a sailor again and spends the entire war doing semaphore and *logarithms*, and my dear what with getting his *latitude* and renaming the stars I *can't* envisage *why*, one *literally never* knows what new horror may not corrode the horizon *any* day, and *none* of them so far as I can see having the *feeblest* effect on the cosmos not to mention the little old *overdraft*, and Mr H himself I think was fairly unfanatical about it himself and sighed somewhat for the old life *mainly* based on the *Study* and the *Local*, however it seemed the done thing to do, to stand I mean, so there it was, well of course we had a *rationally* calm passage ourselves, apart from addressing *thirty* thousand *putrescent* envelopes *and* filling same with Haddock's *interminable* Address, my dear I know a man who's *still* reading it, in *bed*, *doggedly*, but after that well you can spurn the ancient Universities if you *like*, but they *do* have the *sole* civilized election habits, my dear there are *no* meetings, *no speeches*, no *posters*, *no* committee rooms, my dear Haddock hasn't even got a *Committee*, because he says *if* you have a *Committee* at *any* moment they may mass together and proclaim that they've lost *all* confidence in you, whereas not *one* person has ever expressed *any* confidence in Haddock, which I think is *so* right, so at least *nobody* can say he's *lost* it, and my dear *all* you do is to write down *everything* you think about everything and *weigh* it, yes I *mean* weigh it darling because it has to be under 2 ounces or ¼ oz for the troops, and then if your opinions don't weigh *too* ponderously you merely discharge them into the Post Office and pray, and my dear *when* you think of the *squalor* and *torment* of the normal Election my dear *continual* mouthwork, I know people who made *seventy* speeches, and at the end they said they felt like *filthy* sponges, dank and degraded, well when Haddock had been safely delivered of his Address we *circled* about helping in six other places, well when I say *helped* at least *four* of the six were *outed* so who knows but my dear the *meetings*, either sleeping-parties or shouting-matches, and of course *all* the open-airs were arranged to take place on Saturday evening in the rain *too* close to the *largest* pub, and the un-Christian soldiery would cluster outside the pub with *copious* tankards, pay *no* attention to anything said and make the *most* irrelevant *long-range* interruptions, and of course *since* their vote if any was *miles* elsewhere they were simply sabotaging the truth from the local votery, who my dear being *mere* civilry sat *mute* as mice, and of course if *any* speaker so much as ventured to say to some *vocal* warrior Sir *have* you a vote in this division, there was *complete* uproar mutiny and *dis*affection, and honestly my dear *when* I think *how* they behaved and *how* they treated that *sympathetic* James Grigg who Haddock says was the best War Secretary the old cow Britannia has had for *generations*, and the *first* one who won a *real* battle for *several* wars, well honestly I could bear it if some of them were *never* demobilized or anything ever, poor pets, well then of course there was the *unique* Mr —— at Longbottom Nearly where George Pixton got in again in *spite* my dear of Haddock making *six* speeches in aid of him, well this Mr —— said that he was for Churchill *too* but *independent*, well *quite* all he did was to harry and molest poor *George*, my dear he had a *hired* gang of soldiery who *hounded* George from meeting to meeting, *asking* always the *same* synthetic questions from *typewritten* slips, which of course is *so* spurious, and my dear *all* the questions were about their *unimportant* stomachs, I mean did *one* man ever yell *What* about the Empire, and *then* my dear Mr —— went *round* the town *daily* in a loud-speaker van *booming* viperously GEORGE PIX-TON IS A LI-AR — GEORGE PIX-TON et-cet-er-a, the evidence for which assertion being *quite* fallacious and *non-existent*, because *I saw* the *telegrams*, well poor George at last distributes a *writ*, or whatever is the done thing to do with writs, but after the Election he has to *withdraw* it, because it seems by the *infantile* law of libel and so forth when it's a *spoken* slander you have to prove *damage* which as George *won* he couldn't, and that will show you what the *law* is, I mean when you can shout *carbolic* insults through a *loud*-speaker for *days* on end *without* a come-back, in the Courts I mean, because thanks be Mr —— *did* lose his *festering* deposit, well finally there was *Deathsend* where Haddock spoke at the Eve of the Poll meeting in the *most* scrofulous Market to two thousand citizens, some alien soldiery and a *mercenary* gang of hoolies who *with* the soldiery *quite* dominated the proceedings, well when I tell you that Haddock is one of Deathsend's *most* ancient allies, my dear he *opened* their obscene Municipal Baths *before* the war and *with* the Mayor threw a ceremonial blonde into the Bath, not to mention he was *always* disembarking at Deathsend during the late conflict, so he did think in *spite* of the form that possibly he *might* get as far as L and G it's good to be in *good* old Deathsend again, but my dear *far* from it, they *howled* miscellaneously for *five* minutes before he could *utter*, so at last, wearying slightly, he *yelled* into the microphone, *How* many of you have been *paid* for making this *criminal* din, hands up, well my dear *two* well-trained hirelings at *once* put their hands up, at which Haddock says he laughed so much he nearly *gravitated* off the platform, but then he shouted Jolly good show any advance on *two* and three more citizens put *their* hands up, which Haddock found *so* stimulating that *in* the end he shouted them *down* and said *much*, though I need *not* say that his Candidate was *quite* out, altogether perhaps you'll begin to sniff the general *aroma* of the suffrage episode, and *although* no doubt we've got the best Government *ever* one did *just* wonder sometimes if it wasn't a queer way to choose a *Parliament*, or even a dog, however, no complaints, I must say they're *all* welcome to their hot seats, *what* a job, farewell your unstateswomanlike TOPSY.

4 The Moon Party

November 1, 1945

Trix, darling, I couldn't care *less* about the atomic bomb could *you*, I mean on *all* the evidence it's a *fairly* drastic and straightbackward proceeding, there are *no* queues for it, *no* coupons are required it seems, one will *not* spend the rest of one's life weeding *broken* glass from the flower-bed, there are *no* r's in it so one will *not* be rendered raving by my *favourrrrite* announcerrr's announcements about it, the desirability of the cosmos is *quite* dubious anyhow, and my dear as Harry said it was *too* laughable when the old atomic emerged how *all* the woolliest and wettest of the population at *once* vociferated Well *this* will clear the cosmic mind at last, and *then* my dear settled down to talk the *same* wool and wet as they had talked for *centuries*, well now for example they're *dismembering* the American Pres because he won't show the Secret to suffering *Russia*, and no wonder suffering Russia is suspicious and everything if *that's* how the brutal capitalists behave, etc, when my dear if there *is* one thing more patent than another it is that you *won't* get *many* kind words out of suffering Russia, *whatever* you do, well my dear *suppose* the Americans said O K we'll *share* the Secret with *simply* everyone, it's too easy to envisage how suffering Russia would respond *at* once, it would be *There* you go again, giving *all* my neighbours the know-how so as to build the *most* unmatey atomic wall *against* me, *personally* of course I'd make it all *quite* public, if only because *if* one's going to be *obliterated* there's something to be said for having it done professionally and *well*, with *notice*, whereas my dear as long as it's a naughty secret it's *too* likely you'll have old men fumbling about in the mountains and deserts and blowing up the cosmos *messily* without a word of warning, which *perhaps* was what Einstein had in mind, my dear *did* you see, the old wizard said it was *quite* erroneous that the atomic conflict would be the *end* of civilization, because he said we should be *merely* terminated about *two-thirds* and there'd be enough *books* surviving probably for the residuary chaps to start *all over again*, which you must agree darling is *about* the most *lowering* utterance of the *whole* series, because my dear *can* you envisage your little Topsy *waking* up *quite* naked in a dank jungle *miles* away and *starting again* on the New York Evening Post and the Swiss Family *Robinson*, no thanks *no*, by the way darling don't whisper a *thing* because I gather it is pretty confidential still but it seems there is a *definite* movement to evacuate *some* of the British to another *planet*, or at least to start a pilot *colony*, I mean to found a New World *literally*, I *won't* swear but I *think* it's the Moon, which I believe is *too* feasible because *once* you've got the old atomry in *full* action you can *fertilize* deserts and make *granite* nutritious, then of course all these *fantastic* jet-machines, my dear they'll be *so* fast it seems you'll be *in* the stratosphere the day before you *start*, if you see what I mean, the *one* snag I believe has been about reaching the Moon *too* fast because of *gravity* or something, but now they've got round *that* even by *Radar*, because my dear there's *utterly* nothing you *can't* do by Radar, well it seems by Radar you set up a *resistance*-cushion in the Moon on *which* my dear you come down *too* cosily like the *Black* Duchess *planing* into a Charity bazaar, however darling *don't* press me for *all* the details, the stark thing is that the *Plans* are ready, but my dear *apart* from the Red Tape, which Haddock says has been *without* precedent, the *usual* stumbling-blocks at once obtrude, and *that* is *Shall* we tell the suffering *Russians*, because of course they'll be *too* suspicious and wounded about the enterprise, and for *all* we know they may have a *secret* eye on the Moon themselves, or some say *Mercury*, though of course we're *not* likely to hear *many* details in advance if they *have*, however it seems we'd be *most* amenable to unfold *all* if it will help to keep the cosmos sweet, but the drear thing is of course that *if* we tell the suffering Russians we shall have to tell the soft-eyed *Americans*, and then the Yanks will want *bases* all over the Moon, *not* to mention *platoons* of observers, there'll be all that *stupefying* dollar-nonsense again, my dear you *know* I'm not *congenitally* international but *why* we can't *all* use the *same* coins I definitely can *not* envisage, and then I suppose the first babies in the Moon will be *born* chewing, if *not* crooning, which much as I love them, my dear you *should* have seen Eisenhower and Mark Clark taking their degrees at Oxford, my dear what *pets*, what *natural* magnets, as I've told Haddock if either of them raised the *merest* finger I'd be an export *at* once, on the other hand I do think that the New World perhaps *should* start on the right foot, that is *rather* British and *no* chewing, because I do feel that a chewing child in a *New* World might spoil *half* one's pleasure, altogether it *does* look sometimes I gather as if this *utterly* idealistic plan might be merely *one* more elephant in the cosmic *wood pile* if it's *not* handled like one's monthly egg, that is pretty *maternally*, however we shall see, meanwhile Haddock and me are on the *Shadow* List for Founder Members and soon I suppose we shall have to *make* up the reluctant *mind*, what do you think darling shall we *go*, of course if it could be a real nest of *suitables* it might be *quite* Heaven getting *away* from everything, my dear these *builders*, I suppose you'd *never* seduce your Henry from his heaths and spinneys and I *can't* promise *much* about the *shooting* in the Moon, in fact Haddock's a *little* dubious about the *boating* because nobody *really* knows about the *canals*, or is that *Mars*, on the other hand it's *not* like Australia one gathers where you have to *saw* your way into the Bush, or out of it, and of course with the *atom* in your hand you can *practically* have what *scenery* you *require*, I mean you make a *lake* here and a mountain *there* and grow what you *like* in them, so I don't suppose it would be *too* long before we fitted the male appendages with the customary pursuits and hobbies, but of course the *key*-thing is to have the *right* category *personnel*, and my dear *if* the New World is going to be *peopled* with Youth Movements, Government Departments, observing *Senators*, *chewing* children and jitterbugging *soldiery*, and of course *if* the *entire* place is to be run *half* like a Borstal and *half* like a quick-lunch canteen, which Haddock says *is* civilization today, then perhaps there is *something* to be said for clinging to the old familiar planet during its *few* penultimate *years*, and *by* the way there is *one* thing that *when* the Big Bang happens even the *Moon* may not be *too* salubrious because of proximity, however I do think that if one's going to be as *meticulous* as *all* that one would never get *anywhere*, well don't you agree.

So there it is, I must *desist* now darling because I'm dining with Haddock at the *House*, first time since the New Era and *quite* a thrill, that is if he gets a *table* which I believe is *generally* prohibitive, because my dear it seems the old place has become a popular *resort*, not only do all the new Members spend the *entire* day on the premises, *not* having a mass of clubs like the old school it seems, but *all* their constituents swarm upon them daily, *eager* for seats in the Gallery or beer, which Haddock says is *too* gratifying because for years he's been urging the populace to *take* an interest in the despised *talking*-shop, and now it seems they *do*, which of course is *one* valid result of that *fallacious* Election, however no more now darling, you might *sound* Henry about your coming on the *Moon*-party, don't tell him a word of *course*, only the general outline, as it were, farewell your faithful TOPSY.

5 Frustration

Well Trix old evergreen we were *too* right about your *not* coming, because my dear these *builders*, I'm a mere *maze* of frustration and trouble, my dear I *sometimes* think I'm heading for the new *peace*-neurosis which is congesting *half* the nursing-homes, it's not *too* certain we shall get far with this epistle now, no there's another bell, oh what is it *now*.

That my dear was that *melting* man with the dog-like eyes from the Town Hall Mr Fisk, and it seems the plumber's mate has merely *declined* duty and gone to the dogs or pictures, my dear *what* a job Mr Fisk I mean, because he's the poor martyr in charge of *bomb*-repairs and my dear sooner than that I'd *volunteer* to sit in the House of Commons *all* day and listen to *all* the speeches, and *if* you recall how well-developed my powers of *speech-resistance* are that will show you perhaps, well I dare say all this will sound to you like the whistling of *bats* because of course you've no *conception* of peace-conditions up there in the pampered North, but the *basic* horror is that one's own builder is *too* illicit, I mean you remember my boracic Mr *Mason*, I'm sure you do because my dear the day you got locked in the lav he came and *redeployed* you, well for *centuries* when there's been the *least* home-trouble, my dear from porous walls to stubborn obstacles in the *sink*, one merely hoisted the Mason signal and *there* he rapidly *was*, of course there'd be *estimates* and all that ritual, but things did utterly *happen*, my dear there is not *one* square centimetre of this humble ruin that Mr Mason has *not* patched up or painted or played with at one time or another, my dear it's like Stone*henge* to him, the merest *hint* of wet-rot keeps him *awake*, my dear he erected our sandbag-shelter in 1938 which by the way *collapsed* theatrically the very *day* the war I took place in *1939*, however, sorry darling, another blistering *bell*.

That of course was the *piano-tuner* who my dear has an

enviable genius for arriving *quite* unheralded on the *wrongest* day, my new still-life chrysanthemums group *majestically* arranged have to be *banished* from the instrument and *plasterers* in the room, however there's a *dim* hope he may drive the builders into a *frenzy* about which I should be *quite* neutral, because *as* I was telling you Mr *Mason's* men were *all* locals and *too* congenial, my dear they knew *all* the gossip on *all* the neighbours, they remembered the *twins* when they were *one* inch long, there was one *celestial* old carpenter who Haddock says would have done *just* as well as the Archbishop of Canterbury and *looked* it *better*, then of course Mr Mason himself was always BEE*ing* in and out to see that things were maturing, though *quite* needless because my dear the men *took an interest* and toiled like *yeomen*, one sustained them with beer and bonhomy and all proceeded fraternal and *effective*, however *now* my dear the picture is *too* otherwise because for *bomb*-repair Mr Mason is *quite* out-of-bounds, my dear I was *practically* arrested for ringing him the morning after our *rocket*, which *by* the way descended *punctually* in the *early* morning after our *wedlock* anniversary party, my dear Haddock lay in a *classic* stupor and simply *never* heard the thing *at all*, which *when* I tell you that it was the *loudest* missile *just* across the river not *three* hundred yards from the home was not perhaps a startlingly good *show* as from time to time he *half*-acknowledges, as for me I woke up to find the trembling frame *encrusted* in plaster from the ceiling and glass in *all* our quarters for the *fourth* time, well in the dank dawn we waded through glass to the long-talker and got the faithful Mr Mason round, well *he* got a *licence* or thought he did to stave off the elements with cardboard and such, my dear for *years* one lived in *electric* light and *looked* like one of those synthetic *mushrooms* in a cellar, and then of course they couldn't trace *who* had said Proceed, and for quite a time there was almost *national* unpleasantness because as I know now *painfully* the done thing is to wait till they send you someone from the *Pool*, and the Pool my dear at the *present* time seems to be a gang of *non*-local *non*-labourers, *mainly* imports from the *swamps* of Ireland, who my dear could *not* care less if this Borough had *never* existed and remained

in ruins *now*, they're *too* uninterested in *us*, they're *not* paid by
the builders, they're *not* his men, and think he's getting *rich* on
them, because of cost plus or something, they merely *milk* and
mock at the Council, and *we* don't pay anyone so can't utter a
word, except of course to my *poor* Mr Fisk who is quite beside
himself with care and thwartment, *beavering* wistfully to get
all this *pond*-labour to *labour* from time to time, and of course
as Haddock says as an advertisement of State what-is-it it is
not spectacular, because my dear *when* you think that the *last*
relevant missile descended more than *ten* months ago and the
roof's still quite undone, not to mention a *precarious* chimney
which is *too* likely to *dive* into the top bedroom if it blows
at all Haddock says, of course I *know* they had to do the *top*
things first and of course *labour* and *wood* and everything is *too*
insufficient, *all* one wonders is that *anything* gets done under the
pond system, well my dear for *twelve* days they've been at work
on our *blasted* conservatory, well when I say *at work*, my dear at
8.30 two soporific types arrive and have a *prolonged* smoke, at
9 or later two more come *sometimes* and *one* morning they all
toiled *madly* till 11.30, at *which* point there was a *general* exodus,
returning my dear at a quarter-to-two, two of them, so my
dear you can see the Civil Service luncheon hour is spreading
vertically, however *more* often what happens is that only *two*
toilers appear at all the carpenter and the plumber's *mate*, or
sometimes the plumber and the *carpenter's* mate, which my dear
means *utter* inanition because it seems the carpenter can't *move*
without his *mate* and the plumber's *mate* is *too* powerless without
his *plumber*, the point about the *plumber* darling is that the
bathroom waste emerges down a pipe on top of the conservatory
which being now removed *no* bath is feasible without a *cascade* of
soapy water into the *conservatory*, too alarming, well of course
in the *normal* outfit the carpenter would merely *ring* Mr Mason
and say Oy we're Stagnant, but my dear in *these* proceedings far
from it, they're *too* content to sit about the garden enjoying the
view and smoking *endlessly*, my dear I can *not* guess *where* they
obtain such *multitudinous* cigarettes, and the next day probably
it's a *different* two but they're waiting for *material*, which for all

we know may be *too* true, however from time to time if one ventures to take an interest, and Haddock says it's not *too* safe, one rings up the Town Hall and tells poor Mr Fisk one's got two *stagnant* toilers in the garden, but by *that* time of course they've quietly *vanished*, to the local one presumes, well in the afternoon perhaps a *foreman* visits the scene and then if any toiler has returned there's the *most* corrosive wrangle about their *rights* and everything, because it seems on this work they get only *union* rates while similar toilers are getting *bonuses*, which is rankling as one must admit, and by the end of that it's time to put the old tarpaulin over and *withdraw* exhausted, my dear this morning Saturday three toilers attended and sawed and hammered for *quite* half an hour, but my dear they've dispersed *already*, at 11 sharp *away* the toilers went not to return praises be, perhaps it was the piano-tuner, well *after* all this to the *lay* eye the conservatory looks *too* like what it looked like last *Monday*, after the first assault, the *one* difference is that the garden is a *sea* of *chips* and corrugated iron and one of the Irish citizens *inflamed* about his rights fell into Haddock's little pond *quite* wrecking the *last* water-lily of the season, *too* cruel, the *one* gleam is that when you get two *English* locals alone they seem to toil in the ancient fashion, my dear the *painters* are *utter* pets, so perhaps there is *one* ray of hope, and my dear I'm *not* suggesting that our landlord's conservatory is a *top* priority in the Reconstruction and the Worthier World, *all* I say is *if* it's to be done well *do* it because as Haddock says *if* this is a small categorical example it's *too* lowering to think of all the public money that must be ambling down the drain, and *how* they hope to build a *single* house at this rate, and my dear when I think of all that *fallacious* drip about the *profit* motive and how the toiler toils with a *whistle* in his heart when he knows he's toiling for the *community* and not for a *shark-souled* employer like my beloved Mr Mason, well *then* my dear I feel sometimes like hiring one of those *odious* loud-speaker vans and going for a ride round London saying the *rudest* things, O dear, farewell your far from unfrustrated TOPSY.

6 Iodine Dale

November 14, 1945

Trix darling about the *Moon*-Party, you remember I said you might *sound* your Henry a bit, about the *evacuation* I mean, well I do *hope* you weren't *too* communicative because it's *quite* off the *whole* thing, my dear *just* as I foretold *pure* international jaundice prevailing *ubiquitously*, my dear the suffering Russians wouldn't think of *anyone* proceeding to the Moon *at all*, the Americans wanted *ten* Moon-bases, the Australians it seems had *never* been consulted, the Canadians needed *all* the mining-rights, the *entire* tribe of Smaller Nations *not* to mention the *whole* of South America *insisted* on having a *Joint* Committee *not* to mention *observers* and moon-dromes, so my dear by the *end* of the Conference the *one* country with practically *no* claim on the Moon was *poor* old Britain, who conceived the entire *thing*, anyhow it's *quite* off now darling, and perhaps there *is* something in Haddock's couplet If Drake had waited for Whitehall He never would have sailed at all, *too* discouraging.

But I was going to tell you about my pathetic *Iodine*, you remember her *don't* you, Iodine *Dale*, she captained *lacrosse* or something at the old academy, well my dear *too* carelessly she married a *most* dank and insanitary species, my dear I *can't* tell you everything in a *letter*, but anyhow the total effect of the union was *atomic*, *mere* disintegration and septic vapours, however she's got her divorce poor dear or rather she *hasn't*, because of course *all* she's got is this childish decree *nisi*, and *nisi* little rustic I *must* inform you is a *Latin* word signifying *unless*, and when you think of the *thousands* that occur each year well *that* as Haddock says will show you how *dead* the Latin language is, well anyhow Iodine has got this decree of divorce *unless*, and my dear *if* you ask Haddock unless *what*, *all* he can say is *unless* the Judge changes his *mind*, and of course *put* like that it shows up doesn't it how *intensely* spurious, because at *once* you ask why *should* he change the little old mind, and then he says Oh well there might have been *collusion* or *connivance* or *condonation* or one of *those* things, well then I said but *why* didn't the Judge discover such banes and blemishes at the *trial*, so then Haddock said As a *matter* of fact you're *too* right, that's just what he's *supposed* to do, well my dear by *this* time the little head was circulating somewhat, so Haddock gave me the longest explanation which I'll *try* to repeat for you in rustic language, and my dear *don't* think that this is merely *lawyers'* fun because here under my *anæmic* wing *is* this distracted Iodine, half-*bats* with worry *although* the innocent party, policemen at the back door, and macaber figures *lurking* in the shadows, what's more you or yours may be in the same ditch any day *no* darling I withdraw of course your Henry could *never, half* a minute I *must* take a peep outside to see if that *man* is under the lamp-post again.

Yes there he is, *too* fraying, it's the cockeyed lamp the *rocket* blasted, and now I suppose it will *never* be mended, he *leans* against the lamp-post on the shadow side and you *just* can't see his *repulsive* face, I'm *sure* it's repulsive, however to go back, you *may* remember that *years* ago Haddock brought in the old Divorce Bill, and *one* of the clauses he added on his own was to *abolish* this puerile and fatiguing *nisi*-nonsense, which *by* the way it seems they do *not* have in Bonny *Scotland*, I mean there you're divorced or *not* and no doubt about it, where*as* of course for *six* months my *hunted* Iodine is neither one thing *nor* the other, she's *no* husband but she can't *marry*, which is *against* nature and practically *everything*, well to go back *that* clause was *whisked* out at once in Committee, because they said the *King's* Proctor *must* have the six months to probe about for *collusion*, etc, and smell out any *unveracities* or half-lies that may have slipped past the *Judge*, I *should* say *by* the way darling that according to Haddock the King's Proctor is a *lovable* variety and his charm-and-merit group is definitely *high*, well but *then* they said that *as* the law stood the Judge *might* grant a decree *unless* he had any reason to suppose that there was any *collusion* or lying or what-not about, I *think* it's Section 178 of something, so they said it was *too* feasible for the plausible and low-intention type to slip a wicked one past the poor Judge while he wasn't looking, *hence* they said the Decree *Nisi* in 1860 and *hence* how *indispensable* still the Decree *Nisi* in 1937, my dear have you the *faintest* notion what all this is about, *just* read it over and over again darling *quite* slowly, because honestly my dear Haddock says there are *quite* scores of *thousands* of citizens in the same *crazy* quandary as our Iodine today.

Well of course it seems worn down by all this *ponderous* metal poor Haddock had to surrender his little clause and the old Bill *trundled* along, but my dear *this* is the stagger, *what* happened *next*, why my dear they said we *can't* have collusion and everything and *what's* more we *won't* have our judges *deceived*, so they altered section 178 of what-was-it and turned it round the other way, so that *now* my dear it says the judge *shall not* grant a decree *at all* unless he's *too* satisfied there's *no* collusion, lying, etc, my dear if he's the *least* suspicion he must say *No*, you *do* see the point now *don't* you darling, because it means that *if* he's a good judge which one *must* assume darling he can't *possibly* have been *deceived*, whereas you still have this barbarous *nisi*-stuff the *whole* point of which is that he may have been deceived *still*, and of course Haddock says the *nisi*-law is absolutely a *concrete* insult to His Majesty's Judgery.

However *so* much for the law darling, *now* for the gruesome *events*, well my dear the *first* thing was that I get an *appealing* telephone from *tormented* Iodine who is alone in the ancestral villa with her Decree *Unless* and her faithful Nanny, and it seems that *quite* suddenly a policeman appears at the back door and asks the petrified Nanny the *most* mild but *intimate* questions about the Iodine Way of Life so to speak, I mean *how* late to bed, *any* men about and *so* forth, well in the *midst* of the narrative there's a *hair*-curling scream, because it seems Nanny has just reported there's a *hooded man* at the *front* door, well of course I at once offered the poor waif *sanctuary* in Jill's room who my dear I think now will *never* be demobbed or *anything*, I forget if I told you she's a *Leading* Torpedo Wren and knows *quite* everything about Volts and Wattery, besides my dear doing *land*-work and massage in the early stages, the *things* they're up to the Youth Movement nowadays, well to return to Iodine and my *Christian* behaviour, because my dear *wet* paint everywhere and Haddock I *rather* think is *rather* attracted, though of course it's too true that he has a *technical* interest, because you know in *this* Parliament he *tried* to introduce *eleven* Bills, *too* numerous and *quite* fruitless because this *inflated* Government has taken *all* the time for their *verbose* mega*lo*manias, anyhow *one* of the Bills was to *again* abolish this infantile Decree *Unless*, so one can't complain of a *certain* interest, though *when* it comes to striking *utter* strangers at the *front* door, however I haven't told you all, in fact I *can't*, the thing's an *enigma*, my dear *one* theory is that *someone's* written the King's Proctor an *anonymous* letter about the innocent *Iodine*, which it seems is the done thing in this *indecent* world, and *hence* the *policeman*, but then *who* is the *hatted* man who merely *haunts* the premises, *glues* himself to that lamp-post for absolute *hours* and from time to time *darts* across the road, *hammers* on the front door and *at* once vanishes, *except* as I say my dear when Haddock *biffed* him, well the Haddock hypothesis is that he *is* actually the *respondent* Mr Iodine, because Iodine once thought that she recognized the *walk*, though now of course she's *too* tremulous to even *peep* from a window, that it was Mr Iodine who wrote the anonymous letter, to *secure* the policeman, and now does the hooded-man act to keep him *interested*, well of course it all sounds *absolute* bats, but then as Haddock says the Decree *Unless* is absolute bats, and of course it seems that *Mr* Iodine *is* actually that sort of *type*, so there's *no* reason why *quite* anything should *not* occur, and of course the hooded man may *well* be a *detective*, but my dear the drab thing is that Iodine has three months to go at *least*, so *what* will happen in *this* poor home, and if anyone defends these *flatulent* laws, but of course *all* the King's Ministers think about is *nationalizing* this and that, *Oh* dear, farewell your agitated **TOPSY**.

7 Saving At The Races

Trix darling of *course* we'll turn every *stone* about your Maria Whatisitska, but Haddock says you must tell *more*, my dear what *is* she, you say go to the Russian Embassy, but my deluded rustic there *is* no Russian Embassy, at least not in the London Telephone Book, there's a *Soviet* Embassy merely, where Haddock says they speak the Soviet language, and of course if she's *Soviet* it seems she might be Georgian, Kamchatkan, Ukrainian, or even Russian, but then again from what you say she might be an *Estonian* or Lithuanian, and in *that* case who knows what, because it seems *nobody* quite knows if *they're* Soviet or not, anyhow there *is* an Estonian Legation in the T B and a Lithuanian *likewise*, so perhaps that would be the better avenue, it's *too* confusing, and by the way Haddock says you mustn't talk about a Soviet *national* because that at least can mean *quite* nothing, however darling we'll do our best.

Well, my dear we've just had a rather *jeopardous* adventure, *too* nerve-removing, I must explain that *poor* Haddock like other pubs, and when I say *pubs* darling I of course mean public *men*, not houses, my dear I do think there ought to be an absolute *statue* somewhere to *all* the pubs of England, when you *think* of all the fraying toil they undertake for *quite* nothing, I *definitely* can not envisage *why*, and of course the more you do for nothing the more the *entire* population seems to think that you've *nothing* to do but to do things for *nothing*, I mean go weakly onto *one* Committee and *half* the Committees in the kingdom swarm upon you, my dear we know men who spend all their *days* in Committee, whether it's Water Boards or *Catchment* Areas or *Saving* Europe or *Improving* Prisons, and my dear getting *quite* nothing out of it but *national* umbrage and premature tuberculosis, my dear Haddock says he knows *three* men who are *quite* never out of the *Chair*, as for Mr H himself who is a mere *amateur* and short-time pub, well in the old days he never *deigned* to *lecture* except too haughtily for a mass of *guineas*, not that he has the *smallest* urge or even *theme* to lecture about *anyhow*, but now that he's a semi-reluctant pub there is not *one* Society, Gov Department or *Youth* Movement that does not it seems expect him to lecture for nothing *quite all the time*, my dear the letters cascade in daylong, my dear it takes days to say *No* to half of them, not to mention the *lethal* expenditure on stamps, Haddock has a Movement for a *Sixpenny* Post, and *how* the old overdraft is to be equilibrized is *not* it seems a problem that is taken *too* seriously anywhere outside *this* humble home, however *as* I was saying like the other pubs *poor* Mr H from time to time is cajoled and goaded to speak at a *Savings* Week meeting and from time to time does so because it's the *done* thing, which of course is *so* spurious because my dear *try* how we may we do *not* seem to save a *shekel* and one can *hear* poor Mr H's conscience kicking while he *implores* the charwomen to give up their yachting and oysters and invest their all in these *drab* certificates, besides which I am *not* positive that he knows *much* more than I do about *inflation* and everything, which is *about* ZERO minus 14, anyhow I notice there's rather a *skating* movement when such topics are touched upon, however the *key-*point of this narrative approaches *now*, which is that as you *may* or may not remember for *quite* years he's been *going on* about the taxation of *betting*, which does not *exist*, and of course *now* he says *how* incompatible it is all this *Purchase* Tax on everything you *buy*, all this *murderous* mulcting of everything you *earn*, and all this *pontifical* yap about *saving*, when my dear if you put a *hundred* Peppiatts on some *ludicrous* horse you pay *no* tax *at all*, not even if it *rattles* home at 50 to 1 and you win a great *wad* of Peppiatts, which one *has* to agree darling has a *tinge* of *plausibility*, well anyhow *being* invited to address the *Chamber* of Commerce and the *massed* Rotarians of Burbleton about saving he said what *is* the purpose, *all* those respectables will do the old duty *anyhow*, why if I *must* utter not utter on the *race*course where I see the Autumn Gathering will be proceeding, the *Big*

Race is on the identical day, and the untutored proletariat will be *squandering* their hard-earned on *anti-social* and go-slow *horses*.

Well darling *somewhat* to my surprise and apprehension it *was* so, my dear we were parked in the *Silver* Ring or somewhere, *too* close to the *loudest* bookies and with a sort of lectern-arrangement like theirs, only of course instead of the *odds* and so forth *our* blackboard was all about these dreary *certificates*, well my dear Mr H opened fire between the 2.50 and the *Big* Race, with an audience of *about* one man, as a matter of fact I didn't hear *all* his opening speech because I *slipped* away to put a fiver on Love Lies *Bleeding*, which Frank told me could *not* be beaten, and ten bob each way on Diadem for Frank's Nanny, rather a *melting* bookie my dear called *Oats*, and I *rather* think he was *rather* attracted, we still have *remnants* of the old charm darling, however he said *What's* the old bloke belly-aching about lady, which being a reference to my only husband I explained the *Savings* Message *briefly* with the *result* my dear that Mr Oats went *quite* purple and began yelling *Ten* to one the *Field don't* forget the Old Firm lady *Come* to us and you'll have something to *save*, in which I must say I did see the *point* don't you, so then I went back to Haddock who *stung* and galvanized was shouting madly about *certificates* and two and a half per *cent*, which *works* out I gather my dear at about *two* to one after eight years, and the cries of *ten* to one the field and *100* to 8 Diadem did somehow have a more convincing ring, well by this time a rather *acidulous* little crowd had massed round Haddock, my dear some *quite* unChristian and muscular categories, as a matter of fact I *might* have heard my bonhomous Mr Oats say something about Handle him lad to one of his own henchmen, who had a face my dear *exactly* like a whale's ear, anyhow it was *too* clear that the *sense* of the audience was not *utterly* with Haddock, *things* were being audibly said *quite* alien to the Savings Movement, I mean when Haddock got to *inflation* and everything a man would sing out *Forty* to one *Inflation*, or Six to four on *Thrift*, *too* out of keeping, and one man shouted Send for the *police*, which I thought was a *little* harsh on the envoy of the State, well presently there was a rather *pointed* little rush towards the lectern, so of course *all* the motherbird in me rose up at once, I *sprang* to the side of my poor threatened pub and began a private yell of my *own*, my dear I can *not* record all the things I said to those citizens, my dear Parasitical *louts* was about the most *unprovocative* of all my assertions, and of course the *laughable* thing was that suddenly I found I was *too* serious about the *entire* Savings Movement, my dear if you could have *seen* those *uncivic* creatures with their *wads* of Peppiatts and greedy eyes, and my dear the *entire* paraphernalia of horsery is *so* pseudo when you come to think of it, my dear not *one* of those avaricious sportmen had ever touched a horse I *swear*, and of course the *other* laugh was that *whatever* I said about their antecedents and *obscene* appearance I *rather* think they were *rather* attracted, indeed Haddock says that with the little eyes flashing and everything, and I'd got on my new blue two-piece, *18* coupons, the old form was definitely *recaptured*, anyhow they were as mute as newts, and fortunately the *Big* Race beginning they dispersed at last with a few rude cries of *Forty* to one Inflation, well *then* my dear to *crown* all as *perhaps* you remember my *adored* Love Lies Bleeding came in *quite* first, with Diadem a good *second*, so in rather an *astringent* silence I collected *fifty* Peppiatts from the unamused Mr Oats, who said sultrily Mind you *save* it lady, and as a matter of fact I have bought *three* or four of Haddock's *insipid* certificates, which is more than Haddock has, so all's well, etcetera, but what a *day*, farewell your battling TOPSY.

8 The Danes

November 28, 1945

Trix, darling, *where* am I, I'll give you *four* guesses, *right* in
the middle of the *Kiel* Canal on the darkest night in the *most*
appealing *butter*-boat bringing butter and eggs and *bacon*
from the Danes to *England*, because my dear Haddock's been
lecturing in Copenhagen, it's still not utterly manifest *why*,
but concerning that you must ask the British Council and
everything and when I say lecturing he merely rises *without*
notes and burbles bonhomously for *quite* hours, which I must
say the Danes did seem to suffer *gladly*, but then of course they
are the *completest* pets with *angels'* manners and a British sense
of humour, my dear the *shaming* thing is that they contrive to
laugh at Haddock's most *esotteric* anecdotes, and of course why
on earth that *overrated* author made that *bilious* citizen Hamlet
a Dane is *quite* inexplicable, most of them talk English *far*
better than the English and many of them you'd bet *six* pairs of
fully-fashioneds that they were *native* Brits, whereas of course
Haddock and I can say *quite* nothing in their tongue except
Skaal which is Cheer-O and *Tak* which is Ta duckie, and those
of course you say *all* day, my dear Haddock has just *startlingly*
refused a Schnapps at 0900, the children *all* acquire English
it seems, my dear *one* morning at 0400 we were woken up by
small boys vociferating *Tipperary* with which odious ditty they
used to madden the Germans one gathers, and my dear *how*
they abominate the Germans, well *can* you wonder, not only
Tipperary they know *all* the island anthems, my dear at the
60th anniversary of the *English* Debating Club which was the
just cause and excuse for the Haddock sortie, my dear the *drill*
is that *at* the meetings not *one* word of Danish is uttered and
when you think that for *sixty* years all this has been proceeding
it *is* a little wonder-worthy and pride-producing you *must* admit,
well my dear Haddock had brought a *genial* message from
the Speaker and the *entire* company *about* five hundred arose

and *stood* while he read it, *too* stirring, and then at the supper they sang *Auld* Lang Syne and *He's* a Jolly Good, and my dear Haddock *not* content with having orated for one *complete* hour must *now* be upstanding and sing his *Beveridge* song, Oh *won't* it be wonderful after the *war*, which personally I thought was *rather* unprovoked and even out of *keeping*, however my *gorgeous* Danes digested the ditty *at* once and it's now *practically* the new national *hymn*, because my dear the next night at the Students' Union at the *University* where Haddock gave another *inexcusably* protracted discourse about parliaments and everything, my *dear* how I suffered and as a *matter* of fact about *half*-way through I *rather* thought the old man himself would sink into a *stupor*, and *actually* as it turned out he *was* sickening for a *food*-fever which is what *all* the English become a casualty to it seems after about five days of this *enchanting* Danish *alimentation*, well anyhow at the end of *questions*, which I thought were a shade shy and sparkless on the part of the Youth Movement, but then can you *wonder* in an alien *tongue*, well then a far from unmagnetic *froken* petitions Haddock to sing his *Beveridge* which they've read about in the morning it seems, *after* which my dear they all sing *everything* from My *Bonny* is Over to *Loch* Lomond, A *Tavern* in a Town, *Annie* Laurie and The Prettiest Girl I ever Saw sat sucking Cyder through a *Straw*, the last being another *quite* superfluous Haddock solo, well my dear if you could have *heard* those young you'd have sworn it was a bunch of Brits, *no* accent and *what* spirit, *quite* electrical, well we wound up with Auld Langers and the Danish National, and the same day Haddock had a *princely* lunch with a *platoon* of lawyers who he says discussed the most *obstruse* points of English law in *top* English, and this morning my dear while I'm watching one of the seamen burning paint with a *blow*-lamp *what* is the first thing he starts to whistle, When Irish Eyes are *Smiling*, so altogether as Haddock says *if* there *is* going to be a Western *block* or something there could *not* be a *much* better foundation than the Danes, because my dear *after* all the whole Prussian filthery did begin in 1864 it seems, when Denmark was the first unlucky virgin so to speak, and my dear in the *late* conflict I do *not* think one *quite* recalls just *how* tough and unfraternal the Danes were to the septic *Germans*, for one thing as Haddock said in a speech *uncongenial* though bombs may be one does remember saying *constantly* in the blitz-days and doodle-times Well anyhow this is no great *fun* but *how* much worse to have *Germans* about the place, better *two* incendiaries on the roof than one Prussian at the front-*door*, and my dear I can *not* envisage *how* we could have *endured* to see that *contagious* and inflated race *strutting* about the Strand and *swilling* at the Savoy and so forth, well my dear the Danes it seems merely *wore* the vermin *away*, always *too* polite one gathers when they weren't blowing up railways or their own *pet* buildings, or else making the *rudest* jokes, my dear I *adore* the bookseller who put pictures of Hitler and *Mussolini* in his window and in between them the *largest* copy of *Les Misérables*, poor sweet incarcerated of *course*, and my dear *ab initio* there were *Churchill* Clubs in *half* the High Schools, and in 1940 during the Battle of B *three* quarters of a million Danes it seems came out *quite* suddenly into the streets and parks and everywhere and *sang*, merely *sang*, they called it an *All*-Sing, just to *show* the cosmos, which of course the Germans thought was *too* out of place, and *how* I *ache* to have seen their *superb* King Christian *horse*-riding about the streets in the early morning *quite* unaccompanied, *that* is till the Huns interned him, and then of course when the Jew-nonsense began and they said that all the Jews were to wear the *Yellow* Star, the King said in this country there is *no* Jew-problem for we have never considered ourselves *inferior* to the Jews, and as for this Star-Stuff the King and the *entire* Court will wear the Yellow Star *likewise*, so *that* was a flop, my dear what *can* you do with such people, well then in '43 of course they *all* blew up, King, Parliament *and* Populace, they said they were *too* congested with the German race and it could transfer itself to any *appropriate* place as long as it was *quite* elsewhere, well *then* the afflicted Huns had to *invade* the Model Protectorate *again*, the police were turned out, there was sabotage and *anti*-sabotage, because wherever the Danes blew up a *factory* the Huns blew up some favourite place like a Yacht Club or cinema, my dear *too* infantile, and *by* the way you *ought* to see the *Shell* building where the obscene Gestapo gang resided, right in the *heart*, I mean about Trafalgar *Square*, and the RAF came over and *quite* obliterated the lair, *three* minutes before the sirens went, and 200 of the vermin slain, *what* a job, the Danes will *never* forget it, well then there were strikes and *more* strikes, and the Huns decreed a *curfew* at 8 o'clock, my dear in *summer* time, so *what* do you think the Danes came out in the streets and lit the largest *bonfires*, well in the *end* it seems the Germans saw *three* red lights and utterly agreed to *terms*, *no* curfew and who knows *what*, so that will show you what *can* be done by a bijou St George with *top*-guts and no sword at *all*, and as a matter of fact they say if the conflict had continued *much* they'd have had *all* the cooperative *dairies* striking and then the poor Prussians would have had no *butter*.

Well here we are in this almost *invisible* steamer, the dear little *Rota*, my dear Haddock says she's *just* over 1000 tons but swift and *quite* full of bacon and butter for you and yours, the captain by the way who is the *ocean's* darling and I *rather* think is *rather* attracted, was deep in the underground stuff *throughout* the conflict, my dear *smuggling* Danes and our parachute chaps across to Norway and everything, one time he says he had 30 chaps behind the cargo with the Germans ramping about the hold, however I must close now because we're approaching the *ocean* end of the said Canal, the captain says the wind is Force 5 in the North Sea which Haddock says is *quite* enough if not more, so I propose creeping into the *bottom* bunk *forthwith*, a pity my dear because I was *eager* to tell you about the *food* at Copenhagen, the cooking in this ship by the way is a thing to *sing* about and last night we went on a *Skaaling* party round Aalborg with this *magnetic* captain, beginning my dear with sherry *and* port in an antique cellar, proceeding to a *unique* old tavern with schnapps and *beer*, followed by a sumptious dinner with the celebrated Danish cherry *brandy*, fortunately there's *no* skaaling once we leave port so there *has* been a day of rest, but whether the little frame is *quite* attuned to Force 5 in the North Sea is something that remains to be *proved*, farewell, your faintly unconfident TOPSY.

9 Force 5

November 29, 1945

Well Trix darling, we've *issued* from the Kiel Canal at *last*, and now after two days we're in the *North* Sea and *practically* on our way to London, though even now we have to go right up to the *Humber* and then down the *coast* it seems because of *mines*, but then as Haddock says what *does* it matter, my dear I do think he's *so* right about the *overrated* Air, well of course if we'd aviated we'd have been back in four hours, we took *five* coming because of adverse tempests, but my dear *what* hours, that *dreary* noise the entire time, you *can't* move, you *can't* read, you've *no* idea where you are, and as for feeling you're monarch of the air you feel more like a *deaf* prisoner in a third-class dungeon bumping up and down in an *insufferable* din, my dear you can *see* nothing, coming over I had the *minutest* window *thick* with rain through *which* you could see about four clouds and the starboard *wing*, and if there *is* any object more boring than an aircraft's wing, *added* to which of course you see no *life*, I mean you can *roar* over Denmark, Holland and Germany and know no more about the people than if they were *fishes*, whereas in *this* way pottering about by ship and puff-puff, of course we've had the craziest journey because to get from Copenhagen to Kiel we first travelled *west* in a ship all night, then *north* for four hours in a train, then *south* again for a day and a night in *this* bijou vessel, *nearly* my dear getting back to *Copenhagen*, which sounds *too* wrong to the speed-fiends and save-timers, on the other hand *all* the time we've been seeing *Danes*, and *Jutland*, and the farms and railways, and the wrecks in the Baltic which are *quite* phenomenal, my dear the Captain says the ships are *still* going skyward where we were last *night*, then of course there was that *electric* skaaling-party at Aalborg to which no aeroplane could *ever* get you, and Kiel Harbour, what with the *fat* battleships *quite* upside down and the Hun pilot being polite to the Danes at *last*, and the *rather* compelling British naval officer in his *German* launch with a *German* crew and a *German* officer gold-cap and all, *too* satisfying darling, well as Haddock says *how* much of *all* this do you see with a bird's-eye *view*, not *much*.

On the *other* hand of course we may still stimulate a *mine* or two, and your little friend can no longer conceal from herself that we are *pretty* definitely at *sea*, because whether the wind Is Force 3 or Force *13* the undulation is quite *noticeable*, my dear don't think I'm *nauseous* or anything, it's only the faintest apprehension of *unease*, if you know what I mean, and perhaps the *sage* thing will be to lie still and tell you more about *Copenhagen* to keep the *mind* off the dubious tummzy, well darling Copenhagen I *rather* feel is *almost* my favourite city, of course I've not seen Stockholm about which they all talk ravingly, there are the *most* arresting buildings everywhere with *quantities* of the tallest spires and things, most of them in *lizard* green, which they say is because it's *copper* I can *not* envisage *why*, my dear Haddock has just been in and he says the wind is only Force *4* South Easterly but *freshening*, the drab thing will be if I miss the mid-day *meal*, I think there's a dim hope still because my delicious Danes do everything at the *wrongest* time, my dear we *lunch* at 11.30 and have dinner at half-past-*five* which gives one *rather* a protracted evening, but my dear *what* meals, the entire crew is only 21, but you couldn't *comb* Soho for more salubrious cooking and the *most* paternal steward, the *overture* to lunch is like *all* the stories, my dear yesterday I counted *fifteen* things on the table and *all* enchanting, there were *two* kinds of smoked herring and one smoked *sole*, with *onions*, imagine darling, *two* categories of bacon no three I think because one was hot, some fascinating sliced *ham*, some sort of hot *fish*, two types of egg-food, *liver* paté, home made and high marks for succulence, cold pork, and *pressed* beef, sausages in two styles, oh yes and mayonnaise of *salmon* and some sort of *inscrutable* stuff I cannot classify, all this my dear accompanied by schnapps, with *chasers* of refreshing lager, *not* to mention a *mountain* of butter, and of course *just* when you think the meal is over, *not* that you tackle *all* the things of *course*, it's just the *spectacle*, well *in* comes some *hot* pork or beef or somewhat *magically* but *simply* cooked, actually, my dear they do *not* consume excessively but there *is* no doubt they understand the art of *living*, however perhaps one had better *discontinue* this discussion because it's putting ideas into the little *tummy* and it's now *too* manifest that steamers of 1000 tons ought *not* to go about the oceans *excepting* in the *flattest* calm, my dear Haddock who's *indecently* well keeps *surging* in and saying *What* a good *sea-boat* which I've told him not to say again, however to go back to the buildings which *may* be safer, there's one fantastic pale-green spire made of the tails of *four* dragons *twisted* together, I'll send you a postcard and as for the *Radio* House which we went *all* over after Haddock's broadjaw, it's *too* palacious, *Greenland* granite and the *most* beautiful Concert Hall you ever saw, altogether my dear it makes the poor old BBC look like a suburban *pub*, they say they had to *bribe* the German anti-sabotagers not to blow the whole thing heavenward, my dear Haddock has been in again *encrusted* with brine, he says the wind is now definitely Force 5 and *backing*, lunch is on the table and there are two *new* categories of smoked herring and *cured* bacon, but my dear I grieve to say it but I *seem* to have lost *all* interest in *bacon*, I've consented feebly to a small hot *soup* and perhaps if I continue to keep the mind on *you*, well the *shops*, my dear at *that* moment there was a shattering *thump* and the ship did actually stand on its *head*, *quite* all the clothes flew off and the little feet pattered against the bunk *above*, *too* alarming I'm *not* sure but I should think it was a *mine*, no Haddock has since transpired with the soup and *all* he said was *What* a good *sea-boat*, well the shops, my dear I could *not* get any chocolate for you because that's rationed and there are absolute *queues*, butter's rationed too but seems to be prolific by our standards, there's *no* tea, and they ache for tobacco and coffee, my dear an English *cigarette* is practically *manna*, a shilling for one was the done thing recently, then of course there are *no* hot baths because of no coal, which is a fraying detail maybe but affects a girl's life as *you* know, and I mention all this, my dear the soup has cascaded *all* over my night-wear, because I *don't* want you to think that my darling Danes are living *heartlessly* in the lap of lux, far from it, they're doing all they can to do the Christian thing, well *meat* is in *masses*, my dear if you could *see* the butchers' shops, *enormous* cattle and festoons of oxtails, but they can't distribute more it seems because of *transport*, meanwhile as Haddock says it *is* a comfort to see *one* corner of *civilization* surviving, I mean in the way of *eating*, le manger, there are the *most* atmospheric old restaurants and oak taverns, and personally, I should *hate* to see them reduced to *our* abyssmal queueing and scraping, because *after* all it is an *Art*, which ought to be preserved and fostered, my dear the fried sole at our hotel was a *dream*, and as for the *cheese*, my dear the *Roquefort*, oh gosh such thoughts are a fraction *dangerous*, and of course *when* they give you a *special* lunch to show you what the old times were it actually *is* a spiritual *experience*, so is the *skaaling*, Haddock asserts the wind is *abating* but it's not *too* perceptible *here*, my dear there's none of our *casual* sipping and swilling, every drink is a *solemn* toast, you look *deep* and earnest into *all* the eyes and say *Skaal*, then you *bow*, my dear it's more like a religious *ritual*, which again is a sign of *civilization*, well *can* you envisage some of our gin-groups behaving thuswise, however, they're *so* hospitable that to an untrained British tummy the task is *formidable*, and I must say that after *six* days my pathetic Haddock had a pain in the *midriff* which he described untactfully as a *duodanal* ulcer, however it wasn't and *today* as I think I said he's odiously well, he's just announced my dear that we've passed the P10 *buoy* and we've only another *three hundred* and fifty miles to go, the *wind* is freshening again and *drawing* ahead, my dear he also described the whole of his *disgusting* lunch as a result of which my dear I rather fancy the *worst* is about to

It did darling, farewell your suffering TOPSY.

10 The New House

December 6, 1945

Trix darling, I grovel about the pencil, *not* to mention the *squalid* paper, and I shouldn't wonder if this actual *letter* turned out a shade miscellaneous and disordinated, when I tell you where I *am*, my dear I'm waiting in the *Central* Hall at the House while Haddock seeks a seat in the Gallery for me, which I gather is *practically* prohibitive, my dear you've *no* conception of the *multitudinous* conditions in this place now, it is *actually* the National Home for *Queues*, because you know for *years* past the populace have sniffed and snooted at the *whole* institution, it was the *gasworks* and the *talking*-shop and such, and every Member was a *septic* politician, my dear the *meanest* category of personnel, in fact during the late conflict as Haddock used to say, it *sometimes* sounded as if the Populace had *no* use for what they were *fighting* for, if you see what I mean, however now that the Populace have swamped the polls all's well it seems, *too* erroneous of course but satis*fac*tory, my dear there's a *sedentary* queue of constituents *all* down St Stephen's Hall which is *exactly* like a *refrigerator* except for Statues of Burke and Pitt and even they have small *calory* value, sometimes Haddock says the queue *expands* standing into the Street outside, *all* this my dear to hear the whifflings of the *septic* politician in the gashouse or *talking*-shop, *too* as it should be but not unlaughworthy, while in the *Chamber* it seems the Members have to *queue* up to the Sergeant-at-Arms, or should that be spelt with a j, I believe it's the done thing, with the same weird purpose, and as for where I am, my dear it's like *market*-day at Burbleton or Bunbury, I haven't seen any *cows* but *quite* congested, you can't *move* for all these *herds* of electors waiting to extract their Members with *Green* Cards and humble petitions, *rather* stirring as Haddock says because it shows the *interest* but a *shade* fraying for the battered *Members*, because of course it may be the *one* debate they ought to hear and instead they have to hither-and-thither for tickets or tea, *during* which somebody in the Chamber is saying *carbolically* I'm *surprised* not to see the Hon Member in his *place* and so forth, and by the way Haddock says the amount of *superfluous* carbolic about is *too* synthetic and boring, my dear you know how they always say that the start of a new Parliament is *exactly* like a new term at a Public school, well my dear he showed me one of the *Members'* telephone boxes where *two* days after the opening someone had written on the wall in *block* letters 200 TORIES CAN'T BE RIGHT, at which he thought Well the new term is starting with a bang, but my dear the *next* day it seems someone had rubbed out the T in CAN'T so that it *now* read 200 TORIES CAN, etc, and the *next* day the T was back again, the last thing was that someone wrote rather pompously underneath it, *Please* see notice about defacing *walls*, then someone scratched the whole saga out, *too* adolescent don't you think, however so far Haddock says there've been *no* rude pictures or hearts with arrows through them *yet*, though some fiery fellow did draw a hammer and sickle in the dust over one of the lavs, but that perhaps was some volcanic *visitor*, and *by* the way I don't think I *ever* told you about the *one* disconcertment we had in Copenhagen, my dear after Haddock had been interviewed by *quite* all the papers who were *too* nice and non-violent, he happened to see in one of them a column with a heading which *looked* like Stories about *Haddock*, *too* right, because my dear a friendly Dane interpreting it seems they'd attributed to my *blameless* Haddock three or four of those *antique* practical *joke* stories about the *renowned* practical joker Horace somebody I can *not* recall his name, my dear it was Haddock we understand they said who dug the *largest* hole in Whitehall and was a pest to the traffic for *simply* days *pretending* my dear to be someone from the gas or Water Board, like-wise it was *Haddock* we believe who gave his stop-watch to Sir *John* Simon, challenged him to run down a piece of Piccadilly in so many seconds and *when* he had started yelled *Stop* thief he's got my *watch*, my dear *John* Simon of all people *can* you imagine it, and can you *conceive* our blushes, because my dear if there *is* a thing my sunny spouse has *never* done it's practical *jokery*, *too* infantile we've *always* thought, and *now* my dear in a strange city on a *goodwill* mission, my dear we *scarcely* dared to emerge at *all* for fear the *police* would be watching us, though of course in the late conflict there was *no* sort of *practical* mockery the Danes did *not* do to the septic *Germans*, my dear one man put an advertisement in the paper *Quantities* of second-hand furniture to sell *Ring* number so-and-so, the said number being the telenumber of the *Gestapo*, who my dear went *utterly* bats answering applications for *beds* and wardrobes and could *not* ring Hitler or anyone up for *days*, so it may be they thought that Haddock's alleged antics were part of a *Resistance* Movement and took a Christian view.

Well, here I am still, darling and *no* Haddock, a lonely cork on the animated sea, but my dear I could sit here for *days* it's *so* human, my dear the *pathetic* constituents whose Members are *not* here, or can't come out perhaps, my dear like *dogs* waiting for the front door to open, *too* forlorn, and then of course the *Members* hither-and-thithering *manfully* my dear with that sort of *destiny* air they *all* have, bless them, as if D Day might be *any* minute, the dank thing is that nowadays I know so *few* of them, and *snooping* down at us of course those appealing little *stone* kings and queens on *all* the walls, talking of snooping my dear I've just given rather a *glacial* grin to Mr Ferret, I'll tell you later perhaps, however *what* I was saying was that *after* all I *am* sitting in the absolute *bosom* of the Mother of P's, *half*-way between the Lords and Commons, and *just* where the People come to meet the *Parliament*, my dear through the door I can *just* see Mr Pitt at the *other* end of St Stephen's Hall and opposite him is the enormous Mr Fox, *too* alarming, and my dear it *is* rather moving to think that that is *exactly* where they used to jaw and jangle in the aged days, when it was Pitt not Winston, though of course I definitely can *not* envisage that they had *half* the coping to do that we have, my dear have you the *faintest* notion what *Burnham Woods* is about, and then this *quite* inscrutable *Loan*, Haddock says he *rather* thinks that he may vote *against* it because it's the one thing that may stop him *smoking* at last and he could hardly care less if there were no more *films*, though I dare say there *is* a little more in it than *that*, my dear there's that Mr *Ferret* again who Haddock thinks *may* be one of the *pseudo-squad*, it seems that some of the Members have taken to writing articles about this place in the bilious weeklies under *false* names, my dear *too* pompous and *inflated* names like *Judex*, *Liberator* or Titus *Oates*, and some of them say the most *corrosive* things about the other Members, which Haddock thinks *if* it's the done thing it's time it *wasn't*, because he says *however* hot the argy-bargy in the Chamber the done thing is to be fair and frank *outside*, and even *in*, well I mean on the whole you don't chew up a chap who's not *there*, and anyhow it's all *quite* public, so the other chap can bang you *back* perhaps, next time, moreover after a banging-match you can *always* meet over a noggin in the Smoking-room and bang it out again in friendly fashion, when of course you *may* remember all the things you *forgot* to say before and so forth, which in the old days he says led to *many* amiable battles between the incompatibles, whereas now it seems you may be standing a chap a *double* whisky to-night when *last* week he called you a *vested* interest a reactionary what-not or Fascist *lackey*, *not* he says that *that* would matter if only you *knew*, because then you could buy him *another* whisky and matily explain just *where* he was *erroneous*, though personally I should save my Scotch for someone who had *not* called me a vested interest or *even* a reactionary *what-not*, but that I know is *not* the Commons way of life, and I must say there *may* be something in what Haddock says because here I am in a *dubious* state about poor Mr Ferret, who may *not* be one of the pseudo-squad at *all*, and at one time I *rather* thought that he was *rather* attracted, oh dear, here's Haddock at last, farewell your devoted TOPSY.

11 The Prime Meridian

December 13, 1945

Trix darling, one hundred salvoes from a thousand *guns*, this is my *Christmas* epistle to the frozen *North*girls, I don't suppose for a moment you'll get it before *Easter* because of course of the Christmas *rush*, and I won't swear that the *news* in it will be utterly *topical*, because my dear I *did* think *this* year the *septic* Germans being *practically* defeated I *might* have sent you a really *red-hot* Christmas epistle on what the papers call *hard news*, bless them, but my dear *last* night, *did* you hear it, *what* was my dismay and deflation, there was the *most* unencouraging broadjaw from somebody about the *Yuletide* drill, and it said for *pity's* sake don't send any letter after the *August* Bank Holiday, *only* telephone after Whitsun, and *never* telegraph *at all*, as for Christmas greetings on gilded wires, *nothing* it said could be *more* anti-social and everything, and *now* my dear they tell me there are the *largest* GPO vans traversing London today saying TELEPHONE LESS and *never* TELEGRAPH, which my dear is like the *Savoy* putting streamers out to say *don't* COME IN HERE, of course my dear I *know* you'll say all this is *obese* exaggeration, which perhaps it is but *not* much, because my dear that is the absolute *trend* today, I mean the *State* saying we *must* do everything but *don't* expect *me* to do a *thing*, and the private fellow saying I *ache* to do everything but nobody *lets* me, the *result* of which my dear is *primordial* chaos, and here I am composing my *Christmas* epistle to you in *mid*-Autumn, and *quite* unable to tell you *what* happened about Burnham Woods and everything, because I'm posting on Friday morning in the dim hope of reaching you before the *first bluebell*, my dear *don't* think for a *moment* that I'm not *completely* ethical about the post-personnel and *telecommunicationmongers*, because *actually* I'd like everyone to have *six* days off before Christmas, *and* another six *after*, my dear *no* food or posts or *gas* or electricity or *anything*, which Haddock thinks is a *shade* unfeasible though *I* should have said *quite* Christmassy in *spirit*, however *there* it is I can *not* tell you *what* happened about Burbleton Woods and everything because it will *not* have happened until after I caught the post tomorrow, if you see what I mean, which of course Haddock says he is *all for* because he says the *stark* menace to humanity is *easy communications*, and the more the State takes over everything the *less* there'll be of *that*, so to speak, well I mean he says after *about* three centuries the State has worked up to *twopence-halfpenny* on a letter from the Strand to *Fleet* Street, and he says with *all-party support* in a year or two they *may* get it up to *sixpence* or more, besides of course *practically* putting a stop to *all telecommunications*, my *dear* what a word, whereas of course if you put some *frightful* wizard like Woolton in charge you'd have letters *whizzing* in at a penny a time, everybody would get through to everyone *at once* and life on the whole would be too communicative and unendurable, for which I *must* say there *is* something to be said, don't you agree darling, and I rather hope they'll internationalize the *cosmic* wireless and save us from some of this defatigating *news*.

On the other hand, I do confess, Haddock does have qualms about the Prime *Meridian*, of course my poor rustic I don't suppose you've ever *thought* about the Prime Meridian, and I can't say it's *frequently* kept your little friend awake, but *actually* Haddock says the *Prime* Meridian is Longitude Nought, the merest *line* my dear it seems but it goes through *Greenwich*, in the South-East of *London*, well it seems for *years* and more they've been arranging all the navigation and the *Time* and everything by their laughable line which goes through *Greenwich* of all places, my dear if you'd ever *been* there you'd see what I mean, *not* I gather that there's been the *wee-est* trouble about it, in fact Haddock says the simple *mariners* and birdmen have quite a *feeling* for the place, but there it is it's *too* uncentral and bombed to bits besides of course being about a *year's* tram-ride from Westminster and everything, *apart* from which of course the whole thing dates a bit from the bad old *Tory* days, and what with one thing and another they appointed the *most* ponderous Committee, which said that Greenwich was *too* unsuitable and far away, and to *mark* the New Era the *Prime* Meridian ought to be moved to *Westminster*, and pass *if* possible through the *County Hall* in memory of Herbert *Morrison*, well darling *rustic* though you are I *expect* you'll see the point of *that*, but there was the *most* acidulous row in the House, because it seems the astrosophers said they would have to start *all over again*, and how would anyone know where the *Moon* was or anything, to which of course the Gov replied, It's the New Era and Damureyes, which it seems is the done thing nowadays, and if anyone who *knew* anything *said* anything there was a mocking *yell*, which also is the done thing now, however on a division it passed by a *183*, and that was *that*, but *now* comes the rubble and wife, as the Civil Defence man said, my dear I wonder if you're giving the *faintest* attention to my Christmas message, *if* not *do* read it *all* over again *quite* slowly, because honestly my dear you *must* try to keep *abreast* of civilization, *whatever* Henry does in his woods and spinneys, well you see *now* the *cosmos* had to be consulted, and of course the *cosmos* who never had a *word* to say about *Greenwich*, the moment there was all this yap about *Westminster* the *entire* cosmos began to have *ideas*, as you *may* imagine, well first of all the Dominions, my dear Canada it seems said the Magnetic North, whatever *that* may be, was *practically* at her back-door and *how* suitable, etcetera, and Australia said she was *half*-way between the Old World and the New and the *Prime* Meridian ought to go through *her*, causing Haddock says *practically* Civil War between Melbourne and Sydney, *not* to mention Canberra, well then South Africa said what about *Gold*, so they had a *Conference*, which I believe sits still, *meanwhile* of course the remaining humans were *all* muttering snootily *What* is all this British *Imperialism* and *Why* should the Prime be on British soil *at all*, anywhere, my dear the Portuguese were *too* umbrageous, the Americans said *New* York or nowhere and on the whole *Fifth* Avenue, the Zionists of course had *quite* other notions, my dear the *riots* in Calcutta and *Jerusalem*, and so it went on, *finally* my dear the suffering Russians got wind of it, the new idea, and now of course there's a *cosmic* conference in the pot, the *result* of which Haddock thinks will be that the Prime Meridian will be placed in Sweden, *unless* it moves from place to place at *five*-yearly intervals, *thus* driving *all* the astrosophers and navigators *bats*, which only shows as Haddock says how *sage* it may be to leave *some* things *alone*.

Well darling, I do hope my Christmas message may seed and fructify in your *slough* of a mind, if you'll forgive my poetry, it's not quite snowing, but the house is *thick* with fog, the gas is anæmic, my tiny hands are *frozen*, I *rather* think *all* the pipes will explode to-night, gangsters I'm *quite* confident surround the home, Haddock for all I know is *voting* for Burnham *Woods*, the twins are distant and probably *engaged*, but after all there will *not* be no *sireens* to-night, and *peering* through the fog I seem to see Britannia in the *arms* of Father Christmas, *utterly* illuminated by *rays* of hope, so *all* the happiest my oldest turtle, and for Heaven's sake don't *touch* that cheese if you think it's gone a *yard* too far, farewell, good Yuling, your antiquated TOPSY.

12 Good Resolutions

January 1, 1946

Trix, my little sunspot, I'm *quite* moribund with Christmas are you, my dear the *shopping*, and the *coping*, it's *too* satisfying to think we've got twelve *clear* months now before we have to go through it again, my dear *could* I get my poor Haddock so much as a new *pipe*, *not* anywhere though I *ransacked* the city, you would think, wouldn't you with all the *trees* we have in the land we could produce a *few* small pieces of wood with holes in them in which tobacco could be burned conveniently, because after all what *is* a pipe, they're made it seems of French briar, but why not *British* briar my dear you have *so* much surplus space up there I suppose you couldn't get Henry to plant a *grove* of briars for Haddock's pipes, Jill could fabricate them when she's de-mobbed if ever, because there's *quite* nothing she can't do with her hands, she makes the *most* appealing toys for children in the torpedo shed, or somewhere, and as Haddock says, on the other hand of course I need *hardly* say that Haddock has just given up smoking again for *quite* ever, and this time he says it's final because of the *dollar* area or something, nevertheless darling I should go ahead with the *briar-grove* if I were you, talking of *good* resolutions I've been in conference with the better self a good bit recently, and about some things I've made the most *steely* decisions, haven't you, because my dear I do think that *this* year is going to be so *unspeakably* macaber that really one must make an *utter* surrender to the better self and be a sort of *torch* and beacon to those about one, don't you agree darling, the drear thing is it *is* so difficult to get the *practicalities* clear, well for instance you know the new rule is *If* we've got anything we want *export* it, which *may* sound like the signature-tune of a bat to you my dear but *actually* it is political *economy*, and of course every *penny* you spend is the last and fatal step to *inflation*, or perhaps *deflation*, I never *have* known which is which and now

I've abandoned the struggle, well of course the very *first* thing I vowed was to utterly *expel* the juniper-juice and everything from my life, *except* after 6 on alternate Saturdays because, my dear I thought if only we *all* did that what *quantities* of gin we could export to America, well then of course Haddock says he thinks we don't export gin very prolificly to America I'm thinking of *whisky*, which I never *touch*, *too* discouraging, however that is *actually* going to be the way of life this year because of *inflation*, and then of course *accounts*, my dear I've bought the *largest* ledger and I'm going to record *quite* every penny and Peppiatt we spend, of course I know there *have* been years that *started* thus before, but *genuinely* this will be *too* different, I'm going to have *two* columns, one for expenditure which is the Done Thing or unavoidable and another in the *reddest* ink for unpatriotic or *bestial* expenditure like cigarettes or juniper juice.

Well then the drill is at the *end* of the week I show the page to Haddock who will add up *both* columns which is a thing I *cannot* do, and *sign* the page, *after* which my dear for everything in the *red* column we buy an *equal* amount of these soporific *Saving* Certificates, *that* is of course if the cash is in sufficient supply, my dear it *is* rather a satisfying system don't you think and if you and Henry would like to try it by all means, only I don't suppose your Henry can add much can he, I *ought* to warn you perhaps that one small serpent is *just* perceptible, and that is *which* column to put *what* in sometimes, well today my dear what with the New Year burgeoning and the little bosom surging about and *warming* to the fellow-creatures I went to the Festering Gallery and bought rather a *bizarre* picture by Carl and Taffeta Brule for Haddock, you know darling or perhaps you don't poor rustic they're the couple who paint all their pictures *together*, I definitely can not envisage *why*, but there it is they're the most *electric* couple and *quite* penurious, so whenever I can I do the Christian thing, I can *not* pretend however that they magnetize my Haddock *much*, in fact he did once say that he'd swim the Channel on a *cold* night to avoid poor Taffeta, and it's true that the *last* picture of theirs I bought was one of those *rather* triangular women with *green* hair, which did take a *little* time to settle down in the home, though I *think* I do see what they mean now, it's the *pattern* and the composition and everything that *matters*, however *this* picture was quite *unsimilar*, my dear the *Pool* of London with the Tower and *Tower* Bridge and tugs and steamers and two barges with *enchanting* cinnamon sails, which I did think Haddock would like for his *study* because of old haunts and everything, well my dear I *purchased* impulsively and took him to see it, later, *without* however telling him it was a New Year *gift* for him, well my dear he gazed at it with *noticeable* aversion and *all* he said was Where is the *wind*, which of course I ought to have known because he is so tiresome about the wind in pictures, however, I said *Must* there be a wind perhaps it was a calm day, and he said *Look* at the *flags* the wind's easterly at one side of the picture and *westerly* the *other*, which I now perceived was *too* right, however I said I expect Carl painted one side and Taffeta the other only it was on different days, and anyhow I said don't you like the *sails*, at which he said *no* barge would have all those sails up above Tower Bridge and *this* one if the tide's flowing will charge into *London* Bridge and lose her *mast*, he also said the tug's funnel was *four* sizes too large, and *where* was the steamer's anchor-cable or something, so I said Oh well you don't want a *coloured photograph* and he said Yes he'd *much* prefer it, at which darling *gulping* down the tears I was *just* wondering if I could *cancel* the purchase when *who* should roll up but Taffeta and *Carl* all burbulous and grateful, *on* which of course the ghastly facts emerged, you should have *seen* Haddock's face, I must say he behaved *too* well, said quite nothing about the wind, and was *even* affable to Taffeta, however outside, and this is the *point* of the entire narrative, he said In *which* column will you put expenditure like *that*, so I said In the *Done Thing* Column of *course* because it *must* be the done thing to nourish the anaemic and subnutritioned artist even if he does *not* cause *unanimous* raving, so Haddock said Well you may be right my dove of course I *should* have said that *any* picture by Taffeta Brule should be in the *Bestial* Expenditure Column, on the *other* hand

I do know *this*, that every time you buy a picture of a *triangular* woman with *green* hair *fifty* per cent by Taffeta Brule I am *not* going to put an *equivalent* sum in the *Savings* Racket, so there the matter rests darling, I *only* mention all this to show you the *kind* of enigma that may confront you if you and Henry take up the Topsy Loyalist Accounting System.

About my *other* Resolutions darling I doubt if I can reveal the *whole* soul now because on the *first* day of a *new* year as *you* know darling there *may* be the *faintest* indications of *fatigue*, however the *main* thing *as* I have said is the Torch and Beacon Movement, illuminating and beckoning to *all* the comrades and utterly determined *not* to enjoy oneself for *simply* years, of course Haddock says I've gone quite 'masokist' or something, merely because I said *Why* do we women wear all these *garments*, why not *export* the lot to America and let us women go about in smocks and *sandals*, after all you can scarcely *see* a stockinged leg in London today so why not be *logical*, as a matter of fact I've made myself the *most* seductive though spiritual smock and came down to *breakfast* in it, but Haddock says I am *not* to wear it at the House or *anywhere*, which only shows you how difficult it is to be *helpful* economicly, oh dear, the best and briefest of years darling, your *frustrated* masokist TOPSY.

13 Heroic Act

January 9, 1946

Trix darling, a *new* rule of life for you, *always* keep a little *holly* in the hall, I'll explain why in a minute, *by* the way my dear *what* about the good *resolutions*, I *noted* sardonicly what you said about making Henry join the *Rotary* and circulate a little more, because I don't suppose a *thing* has happened and if I were you I'd abandon the *entire* aspiration, for one thing one has to attend on *all* the Fridays except about *one*, and Henry will only be *expelled* for non-attention like Haddock was, or do I mean *as* yes Haddock says I do, it's *too* clear from what you say that your Henry's reaching the *ungregarious* stage and when he's not *squelching* about his woods and spinneys prefers to be *quite* reticent and ruminative in the *home*, I know the signs, of course I don't mean that you mustn't do your best to *make* him utter from time to time, though *never* at the morning meal, and as for *people* my dear have a few *sprigs* and blossoms in from time to time and you'll see him expand like a *rose*, especially if they go slow with the *Scotch*, but Rotary or anything like that no *definitely* no darling, Haddock by the way is already smoking like a *volcano* again, only more regular, in *spite* of the dollar area, and as for my *accounts*, well they began *meticulously*, but *what* a pest and martyrdom they are, however about the *holly*, well I expect you've read about the wave of *delinquency* in our afflicted city, my dear *too* alarming, one day it's *jewels*, the next day it's cases of *tea* far more dejecting, and they took 57 turkeys from a local meatmonger, it's called *bulk*-purchase I believe, and of course *how* they flash about the city with all these *massive* ill-gotten cargoes, because my dear the *crowds*, one can scarcely *stir* with the merest *parcel*, and as for 57 *turkeys*, my dear *where* all the people come from and *where* they sleep is something I *definitely* can *not* envisage, well among them it seems are *exactly* ten thousand *deserters* who having no *ration-cards* are compelled to exist by grabbing diamonds, etcetera, I do *not* follow the reasoning utterly but there it is, my dear the other day the police *flooded* the West End and Haddock's identity things were scrutinized *four* times in half a mile, *too* thorough but as he said not *totally* convincing, because after all these deserters have to sleep *somewhere*, why not make the *most* loud and *alarming* pronouncements about *harbouring* deserters and let *no one* sleep a chap without examining a chap's *papers*, however I dare say there is a little more to it than *that*, and of course as Haddock says what with all the chaps having been in the Army where private property does not *exist* and all the chaps at home being told that private property is a kind of *crime* invented by the wicked Tories, it's not too surprising to find the *sense of property* a shade *sluggish* here and there, though of course in the same circles the bestial *profit-motive* does seem to struggle along somewhat, anyhow my dear in liberated London now we all look under *all* the beds, especially of course my *hunted* Iodine Dale, Oh I forgot, I *did* tell you didn't I that she's working out the last months of her *decree nisi* and is *quite* satisfied that the *King's* Proctor is after her because of the *hooded* man who lurks under the lamp-post the *rocket* blasted, doesn't it all sound *too* macaber and moving, personally my dear I think she's bats, but what can you expect and there after an absent week or two he definitely *is* again, or someone *like* him, I've *implored* Haddock to *visit* the King's Proc and find out for certain if he has any *hounds* about, but Haddock says *if* the great *wheels* of Justice are in *fact* in motion it wouldn't be the done thing for a *Member* to poke the old nose in *much*, if *any*, meanwhile the poor victim is in *such* a state of *nisi-neurosis* she makes me open *all* her letters in case it's the King's Proc or somebody and will *not* open the front-door if it's to take in the *bread*, though *too* helpful in the home elsewhere, in fact a godsend, because my angelic Mrs B is *quite* distracted with all her family demobbed and *how* to feed them, well my dear *last* night I said to Haddock, *Take* the pathetic waif to the pictures or somewhere before we all have an attack of *battery*, I'll guard the fort, so off they went, and my dear feeling *noticeably* Christian because there have been moments when I *rather* fancied he was *rather* attracted, I thought it's at least the *Fourteenth* Night let's get the Christmas vegetation down, so after a *heroic* act with the step-ladder up the basement stairs I did the schoolroom and the hall, *beginning* with that barbarous *holly*, which they say this year is more lacerating than ever, *too* right, quite agony, well then my dear when half-way up the ladder to dismantle the mistletoe there's the *rudest* knock on the *front* door *three* feet away, my dear the little heart missed *seven* complete beats and then fell into the larger intestine, the *brain* however was working like a *rocket*, I thought Well it *may* be the King's Proc, or it *may* be one of the new *inspectors* about erroneous war-works or *billetees*, but intuition tells me it's a *bandit*, because you know darling *sometimes* you absolutely *know* you're right, well I thought the done thing is to ring up that *magic number* for the *police* and *hold* the bandit till they arrive, only *could* I remember the magic number, *no*, yes I know now it's 999 but *all* I could think of was Terminus *1234*, so my dear I *slunk* into the schoolroom and dialled *that* which turns out to be the *Sunday Times*, well while I'm explaining to a *baffled* watchman or somebody there's another shattering knock at the door, and I think *Let's* face it *after* all it may be the Ministry of Health or *carols*, because my dear in these parts carols begin in November and go on till *March*, so I snatch up a bosomful of *excruciating* holly, *turn* the latch and scuttle back and up my *ladder* again, well my dear in at once comes the *most* scrofulous little man with his *hat* over his eyes and *shuts* the door, and he says *very* American, *This* is a hold-up, *stick* 'em up, well by this time believe it or not darling the little brain was working *exactly* like a *ball*-bearing and I said *That's* no way to talk to a British matron under the *mistletoe*, to which he answered Cut it out swell dame are you Mrs *Elkinstone*, so I said For that matter are you the Ministry of *Health*, and he said *Are* there any *guys* in the house, my dear believe me this is absolute *verbatim*, so I said *Several*, and I *then* perceived that the little vermin was trembling like an *aspic*-leaf, so I thought This is one of the *amateur* bandits, no more American than Stonehenge or *me*, so leaning gracefully over my ladder I caught him the *most* unfriendly slosh in the face with about *five* shillings' worth of holly, I then fell on top of him, *ladder* and all, my dear I'm *nothing* but scratches and bruises, but I was *on top* so I hollied him a *little* more till my dear he *mewed* for mercy, when leaving the body *entangled* in the ladder I darted to the phone and shouted *Bandits*, well of course I was still through to the *Sunday Times* man who was sweetly helpful and told me *all* about 999 which we arranged for *him* to ring but of course I'd hardly *begun* to give him my address and everything when we were cruelly *cut off*, and by then the *anaemic* bandit had crawled to his feet and *evaporated* into the night, *too* disappointing but *rather* a triumph don't you think, though of course Haddock and me are *scarcely* speaking because he doesn't think it was a bandit *at all* but some sort of *divorce* detective, who thought it was a *sage* way to get *evidence* of any illicit *man* on the premises, who of course would rush to repel *bandits* but not the Ministry of *Health*, but then I said Why *me*, well it seems there *was* a Mrs Elkinstone in these parts *years* ago, so probably it's some utter failure in the filing system, they've got the *wrong* address in the wrong Borough, and if so it means that my *haunted* Iodine has no more to fear from the *hooded* man, which is a *big* thing to the good, on the other hand Haddock says that for all we know I *may* have mangled one of the *King's Proctor's* men, which may be *high* treason or something, I must say I could hardly care *less*, farewell now your big bedridden bruise TOPSY.

14 Timothy Brine

January 16, 1946.

Trix, my distant woodpigeon, *sensation*, what *do* you think, I'm going to write a *book*, or part of it, or anyhow be *in* it, I know you never *glance* at my letters, but Henry does I *hope*, and perhaps he'll remember I told you about my *bandit*, the small-sized weasel I lashed and dispersed with cruel *holly* in the hall, well *what* was my astonishment yesterday he *telecommunicated* and asked if he could 'contact up with me a coupla minutes', my dear as Haddock says it's *too* bizarre the *words* they waste these tough and snappy categories, because *contact* was pompous enough and *meet up with* was worse but when it comes to *contact up with*, when all you mean is *see*, however I said whatever *for*, and he said he reckoned he had to hand himself a *coupla* basinfuls of humble pie, by which my dear I gathered he meant *apologize*, so never yet having had an apology from a *bandit* I did the gracious, which Haddock to my surprise supported, so we made a date when Haddock could be there, Haddock by the way insisted on digging out the *rustiest* German weapon he brought back from the last war but *one*, for which praises be he has never had an *inch* of ammunition, because he said for *all* we knew there was dirty work in the offing still, he knew the type, which of course is *so* spurious, but my dear I must inform you that Haddock to my *mortal* shame reads absolute *leagues* of all this toughery stuff, moaning the *entire* time What *muck* what *utter* muck but *wallowing* deeply and quite inconsolable unless there's a new Timothy *Brine*, who is perhaps one of the *least* intolerable, I did actually wade *womanfully* through one of his, but my dear *what* squalor, what *insanitary* English, nobody is *ever* shot except in the stomach, *everyone* talks like a hairy ape, there are *no* women only *dames* frails and floosies, and every third paragraph the detective has a *slug* of rye or *four* fingers of *Scotch*, my dear *where* they get all the whisky and *how* they do any *detecting* on it, in one book Haddock calculated in *one* night and day the G-man hero got rid of four bottles of Scotch and one of *rye*, and this was in the Home Counties *1944*, however *as* I say these works are manna to my respected Haddock, *what* is more it now appears he *rather* fancies himself as a psycho-whatisit *student* of the underworld, anyhow he said he must sit with the gun in the *back* drawing-room in *case* my humble pieman was not on the *level* or the up and *up* or something, my *dear* what expressions, well at last my *adored* Mrs B who is doing a *brief* chore or two again now her breadwinner is better brings up the little bandit, who my dear *without* his hat looks littler than ever, practically invisible, and what with the *holly*-scars on his poor little face which is like the face of a backward *mouse* all the mother-bird is beginning to stir in me, when *judge* darling of my astonishment and dismay, before the bandit-waif has had time to open his tiny mouth I hear Haddock say *too* savagely *Stick* 'em up pal, and out of the shadow he comes with that laughable *pistol*, my dear *imagine* all this in a girl's *own* drawing-room, W6, well the little bandit puts his hands up and says *Look* dame, I kinda thought you and me was on the up and up, I thought maybe you'd let me get next to you *alone*, but now I guess I gotta take what's coming to me, well then Haddock said What's *beefing* you chum, or something, I'm gonna *frisk* you, maybe you pack a *rod*, at *which* my dear I merely *flopped* on to the sofa in a state of wonder and blush, too lowering, well Haddock went through all the little bandit's pockets, he found a tobacco-pouch, a *spectacle*-case, two pipes, a bit of *string*, a wallet, a box of matches, *quite* empty I need *hardly* say, and an envelope which he read out *too* suspiciously, To Timothy *Brine*, he said, Whadya know about Timothy *Brine*, well then my dear the little bandit said softly in the sweetest little Cockney voice, I *am* Timothy Brine, my dear I thought then that *Haddock* would fall in a faint, but it seems he told me afterwards it's the done thing with bandits never to show *surprise* at *anything*, anyhow all he said was, Look pal could you use a shotta *Scotch*, and the little man said Thank you sir, with *lots* of water, and look here you needn't keep up the American I'm no more American than Westminster Abbey, even then darling it seemed Haddock could *not* throw off his part once started, because he said something like Listen boyo no funny business or I'll drill you so full of holes a *culinder'll* look like it could hold a gallon of *rye*, which my dear will show you how *much* he's absorbed of this *unspeakable* imbecilery and *just* how deep the canker's gone.

Well, darling, while he's 'fixing' the drinks as he now calls it I get the little ex-bandit to sit down and sorta draw him out, O gosh I'm *catching* it, my dear it's the *most* affecting story you *ever* heard, it seems he really *is* Timothy Brine, or rather he *isn't*, because his real name is *Cuthbert* something, he's a *library* assistant at *East* Wansey, and he has a widowed mother who's been dying for *years* and has to have *constant* operations and oranges and everything, well in off-hours at the library he read *all* the Tough Guy and Stomach-shooting School one after the other, till at last he said a little voice inside said *Cuthbert* boyo *you* can do this, *which* accordingly he *did*, though my dear he's never been *near* America, in fact the longest he's *ever* been absent from mother was a day-trip to Southend in *1939*, but you see he's *utterly* absorbed the atmo and the lingo from the *books*, which shows *how* pseudo it all must be, on the other hand he must have a little *swamp* of an imagination because my dear *some* of the episodes in the *early* works, however darling you know how they *sold* perhaps, and you must *always* remember that *all* this was in aid of a poor sick *mother*, but my dear *now* comes the thumping tread of tragedy and gloom, the poor sick mother *declines* to die, resuscitated of course by these *miasmic* but cash-creating books, what is more she now has such a *high* standard of dying so to speak, meanwhile my poor little chum thinks he's *drying up*, he's done the same thing over and over like they *all* do, yes my dear I *know* I mean as, and now he wants some more *reality* to mine and quarry, but of course he *can't* go to the States because of poor sick *mother*, and besides he'd probably be *slaughtered* by the stomach-shooters *not* to mention the *authors* if they only knew, so the *pathetic* sweet has been picking the dust-bins for reality *here*, Haddock was *too* right the first thing he tried was *divorce* detective because nothing he thought poor innocent could lead a chap deeper into the cosmic midden, whereas nothing in *fact* it seems could be more respectable and *drab*, but he thought Well anyhow what a good '*front*' as they call it for burglary or banditry, moreover says he a chap who is practically *always* writing about hold-ups etcetera *ought* perhaps from time to time to do one *himself* if only to get the *psycho–whatisit* accurate, which I think is *so* right don't you agree darling, *hence* anyhow as I've told you he makes his *trembling* assault upon the Haddock home, and of course *how* fruitful because I'm too sure that half the time the bandit's *bleak* with apprehension but no one *says* so, well then it seems he's *so* impressed with the Topsy technique and her *heroic* holly act, *about* which he's *quite* unresentful, he thinks I *must* get next to *that* dame, my dear *what* language, so the idea is, I gather, only of course there's *Haddock* who's *too* disappointed it's not a *real* bandit, *thrilled* up to a point to meet Timothy Brine, but slumped no little to find he's a Wansey *librarian*, and how far he'll be *quite* keen on my being the chief dame frail or *floosie* in a new Timothy Brine is an avenue still to be *explored* so to speak, however we've both promised to aid the little bandit *all* we can, if it's only some sage advice on dress or drink, and who knows we *may* reduce the stomach-shooting ration, and *even*, though too unlikely, get a word or two of *English* into the works, farewell your battling patriot TOPSY.

15 The Dogs

January 23, 1946

Trix, you little *land-clam*, I'm *too* wounded about your reticent responses, I *empty* my bosom at you and *all* I get is an *unreadable* postcard, my dear for another halfpenny you can send an entire *letter* free of tax, but of course if you've taken to your *horse-hobbies* again I suppose you're *practically* always in a healthy *stupor*, by the way darling we were wondering the other night *has* anyone ever tried *eating* the fox, because after *all* that exertion, and surely the whole *conception* of the hunt is *food* for the hungry squaws and squawlers, of course I suppose it would disappoint the *dogs*, and Haddock says he thinks it might be *tough*, though *why* is an enigma because one gathers they eat *nothing* but the *most* expensive poultry, anyhow why don't you and Henry start a new breed of *eating*-foxes, *three* sizes larger, and make hunting a definite *drive* to supplement the *meat*-ration, in which case it might have a *permanent* niche in the *planned* economy, whereas otherwise it's *too* likely to be anti-social and the undone thing, if not denounced by *Uno*, the only *other* hope for you Haddock thinks is to somehow bring *betting* into it, because he says anything with betting in it is bound to flourish and *no* Government *dares* to so much as *sniff* against it, so perhaps you could have Four to one on the *Fox*, and *Ten* to one against Mr Peasepudding witnessing the *Kill* and so forth and of course *mounted* bookmakers *galloping* among the horse-men, changing the odds and *stimulating* the stern-most, honestly my dear you must confess there *is* a sort of *marginal* sanity to my at first sight *esotteric* and even *certifiable* suggestion, well for example glance for a moment at these inconceivable *greyhound-contests*, to which my dear I used to *guiltily* creep from time to time before the late conflict, and as a *matter* of fact I've *just* begun to more or less *resume* the wicked ways, *not* of course for self-*enjoyment* darling far from it, because my dear following the dogs, which *by* the way is what you call *your* quaint proceedings isn't it so you see we have got a *few* spots in common, well *actually* it is about the *most* exhausting form of human *toil*, my dear not a *moment's* peace, *incessant* arithmetic which as you know was never my *ace* activity, and constant bodyjostles with swarms of VUPs, which is short of *course* for Very Unmagnetic Persons, no darling it's *purely* part of the *drive* against the *overdraft*, because as Haddock *wistfully* reiterates betting in this *bat-conducted* world is the *one* form of cash-creation which is not taxed *at all*, and actually before the conflict I did one year *create* enough to take the *entire* tribe of Haddock to France, *too* satisfying, and this year if the twins are back I *do* want them to have a halcyon holiday with *weeks* of ozone, my dear I can *hear* you cackling but many a night as Haddock will confirm when *yearning* for a *nice read* in a soporific seat I've obeyed the better self and marched away to martyrdom among the VUPs, who of course one *must* admit may *all* have prolific families who are aching for the seaside *too*, so perhaps it's not *quite* so anti-social as you *think*, though when one sees the *figures* not to mention the VUPs, my dear do you realize, Haddock says the dog-totes are taking nearly *twice* what they did before the war, *seventy* millions a *year* I think he said though of course a *mass* of that comes back in *winnings*, but my dear *when* you think that in *three years* the money we put on dogs and horses and *Arsenal* and what-not is more than the *entire* American Loan one begins to perceive *just* what the national hunger for the seaside must *be*, so to speak, and they say *why* there are *quite* no taxis in London is they're *all* waiting for wad-hunters at the *dogs*, I couldn't tell.

Well darling I don't want to ululate *too* soon, because it is *so* flattening when you think you have the *longest* holiday *practically* in the bank when suddenly those *irrational* beasts begin to do the *wrongest* things and day by day the little gainings dwindle, but *actually* at the moment we are about *ten* Peppiatts on the way to *Cornwall*, of course I'm behaving *quite* cautiously at present, sort of taking the *pulse* of things so to speak, but I rather think it's going to be *less* laborious to win a wad than it *was*, because you see in the old days one made an absolute *study* of the form and everything, *utterly* of course against my principles and *nature*, my dear I do feel in some things the little *intuition* is *practically* infallible, you can't *guess* how many times when I hear what's won the *Big* Race I say Yes I *thought* so I chose that horse this *morning*, by the *name*, in fact as Haddock says if *only* I'd backed them all we'd be rich enough to pay the *income-tax*, at one time that was my absolute *method*, because say what you like a good name is *half* the struggle, by the way darling *did* you see we're now talking about the *Soviet* Ballet which Haddock says is the utter *terminus* of twaddle, game set *and* match, because if there was one thing you *might* expect to go on being merely *Russian*, however he's got a bet with *two* Ambassadors that *before* Easter we shall hear about the Soviet *language*, and people will say they're learning *Soviet*, well to go back to my philanthropic dogs, by the way darling stiff and *stupefied* though you *may* be with indifference to *my* poor dogs you must recall what *weeks* of agony in time past I've suffered with a smile from hearing the news about *yours*, my dear shall I *ever* forget the day you found in Twillington *Bottom* and killed in Somebody's *Patch* after a *celestial* run, and Henry narrated me over *about* five counties, in and out of *covers* and ploughed fields, with hounds *feathering* and *faltering* and *footling*, is *that* right, my dear *too* defatigating, so darling put *one* more pillow behind the old back and *try* to concentrate on the primitive customs of the *capital*, I can see *no* plausible cause for your peering *snootily* at my little dogs, after all *all* dogs are *dogs* and it might be said that Henry and me were *twin* facets of British dog-love, not to mention the *chase*, because it's all very well for you to say that my dogs are hunting a merely spurious *hare*, half the time *your* dogs are after an imaginary *fox*, and anyhow *as* I was saying you bring *no* more back to the larder than *I* do, so, sorry darling I must look back to see where I *was*, Oh *yes* about the *form*, well when I began this *quite* serious dog-following phase I read *all* the dog-columns in *invisible* print, the little eyes became beady and dim, my dear I wouldn't *think* of backing a beast at *Wimbledon* unless I knew *exactly* what he'd done in the last *six* races at Harringay and *How much, what* he beat, *which* trap, *how* fast, and what was the *weather*, my dear *protracted* and *lethal* labour, however *now* I gather, I expect you've read in the papers about the bizarre behaviour, my dear *sub-ethical* men spending the *night* in kennels and issuing suddenly with obstruse *drugs* so that every dog but *one* in a race resents running *about* half- way round, *too* ingenious, and now there are rumours of *more* uncivic devices, my dear in the old days one could stand *close* against the track and have a stirring view of the little yelpers, which is *actually* a decorative spectacle, *even* my dear when a girl's own dog is bitten at the corner and *then* beaten by a short nose, but now it seems they're going to push us *back* because they think *some* citizens may throw small rats, guinea-pigs, invisible *mice* or even *lizards* onto the course, *not* to mention drawing-pins and lumps of *glue*, so as to distract the doggies and frustrate the bookies, though *how* you can arrange for one dog to pursue a rat but not *another*, however personally I'm positively in *favour* of all this, for one thing darling it brings the *whole* thing don't you think into line with *your* sport, the chances of the *chase* I mean, like the fox-dogs going off after a *sheep* or the fox being *headed* by an ugly governess, in fact if I were the management I should have *surprise* items in *every* race, *wild-cats* my dear and old bones and explosive *hurdles*, because think what a fearnought breed of *dog* you might develop, and then perhaps we could *export* it to America, *ranking* who knows with Scotch W and the *race-horse*, but of course the *main* claim for the new technique is that it will cut out *nearly* all that petrifying nonsense about *form* and so forth, the whole thing will be a *genuine* gamble, I shall *merely* choose a *nice* name like I used to or sometimes possibly a nice-coloured *dog* and trust to intuition and natural *justice*, anyhow I must be off darling, I'll put ten bob on the *third* race for you, and tell Henry to think out about getting some betting into the *fox-field*, you must see what a *political* asset, I'm late farewell your industrious TOPSY.

16 Jack and Jill

Trix darling, *such* news what *do* you think *both* the twins may be out by *Christmas*, I've had the *longest* letters, by the way darling have you the *faintest* notion what a *Flag* lieutenant does, personally because they all call him *Flags* I thought our Jack would be in charge of *signalling*, well I know when they talk about *Pills* that's the *Doctor*, and *Guns* is the Gunnery King, and *Sparks* is the Wireless, so what would *you* think, although of course I ought to have known that *pure* logic like I *always* use is *quite* misleading and *redundant* in the Navy, because when they talk about *Number 1* they don't mean the *Captain* like I and you would, they mean Number 2 or perhaps not *that*, anyhow I forget if I told you Jack was *torn* off his beloved destroyer in the East and ordered to be this *Flags* in Australia, which from all I hear means a sort of *Mother* to an Admiral, who is it sounds the *most* lovable category, in Charm-and-merit group undeniably *One*, because Haddock met him at that *Mulberry* place, well Jack we gather has to nurse him through parties, the poor Admiral it seems being far from a *party*-type and creeps into corners *whenever* possible, *too* moving, Jack I suppose has to goad and *mobilize* him again into social combat, *what* wouldn't I give to see it, wouldn't *you*, anyhow he's having the *most* fruity *experience* and one gathers a congenial *time*, though *rather* yearning of course to be back on his little *bridge*, but my dear the Australians have been *too* wide-hearted and wondrous to *all* the Navy *manifestly*, bless them, and if he doesn't come home with at least *one* Australian bride, which Haddock says he might *well* have done himself *but* of course for rather a *Topsy* priority, and of course *all* this is the *most* phenomenal coincidence because my dear I was *too* affected by what you said about your young and ours, and *numerous* salvos for the new *photos*, of *course* it would make me *medievally* happy to have a four-square wedding, *your* Fidelity and Jack, *your* Phil and Jill, my dear it sounds like a *nursery* rhyme, *too* touching, but how *could* you give that poor child a name like *Fidelity*, my dear *Punctuality* I could understand, *Tenacity*, *Veracity*, or even *Fertility*, but *Fidelity*, what a *bunker* to put on the green, my dear it's like labelling a hotel *Temperance*, when of course the *nicest* gentlemen will keep away *even* if they've no *desire* to drink, and of course *what* will happen when the poor child's *married* and her spouse perhaps is on the *China* Station, *nothing* in trousers will venture *near* her, because can you imagine any *nice* man *telecommunicating* to a grass-widow and saying *Fidelity* dear come *out* for a dine and dance, you might *just* as well have christened her *Nun* or *Goldfish*, and perhaps of course that was you and Henry's *plan*, however darling *don't* let us go into all that *now*, honestly I never meant to say a *word* about it, and of course I must tell you that Haddock is *absolutely* with us, I mean about the tribal *nuptials*, the only thing is I *do* think we don't want to *rush* things don't you agree my dear, because after all what *do* we know about the Young, honestly my dear in these days I find the Young are *so* inscrutable that I sometimes feel by the time we *understand* them they'll be practically middle-*aged*, and I do think there *may* be such a thing as incompatible *what* is the word, I *know* you'll understand darling, and then of course there's *environment* and everything, I mean just because you and I were *bosoms* at the old academy and *since* one mustn't be *too* sure about the next litter *must* we, pardon the metaphor my dear, as you know I'm rather *dog-minded* these days, by the way *last* Wednesday was a *pattern* of calamity, only *one* of my selecteds won and then it was a *foul* or something, *too* deflating *all* the little winnings went and I *do* so ache to finance the Haddock holiday, however as I was saying, well Jill for example, Jill and your Phil, my dear I can see at once he's the *grandest* boy, and *how* they've both filled out at Medicine *Hat*, or was it *Moose Jaw*, I suppose you *couldn't* have done anything about those front tusks darling, Jack had *much* the same formation at school but suffered *plates* for centuries, and *now* as you'll see, too sorry it's only a snap my dear and *not* in uniform, the *second* girl from the right we gather is a *rather* aromatic Wren Second *Officer*, no tooth-trouble *there* by the way, however what are *teeth* it's the *temperament*, isn't it, and *that* in passing is the word that baffled me *before*, well of course it *shines* out that your Phil is going to be a *country*-boy, which in theory I'm *utterly* for, my dear you know *whatever* I say I'm *never* so happy as *knee*-deep in mud or sneezing in the new-mown *hay*, Jill by the way my dear is a hay-feverite *too*, they say it's hereditary from Haddock's *great*-uncle who was the *first* Bishop of Sudonesia, which is some *leprous* segment of the *South* Pacific, of course I can *see* your large Philip *striding* through the spinneys with a gun like *Henry*, and it's *too* true that our little Jill has rustic trends *likewise* because for the first year and a *half* of the conflict she was *officially* a *Land* Woman, and they say she has the *most* magical touch with *cows*, for one thing in the *dank* and insanitary dawn she used to recite *pet* pieces from Haddock's *poems* to the cows, with it seems the *most* noticeable effect upon the *milk*, one time I *think* she said she got a prize for *octane* content, or is that *petrol*, it's all so *confusing* these days, anyhow that *is* our *Jill*, I mean with *any* animal she's like the Pied *Piper*, you can't walk down the *street* with her without a *platoon* of cats behind you, *too* embarrassing of course but *moving*, give her a moribund *sea-gull* or a half-drowned *fish* and she'll spend *days* with a brandy-bottle and *hot* wool *resusiuscitating* same, my dear what a *word*, and as for *dogs* they merely *swoon* at the sight of her and *lie* down in front of buses with all four *paws* aloft, actually my dear if you let her loose in one of your *fox-fields* I think it's too likely you'd find the fox and *all* the dogs in a voluptuous huddle on her *lap*, with *all* the horses queueing up for *sugar*, so at first sight you *might* say, I *couldn't* disagree with you *less*, that here you have two environmental *fits* or twin-souls, on the *other* hand one *has* to recognize, and I know my dear you won't for a *moment* suspect me of would-be *woundings*, the *one* thing the dear girl *never* does with her animals is to *shoot* them, and although of course *like* me she can wolf a roast bird *hot* or cold with *ill-concealed* relish, there it is I'm *too* afraid that if on the *first* day he takes her for a *spinney-stroll* with a gun and comes back with a bleeding *otter* or mutilated quail the tender child will give *three* screams and scurry back to *mother*, besides which she's *immersed* in music and could *not I* think live through a winter in the North without *hungering* for the Albert *Hall*, *don't* think I'm making difficulties darling, but it is just as well to face *realities*, as the burglar said to the bishop in the bath, of course you *may* say that Phil could get a job and settle in the *capital*, but *that's* a sacrifice if it was me I wouldn't *hear* of, my dear one thing a girl must *never* do and that is to stand between a hubby and a *hobby*, if you'll forgive that *pestilent* word, hubby I mean, no darling I'm *too* sure your Phil *must* stick to his beaver-shooting and everything, and the estate-agent job you mention sounds like *Nature's* niche for him, then of course there's the *age* conundrum, I don't know about your Fertility, but Jill will scarcely *notice* a man under *about* 43, I suppose it *is* true that the boys are backward especially the Brigadiers and *Wing*-Captains, bless them, anyhow *don't* let's worry or rush for an *instant*, the *moment* they're all present we'll have a *mass*-rally, give the little things their heads, and *philosophically* behold the outcome, but it *would* be magical I *do* agree, farewell Mrs England, the *nation's* matron TOPSY.

17 Keeping Fit

My dear Trix, I *do* wish I had a *single* clue to your *maze* of a mind, honestly my dear how *could* you be umbrageous about my *dove-like* letter, you know I meant *quite* nothing about poor Phil's teeth, *actually* I can't recall a word I *said*, only *as* a mother one does tend to *notice* little details *doesn't* one, but of *course* he's 'good enough for Jill' you little clucking-duck, the only *phantom* of a doubt was about the adjustability of *environments*, I mean a boy might have teeth like a champion *crooner* but if his *main* delight was *eliminating* badgers he wouldn't *necessarily* be the best bet for *my* sensitive offspring, and even there I'm *far* from dogmatizing, because who knows, my dear at one time I couldn't handle a naked *plaice*, but two Yules back, with the aid of fire-water and a gas-mask, I disembowelled an entire *goose*, so it only shows, anyhow *all* I meant was to *mildly* deprecate undue *precipitation*, my dear in these days *never* cross your bridges till you're *quite* the other side, and of course *personally* I wouldn't *presume* to give advice to *either* of my young, so what *is* the benefit of you and me beginning an unnatural bicker in the *dark*, you *do* understand darling, and perhaps if you think over your *mortifying* letter you'll put on the snowshoes, *slide* down the village, and send me the *softest* little *golden* telegram of grovel and *regret*, however not a word more about that *now*.

My dear it's *too* shaming, after a *mere* month the Topsy accounting system has *quite* disintegrated, for one thing the entries in the *red* column became *so* numerous that Haddock mutinied about buying *Savings* gadgets to *match*, I *dare* say by now darling you've utterly forgotten what the system *was* and if so it's *too* immaterial, because suddenly in the bath I had a luminous *moment*, I said *What* after all are these squalid accounts *for*, for nothing but to show if you're spending *too* much, and *what* is the purpose of having a *Bank* and an overdraft and all those *enervating* documents about *Self* they send you, except to give the same grim information, *officially*, my dear as Haddock said *why* keep a siren and yell the little *lungs* out, anyhow my dear large ledger is now in service with Haddock for *press-cuttings*, so closes another epoch in the upward struggle, but *don't* think for an instant there's any *general* weakening, *quite* otherwise, not *one* cigarette has sullied the lips this *year*, in fact I'm now *practically* in the *offensive* stage when one looks *scorpions* at the loose-livers who merely *offer* you a smoke, yesterday my dear I *positively* heard myself saying *Oh* no I *never* do, with the little nose trending skyward *noticeably*, about the juniper-juice the record is not *exactly* parallel, but considering the *ice* and *snow* and everything, and my dear at these *public* dinners one simply *has* to have an anæsthetic of *some* sort, in fact I find *wherever* one has *much* discourse with strangers of the human tribe, do you find that darling, do you *never* feel you'd like to withdraw to a nunnery with a nice *book*, and nowadays I've met *so* many people I simply *cannot* recall who any of them *are*, *too* embarrassing, whereas after a *reasonable* juniper-juice or two one either remembers or it couldn't matter *less*, by the way it's *too* heroic to hear that Henry's joined the *Rotary* after all, but *don't* be surprised if he comes back and drinks *heavily*, because I'm *not* persuaded that he can stand his fellow-men in the mass for *long*, unless perhaps it was in woods and spinneys, and even then, where was I, Oh yes, well in *spite* of the set-back mentioned there's still a spectacular drive for the *care of the body*, which is the main thing *after* all, my dear the scales have *scarcely* fallen from the little eyes when I'm *rolling* the *abdominal wall*, in *bed*, that's the beauty of it, of course darling I don't suppose you've ever given a *moment's* reflection to the abdominal wall, which is *so* shallow of you, because it is the absolute *foundation* of human goodery, my dear you know those muscles down the *sides* of the tummy, I dare say after all your horse-work you've got *steel girders* there but of course we poor townswomen, well it seems it's like a *paper-bag*, if you *don't* keep those muscles tough *quite* all the inside *gravitates* to the bottom of the bag, and *hence* the middle-aged *spread*, well there are two *mellifluous* exercises Haddock got from a man called *Hornibrook*, who says it seems we were never *designed* to go about *upright*, which accounts for everything, and one must admit you never see a *horse* with a middle-aged spread, or *do* you, I shouldn't know, whereas the only *humans* who escape are the *savages*, because they do *ventrifugal* dances, *thus* toughening the abdominal *wall*, well they're *too* easy and require *no* standing about in draughts and *undies*, you can roll the old wall in the *bed* in the bath or *anywhere*, in fact Haddock says he *has* rolled his in the House and on the Underground, and he says a *delicate* roller could make a speech from the Front Bench rolling the wall the *entire* time and nobody would *know*, though whether it would be the done thing, anyhow the little abdo is as flat as a *floor* and even Haddock's is *practically* invisible, besides which I must say the whole interior economy could *not* be more efficient if it was *nationalized*, so darling if you have the flimsiest doubts about your abdo I'll show you the *whole* drill when you come up, but then of course comes the macaber moment when one has to leave the hot-bottle and do the *normal* exercises in a Siberian *draught*, to which I still stick spasmodicly, though according to the Hornibrook School their merit is meagre compared with abdo-rolling, I mean the toe-touchers and *trunk*-twisters, and complex deeds with *chairs* and towel-horses, my dear there's one *captivating* exercise where you put *both* feet in the handkerchief drawer and stand on your *hands* with the *eyes* shut and everything *utterly* relaxed, I forget who told me about it but it's supposed to *liquidate* the entire frame besides mentally at the same time putting the *cosmos* in the true perspective first thing in the morning, and I must say *after* it I feel I can face the Queue Age with a *whistle* in the heart though *too* terrified that the hanky-drawer will descend on me *again*, which it did on *Boxing* Day when demonstrating to Iodine Dale, then of course there's the *mental* gymnastics, because I do agree it's *too* fallacious to care and cosset the *body* merely, I mean it may be malnutrition or the Arctic air-conditions, but I *sometimes* feel the little *mind* is *wizening*, you know like a neglected *walnut*, or perhaps the little soul is at last asserting itself, because my dear I'm *too* contented having esotteric *brooding*, but *can* I remember anybody's *name*, and *can* I concentrate on a funny story or an article on Bretton *Woods*, my dear *yards* before the point approaches I can feel the eyes glazing and the *soul* is reaching for the stars *elsewhere*, which of course is *quite* anti-social, so we've started a *joint* mind-and-body Movement, with special drills for *memory* and *concentration*, well for instance *every* day we learn a *piece* by heart, it may be Byron or Beachcomber or a *few* lines from the *Telephone* Directory, and the done thing is to say it off before *bed*, then whenever Haddock hears a laughworthy story he has to swear to *exactly* repeat it, and when I catch him at a leading article I say *Briefly* explain what it was all *about*, which *too* often has the poor man *yammering*, as for me I learn special verselets of an *exalting* category to recite during my *exercises*, thus you see bringing mind and body into *utter* harmony and dedisintegration, so altogether you see we're not *letting* go, all the same I've still got the *most* barbarous *vibrositis* in the back of the neck besides *occasional* pangs of intercostal or ribby *neuritis*, which Haddock attributes *entirely* to the *exercises*, Oh dear I must go and take my Vitamin Bro, farewell you *have* abandoned your umbrage *haven't* you, *several* salvos your tenacious TOPSY.

18 The Canaanites

February 13, 1946

Trix darling for sheer miscellaneous *frustrating* mess the last week has been the *conqueror*, for one thing more *Iodine* trouble, but I think about that a little *reticence* perhaps, you *do* understand don't you, because my dear between you and I it seems the King's Proctor is *actually*, my dear the hunted child sees detectives *everywhere* and yesterday she screamed like a pig at the cannery when she opened the door to my melting *milkman*, and I forget if I told you about the policeman and Mrs B, as a result of which, however *no* more now dear I promised *positively*, another *major* trauma is that Haddock's secretary has got *maniacal* influenza or something, so once more I'm *floundering* in the *swamps* and fogs of his *correspondence* like I did *quite* all the war, while you were stowing the calories away at Medicine *Hat*, or was it *Moose Jaw*, my dear you've no *conception* the *letters* these poor publics get, heart-aching life-tales to which there's *no* answer, divorce-narratives by the dozen and the *mile*, *page* after page, with *quires* of enclosures, sometimes my dear it takes an *age* to hound down the *point*, and then you find the poor pathetic has been to *three* solicitors and turned down by the Courts, so *no* answer again except *Too sorry, quantities* by the way about the old decree nisi, to *which* we answer *No* more Private Members' Time *ask* HM Gov love, then of course *prolific* moans about demobbery and *students* and *housing* inequities and India and the GI *widows* and Palestine, my dear why don't you *make* the Gov do this that and *everything*, well if the letter's *legible* and not *too* corrosive or crazy you send it on to a *Minister*, and *how* I pity them, then you tell the *chap* what you've done and *bang* goes twopence-half-penny, the Minister *ultimately* sends you the *sweetest* answer which you forward to the *chap*, *another* two-and-a-half d, and *till* recently of course *another* for the letter to the *Ministry*, which is now *privilegious* and free thanks be, though it's true the stamp-bill is still *stupendous*, and of course *if* the chap gets an *effective* answer he generally writes to *thank* us etcetera and asks us to be dynamic about some *new* conundrum, so my dear it *quite* never ceases, and sometimes I do a *little* ache for the good old *bombdays* when we did actually lose a complete *slag-heap* of unanswerable letters by fire and water and the King's *enemies*, bless them, and as far as I know *no one* was *noticeably* the worse, well then besides of course *all* the loons and fearnought *pioneers* seem to write to Haddock, in *procession*, the other day there was the *most* protracted letter from an Indian asking Haddock to propose *polygamy* in the House, and my dear *too* plausible and public-minded, because of the *two* million redundant women and the reluctant *birth-rate* and everything, and he said if the B Parliament does the high and haughty about polygamy well what about the B *Empire* which merely *swarms* with polygammers, *too* awkward to answer I thought, so I sent it on to John Simon's *Population* Commission, and I *do* see, well for one thing it *would* mean a little *help* in the home, which otherwise on all the evidence will *quite* never happen *again*, only I've told Haddock that if he *does* have two she must never *enter* my kitchen except *after* meals, when I shall be *drier* and she'll do the *sinking*, *she* shall answer *all* the letters and hardly *ever* speak, and I will *not* have a neurotical type like Iodine *Dale*, that's all, well then there was the indignant old boy of *73* who was *too* inflamed because he couldn't marry his *step-niece*, 59, which as far as Haddock and me knew he *could*, why *not*, but that will show you, *not* content with wanting you to alter the *laws* they expect you to alter the Forty-nine *Articles* then of course my delicious Canaanite, who my dear has a *complete* solution for the Palestine enigma, game set *and* match, because he says all this chat about the Israelites and the Arabs is *too* misleading and *unhistorical*, because what about the Canaanites who were there centuries before *anyone* and were the peaceful victims of unprovoked *aggression*, which one must admit if you forget about the Promised Land is *one* way of looking at it, of course the Philistines have always had a bad press but even they were there *first* though aggressors *likewise* one gathers, my dear it's all *too* complex what with Phœnicians and *Hittites* and Aryans from *Crete*, and the old boy sends us *immense* geological *trees*, because he says he's a *pure* Canaanite and lived at Joppa till the Zion-troubles when he left in umbrage with his *Committee*, who it seems are *all* Canaanites, including one Phœnician and two *Hittites* I *think* he said, my dear I believe they're *all* at the *Savoy*, anyhow their signature-tune is *Canaan* for the *Canaanites*, because he says once the *principle* is accepted the *other* controversy would be out-of-date and morally short-*circuited*, though no doubt he says the Canaanites would graciously agree to *partition* the land between the Jews and *Arabs* which some say is the only way, so that *theoreticly* perhaps, anyhow he wants Haddock to take him to see *Bevin*, and then for Bevin to go into the *entire* Canaan 'incident' at *Uno*, my dear *who* was the *aggressor* and everything, under one of these unreadable *Charters*, well you *may* sit up there darling in your rustic sanctuary and say Of course the man is *bats* or *bottles*, which I must admit was my own *immediate* repercussion, because Haddock seems to be the main *target* of the bat-population, one poor woman writes weekly to say that 9½ *years* ago he made a *solemn* vow with the Editor of *The Times* to care and foster her, another says she's Queen *Elizabeth* and the people ought to be *told*, but Haddock says that a public fellow *can't* be too careful, because he says how *few* the New Movements which *didn't* seem to be utterly bat-like when they *began*, and it *may* be his *duty* and everything, however I must say he's been *too* uneager about his duty *so* far, *quite* declining to answer the letters or even *look* at the geological *trees*, *I* have to write *boracic* postcards to say that Haddock's in *Denmark* and flying's prohibitive, *now* he wants me to explore the avenues and ask the Canaanites to a cocktail somewhere, which seems to me to be *too* unsuitable, the name by the way is *Moussa* which reminds me of something I can *not* think *what*, I've searched through Exodus and most of *Judges* but Moses is the one name near it and he you see was the other *side*, of course *one* hypothesis is that it's a *new* move in the *crime*-wave, like nearly *all* things, my dear these days one doesn't *think* of smiling at a stranger, and as for giving a *lift*, for fear of being *held up* or *pulped down*, or of course it *might* be one of the *King's Proctor's* men, a *diabolical* move against poor *Iodine*, Gosh I've had an *idea*, stand *by*!

Darling I've *just* telecommunicated to my little friend *Jean* who practically *runs* the Savoy, I *think* you met her at that fraternal *chemist's* the day Henry had his *classic* hangover and we gave him pharmacuticle *pick-me-ups*, anyhow she says there *is* a man called Moussa in the hotel, but no sign of a *Committee*, and no *Hittites* or *Philistines* as far as she *knows*, but she says he does look *exactly* like a Canaanite, as a *matter* of fact it seems he got his room by *mistake* because they thought he *must* be one of their *Unos*, *too* secretive it seems, has *all* his meals upstairs, and stalks out at *nightfall*, Oh yes and they *rather* think he's got an *animal* in a *basket*, which of course bangs an absolute drum with *me* because I now remember *Moussa* was the name of the *snake-charmer* we saw at Luxor, it's *too* true that Haddock says *our* Moussa is *dead*, but it's all *beginning* to check up a *little* don't you think, though whether the *snake* is intended for Iodine or *Uno*, however more later your distracted TOPSY.

19 Stiff Lips

February 20, 1946

Trix darling it's *too* likely that *this* despatch will read like the ravings of a sick *bat* or the *dribbling* of wolves in the Soviet forests, because the fact is I've got the *most* insanitary and stupefying *cold*, which of course is *so* deflating, because last autumn for *weeks* I had those fallacious *injections*, now I've taken *Nazrine* and *Noblo* and *Eumucia* and *Antitarrh*, which Haddock says is the *most* odious violation of language *yet*, in spite of which I'm still a mere perambulating sneeze, *all* my hankies and most of Haddock's are a *swamp*, and the washing these days comes back *half-yearly*, and of course if only all those *obscene* professors would stop mutilating the atom and do a *drive* against the cosmic *cold*, by the way darling you know what a *trend* I have for being right and you *may* remember what I told you *seasons* ago about their doing radar to the *Moon* and the British *Plan* for an expedition and everything, because you were *too* incredulous and septical at the time, but now the first part has been released *official*, about the radar I mean, so who knows about the *rest*, not *yet* of course because the first result would be a scene in the *Security* Circus and as a matter of fact though don't *whisper* about this they *rather* think *Kamschatka* may have got wind already and raise the whole question of planetary spheres of influence *quite* soon, anyhow darling do try not to sniff *too* loudly at our humble efforts to enlighten and *prepare* you, which reminds me *years* ago deny it or not the *moment* you were redeployed from Medicine Hat I told you that *almost* everything looked like being far worse than *ever* in the war, *too* right, my dear even the *Cabinet* have noticed it now, of course I think you're *so* sage not to *glance* at the papers, because these days honestly one sees a death sentence in every *column*, every day some childlike Minister discovers there's *no* coal, *no* fat, *no* wheat, *no* rice, and *no* houses likely for *several* years, that's the latest, and *quite* soon it seems it may be *no* films and no *fags*, well of course *as* I've said we never expected it to be *much* different, in fact Haddock wrote *before* the Election *God* help the men who rule the coming years, *whichever* party, as you know I *always* think the Christian thing, and one *can't* be un-sorry for the wistful Ministers crashing and splashing in the cosmic bog, the only thing is that if there'd been *rather* less cockahoopery about *planning* and everything and a *little* less carbolic yap against the other fellow, the other fellow my dear being half the population, well perhaps the burning tears of compassion *might* flow more cataracticly *still*, as it is they're *mainly* devoted to the afflicted British wife and *matron* whose belt by now is so full of holes it's practically *porous*, and of course the *cardinal* thing is how it all mounts *up*, my dear in the old days with this *mephitic* cold one would merely have crawled into the bottom of a bed and lain there *moribund* with *two* bottles till consciousness returned, whereas now one has to be up and coping if one has the *bubonic* because my dear queues and coupons wait for NO girl and what with stiff-upper-lipping in a bronchitical queue, and searching the snow for *nutrimentary* fragments the cats may bring in from propinquous dust-bins, yes darling that may be the *faintest* atom of exaggeration but *not* more, and if anyone says *Dunkirk* to me again I shall *scream*, *four* times, though of course I do agree that the only *authentic* targets for censure and corrosive talk are the *septic* Germans and the leprous *Japs*, in fact if all else fails and the little upper lip relaxes somewhat I merely mutter *over* and over again, 'GDG' and 'GDJ' which my dear I will *not* interpret in case your Fertility, *too* sorry, Fidelity sees it, but the *last* letters stand for 'the Germans' and 'the Japs', *do* try it darling if you suffer *ever*, you'll find after about *seven* times you see the cosmic mess in *absolute* proportion with *warm* feelings for HM Gov, *always* excepting of course that *phenomenal* blot, my dear you know how I *hate* to say an unkind thing and even now I will *not* use *names*, but my dear *if* you guess I do think you'll agree that his charm-group is *not* high, in fact there is *something* to be said for the Haddock theory that he *is* congenitally *unmagnetic*, but that I know is *not* warm-hearted forget *quite* everything I've said.

Haddock my dear I hardly *see* these days, not that with this blinding cold I should always *recognize* him, partly because he's *too* busy preparing for the *Siege of London* when he says there may be no *Anything*, one hypothesis he harbours is that there may be *edible weeds* in the bed of the Thames, which of course has its plausible aspect, when you *think* of all the organic whatisit, I mean all the vegetational stuff from up the river, the *dead* cats the live gulls and all those millions of revolting little *pink* worms we use for newt-nutrition in the *summer*, anyhow at low tide he digs *doggedly* in the darkest mud, and boils his weeds for *twenty-four hours* though on *what* principle, anyhow the house is *permanently* dank with the *most* discouraging *alluvial* smells, after which we have a *tasting* to see if edible, *if* not which praises be has always been the verdict *so* far, the *next* investigation is *is* the weed *smokable*, which my dear means *protracted* dryings *all* over the kitchen and my *own* oven *too* inaccessible because of *steaming* water-growths smelling like I can *not* envisage what, my dear *too* redolent, *not* content with which he does *poisonous* experiments in the old pipe with *ground* bulbs and *dried* carnation leaves, my dear my beloved winter-plants are *quite* naked not to mention the cat who eats them *shamelessly*, then of course there are the *roast* bay-leaves from the neighbour's tree and blotting-paper *boiled* in vinegar and dried *slowly* over gas, which Haddock says is perhaps the best, though as I *did* murmur *how* he expects to find enough blotting-paper and vinegar to supply the *nation*, not to mention *gas*, but there it is he says the days are coming when there'll be *quite* no *tobacco* to smoke and *how* degrading if a nation of fumigators is caught without *alternative*, which of course I do *so* see, because HM Gov you can bet a billion will open wide their virginal eyes and be taken by *astonishment*, all the same I do wish *some* of the experiments could be done in a Government *wind-tunnel* or somewhere *quite* elsewhere, the *one* ray of hope and solace is that after all these experiments Haddock seems to be developing almost an aversion to the smoking act, I mean after the *bay-leaves* I could *not* induce him to use the *gift-cigar* from my delicious Dane the captain of the *Rota*, who has been over again with *tons* of butter and miscellaneous pig-fruit though not it seems for you and me but the Combined *Food* Board, which means I suppose some unworthy *foreigner*, what a *redundant* nuisance that Continent *is* well don't you agree darling, when you think of the *centuries* they've caused us trouble, and if *only* Adam had been an Englishman what *worlds* of worry would have been *quite* eliminated, by the way I've heard not a *word* more about the Canaanite, and so far the King's Proc has made no *positive* move against my *persecuted* Iodine Dale, who still has spasms when the *postman* knocks, altogether darling the turmoil of Peace is by no means abated, I was going to say well anyhow there are no sireens or doodle-bugs only whenever I do say that I dream about them *at* once so I won't, and of course the *sterling* solace is to think *how* often before the *best* people have seen the *end* of everything *just* round the corner, whereas peeping round it I seem to see an endless vista of the largest *hams* with mountains of enchanting *butter*, on which heroic note farewell your tight-lipped little TOPSY.

20 Movements

Trix darling that *garrulous* Uno has departed *at* last and now perhaps we may have a little *peace*, my dear not a *moment* too soon one gathers because Haddock says the *next* thing was to be *Patagonia* presenting a letter from *Brazil* protesting about there being Russian troops in *Bornholm* which belongs to my delicious *Danes*, by the way darling I don't suppose you could care *much* less but why all this *incessant* twitter about *Indonesia*, in the old days there used to be an island called *Java* because we nearly went there from Ceylon and didn't they grow *jellies* there or was it chutney, and *Java* it seems is what they nearly always mean by *Indonesia*, anyhow that's the place where *Surabaya* is because I've just *hunted* it down in my bijou Atlas, but why *Indonesia* always, because I've looked *that* up in the Encyclopedia which my dear is *so* flattening because it's *quite* always the *wrong* volume and nothing of the flimsiest interest is ever *mentioned*, however *estimate* my astonishment it says that Indonesia means *eight* different areas, from *Madagascar* to Borneo and the *Philippines*, so you *might* think from the papers that our *ubiquitous* troops were fighting in Madagascar which is *French* or bombarding the Philippines which is *Yankland's*, *too* ambiguous, well then I looked up little *Java* where it says the people are the *Javanese* 'proper' the Sudanese and the Madurese, my dear not one *word* about Indonesians, Oh and it says that Java was first mentioned in the *thirteenth* century, which *if* so *why* must we have the longest new name for it *now*, honestly my dear as if there wasn't enough *natural* chaos in the news, to mislead and mystify with *synthetic* hares of that sort should definitely be the undone thing, and *Indonesia* Haddock says means *Indian Islands* which of course makes the entire fuddlery *too* clear you *must* agree, Haddock by the way has internal umbrage because he's *always* said he's the *one* man of letters who's swum from Waterloo

Bridge to *Westminster*, but now he's discovered that *Byron* swam from *Lambeth* Bridge to *Blackfriars*, so he's merely counting the days till he can swim from Vauxhall to *Southwark*, my dear these *men*, I only hope he doesn't start laughing and *sink* like he did last time and *all but* drowned off Cleopatra's Needle, have you noticed that my dear, no I remember you were never a *convincing* nymph in the water, but personally if I laugh in it I go to the bottom like a shiny little *stone*, meanwhile we're an absolute hive of *Movements*, not content with Liberate Bornholm, about which we're giving a *Foodless* Dinner with *No* Speeches, my dear I think it's *such* a sanitary notion don't you, because honestly how *few* the Movements which have *not* been practically *wrecked* by a Lunch or Dinner in aid of, one's pinned down between some *unelectric* stranger in charm-group *53* and some poor sweet who's doomed for a speech, *mutters* vacantly whatever you say and can't pass the *mustard* without intimidation, the feeding takes so long there's no time for even *one* sufferable speech, there are always *exactly* three times too many with *as* a rule at least two *shockers*, and *no* hope of slipping out for a *wash*, meanwhile in these days one drinks toast after toast with *nothing* in the glass which I think is *so* barbarous and Haddock says is *too* likely to set up a *lasting* frustration-canker in the *sub*-conscious, well as the hours pass one develops a slow but *smouldering* antagony to the Cause *whatever* it is, my dear I remember years ago going to an *Anti-Noise* dinner which Haddock was entangled in, and at the end of it I merely *ached* for noise, I was *starving* for noise, my dear I went out into the street with Haddock and *shouted*, he thought I was *dehinged*, I sang in the Tube and *safe* home I turned on the wireless put on a record and played the *piano* until my dear forcibly *restrained* by Haddock, so that will give you a *kind* of clue to what I mean, well my dear you remember the *prelimary* stages of a public meal, when everybody's *just* arrived *too* bright and bonhomous, the frock fits, the face-work is *intact*, a little juniper-juice is available, one meets an ancient bosom or *apprehends* a new, if one is introduced to the unelectric or submagnetic type one can slide away *shortly*, and for a *brief* space one is *practically* content to be among one's fellow-creatures, but *then* comes the *lowering* moment when they say *Dinner* is served, at *that* moment one finds one has *no* hanky, Haddock comes back from the eating-map and says he's sitting *about* a quarter-of-a-mile away, and I am between the *only* two *incurably* septic men he *knows*, the starboard shoulder-strap carries away, and one rather wants to be *slightly* sick, well darling the plan is that at *that* moment we *don't* go into dinner after *all*, in fact it's not settled utterly but I *rather* think we shall have it announced, Dinner will *not* be served, because I do so love to give happiness and *see* it happen, and I can *just* envisage the *wave* of radiance going over the faces when they realize they've *not* got to sit through a festering dinner or suffer a *single* debilitating speech, they can trickle away to the club when ready or have a *cosy* sardine over the fire in the home, *meanwhile* of course the juniper-juice will circulate briskly and one will wander about and whisper *Bornholm*, I can't *think* of a better technique for keeping a Cause warm and fragrant in the mind can you, of course you *may* say it's only a cocktail-party *disguised* but personally I see the most *esotteric* difference, for one thing it has the element of *surprise*, and then of course one will wear one's pretties and you'll have the *dignity* of the one and the brevity of the *other*, then of course I'm *too* concerned about Haddock's *Beacon* Movement, my dear you remember or don't you the Belisha Beacons, which however mocked were a *meritorious* notion and the one thing that gives a pedestrian any *hope* of a future, because as long as he gives reasonable notice it's *not* the done thing to mow him down between the studs, in fact the motors are supposed to *slow* and let him over, nor darling does it *matter* one hoot, as you'd better tell your Henry in *case* he brings the car which I do *not* advise the streets being *quite* impassable and insanitary with car-purloiners, where was I, Oh yes it does *not* signify if the orange blob is absent through blitzing because they made a *special* law in the war, but my dear as Haddock says does a *single* driver know all this, or if he does could he *conceivably* care *less*, *too* often he says when making a stately passage through the studs he's merely *blown* off by the rudest hoots and has to leap a cubitt or two to escape some *rocketing* vehicle, on one occasion *quite* splitting the gastrocnemious *muscle* and he was a cripple for *weeks*, and of course the town is full of the *most* alarming *demobbed* drivers who still feel they're in charge of *tanks* or *ten-ton* lorries, and as for pedestrians they might just as well be *Belgians*, my dear Haddock was in one bus which *quite* evidently the driver thought was getting ammunition up to *Arnhem* under *fire*, roaring round the corners on *two* wheels, uprooting lamp-posts and scaring *half* Chelsea into their *basements*, well Haddock says the police can do *nothing* being *far* too few and the one thing is for the citizen to *act* and *educate*, because apart from the drivers he says there is not *one* doe-pedestrian who *dares* to exercise her rights, they merely *huddle* on the pavement in the usual way until there are *no* cars visible when they scuttle across like frightened serfs, so my dear he meanders round the town solemnly crossing *all* the Belishas he can find, *noting* the behaviour and making *indignant* gestures if the vehicles swoop on impervious as they *nearly* always do, my dear one day I *know* he'll lose a hindleg or *worse*, well then he *yells* after the ruffian like a mad thing, and *if* he stops which they *sometimes* do they have the *most* carbolic altercation, *too* fruitless because most of them have not the *faintest* what H is talking about and *if* they do they say it's *nonsense* because of course the mere *conception* of *any* vehicle slowing down for a mere *foot-serf* is *against nature* to most of them, however that's the *Movement*, Haddock says if he *does* die on the King's High Way which is a safish bet at least he'll have perished for the *people*, and now he's made a new Will to say he's to be *cremated* and the ashes scattered over the driver who kills him excuse the macaber note darling, no more now TOPSY.

21 Ulcerous World

March 6, 1946

Trix darling what an *ulcerous* world this is, don't you agree, what with *Quit* This and Quit *That* the poor old Briton seems to be cosmicly *redundant*, and the next thing *too* likely it will be Quit the *Planet*, for which *personally* speaking I'm almost ready at *once*, because my dear the festering inflated men who seem to breed in almost *every* latitude, of course the *loudest* laugh for *several* centuries was when we read about 'the *wave* of national aspiration' in Cairo, which my dear would have been a *fraction* more impressive perhaps in 1942 when Mr Rommel was practically at *Shepheard's*, you know my dear how I *hate* to say an unkind thing and of course it's *too* possible that *bags* of evidence may have gone *astray*, but I can *not* recall any *epic* narratives about the Egyptian urge to battle against the septic *Germans*, now however I see that *all* the students are declaring war against the brutal *Briton*, by the way darling a thing I'm always *aching* to know, can you tell me *what* part of the day the foreign student spends in *study* because from all accounts he puts in *so* many man-hours at demonstrations, *barriers*, stone-throwing and *ultimatums* he can't have *too* much leisure for *lectures*, I now see that 2,000 *Chinese* students have been vociferating Quit *China* to the Russians, Haddock my dear says the *laughable* thing though perhaps not practical would be if suddenly we *did* quit everything, not utterly he says but just put all the soldiers in the ships, stand off about *six* miles, sardonicly observe what happens and wait for the SOSs, meanwhile he's got a new Quit Britain movement for the EAW, which means I *know* you've guessed the England's Always Wrong boys, because honestly *why* they don't go to Jugoslavia or somewhere, my dear have you *seen* the sort of thing they say about that poor sweet General *Anders* who has been wounded at least *five* times altogether fighting the septic Germans, my dear in 1939 he fought for 28 days incessantly until can you believe it he finds he's being attacked by the Germans on one side and the *Red* Army on the *other*, he's then captured by the Russians and kept in jail for *quite* two years, until of course the suffering Russians are *driven* into the war, he's then *graciously* permitted to fight the Germans *again* and he and his lads do hero-stuff from Cassino to Bologna, now if you please the Polish Government says that his troops are not entitled to wear their *emblems* even, and he's *not* far from being a Fascist *monster*, all of which of course is grist and gospel to our own toxic EAW *too* few of whom have *ever* lifted a gun against the *Germans*, and if it comes to totalitalitarian ideas, I never *shall* spell that *ribbon* of a word, could give *numerous* points Haddock says to *Mussolini*, Haddock by the way struck an abortive blow in the Quit Bornholm campaign and asked the Foreign Secretary how *many* R troops there were there approx, but Bevin said he was not in a *position* to *say*, which considering that *we* liberated Denmark and *no* other is a *noticeable* circumstance you must agree, assuming of course which I do *not* that you have the faintest interest in the cosmic ulcers, how are the fox-dogs, and have you done a *thing* about the *briar-grove* for Haddock's pipes, I suppose you're madly cashing in on the alimentary situation, we're growing *spring* wheat in the window-box, and I'm *too* afraid I may have to sow *barley* in my little herbaceous plot, though not before the Boat-Race I *swear*, because my *bulbs* already are behaving electricly, it gives me a *pain* to see them, and yesterday I planned out the *summer* holiday, the old boat is back from the wars, my dear Haddock *towed* her back in a dinghy like the Fighting Whatisit, and we think we shall all tutter-tutter up to Oxford like we were going to in '39 but of course the septic Germans, there's just a *ray* of hope that *Jack* may be back in *June*, we've had the longest letter from *Tasmania*, which he *quite* loved, Haddock says it's the *most* cosy little island where all the names are *English*, I mean not *one* reference to Warra-warra, the only thing of course is that everything is in the wrong *place*, you motor out of *Cumberland* County into *Cornwall* and on into Lincolnshire, and as you go through Epping Forest you look up and see a hill which they say is *Ben Lomond*, *too* confusing but *enchanting* they both say though not *many* stone-throws from the South *Pole* one gathers, darling it's throbworthy to hear your Henry is really *digging in* at Rotary, but no my dear Haddock will *not* come and speak for him about PR or even Newfoundland because he's made an absolute vow against *all* public utterance *except* of course an occasional *special*, and even they accumulate *leprously*, yes my dear I know *all* that about *too* informal and say *anything* he likes and everything, because that's what *quite* everyone says, which H says is talking cabbage-water because *how* rude to merely rise and burble amorphously after a *free* meal, and as a *matter* of fact these informal jaws *nearly* always mean a morning's work not to mention *nervous* expenditure *frantic* boredom and dangerous *frustration*, because the whole time he's thinking WHY am I making this *dreary* utterance for *nothing* when I might be *winning bread* in the home, which in view of the little overdraft I could *hardly* second more *warmly*, you do understand don't you darling, and *please* tell them that if there's *one* place where deep down he's aching to utter it's the Rotary Club of Little Yattering, only you know he's got entangled in theatricals again, about which more later, and apart from that he's *embogged* in miscellaneous mush, for one thing it seems there's to be a *working-party* for the *publishing* trade, and H is beavering about for there to be an adequate ration of *writers* on the workers' section, because after all the authors are the absolute *pitmen* of the industry, I mean *hewing* the raw material out of their pathetic heads, but he says if they're not *too* careful there'll be *one* speechless author on the w-p and *fifteen* printers binders and booksellers, and besides it seems they have the most *rodent* grievances, my dear thirteen books counting as a *dozen* and so on, as Haddock says *what* would the Income-Tax bandits say about counting thirteen *pounds* as a dozen, then of course *no* Three Years' Average which means if a book takes *three* years to write and then goes well you're taxed like *Crœsus*, and of course *no* allowance for wear and tear of machinery and *plant*, the creaking brain and body I mean, which I think is *so* savage to *all* professionals, take *doctors*, my dear if a soap-maker's ill the soap-factory goes on *churning* out the soap and the income flows *continuous*, but if Haddock or the *doctor's* ill the whole works *stops*, besides which he says the soap-chap keeps on making the *same* soap whereas he has to think out something new every *day*, so he ought to be taxed *too* differently and have the *largest* allowance for wear and *tear*, though whether all this will be in order at the *working-party*, but he says why not it's part of the *export* drive and if you give the authors a *square* deal and quantities of paper they'll do as well as *whisky*, and it's *too* true that in Copenhagen there were masses of English books, only *all* fabricated in Sweden or the Yankland, then he says there's a rumour they're thinking of having a *standard* book for export, because HM Gov thinks the present system is *too* ununiform and anti-economic, I mean all these *different* authors writing *different* books for *different* publishers, and of course they all have to have *different* type and covers and everything, whereas of course if you had about *one* standard British book every *year* it would save *yards* of expense and could be *mass-produced* with the *same* cover and a foreword by S Cripps or H Morrison, which though *eager* to cooperoperate, that's *another* pest of a word, Haddock is not *too* sure would be a wonderworthy idea, because *which* book S Cripps would choose to be the *standard*, personally, of course I think it's *too* likely the whole thing will be *nationalized*, because at the present rate after *about* two years there'll be nothing else *to* nationalize, Haddock I suppose will have to clock in daily at the Ministry of Fiction and Fun which if *no* smoking's allowed will do him *lots* of good, anyhow now perhaps you do understand about the speech darling, farewell there is *ice* on the newt-pond but *two* rose-buds in the next bed, *too* symbolic, your subvernal TOPSY.

22 Haddock In Trouble

March 20, 1946

Trix my little winter-cabbage there's rather a bizarre yellow *gleam* in the garden which Haddock says is the *sun*, I shouldn't know, I'm still a walking *refrigerator*, all the same *deep* down I do feel the old bones stirring somewhat, like something you've had at the back of the fridge so long you've *forgotten* it, for one thing we're all talking about the *Boat* Race which is the absolute *herald* of the Spring in these parts and *quite* the maddest event of the year which I think is *so* suitable, though of course Haddock says if coal gets any *shorter* in supply the 8-oared boat may very soon be a major element in London *transport*, then my dear we had an *electric* evening when the *Ballet* opened, which really *did* feel like the bad days dying, *everybody* there one's ever known and the *entire* Cabinet relaxing bless them, we had a sisterly Scotch with Herbert Morrison who I *rather* think was *rather* attracted, H M by the way Haddock says was *so* boracic and brotherly in the House the other day that half the Tories wanted to *cry*, which is more than can be said of my volcanic *Nye* who I *do* so want to see build *masses* of homes only they say he has congenital *polemicomania* and even if you *agree* with him it's a Tory *plot*, and as for *rudeness* is not the poor PM's *top* ambassador for the *Dunkirk* spirit, however *what* a job and it's somewhat wonderworthy that *all* the Ministers are not stark *staring*, Haddock by the way went practically *certifiable* about the *Lilac Fairy* and was *incandescent* for several hours because she got no *flowers* at the end, he swore he'd go again the *next* day with a *lorry-load* of vegetation and I *quite* feared a cosmic scandal, however *fortunately* he had to play in a *skittles* match at the local, which if you ever *do* penetrate to the capital you *must* see, they throw the *most* ponderous *cheeses* weighing eleven or twelve pounds, I can scarcely *lift* one, and though Haddock thought perhaps it was *too* old-fashioned and laborious for the Century of the Common Man, as a *matter* of fact the interest is *dynamic* and they have *more* members than ever before the *war*, which only shows, though of course whether a *rust-encrusted* warhorse like Haddock, because this week he had his *first* instalment of *sciatica*, and what with *three* speeches in *two* days, *four* visits to the fang-man, and five hours at his bone-setter's, my *dear* what a week, *incessant* umbrage, nor *can* I blame him, because my dear those *speeches*, one about the suffering *artists*, and one in a pub about *what* he wasn't *too* sure, and one to an absolute *battalion* of doctors, and in between *hobbling* through the snowy Streets from the *tusk-man* to the *bone-man* with sciatica and *no* hat and my dear tottering home in such a *typhoon* of a temper that my *one* hope was to remind him of the Lilac *Fairy*, and even *she*, however meanwhile this *magical* bone-man, who Haddock *swears* by and I did once go to myself about my *barbarous* rheumatism, and my dear there's *no* doubt he is a *sorcerer*, but *too* alarming for the tender *doe*, because first of all he reduces you to a cinder with radiant *rays*, followed by *inhuman* massage, my dear if there *is* a soft spot or malignant *nodule* in the shrinking frame he *finds* it and *grinds* it, *agony*, then he says Relax *utterly* and pulls *both* legs off, or *else* which is worse he folds them up singly behind *each* ear and snaps them off at the *knee*, finally he grabs you like a gorilla says *Relax* and *litterally* breaks your *neck*, you can hear it crack, the drab confession is that though I did feel *years* better I've never *ventured* again, *too* pusillanimous, however Haddock being sterner stuff the little wizard *quite* dispersed his sciatica in 48 *hours*, whereas *nearly* always it seems you're a cripple for weeks, the only sour note struck was when Haddock addressed the massed *doctors* he said he'd *just* been cured of sciatica in *two* days by a *bone-setter*, an utterance one gathers in about tact-group *79*, the abominable bone-men being like a stoat to a *rabbit*, anyhow Haddock says it's the *last* speech he's making *this* century, you did explain to Henry about Rotary *didn't* you, however we do not struggle *quite* for nothing, my dear it's *too* startling the Attorney-General says that the abolition or *modification* of the decree nisi is under *consideration*, my hunted

Iodine Dale of course is *stuttering* with chagrin because her time is *nearly* up now and she *rather* feels she'd like *everybody* else to have the *same* degrading torments only rather *longer*, which I've told her is *not* a prosocial state of mind, because the Attorney-G says the King's P has only intervened in *161* cases since January 1938, which when you think of the *totals* Haddock says is *not* an economic *yield*, and how many *thousand* man-years and woman-months of *needless* frustration and general Iodine trouble *not* to mention toil and treasure for the law-lads have been suffered for the sake of *20* cases a *year*, the Canaanite at the Savoy by the way Jean says has folded his tents and gone back to *Canaan* to give evidence before a *Commission* or something, and I do not myself think he had any *long-term* designs on Iodine, and so far the King's P hasn't moved a *muscle*, meanwhile Iodine has got a sort of walk-on part in Haddock's theatricals, I cannot *clearly* envisage *why*, being my dear *completely* tone-deaf and can *not* I believe distinguish between God Save and Danny Boy, of course I *know* they want a few dumb lovelies and statelies for the *Palace* scene, but I should *not* have said that Iodine was up to *that* standard would you darling, I mean stateliness is one thing but *anæmia* is another, and I never noticed till the other day on the stage that one shoulder is *much* lower than the other and the *knees* definitely do not meet *at all*, however fortunately it seems she's to have the *longest* dresses, and my enchanting Mr Figg who's putting it on knows best no *doubt*, I must say she did *quite* a convincing slink across the stage at the audition and the competition was *not* severe, my dear have you *ever* been to an audition, *don't*, my dear it tears the *tummy* out of you, the *swarms* of personnel of *all* sexes merely *aching* to be in the *chorus*, they all bring *interminable* songs, and of course there's *no* time to hear them *all* through into the third verse or even the *second*, so they have to be stopped *half-way*, which though done with *loud* Thankyou's and *courtly* politeness must be *too* wounding to the *auditionee*, especially as quite often she's on her *top* note, the utter *apex* of the verse and everything, with her mouth *wide* open and her *soul* soaring about her *dreams* and what-not when the *suffering* musical man can bear no more the said top-notes being *yards* out of tune, he gives a signal like an executioner, the stage-man *claps* and the poor sweet's muted in *mid-yell*, *too* embarrassing, my dear *I* sat in *tears* with *Mrs* Figg whose bosom is *even* tenderer than *mine*, and whenever some *pathetic* tenor was cut off by that *stony-stomached* man at the *climax* of one of our *favourite* songs, my dear like *Jerusalem* or the *Lost* Chord she'd whisper wistfully But I thought he was such a *nice* tenor, or Didn't you think he was a *sweet* man I should have liked to hear *all* seven verses, and my dear I was *quite* with her always, on the other hand of course that was only *one* audition and the brutal management has had to hear about *twelve*, and about one in fifty of the poor pathetics is anything like what they *want* I gather, so no wonder they can't take the *whole* of the Lost Chord *always*, not to mention that *repulsive* ditty about Dreams which is *almost* the only song that youth seems to *know*, one thing anyhow as Haddock says is with such *battalions* of *both* sexes eager to sing on the stage no one can say the British urge to *music* is dead or the *theatre* either, though when it comes to *Iodine Dale*, no darling *forget* I said that, it's cancelled *utterly*, with malice to hardly *anyone* your warm-tummied TOPSY.

23 The Speech Sweep

March 27, 1946

Trix darling, *quite* honestly *do* you feel that *parts* of this missive look less unreadable than sometimes, because my dear I'm using my magical new *pen*, which is *such* rapture *British* made and even now I do not utterly *believe* it, you know what *torment* a fountain-pen can be, all those *sordid* little pumps and bottles, either there is a *total* drought or *floods* of ink in all your quarters, whereas with this my dear there's *no* nib only a *ball*-bearing they say though *why*, and no ink-work whatever, it merely *flows* out supernaturally for weeks and weeks, and by the way no *blotting paper* because it dries the same *second*, my dear it's *wonder*-work, so that in these days when there's *snow* in the drawing-room one can *huddle* in a chair over the embers if any and write untramelled, *how* many l's, by the normal nonsense, and by the way the whole thing is pretty Heaven-sent because of Haddock's experiments in *smoking* blotting-paper in case no Loan, he's now trying a mixture of *shredded* blotch and pencil shavings with a little *chopped* bayleaf *boiled* in onionwater, as a *result* of which, at least *I* say, he's having long-term *tusk-trouble* besides the most *enigmatic* swelling on the jaw where there were *no* tusks extant, because of course poor sweet the survivors are *too* few and could be counted on *one* hand, and a *half* perhaps, and from what one gathers the dentist would gaily eliminate the *lot*, because there's no doubt they have a congenital *contempt* for *Nature's* teeth, and I should say *Too* right, *what* an inept and *sadistic* arrangement, however H rather hankers for his *scanty* native gnawers because of the *pipe*, besides which it seems he has a concrete *jaw* from which it's *too* impossible to excavate the fangs without *explosives* especially if the tusk disintegrates, once my dear during the late conflict he had one hour and a *quarter* under a local what-is-it, with the tuskman, who my dear is a *top*-wizard, *drilling* away *quite* down to H's *chin* and the anodyne running out at intervals and finally Haddock opens his eyes and sees him advancing with a hammer and *chisel*, which of course one's *heard* about but never *guessed* could happen to anyone one *knew*, well in spite of *heroic* efforts by the fangman not to mention Haddock an absolute chunk of masonry had to be left behind after *all*, so you can understand we're not *fanatically* keen on *further* excavations even with *gas*, because of course one's *too* likely to wake up with a shattered jaw or a circular *saw* in the mouth, then of course in these days the staffwork is *so* interminable because of attaching the new tooth to the denture which means hunting for *old* dentures among all the chaos of the blitzes, I have found his *tops* in a nail-box in the dug-out but the bottoms still *defy* discovery, talking of *extractions* there's *warming* news *have* you seen the suffering Russians they say are positively *quitting* Bornholm 5,000 of them and of course we're *too* sure its *primely* the Haddock Liberate Bornholm Movement, Haddock of course says it's *high* time Uncle Joe came to *London* because my dear *there* he sits like a great *spider* in the heart of his web thinking every *fly* that comes near it is a *wasp*, whereas in London he'd have a *fabulous* welcome in spite of *all*, and if only he could see all the *shelters* coming down the old *suspicions* perhaps might be abated somewhat, though *what* he'd think of the *Licensing* laws, as for the *atomic* what-not Haddock says it's *infantile* for him to brood and hanker for *that*, because after all if the suffering Russians are to have it why not *quite* everyone, and *if* everyone then everyone is *equal* and *what* is the worth of Russia's *Security* Belt, then of course *I* must say one is beginning to *faintly* weary of our beloved *Greeks* who seem to be *quite* incapable of adult behaviour and have got political *liver-disease*, but Haddock says they've been just the same *about* ever since the Trojan *War* poor sweets, altogether the Continent becomes increasingly redundant, and *why* Haddock says do we not get any *Hock*, because what is Germany *for*, and personally I think it's *too* right for France to have the *Rhine* and we to have the *wine*, because it's *quite* manifest we shall get nothing *else*, my dear if it had been the suffering Russians we should have had *all* the

Hun-wine ab *initio, last* night I *confess* darling we behaved *unworthily* at a public dinner, though Haddock having fang-pangs I shall *always* say that there was *some* just cause and excuse, and as a *matter* of fact I couldn't I *swear* it wasn't my own rather unscouty *suggestion*, because I've often *heard* about his Speech-sweepstakes but never *saw* one in all its deplorable *reality*, I must say I think it's a *diabolical* contrivance though with noticeable fun-values, well my dear this was a *Birthday* dinner for the Burbleton Progressives, well of course it was an absolute *concentration* of Progs the *most* unsucculent provender and *uncountable* speeches, my dear after *one* look at the list H said we shall be here till *tomorrow*, so we arranged this *sweep* about a dozen of us, the *principle* is that you draw for *speakers* instead of *horses*, my dear your Henry would be *thrilled* though I do *not* commend his trying it at *Rotary*, and then you have prizes for the *Longest* speech and the *Shortest* speech, one for the Best *Laugh* one for the Worst *Cliché*, like avenues or turning stones, and one for who says *co-ordination* most times, the *result* is that every speech is interesting *however* destimulating or yawnworthy, and *in* a way I do think the speakers ought to be *grateful* to the organizers though *that* Haddock says is not the *habitual* reaction when they get to know about it, the *discouraging* element is that Haddock will *cheat*, at least *I* say it's cheating and he says it's part of the *game*, well I'll explain I drew the first speaker, my dear I will *not* mention names because you know how *odious* I find it to say an unkind *thing*, but he is the *Ace* of Progs, my dear he can't utter the *noblest* sentiment without somehow giving it a bad *smell*, like so many of the top-Progs do, and quite *tumescent* with pomp, my dear an intellectual *carbuncle*, and of course the first speaker *always* feels he has the whole *night* to play with, so I was *too* sure of winning the Longest *easily*, but what was my dismay he hadn't oozed for more than *20* minutes was oozing strong and looked good for *40*, when Haddock develops the loudest *cough*, which I must say was news to me, and you know if you have tusk-ache all other troubles seem to *utterly* dwindle, anyhow he coughed *on* and *on* with occasional indignant *mutters*, and you know what coughing is *by* degrees the *entire* Proggery began to cough and mutter likewise, the speaker began to deflate *significantly*, and Haddock said *too* sweetly Speak *up* Sir *twice* than *which* he says there are few more sabotaging things to hear, and before I knew what my *fallacious* Prog had sat down suddenly after merely *24* minutes, *too* disappointing though of course a public *service* to the *main* community, well then there were two or three quite *sufferable* speeches by *minor* Progs, *one* indubitably in laugh-group 7 or *8*, and *poor* Iodine Dale I shall *always* say might well have got the Best Laugh Trophy because *her* horse was telling one of the *most* hoary narratives which Haddock says never *fails* to cause a roar, not *even* at the Licensed Victuallers' who know them *all*, when *just* before the point and climax H starts a perfect *barrage* of coughery and *claps* in the *wrong* place, *quite* killing any *signs* of merriment, meanwhile his *general* strategy was a shade confusing because I forget if I've said he'd drawn the *last* speaker of all who it's odds *on* ought to be the *Shortest* especially after a protracted *battery* of speeches when everyone is *supersuicidal*, so H on the whole was for spinning *out* the middle ones and whenever a man looked like being *too* brief he'd get an electrifying 'Ear, 'ear from Haddock and yatter along *refreshed* for a bit, meanwhile of course we were having the most *hissing* altercations about the Haddock behaviour and was it the done thing and everything, nor would I swear a *binding* oath that we were the best-loved *table* in the room, well darling *about* dawn the *last* speaker at *last* arose, with Haddock all ready to collect for the *Shortest* having nothing but 9 minutes to beat, but my dear it only shows you *how* inscrutable the hazards of sport *can* be, because *quite* soon it *shone* out like *several* beacons that Mr H was on the *wrong dog*, *too* satisfying my dear the man was the last President but *two* and *swollen* with streptococcal utterance, beginning with the *babehood* of the Club and *all* its contemporaries, my dear with anecdotes of *high* narcotic content, then of course he wanted to *quit* Greece and *invade* Spain, *that* kind of cantankerous *unreasoning* Prog, well at that point to my *unspeakable* anger Haddock suddenly reverses his policy and goes for the *Longest*, and though of course the man is an open *ulcer* to him he noisily applauds *quite* everything he says, with other *unpardonable* devices, I mean if the ulcer said there were *twenty* thousand troops H pipes up *Thirty* thousand and the ulcer stops to justify his figures, well so it goes on for 23 minutes and I'm thinking I shall win the Longest *after* all, because the man is *manifestly* weakening, in *fact* he says the hour is late I must not detain you *longer*, but then *what* does the *base* H do he simply *hammers* the table and yells Go *on* go *on* go *on* Sir, *regalvanized* by which my dear the pest begins on relations with the *Soviets* and carries on like a cataract for 29 minutes, so I *lost*, my dear I've scarcely *spoken* to Haddock since except I've *dared* him to do the same devilry in the House of Commons, I must say it made him *quite* forget about his tusk-ache, there *are* limits however, meanwhile Haddock's theatricals are *trundling* along, yesterday they had a *reading* of the dramma to the entire company, *too* gruesome because my dear there's been a perfect *plague* of tusk-trouble, the leading lady was *quite* speechless after having an *infracted wisdom* fang *excavated* in hospital, the composer had lost *two* fangs and could merely *mumble*, whereas as a rule he sings all the songs like an *angel* and plays electricly, the musical director had *two* out likewise and still having fang-pangs, Haddock was minus *one* merely but it seems the new denture has a *malignant* trick of from time to time nipping the largest chunks out of the upper *lip*, so in the middle of love-scenes he gives the loudest *yelps*, and of course he never *was* the world's *ace*-reader, though one does *not* dare to *hint* it, however all went wellish, but my dear *how* any man can so much as *contemplate* starting a musical play, the *protracted* torment, and when you think there's a special *tax* on it, my dear a *normal* dramma is agony enough when you have one bit of scenery *seven* actors *no* band and ordinary *clothes*, but a *musical*, my dear first of all the composer and the word-monger yapping round the piano for *quite* months about *quavers*, though I must say Haddock and V have never had a carbolic word, in fact they will sing their favourites over and over *again*, my dear *no-one* thinks about an author's *wife* who by the first night has been hearing the *new* tunes for centuries, well then it all has to be *orchestrated*, my dear *millions* of little notes, and paper *practically* unobtainable, meanwhile the *pathetic* manager, my dear you *must* meet my *seraphic* Mr Figg who is the *nation's* pet, is scouring the by-ways for tenors of the right *shape* and everything, *not* to mention sopranos who are not *too* circular, and of course the *moment* he's engaged anyone all the *keys* have to be altered, and everything one gathers has to be orchestrated *again*, at any rate the musical men go about with *set* lips and unfraternal *mutters*, then of course the *chorus* have to be amassed from somewhere which means a *campaign* of debilitating *auditions* like I told you about, and when an *authentic* lovely is discovered she's either got *quite* nothing in the skull or sings like a beetle or has been *lassooed* by the films, *too* discouraging, meanwhile the *scenery* they find it's *too* impossible to change from the *law-court* scene to the *palace* scene under *about* half an hour, so the word-merchant has to write a *shattering* new scene about nothing *special* with none of the top-actors who will all be *changing*, Oh and of course the *dresses*, *scores* of bodies to be measured and fitted for three or *four* outfits, *how* they get the material I can *not* envisage, then my dear as a rule *all* the principals want to wear voluptuous *evening* dresses in the *prison* scene *and* crossing the *Alps*, and there are the *most* incendiary altercations, though praises be not *so* far, and when at last rehearsals begin they all have *lethal* colds or *several* teeth out and crawl about in scarves and shawls poor sweets, *husking* a few words *tuberculously* now and *then*, and it's *too* dubious if any of them will be *audible* on the *night*, though as a rule they emerge heroicly, all this of course *assuming* that the martyred manager has got a *theatre*, which today my dear is like looking for a silk *stocking*, it now appears that someone has already written a play with the same *name*, fire breaks out in the scenery place and *most* of the Palace scene is a *cinder*, the LCC say that the *new* curtains are *too* inflammable and the censor wants to cut out the *entire* point of the dramma, then the band arrives which is *about* the one enjoyable moment only *all* the keys have to be altered *again*, so *chaos*, rehearsals *rage*, the play is *three* hours too *long*, the comic man gets *laryngitis* and I remember once at the *last* minute the soprano was stung by a wasp *all* over her *nose*, at this point the *complete* tribe and outfit have to be transported to *Manchester*, and *as* a rule war is declared or a General Strike *about* the second night, this time he thinks there'll be no coal for lights and they'll have to use *torches*, altogether he says a *Treasury* man ought to be attached to the management from first to last and after the *last* Dress Rehearsal the *martyred* manager should say to him, My *dear* Sir do you *really* think there ought to be a *special* tax on all this *agony*, however somehow or other the bizarre institution does seem to *survive*, farewell your philosophical TOPSY.

24 The Dogs Again

April 3, 1946

Trix my dumb darling unless I get the most *copious* letter from you *quite* soon I shall *terminate* relations, *one* utter from you in three weeks is *not* a ration, and that about your pestaceous friend *Fork* who Haddock says *No* he can *not* ask a question about he must go to a *lawyer*, and yes it's *too* right it seems a man can't marry his *divorced* wife's sister though if it was *deceased* but Haddock's out and *why* I have *no* clue about, as for *Fork* H said if he'd gone to a lawyer *ab ovo* he might not now be in such an inscrutable *mess*, anyhow there are *far* too many Questions nowadays and Members believe it or not can *not* interfere with the decisions of *Judges* neither in the New Era can they germinate *Bills*, as I *think* I've told you uncountable times, tenthly and lastly Haddock said *why* doesn't *Fork* write to his *own* etcetera Member, sorry darling for this comparatively *barren* response, but you tell me *quite* nothing about the children, have you done a *thing* about Phil's teeth, no darling *no* cheese has won through yet though Haddock had a *moving* parcel of tinned provender from an old flame in Dominion *Australia*, here in Parliament England, that by the way is the said thing now because of *Soviet* Russia, Oh yes and Congress America, well here in Parliament England a few *frightened* daffodils are peeping round corners, *two* newts are courting in the pond which whatever the poets say is the first *sure* sign of the Parliament English *Spring*, and by the time you get this the Boat Race will be over, that is if *both* crews don't sink in a snowstorm, and of course *why* they have *all* these events in the *rudest* weather, school *Sports* for example those *mournful* waifs in *less* than undies, with *bright* blue calves and their little noses steaming like *horses*, and of course icicles all *over* the audience, talking of sport we had a *hilarious* though uneconomic evening at the grey-dogs yesterday, Haddock by the way is enraged because they're putting a cruel *purchase*-tax on *sailing* boats which they say are *Sports* requisites, though how they expect to have a nation of Dunkirkers, and Haddock says if boats why not race-horses and *race-dogs*, my dear what *mountains* of taxes you'd amass when they sell those fabulous *stallions* and things, and for that matter what about when Arsenal or Charlton buys a *centre* forward for £15,000, than which *few* things could be more like a sports *requisite*, anyhow about the grey-dogs, I goaded Haddock there for the first time since '39 because it was Jean Dee's *birthday* and I *rather* think he's *rather* attracted, *some* bait there had to be because you know he's rather *aloof* about betting, that is till he begins and then he *dives* in like a mad thing, personally of course I'm a *congenital* gambler and my *spine* tickles when the old tote starts clicking, my dear you *must* come one day, it's *quite* decorative and rather *Roman*, because you *dine* while betting and view the proceedings cosily through *acres* of plate-glass, in fact a bookie comes along and *collects* your bets if you like, so you need never stir from the trough which would *so* suit your Henry, who'd sit there feeling like the Emperor *Nero*, only then of course the whole party knows what you're *doing* and personally I like having *secret* inspirations and prowling up to the Tote myself, well when they turn the lights on it's *too* scenic, like the largest *race-game*, the little dogs come out and *march* round with six white stewards, and *parade* in front of you, when my dear I *nearly* always have the *profoundest* intuition about one of them, my dear you may laugh but I am quite a *sage* judge of a grey-dog, only of course by that time one has already backed *three* other beasties according to the *form* and everything, I should say by the way darling that dog-following is no *idle* pleasure, one works like a *slave*, my dear I'd studied the *naps* and things in *three* papers, all *too* different, then of course some *wide-hearted* man comes and marks your *card*, quite different *again*, and then I have my last-minute *intuition*, so as a rule there are *few* beasties I have not got *something* on in the end, which Haddock says is *girl's* gambling, though if he's an example of *man's*, there are only 20 minutes between the races and what with collecting on the *last* race and deciding on the *next*, life is *asthmatic*, it's like doing an arithmetic exam against *time* not to mention *dinner*, one canters off to the Tote in the middle of a mouthful, the table is a mass of race-cards and *naps* and tote-tickets get into the *soup*, then they put the little dogs in the cage and the *fairy* hare starts circulating, and *when* my dear it whizzes past the cage and they *cataract* after it, *about* two-thirds of the little tummy stops working and does not resume till *minutes* after the finish, so after about three races I have *barbarous* indigestion however it's all in aid of the summer holiday, so one suffers *gaily*, Haddock at first was *too* lofty and *quite* content with Jean and a juniper-juice not to mention some *rather* palatable turbot, though somewhat vexatious about the *Betting* Tax in which none of us at that time could be *much* less interested, and after every race he would say he'd *diagnosed* the winner *at sight* during the parade, and if he'd been betting and so on, the bleak thing was that after the turbot he really began to *believe* it and started wagering in a large way, my dear talk about *girl's* gambling, first of all he'd choose two grey-dogs with nice *names*, you could *not* get him to back a beast with what he calls a bad name if it had a half-mile *start*, then he picks one because of its lovable *walk*, and nearly always he does Number *two* because it has a *blue* wrapper and he's sensitive to blue, then he asks what I'm on and invests in that *likewise*, so at the end he's on *all* the runners but one or two, *which* of course finish *quite* first, my dear *calamitous* because *till* then I'd been raking in *reasonably* and the summer holiday was about *six* Peppiatts nearer, but now Haddock is on my hounds not *one* thing goes well with them, my dear they're *jostled* at the bend or fall *fatally* at hurdles, the hurdling by the way is *quite* electrical and while they're doing that one *practically* forgets one's degrading *money*, there's the closest finish *twice*, my dear *three* little snouts on a half-sheet of notepaper each time of course I could have *vowed* that my *pet* beastie was first, though of course *too* prohibitive to be sure, because Haddock says by his slide-rule which I do not utterly believe in they're doing about 35 miles ph, I should have said *sixty* myself, so now they have the *photo*-finish which is *absolute* magic, we saw the works, and in *quite* no time you can see a *dry* print, only of course each time my pet *intuition*

hound owing to the *baneful* Haddock influence was *third* and
out of it by *two* hairs or half a nostril, *malignant* luck, and so
it went on, Haddock my dear wagering wilder and wilder and
your little friend's winnings *quite* melting away, *what* Haddock
lost has *not* been promulgated, all he said was that he would *not*
have minded if there'd been a *Betting* Tax and he'd contributed
something to the *Exchequer*, which in all the circumstances the
rest of us did *not* think was Utterance Number *One*, Jean and
her mate being downish likewise and quite unallergic just then
to the *Exchequer*, as for me I have rarely felt *less* cordial to the
Exchequer, we then withdrew for *solatious* draughts with some
of the dog-heads, and the sequel is comparatively *nebulous*, only
I seem to remember something being said about our *acquiring* a
race-dog, I can not envisage *why*, because *where* are we to keep
it and what will it *eat*, anyhow it's *too* sure to be last *always*, if
you're *not* careful I shall call it Tongue-tied *Trix*, no more now
TOPSY.

25 Radiant Day

Trix my favourite clam I'll forgive your *wordless* letter because
of your electric *news*, my dear it's *lyrical* to hear that you're
coming to the insanitary capital, yes we can bed you for a *bit*
while you're seeking stable-room, Haddock says he *thinks* he can
tolerate you both for *about* a fortnight, but have courage I *dare*
say he'll make it more only of course you must vow not to *utter*
at *all* at breakfast-time when he reads *seven* papers and indicates
his wishes with animal noises *merely*, as a *matter* of fact it must
all be a benign piece of celestial *planning*, because Iodine Dale
has *just* got her absolute at *last* and is packing *now*, praises be,
so you can have *her* room over the river, no nightingales I *fear*
darling but ducks and tugs and *herons* vocal, there's a rather *bleak*
bathroom behind with a pre-Crimean geyser which fills the
bath the *next* day, however I remember you and Henry are both
leisurely dressers and Henry shaves at *dictation* speed, whereas
we both detest the business and *scuttle* through it, in fact the
first thing Haddock said was Henry is *not* to use our bathroom,
so you might *tactfully*, I'm *too* joyful about Henry's new *job*, I
should think for a time he'd make a *pet* Club Secretary, though
won't he have to do *arithmetic*, Haddock says he's never *heard* of
the Elephants, is that the club where they all have to have shot
two tigers, and by the way what *will* your Henry do without
his woods and spinneys, there's rather a swampy island just
above us all mud and *osiers* where Haddock says he could land
in the dinghy and stumble about at week-ends, only he mustn't
shoot the *swans* which belong to the *King*, of course *how* you're
going to find *permanent* sleep-space, it's *too* prohibitive, however
we'll keep *all* eyes lifting, the one hope is to meet someone by
accident at a party and *shame* them into a Christian arrangement
with *cataracts* of juniper-juice, otherwise if it's only a hen-coop
they want the earth *and* all the planets, the other thing is if

somebody dies one makes *ghoulish* passes at the *widow* before she has time to *think*, only you have to be *too* prompt and pitiless, we've lost *two* good houses for friends because Haddock said it was the done thing to wait till after the *funeral*, it *isn't*, by the way can Henry do *carpentring*, because I wonder how you'd like to live on a *boat*, there aren't any, but they are going to sell some of these *naval* things they say, only then of course you can't get a *mooring*, it's all *fairly* difficult, here however I must say the general note is *buoyant*, my dear Jill has been decanted from the Wrens at last, *yards* longer and *quite* lovable, and Jack will be back from Australia in May, so with *both* twins you see we shan't have any *excess* cubic *space*, but darling you can imagine what a *spark* one feels, then of course I've *two* more fairy-tales to tell you, the *first* is after *quite* years of solitary servitude I've got *help* in the home, the *most* appealing and meritorious *couple*, my dear talk of working with a *whistle* they make the bees look lazy and *bored*, my dear it's *such* bliss *not* to have to do the front-door and the washing-up and cook and scrub *incessantly*, I've stopped already having the cramp *all* over, not to mention savage *heart*-leaps at night, honestly my dear one can not *envisage* what one's been doing all these years, and if the couple *ever* leave us I shall merely dig a *small* hole in the corner of the garden and *creep* into it without a word, though of course to you having weathered the war in Medicine Hat, or was it Moose Jaw, all this I suppose is merely *bat-song*, and the *second* fairy-tale is even more affecting, because my dear we *suddenly* discovered that our *lease* was up *too* soon, my dear have you ever the *faintest* notion where a lease is and as for *insurance* policies, well my dear our *sweet* old landlady came up to see us about a *renewal*, which she said she was *quite* willing about, and *then* she said, I'll give you thirty guesses, she'd like to *reduce* our rent, repeat *reduce*, because we'd had such trouble in the *war*, my dear when we'd got our breath again we refused *tearfully*, because the rent as you know is *not* ruinous, and she is *not* rich, far from it, but you must agree as Haddock says it was an episode of *cosmic* import, throwing an absolute RAY of hope over the entire human swamp, because *when* you hear of some of the stoats and monsters about and *what* they're asking for imperceptible flats and *medieval* cars, to hear this aged angel suggest *reducing* the rent, it was like seeing the *most* luminous rainbow in the middle of a *dense* fog, it does show you doesn't it that there are still *some* unrapacious and golden souls in currency, Haddock says there ought to be a *monument* to The Lady who wanted to Reduce the Rent because her Tenants had Trouble in the *War*, because he says if it once got public there might be an absolute *wave* of Christian dealing, *sane* prices would be asked for houses, Goering would admit that he was sometimes wrong, and the suffering Russians might give Poland to the Poles, anyhow it was a warming incident for *this* little bosom and the old lady stayed for the *Boat* Race, which my dear was a *radiant* day, I don't suppose you saw but *Oxford* won, *noticeably*, we had the hugest party and *stage* weather, *all* my daffodils and hyacinths came out unanimously *just* in time, in fact most people thought I'd been buying them in *pots*, Haddock covered the house with *flags* making the race invisible from *most* windows, the PM came and the Speaker, and Members of numerous parties all bonhomous and beaming with Haddock's theatricals and some dazzlers from the chorus, and of course *swarms* of ancient bosoms one had scarcely *seen* since the last time in 1939, *too* moving, though of course everyone invited brought *two* nieces or more, or an *old* friend from the country, so the catering problem, however the sandwiches which we began at *dawn* held out, my dear we were all mere *shadows* at the end and even Haddock had been *scrubbing* for days, however *nothing* mattered because it was the *Boat Race* again and a *magical* day, there was Haddock's old boat *still* afloat and in her Oxford blue again after *six* years of battle-ship grey, no more machine-guns and stokers but *alive* with *children* not *one* of whom fell in, *pure* miracle, there was the *obscene* spot across the river where the *rocket* fell, but now a man playing a *trumpet*, and there was the skeleton of Haddock's buoy where the *bomb* fell, and there *most* wonderworthy was the old house still erect with *all* its windows in and *bursting* with *congenial* people come to see the crazy *Boat Race* again, no one on the *roof* this time though because of the incendiaries and dubious *slates*, but altogether my dear it simply *was* the old world *creeping* back to life again, an utterly symbolic what-is-it, of course I hardly *saw* the poor crews *straining* their stomachs to get to Mortlake, one *never* does, what with *squeezing* late arrivals into non-existent spaces, and of course in agony about the *children* falling in when the big wave came, but I did snatch a glimpse of them as they *melted* into the mist, *Oxford* leading as I *think* I said, and my dear I remembered one night when we saw *two* doodle-bugs go by, one chasing the other up the river *likewise*, and we had *bets* about which would win, and I thought when *next* I hear some dreary unmagnetic ullage say *What* exactly have we got to *celebrate* about I shall say a few brief detonating *words*, fare well and bless you till we meet, your tough but tender TOPSY.

Notes on the text

BY KATE MACDONALD

1.1 A Brush With The High-Brows

That Kipling bit: probably Rudyard Kipling's poem 'If', first published in 1910, one of his most well-known poems, often prescribed for memorising in the school-room.

1.2 The Simple Life

The Electric Hare: at the greyhound track the dogs race after an electric hare.

Betty Nuthall: one of the top English tennis players of the day, ranked in the world top 10 in 1927, when *The Trials of Topsy* was published.

1.3 Nature

Catherine Parr: the sixth wife of Henry VIII, who died in 1548.

1.5 Good Works

settlement: APH had worked at the Oxford House Mission settlement in 1914.

Halma: a quite basic board game in which counters jump over each other.

Gadarene: as in the Gadarene swine, into which Jesus cast a host of demons, and then the pigs ran off over the edge of a cliff (Mark 5 1–13).

1. 6 Hymen

Hymen: the Greek god of marriage and its celebrations.

butterfly-collar: much like a modern shirt collar, with the collar points pointing downwards, unlike the more conventional collar, at this period, which was a separate upstanding celluloid and linen contraption that fastened with studs to the shirt itself.

tail-coat: part of a morning-suit now only seen at formal weddings and Court events, always worn with a top-hat.

law about not getting married until after three o'clock: the Marriages (Hours of Solemnisation) Bill of 1886 prevented marriages in England and Wales taking place after three in the afternoon. The Marriage (Extension of Hours) Bill of 1934 extended the legal period for solemnising marriages to six in the evening, a move that Herbert had been campaigning for in print for many years.

clandestine marriages: Lord Hardwicke's Act of 1753 made it illegal to solemnise a marriage not conducted in a church or chapel, or by special licence, within certain hours, to prevent clandestine marriages.

the Jews can be married at midnight: the Jewish community in England were not restricted by Lord Hardwicke's Act of 1753, as this was solely concerned with marriages conducted by the Church of England.

Talullah Bankhead: stage and screen actress, working on the London stage during the 1920s. Her publicity photographs were probably in quite wide circulation.

1.8 Reducing

Reducing: going on a weight-reducing diet.

T B: APH believed in the restorative power of Turkish Baths all his life.

1.9 Going To The Dogs

the dogs: the greyhound races.

1.10 Ideals

ghastly League: the League of Nations, founded after the First World War to prevent another war.

Guardee: slang for an officer of one of the Guards regiments, at this period young men of a conservative and upper-class background, selected for their height, background and ability to carry out orders.

short hair and short skirts: fashions for women changed radically after the First World War when women 'shingled' their hair to a modern-day bob, and skirt hems rose above the ankles to the knees.

1.11 The Origin of Nieces

Deposited Book: a resolution to present a revised version of the Prayer Book for use in Church of England Services to the King was defeated in the House of Commons in 1927, and the draft version, the 'Deposited Book', and its offending element, of introducing the practice of 'reserving' the unused sacrament, became an object of contention between Catholics and Protestants.

monkey-trial: the Scopes Trial, or The State of Tennessee v. John Thomas Scopes, which brought a high school teacher to trial for teaching human evolution along Darwinian lines, which American fundamentalist teaching disagreed with.

1.12 The Superfluous Baronet

Spartan mother: the Spartan mothers were legendarily expected to require their sons to come back dead from the war rather than be taken prisoner. The Spartan boy with the fox, with which Topsy is confusing the mother, refuses to say he is being eaten alive rather than admit he has a stolen fox under his cloak.

1.14 The Fresh Mind

Harrovian: an unexpected slur against the former pupils of Harrow School. APH went to Winchester College, a rival establishment.

1.15 A Run With The Yaffle

Cadogan: as in Cadogan Square, a grand address in Mayfair populated in Topsy's time by wealthy landed families with fixed ideas about social codes. She herself is Cadogan, if not Berkeley (Square).

we sat out: sitting out a dance with her partner is an excellent opportunity for intimate chats and exploratory amorous glances.

Sybil Thorndike: one of the great English Shakespearean actresses of the period, who would have been in her late forties when this book was published.

1.17 Good Women And True

ullage: the space unfilled by liquid in a sealed container, for example a barrel of beer. Used here, possibly, to suggest a waste.

hairy at the hocks: a snooty term from the world of horses, to disparage someone for not being well-bred, coarse in appearance, unsophisticated.

1.18 Charity

C B Cochran: one of the great theatre producers of the London stage.

monkey glands: the popular 1920s fashion for grafting slices of chimpanzee testicle onto human testicles to increase testosterone production ended by the 1930s. The chief proponent was a Russian surgeon, Serge Voronoff.

selling plater: a horse that is only suitable for entering into a selling race, the winner of which is to be sold at auction; a horse of low quality.

1.20 The Ephemeral Triangle

hinc illæ: Latin, hence therefore.

carbolically: Topsy often uses 'carbolic' as an adjective, meaning 'non-harmful'. In this case she may also be referring to the red colour of carbolic soap, reflected in the red-lipsticked smiles of the antagonists.

too Ramsay Macdonald: Scottish leader of the Labour Party from 1922, and as the Scottish song 'Auld Lang Syne' is traditionally sung at New Year, Topsy naturally alludes to the only Scotsman she has ever heard of.

1.22 The Untrained Nurse

the VAD: in the First World War, society girls flocked to become Voluntary Aid Detachment nurses, and were looked down on by the professional nurses they worked with.

boracic: another of Topsy's favourite hyperbolisms, meaning 'harmless' or 'good for you', derived from boric acid, a common household antiseptic used in wound dressings.

1.26 End of Act One

g h p: possibly Good Hearted Public?

Topsy, MP

Sir Leslie Scott: senior judge and Conservative Party Member of Parliament for Liverpool Exchange, who retired in 1929.

Sir William Bull: solicitor and Conservative Party Member of Parliament for Hammersmith South until 1929.

2.1 Becomes A Member

Cambridge: light blue.

House: the House of Commons.

Hicks: William Joynson-Hicks, reactionary Conservative Member of Parliament, in this government representing Twickenham, with the nickname Jix.

2.2 Goes Shooting

Arras: French site of several major battles during the First World War.

2.3 Flies Half The Atlantic

routs and swarries: routs and soirées are archaic terms for semi-grand evening parties.

fly the Atlantic: the first east-west transatlantic flight (held to be harder as it was flying against prevailing winds) was made in 1919 by the airship R34 piloted by Major Scott. Amelia Earheart was the first woman to cross the Atlantic by plane, as a passenger, in June 1928, from west to east. The first non-stop fixed wing flight from east to west between the European and North American mainlands took place in September 1930, by Costes and Bellonte. Topsy was very much ahead of her time.

2.6 Goes Hunting

Master: the Master of the Hunt is usually an intimidating individual who funds and directs the Hunt, not someone to annoy.

bowler: women riding to hounds wore a bowler hat as the feminine equivalent of the men's top-hats, for its hard protective surface. Veils were a rather glamorous accessory that might disguise the clots of mud spattered over the face.

playing the cornet: giving the hounds commands, and letting the rest of the hunt know where the fox was.

2.7 Passes Poxton

Williams Ellis: Clough Williams-Ellis, Welsh architect, author of *England and the Octopus* (1928), which deplored the way villages were losing their cohesion, and the increasing spread of towns into the countryside.

Auntie Jix: see Hicks, above.

2.8 Is All For Al

Al: Alfred E Smith, Al Smith, a Catholic, served four terms as the Governor of New York and ran against Herbert Hoover as the Democratic candidate in the 1928 US Presidential election.

bloater: a bloater is the English version of the kipper, a smoked herring.

Eighteenth Amendment: voted in in 1919, the Eighteen Amendment to the US Constitution prohibited the production, transport and sale of alcohol in the USA.

wowsers: people who try to prevent other people enjoying themselves in ways that the wowsers consider to be sinful or immoral.

2.9 Takes Her Seat

Amami morning: the Amami setting lotion for hair was a top seller for decades, fixing curls and waves.

Winston: Sir Winston Churchill, at this point Chancellor of the Exchequer for the Conservative government, of which party Topsy is also an MP.

Sir Robert Horne: Unionist Member of Parliament for Glasgow Hillhead, former Chancellor of the Exchequer under the Coalition Government until 1922.

Captain Eden: Anthony Eden, later a Conservative Prime Minister, at this point a rising star in Conservative politics.

Harcourt Room: a dining room used to entertain visitors to the House of Commons.

2.10 Hauls Down The Gold Standard

non sine pulvere: Latin, not without dust.

2.11 Has Words With The Whips

£ s d: the symbols for pounds, shillings and pence.

2.12 Knows Too Much

asked the Whips for a pair: asked the Whips' office to arrange for the MP from the Opposition benches 'paired' with her to not vote in her absence, so as to not lose or gain any advantage.

2.14 Behaves Badly

Total Abstinent Sons of the Salamander: Herbert's spoof of a Temperance Society dedicated to not letting people enjoy themselves.

Amalekites: a desert people in the Old Testament, a hereditary enemy of Israel.

his own paper: his own notepaper from his home, which would have had his name and address stamped or printed thereon.

2.15 Plays Golf With Nancy

Bernard Shaw: one of the leading playwrights and radical spokesmen of the late Victorian and Edwardian periods, a Grand Old Man of vegetarianism and intimidating intellect by the late 1920s.

Why don't Americans: Lady Astor was American by birth, married to an Englishman.

Band of Hope: the leading Temperance movement for children.

2.17 Converts A Whip

revoltage: the Central Electricity Board was established by the Electrical (Supply) Act 1926, to consolidate all independent power generating systems in England and Wales. The early stages of this would have led to adjustments in the voltage to make this consistent across the network.

complete blanket: a complete wet blanket, entirely negative.

corybantic: corybants performed wild and frenzied dancing as a votive performance in pagan ritual.

Savonarola: fifteenth-century Florentine friar, a byword for Christian zeal urging the prohibition of joys.

2.18 Is Unlucky

caught the eye: the archaic practice of the hostess catching the eye of the women present to lead them out of the dining-room after dinner, while the male guests remain with the hosts to smoke, drink port and discuss manly matters.

2.20 Starts A Salon

KCB: Knights Commander of the Bath, members of the fourth most senior British order of chivalry.

Arnold Bennett: author and editor, a ubiquitous and well-liked member of English literary society.

Maxton: Scottish socialist politician, Member of Parliament for Glasgow Bridgerton, and at this time Chairman of the Independent Labour Party.

Kirkwood: David Kirkwood, later Baron Kirkwood, Scottish engineer and socialist, and Labour MP for Dumbarton Burghs.

feudal home: Topsy has not mentioned her father's title in these letters since Trix of course knows exactly who he is, so all we can deduce that as Topsy has a title in her own right her father is a duke or a earl.

the Stores: the Army and Navy Stores, one of the London member-ship Stores, open to the middle classes and the gentry supplying household goods for all circumstances, for hire or purchase.

Elsa Lanchester: English stage and screen actress, in 1928 at the beginning of the rise of her career, about to marry Charles Laughton, and starring in plays by Arnold Bennett and H G Wells, among others.

H G Wells: novelist and public intellectual, about as ubiquitous in literary life as Arnold Bennett and Shaw.

Ellen Wilkinson: socialist, former trade unionist and the only Labour woman Member of Parliament elected in 1924.

a cigarette of all things: the Prime Minister, Stanley Baldwin, was famous for being a loyal pipe-smoker.

chaperones: when unmarried young women attended social engagements they had to be accompanied by an older woman as a chaperone, who may have resented this duty.

2.21 Trouble In The Home

Chiltern Hundreds: the traditional means of enabling an MP to resign their seat by being promoted to an office that precludes their representing a constituency, in this case the ancient office of the Crown Steward and Bailiff of the Chiltern Hundreds, which doesn't actually exist.

2.22 Asks Questions

Dora: the Defence of the Realm Act, first established during the First World War, which contained an unexpectedly wide range of prohibitions which might in wartime have prevented helping the enemy, but in peacetime were a burden on normal living.

raid on Arcos: in May 1927 British intelligence had raided the offices of the All-Russian Co-Operative Society (ARCOS), the body responsible for organising trade between Britain and the USSR, to retrieve suspected confidential documents. This caused the termination of diplomatic relations between Britain and the USSR.

Terence O'Connor: Conservative MP for Luton.

Virgin's Vote: the first law to give the vote to women in Britain, in 1919.

Roedean: prominent fee-paying school for girls in Sussex.

2.23 Loses The Whip

General Election: there was to be a General Election in 1929, which would see a change of government and the retirement of many politicians.

Ullah family: Amanullah Khan was a reforming and modernising king of the Islamic nation of Afghanistan until early 1929 when he abdicated.

Labby: Before Topsy the atheist MP Charles Bradlaugh was held in the room in the Elizabeth Tower of the Palace of Westminster (the Clock Tower), in 1880.

2.24 Does Embroidery

Boat-Race Night: the Oxford and Cambridge (universities') Boat Race takes place on the Thames, and the night of the race used to be a traditionally drunken event for supporters of both teams.

2.25 Becomes A Mother

Byron: Lord Byron achieved overnight fame with the publication of his poem *Childe Harold's Pilgrimage* in 1812, when he 'awoke one morning and found myself famous'.

Hampden: John Hampden, one of the Members of Parliament who led the resistance to Charles II's autocratic rule as absolute monarch, leading to the English Civil War.

Sankey and Moody: two celebrated American Christian fundamentalist preachers who brought a gospel mission in Britain in the 1870s.

Derry and Tom: Derry and Toms was a well-known London department store.

3.1 Peace!

Medicine Hat, Moose Jaw: towns in central Canada, both on the same major east-west highway, but to Topsy they may as well have been on the moon.

Golders Green: Golders Green crematorium was and is the most-used crematorium in England.

doodle-bugs: the V-1 flying bombs launched by the German army against the UK in the last 18 months of the Second World War. They screamed as they neared their target, making them particularly unnerving as well as unpredictable.

Black List: the 'Black Book' listing prominent individuals in the UK who were to be arrested after the German invasion.

blast: the effects of bomb-blast on the body and on unsecured items in civilian areas were varied and sometimes bizarre, and the official guidance about the posture to adopt, if there was time, was also considered derisory.

belay there: sailing slang meaning to stop, in this case talking. Herbert was an avid sailor.

Alamein: the Second Battle of Alamein ended on 11 November 1942, and was a landmark Allied victory.

3.2 Consolations

bath-water: incendiary bombs caused fires, which the bath-water could be used to extinguish.

black-out: early on in the war a black-out was instituted across Britain, requiring all house-holders to use thick black paper or curtains across windows at night to prevent light escaping, which might serve as a guide for enemy planes, or be fined.

types with Thirds: passengers with third-class tickets taking up places in the First-class carriages, and refusing to move.

3.3 The Suffrage Episode

Galahad: the purest Knight of the Round Table.

ancient Universities: like APH Haddock was a Member of Parliament for the University of Oxford, one of several university constituency seats that were abolished in 1950. Candidates needed only to post an Address to the voters; no meetings were required.

James Grigg: a highly effective senior civil servant at the Treasury and during the transition to self-rule in India, he was appointed Secretary of State for War by Churchill in the government shakeup of February 1942 and was well-regarded. He lost his seat in Parliament in the 1945 general election.

hoolies: hooligans.

3.4 The Moon Party

Swiss Family Robinson: early 19thC novel about a pious and resourceful family who survive after shipwreck by careful husbandry of salvaged animals and knowledge of how to make and use tools.

Eisenhower, Mark Clark: General Eisenhower, lately the supreme commander of the Allied Army in Europe, and General Mark Clark, commander of US forces in Austria, both received honorary degrees at Oxford University in October 1945.

3.6 Iodine Dale

decree nisi: Iodine has been granted notice that her divorce may take place if within six weeks no evidence is presented to show that it should not, in this case evidence that she was being adulterous, or that she and her husband were conniving to secure the divorce against the principles of the then law. APH was still campaigning for the reform of the divorce laws.

3.7 Saving at the Races

Peppiatts: Kenneth Peppiatt was Chief Cashier at the Bank of England from 1938 to 1949, and his signature adorned four one-pound bank notes released during this period, called Peppiatts by coin-collectors.

3.8 The Danes

Kiel Canal: the Nord-Ostsee Kanal links the Baltic Sea at Kiel to the North Sea at Brunsbüttel, allowing shipping to cut through in a day rather than spend several days sailing north around the tip of Jutland.

froken: Danish, miss, young lady.

3.9 Force 5

British naval officer: Kiel was captured by a British-US force in May 1945, to gain control over the port and its shipbuilding and technological capacity before the Soviet Army reached it.

backing: the wind is travelling anti-clockwise.

3.10 The New House

Sergeant-at-Arms: the Serjeant-at-Arms at the House of Commons retains the 15th-century spelling of his name.

Sir John Simon: one of the most senior judges in Britain and a Lord Chancellor.

Burnham Woods: Topsy is confusing Burnham Beeches, an area of beech woodland north-west of London which was in the news for having been requisitioned for the safety of the public, with the 1944 international conference at Bretton Woods, Massachusetts, to rebuild the international economy after the war.

3.11 The Prime Meridian

Woolton: Lord Woolton, a former businessman and very competent Minister of Food during the war, and later Minister of Reconstruction.

rubble and wife: a variant on trouble and strife, Cockney rhyming slang for wife, though Topsy's meaning is trouble.

3.13 Heroic Act

Rotary: the Rotary Club, a male business and social club.

Fourteenth Night: against tradition Topsy has left the Christmas decorations up past Twelfth Night.

999: the British emergency phone number of 999 was set up in June 1937, so Topsy is rather casual about remembering it.

3.14 Timothy Brine

W6: the post code for Topsy's district of West London, a respectable and mundane place.

3.15 The Dogs

Uno: one of Topsy's more elusive references, it's possible that this is the United Nations Organisation, whose first Charter had been signed in July.

3.17 Keeping Fit

Hornibrook: F J Hornibrook popularised the Hornibrook belly rotation exercise in his *The Culture of the Abdomen* (1924).

3.18 The Canaanites

quires: stacks of writing paper.

two-and-a-half d: two and a half pence.

Canaanites: a prehistoric tribal group who were, according to general usage in the books of the Old Testament, wiped out by the Israelites. However Topsy's Canaanite correspondent is a member of the Council of the Coalition of Hebrew Youth, a modern Hebrew ideology that resisted Zionism and advocated a new non-Judaic Hebrew nation in the Middle East. It was influential but had few members.

3.19 Stiff Lips

washing: before the availability of relatively cheap and easily-installed domestic washing machines, most households who could afford it sent their washing out to private laundries, which could take a long time to return it.

3.20 Movements

Bornholm: a strategically important island in the Baltic, this was occupied by the German army until May 1945, when, despite German intentions to surrender to Allied forces, the island's towns were systematically bombed and it was captured by Soviet forces.

Indonesia: Indonesia had proclaimed its independence from Dutch colonial rule in August 1945.

jellies: Topsy is possibly thinking of guava jelly.

Belisha Beacons: flashing lights at the roadside to signal pedestrian crossings, marked by studs on the pavement, established in Britain in 1934.

3.21 Ulcerous World

Quit: most famously used in the Quit India movement that began in 1942, the slogan was in the news again in early 1946 with new elections in India, and the British government's slow realisation that it could no longer rule this colony.

Mr Rommel: General Rommel, commander of the German Afrika Korps, did enter Egypt but was forced to retreat.

Shepheards: the famous English hotel in Cairo, with a long bar that produced even longer queues for a drink.

students declaring war: Egypt was a British protectorate at this point, but King Farouk was regarded as a puppet of the British government by the Egyptian population.

Anders: Polish general in exile who commanded Polish forces for the Allies as a leading commander.

Fighting Whatisit: the painting by J M W Turner of one of the great ships of Nelson's fleet that fought at Trafalgar, *The Fighting Temeraire*, shown being town up the Thames to be broken up for scrap metal, by a paddle steamer.

S Cripps, H Morrison: Sir Stafford Cripps, Labour politician, at that time President of the Board of Trade. Herbert Morrison, Labour politician, Leader of the House of Commons and de facto deputy Prime minister to Clement Atlee.

3.22 Haddock in Trouble

Nye: Aneurin Bevan, the Minister of Health, which also included housing, in the Labour government. He was a passionate speaker and a fiercely effective politician, at this time creating the National Health Service.

Lilac Fairy: the Haddocks are at the first performance of the newly reopened Royal Opera House, at which the Sadlers Wells Ballet are performing *The Sleeping Beauty*. The Lilac Fairy plays a leading role.

3.23 The Speech Sweep

LCC: London County Council.

3.24 The Dogs Again

ab ovo: Latin, from the egg, from the beginning.

naps: betting term meaning the strongest position or candidate.

Business As Usual

by Jane Oliver & Ann Stafford

Jane Oliver
& Ann Stafford

Business As Usual

Business As Usual is a delightful illustrated novel in letters from 1933. It tells the story of Hilary Fane, a newly engaged and also newly unemployed Edinburgh girl who is determined to support herself by her own earnings in London for a year, despite the resentment of her surgeon fiancé. After a nervous beginning looking for a job while her savings shrink, she finds work as a typist in the London department store of Everyman's (a very thin disguise for Selfridges). She rises rapidly through the ranks to work in the library, where she has to enforce modernising systems on her entrenched and frosty colleagues.

Business As Usual is charming, intelligent, heart-warming, funny, and entertaining. It's also deeply interesting as a record of the history of shopping in the 1930s, and for its clear-eyed descriptions of social conditions, poverty and illegitimacy.

Jane Oliver was the pen-name of Helen Rees (née Evans, 1903–1970). After working as a PE teacher and as Clemence Dane's secretary and learning to fly, Helen became a successful historical novelist. She was the widow of John Lllewelyn Rhys, in whose name she founded the John Llewelyn Rhys prize for Commonwealth writers from her own royalties. (Handheld also publishes his complete works.) Ann Stafford (the pen-name of Anne Pedler, 1900–1966) also became a successful novelist. Together they published at least 97 novels.

£12.99, ISBN 978-1-912766-18-5